ALONG THE FAR SHORES

A CELTIC KNOT NOVEL

KRISTIN GLEESON

An Tig Beag Press

OTHER WORKS BY KRISTIN GLEESON
In Praise of the Bees
CELTIC KNOT SERIES
Selkie Dreams
Along the Far Shores
Raven Brought the Light
A Treasure Beyond Worth (novella)
RENAISSANCE SOJOURNER SERIES
A Trick of Fate (novella)
The Imp of Eye
The Sea of Travail
The Quest of Hope
HIGHLAND BALLAD SERIES
The Hostage of Glenorchy
The Mists of Glenstrae
The Braes of Huntly
Highland Lioness
NON FICTION
Anahareo, A Wilderness Spirit
Listen to the music while you read- go to www.kristingleeson.
com/music and download the files.Receive a FREE novellette
prequel, *A Treasure Beyond Worth,* and
When you sign up for my mailing list: www.kristingleeson.com

PART I

––––––––––

KINGDOM OF GWYNEDD, WALES, 1169

1

————

á brón orm. The words of mourning in her Irish tongue
hung heavy on Aisling. They'd followed her as she
travelled along the fields and through the woodlands
on the broken nag with her servant and then across the sea to
the kingdom of Gwynedd. They lingered now around the castle
hall, mingled with the smoke from the fire and grew stronger,
joining the sorrow of the passing of the Gwynedd king.

'Was it the plague that took your mother, our kinswoman?'
Prince Hwyel, one of the dead king's sons, addressed her in
Latin, for she knew little Welsh.

She could hear the sharp intake of breath from those around
her. Some edged away, while others were more overt in their
panic, putting hands to their mouths and noses. With a brief
flash of anger, she thought of the comments she could make on
the ripe odors coming from their elegantly laced gowns and rich
tunics.

She caught her brother Cormac's fearful glance from
where he stood at the far end of the hall. They were some
ways away from Hwyel, who sat at a small table with some of
his brothers and other relations to discuss the succession. It

was his mother who'd provided the connection years before so that her brother Cormac could be fostered here, far away from their home in Leinster. She'd hoped to escape Hwyel's notice for a little longer, feeling that he would have no interest in a newly arrived sister of his poor and distant kin. But his dark, piggish eyes had missed nothing and she had felt his periodic scrutiny for some time, until after inquiry he'd been told who she was.

Everyone's eyes were on her, waiting for her answer. She resisted the urge to smooth her hair, held in place only by a plain band around her head, or tug on the sleeve of her woolen dress, which, though finely woven, was fashioned in the simple, loose style of her home and no match for the women here.

'My Lord...Cousin,' she said, uncertain what title to give him. 'It's true my mother died of a fever, but it was not the plague.' She responded in Latin, glad for once that her brother had made her learn it, so that she might let everyone know she carried no contagion.

She felt some of the tension ease as false smiles and nervous chatter erupted when Hwyel, seemingly satisfied, resumed his conversation with his neighbor. Aisling felt some relief that attention had shifted away from her, but she could not push aside her astonishment that Hwyel had not even pretended to observe the custom to offer condolences on her bereavement. She looked over at Cormac to see if he found Hwyel's words as lacking in sensibility as she did.

He smiled at her, his face full of determined reassurance, and made his way towards her. He was fair, like she was, though he appeared almost angelic with his honey colored curls and beardless face. She noticed his hands still possessed the slender grace she remembered. Though it had been more than three years since they'd been together, she still found that her heart swelled at the sight of him. Her dearest younger brother. He was all she had left now.

'We'll go to the chapel later and say prayers for our mother,' Cormac said when he reached her side.

She studied her brother a moment, puzzled. 'Yes, of course.' Why would Cormac suggest such a thing? She'd only had a few moments with him since she'd arrived. Just enough time to embrace him and pass on the awful news, before she was told she must go to the hall before Hwyel and his brothers. But surely Cormac remembered that her mother wouldn't have wanted them to pray in a chapel. She'd kept the ancient customs and had paid only lip service to the Christian beliefs to please their father. Perhaps it was the only way he could speak privately to her.

She stood restlessly, waiting for the princes to leave so that she might speak to her brother alone, share with him all that she and her mother had endured these many months. And there was much to be done. She must not lose sight of that. All that time her mother had made her promise to refrain from writing to Cormac had been precious time wasted.

Finally, Hwyel and his brothers rose and made their way out of the hall, dogs crowding their feet. Some of the women followed them, while others lingered, forming small, whispering groups. Cormac moved closer and took her hands.

'Come, I'll take you to the chapel.'

She nodded and followed him through the hall out across the courtyard to a small building. Aberffraw Castle had astonished her when first she viewed it after the rough sea journey. The large stone keep stood atop an outcropping surrounded by a moat and also included a small stone chapel, kitchen and some wooden outbuildings.

She entered the chapel and shivered at the cold. The long, dark winter seemed to have lodged in the stones, and neither the many mass candles wedged in the makeshift rack, nor the feeble fire in the small brazier beside the altar alleviated it. The short rows of wooden benches looked uninviting. She watched

Cormac approach the altar, kneel and cross himself. She sighed, despite knowing that it was impossible to think that Cormac might have set aside his deep Christian beliefs in the years they'd been apart, but still she had hoped. It had been one source of difference between them and one that she knew had secretly disappointed her mother. She took a seat on one of the benches and waited for Cormac to join her.

Should she try to pray? Pray for her mother, pray for her father so brutally murdered? Pray for all the land stolen from them, seized by ruthless noblemen warring with the King of Leinster? Whom should she pray to, anyway? The Christian God or the ancient gods of her mother?

'Aisling.'

She jolted and looked at Cormac, realizing that she'd been caught up once again in the staring absence where no thoughts came to her, where nothing could touch her—no rage, no despair, no sorrow. She took Cormac's hand.

'Ah, *mo chroí*, how I've longed to see you again.'

Tears filled his eyes, those lovely sea-blue eyes she remembered. 'And I've missed you so, and now to see you once again only to be told our mother is dead.'

She nodded and stroked his palm, trying to bring some comfort.

'I will ask Madog if we may have a mass said for her soul.'

She gave him a curious look. 'You know she would never have wanted that. She died unshriven.'

Cormac's eyes darkened. 'I'll pray for her then.' He squeezed her hand and gave her an intent look. 'And you will, too.' She could detect a note of pleading in his tone, so she refrained from adding anything more and merely nodded. She told herself she cared nothing for the prayers that might be said and to whom they were said.

'Thank you,' he said, his face softening. 'I know that mother has misled you in her own beliefs, but now we can begin to redress that.'

Irritation pricked at her despite her efforts. 'Redress my beliefs? Have you become so much a part of this *Bretnais* court that you have forgotten who your people are?'

Alarm flashed across Cormac's face. 'No-no, you must not think that I am not proud to be Uí Bairriche of Leinster, son of Eoghan. But you should put aside these old ways, forget that our mother wanted you to be a seer.' He eyed her carefully a moment. 'You haven't had the visions come yet, have you?'

'So you still believe it's possible, do you? You haven't entirely given yourself over to the Christian beliefs, then.'

'Yes, I mean, no.' He flushed heavily. 'I have taken the Christian faith deep to my heart and set aside all the old beliefs. But I would warn you that you must keep any talk of visions and seers to yourself.'

She glared at him for a moment, and then relented. Why should she mind about it after all? She'd had no visions; she was not a seer, despite all her mother's hopes and efforts to make it so.

'Let us not quarrel, *a stor*,' said Cormac.

She smiled at him. 'You're right of course. We must make plans instead. There is no time to lose. The rumors are already rife that there will be more fighting in Leinster. Macmurrough thinks to get his kingship back. We can use that opportunity to get back our lands. You're of an age, you can fight—offer your services.'

Discomfort filled his face. 'I know it seems pressing to you that we should return, but it's not that simple. We can't just go. We have nothing, you say. It's all gone. No money, no land, no cattle and no home. Just the few possessions you brought with you. So we're dependent on the favor of this court and now it's in turmoil. The king left eleven sons and many of them feel themselves fit for the throne. They gather like crows to carrion, some circling from afar, waiting for their chance, while others try to shove and peck each other out of the way. There's a battle coming. Alliances are forming.'

'And which side are you on?'

Cormac gave an uncomfortable smile. 'I'm on no side. I'm on the side of peace, like Madog.'

She stared at her brother, trying to reshape the boy she'd known into this young man that stood before her. He was fifteen, come fully into his height and filled with some of the discernment that life spent among the nobly born required, yet here he was proclaiming himself on the side of peace. Was this the full blooming of the boy poet she remembered? She was more in need of a warrior, though, not a *fili*.

Before she could say more, the door opened and allowed a gust of wind to sweep through. A dark, slim man stepped across the threshold, his footfall quiet and reverent. He moved forward, and, like Cormac before him, knelt before the altar on one knee and crossed himself.. His movements were deliberate and spoke of a great calm, his closely barbered brown hair catching the full light of the mass candles on his bowed head so that it seemed to halo him.

He took a seat on a bench at the front, near the altar and bowed his head. With folded hands, he began to mouth a prayer. His lips moved silently, forming words carefully, his knitted brow betraying their intensity. Here was a man who desperately wanted what he prayed for. Aisling found herself smiling at his earnestness. There was something pure and unsullied about him and she liked it.

Beside her, Cormac folded his hands and took up a posture similar to the man. It was clear he felt he couldn't speak with this man present, so she turned her attention to the front and observed him further.

The prayer took longer than she would have thought and its earnest quality never faltered. When he finally did finish, he rose, turned to them and fixed the most transparently blue eyes on her. It was as if he saw through to her innermost self when he looked at her.

'My lord Madog,' said Cormac. He flushed when Madog shifted his gaze to him. 'I would be pleased to introduce you to my sister, Aisling.'

Madog gave a small bow, which she returned. She had no notion of the customs of this land but she'd been surprised to hear Cormac speak his introduction in Irish.

'You speak our language, my lord?' asked Aisling.

He gave her a warm smile. 'A little. Your brother has taught me.'

Aisling gave him an appraising look, noting his rich but sober-hued garb. This was the Madog whom Cormac had spoken about earlier. The man who would arrange the mass for her mother. The man who spoke of peace.

'Are you a religious of some sort?'

'No, no,' Cormac said quickly. 'He is King Owain's son.'

'One of his many sons.' Madog gave a wry grin. 'I could never aspire to the purity of a holy man.'

'Oh but my lord, you're just as holy as any priest,' Cormac said.

'No, I would never entertain such blasphemous thoughts.'

'Of course not...I only meant that—'

'I know my dear boy, and I appreciate the kind intention by the remark.'

Aisling watched this exchange with wonder. She hadn't remembered this man as one of the identified brothers at the table in the hall, but there was no doubt to his princely bearing. Clearly Cormac had found a mentor he could admire and look up to, but hearing their exchange made her a little uneasy. Was anyone that perfect?

'I'm glad to meet you, my lord, in any case. My brother clearly holds you in great esteem and that alone is sufficient to recommend you.'

'And I'm only too glad to finally make the acquaintance of his treasured sister, though I am sorry it's the loss of your mother that makes it possible.'

His eyes were full of compassion and she blinked back the tears that suddenly came. She could bear the rudeness, the oversights; it was the kindness that was difficult. While she had nursed her mother in the corner of a squalid hut on the edge of a farm belonging to distant kin, she could manage to face each slight or difficulty with a semblance of equanimity. Now, in the face of true sympathy, she nearly came undone.

Brushing the tears aside, she forced a smile. 'I thank you for your words. It is a sad occasion that causes this reunion with my brother.'

He nodded and glanced at Cormac. 'I will add your mother to my prayers.'

'That's most kind of you,' said Cormac. 'And I will pray for peace, as you do.'

Madog smiled. 'Pray for peace and the success of our venture.'

Cormac's face lit up. 'Our venture? It's been agreed?'

Madog nodded. 'I may begin outfitting the ship as soon as I would like.'

Unease stirred in Aisling. 'What venture is this?'

Cormac gave her a guilty look. 'Prince Madog has read of the voyage of the blessed St Brendan. Some time ago, when we were talking about long journeys to strange and exotic places, I told him the tale of St Brendan's voyage. Well, what I could remember from Father and the bits Bishop Aidan told me on his visits. Madog found them so interesting he wanted to know more, so he wrote to various religious here and abroad and gathered all the details he could. He eventually obtained a copy of *Navigatio Sancti Brendani Abbatis*. We read it through together.'

Once again she was reminded how different Cormac's

upbringing was to hers. Regular visits to a priest had given him his education and foundations for life as directed by her father and grandmother, while she had taken an entirely different path guided by her mother.

She gave a pained smile. 'I'm glad you both found it to your liking.'

Cormac showered Madog with an admiring look. 'Prince Madog has been a very good friend and more. He has guided me well these past few years and shaped my skill with words and sword. And now he's asked that I help his dream be made real.' He looked at Aisling, his face shining with purpose and belief. 'He would have me join him on his voyage.'

'Voyage?'

'To retrace St Brendan's journey. He wishes to go to the western lands.'

She was too stunned to say a word at first. 'The western lands? Why?'

Madog put a hand on her arm briefly. 'I know it's hard for you to appreciate how important this is to your brother and to me. We have studied his text these many months and have caught the wonder of his feat. I have prayed long and hard over this and I have felt God's desire that I should seek out these lands. Lands that are unmarred by the strife, the greed and grappling for power that riddle this kingdom and those around us.' His eyes took on a fire that she hadn't seen before. 'There we could establish a new life, one filled with harmony.'

She gave a small nod, uncertain how to respond to something as drastic as he proposed. 'Will there be many of you on this voyage? And will it be far?' As she waited for the answer, the story came back to her, a vague impression of a long sea journey encountering fantastical creatures. She glanced at Cormac and saw the eagerness.

'There are at least twenty men who are willing to accompany me, and now I have a ship and the means to outfit it. As for the length of the journey, I'm not sure. It may take months, maybe more, before we get there.'

Months? That meant many months going and many to return. Something of what he said before came back to her. 'You mean to return, don't you?'

'Of course. Once we've established ourselves. We'll come back for anyone who wishes to settle in this place of peace.'

It could be years before they returned, if they returned. What would happen to her if Cormac accompanied him on this journey? Her mind reeled. This wasn't what she expected. She'd hoped that once Cormac had heard of their true situation back home in Leinster he would do all he could to get some or all of their land holdings back. She hadn't realized his years here had loosened his connection to home so much.

'And you say you have been given approval? By your brothers?'

'Hwyel and my brothers who support him—Morgan, Llewellyn, Rhys. I would guess the others would have no quarrel with it either.' He gave a rueful smile. 'It is one less brother in the way while the kingship is decided.'

She understood more of his desire and the urgency of it. But it didn't detract from her situation, or the hurt she felt that Cormac would wish to part from her once again.

'And in the meantime, while you go off with my brother seeking this land, am I to remain here amid the strife, the greed and grappling for power?' She fought to keep her voice in control. 'That's if your brothers allow it. Take pity on a distant kinswoman who has nowhere else to go, for as I have just told my brother, our lands are lost and must be reclaimed. I cannot do that on my own.'

Madog put his hand on Cormac's shoulder. 'I had no notion that your circumstances have come to such a pass.'

Cormac stiffened. 'Of course, I had not thought for a moment, forgive me, Aisling. I didn't mean to push your welfare aside. I will of course remain behind, with you under my protection, that is, if it's permitted.'

Madog squeezed his shoulder. 'I'm certain Hwyel will allow you to remain with your sister for as long as you like. I'll speak to him.'

Aisling heard the exchange and tried to set aside her dismay that Cormac remembered her position only after she reminded him and Madog expressed his sorrow at it. She weighed the options of Cormac staying behind on sufferance and found that she still preferred that to the separation and the danger he might never return.

'Thank you,' Aisling said. 'I appreciate your help in this.' She noted the barely concealed disappointment in Cormac's face. She sighed, hoping she might find some way to make it up to him. She loved her brother too much not to wish otherwise.

Aisling smoothed her gown, trying to remove the wrinkles evident in the strong sunlight of the castle solar that also functioned as sleeping quarters. The dress's disgraceful state owed in part to its journey across the sea in the small sack that contained her belongings. The old nag of a horse that had taken her across country had barely been able to carry the two of them, let alone the sack. And now the nag and Tomás were already making their way back to Ireland.

Thinking of it, a small tear caught in her eye. Perhaps she was better served to wear the salt-stained gown that she'd worn these past few days since her arrival. She cast a glance at the group of women who sat sewing along the benches encircling a blazing fire in the brazier that took the sting out of the cold morning air. The women regarded her mostly with mild curiosity, though she could detect a trace of suspicion among a few.

'Would you like to borrow a gown? I'm sure Glennys would lend you one.' It was the late king's daughter, Lady Blodwen, who asked the question, green eyes tightening in an unbecoming manner.. Her thin lips narrowed as she tried to sweeten the barbed question with a smile. 'Perhaps you might also like a shirt to mend, to pass the time.'

Aisling refused both offers, imagining what kind of gown the large-framed woman who attended Lady Blodwen might possess. Even if it was suitable, she couldn't bring herself to don something in the fashion these women wore, so tight across the body, revealing all their curves. How strange they looked, so different from the women at home. It seemed as though they wished to bare all to the men. That was the last thing she desired, to give any hint of her body's curves so that one might take an unwelcome fancy to her and agree to take on her care.

The women, so eager to gossip as they plied their needles mending or, in the noblewomen's cases, fashioning embroidered coverlets, hangings and other luxuries, revealed more than either Cormac or Madog had about the events that pressed in upon them. Hwyel was one of the main contenders for the throne, not that she hadn't guessed, but the women seemed sure he was in the strongest position with his brother Davydd the only other serious challenger. And Davydd was at this moment gathering his men, preparing to make his way here and challenge his brother for the right to the throne. She'd gathered this much in the Latin mixed with only a sprinkling of Welsh they spoke, in deference to her presence.

'What think you of Madog's plans to visit these western lands?' This question came from another of the king's daughters, Gwendolyn, whose soft brown eyes reflected the gentle nature she possessed.

'He seems to have worked hard to ensure its success,' Aisling said. It was not the answer the other women hoped for, she knew, but she would never betray the distress it caused her. Though Cormac had resolutely held to his determination to remain behind, over the weeks she'd noticed a slight weakening when Madog spoke with him about the plans, thinking by including him, Cormac wouldn't feel excluded as much. Madog had also assured her privately that he'd spoken to his brother about the two of them remaining behind and had been surprised when Hwyel had only said he would consider it. Had Hwyel other plans in mind?

'But don't you find the idea of sailing off in search of these lands terrifying? What if they should sail to the world's end? Fall into a great abyss?'

'I think it's exciting,' Glennys said.

'Don't be foolish. How could something so dangerous be exciting?'

Aisling didn't know the round-cheeked woman who had spoken. The woman's head covering obscured every trace of hair, chin and neck, but the fine quality of her dress indicated she was as noble as Blodwen.

'I don't know, it's just the thought of sailing away, seeing new lands, new people. An adventure.'

'Heavens, child, you'll be telling us next you want to go along,' the round cheeked woman said.

Glennys blushed. 'Oh no, I would never wish for that. I just would love to hear about it. Think of the tales they will have to tell when they return.'

'If they return,' said the Lady Blodwen.

A few of the women cast sideway glances at Aisling.

'The Lord will protect them,' said Gwendolyn.

The Lady Blodwen put down her needlework for a moment, her face a semblance of kindness. 'This must cause you some concern, my dear. The thought that your brother might not return. And what will become of you?' She reached across and patted her hand. 'You must not fret, though, my brother is in the process of arranging a match for you with a fine man, Ivor ap Llewellyn, a landholder near here.'

The other women gave her pitying looks. Aisling flushed, her thoughts in turmoil. 'I-I'm sure there is some mistake. My brother means to stay here, now, so there is no need for a marriage.'

'I believe that Prince Hwyel saw fit to make other arrangements,' Lady Blodwen said. 'Your brother is to go with Prince Madog, as originally planned, and you are to be placed under the care of your new husband.'

'Was Ivor truly the best Hwyel could manage?' asked Gwendolyn.

'Sister, you know Hwyel has need of all but the most infirm of his supporters on the battlefield. Ivor is a good choice because there is no doubt that he will survive any encounter with Davydd. He is simply too old and infirm to hold a sword. And all those children need a mother.'

'There's no fear he would lose his looks if he was to go into battle,' Glennys said in a wry tone.

The round-cheeked woman frowned at her. 'There is no need to mock the man's deformity, may God have pity on him.'

Aisling absorbed this exchange with growing horror. What other slights would be heaped on her? She suddenly wished that she'd accepted their offer to give her a shirt to mend. She had a great wish to stab something, even if it was a needle into cloth.

She endured their chatter, making no comment. They seemed content to leave her be, now that they had imparted all the barbed and spiteful news they could muster. She allowed her thoughts to dwell in the misery she felt, her hands clasped firmly, her nails digging into the palms of her hand. Finally she could sit still no longer and excused herself to take some air. She needed time to think alone, away from observing eyes.

BIRDS PERCHED in the trees that surrounded her sang spring courtship songs, reminding her it was a time for hope. Though only a short walk away from the castle, the forest was a place to soothe, and it was away from the tension and watchful eyes of the king's court.

Aisling located the holy well with ease, its small pool of water reflected the afternoon sun that shone through the small clearing ahead. Approaching the well with a mixture of curiosity and anxiety, she knelt beside it and stared into the clear water to the silty bottom below. There was no danger of a vision here, no chance that without employing any of the rituals she'd been taught, the gift her mother had longed for would now manifest itself. Nevertheless, at this moment she couldn't help but wish that she might see something of her future. Some kind of sign that all would be well. She peered closer and saw nothing. Angrily she dashed the water with her hand, disrupting the stillness. There was no point in wishing what could never be. What she no longer believed in.

'Sorry I'm late,' said Cormac. His face was red and he was breathless. 'I was delayed by one of the men who are assembling supplies for the journey. He thought to ask me some questions about cattle.'

She rose and refrained from commenting on an action that seemed as absurd to her as it would have been to her father. Cormac had never had an interest in cattle, despite all her father's efforts. He found playing the harp a much better pursuit.

'And you were helpful?' she asked. She tried to keep her tone neutral.

'To some degree,' he said. He gave her a sheepish look. 'I tried to recall as much as possible what Father spent so much time forcing inside my addled head.'

She nodded, softening. 'You had other interests then.'

He laughed. 'That's a kind way of putting it.' He laid a hand on hers. 'I have been meaning to speak with you all morning, but have been kept from it by pressing concerns. But you speak first. What was it that caused you to ask me to meet you here in private?'

Taking a deep breath, she grasped her brother's hand. She'd thought long and hard how to form the words, plead her case with her brother. 'I'm not certain if Hwyel has told you, for I've only just heard it from his sister this morning, but he has decided to arrange a marriage for me.'

Cormac flushed. 'I had thought as much from what Madog said and I meant to tell you myself. It appears that Hwyel thinks it better that you help seal Ivor ap Llewellyn's allegiance by a marriage. Though you're distant kin, you are kin nonetheless.' Cormac sighed. 'Madog said he would settle a respectable dowry on you as well.'

'And you are to leave me and go with Madog now?'

Cormac nodded, a hint of sadness in his face. 'I'm sorry that I must leave you to this fate, but Hwyel insists that I go as well.'

'Wouldn't he prefer you to remain behind and help fight his cause?'

'My fighting skills are such that I won't be sorely missed.' He smiled a moment, a brief flash of humor that allowed her to glimpse the young boy she remembered. He sobered a moment later. 'No, I think Hwyel may have other plans in mind. Perhaps he wants to stake out claims to our lands once his throne is secure. There are other Welsh lords eager to help the old Leinster king regain his throne. Why shouldn't he use this opportunity to get our lands back but keep them for himself?'

She took in all he'd just explained and tried to see the way through it. 'Take me with you,' she whispered. The words were out of her mouth before she could stop them. She knew she could never consider anything else, especially not marriage to an old man with seven children.

Cormac searched her face and bit his lip. 'You know it's impossible. I will talk to Madog, if you like, and discover if this man is honest and good and really suitable for you.'

She sighed. She'd have been surprised had he reacted any other way. But she would rather risk the men, the danger and be with her brother than remain here at a court full of women who disliked her, and men who sought to marry her off to some wretched old man with seven children. Madog was courteous towards her, and his religious and peaceful nature ensured that she would be afforded protection, whatever other dangers she might face. There was no alternative, she must choose the other course of action and leave behind all thoughts of reclaiming what belonged to her family. She would not be separated from her brother again.

She forced herself to smile. 'You are right, of course. It was only wishful thought, spoken in haste, but very impractical. Forget I spoke.'

AISLING PULLED her woolen brat tighter around her against the night air, glad that its dark length extended to the edge of her gown. Though spring had come these past weeks, tonight she still felt the lingering bite of winter. She glanced up at the clouds that raced across the night sky, momentarily obscuring the half-moon that shone out brightly. It was wise to make her move now, leave her hiding place and board the ship under the cover of darkness.

She clutched her small bundle of provisions and made herself creep forward, ducking behind the remaining barrels that lay ready to be loaded on the ship before it began its journey downriver on the early morning tide. Her heart raced as she pushed the small curragh into the water as quietly as possible and took up the oar. With as little splash as possible, she rowed the boat towards the anchored ship, scanning the decks for the man she knew was assigned there as guard. She located him at the far side of the boat and breathed a sigh of relief. At least fate had smiled on her so far.

When she was close enough, she banked the oars and allowed the curragh's momentum to carry her the rest of the way. She grabbed the knotted rope that served as a ladder and with her bundle securely in one hand, kicked the boat away towards the bank and climbed up the rope ladder. It was an awkward progress with gown and the linen *léine* underneath it threatening to entangle her legs, but she eventually managed to reach the top and haul herself over. She landed on the deck with a thud and for a moment she held her breath, certain she'd alerted the man keeping watch. After a while, when no alarm had been raised, she made her way across the deck.

It took her a while to locate the trap door that led to the storage area. She'd questioned Cormac thoroughly about the ship's layout, under the pretense she wanted to know as much as possible about the voyage he was to make without her. Now she put this information to full use. Once she found the trap door, she took the iron ring and heaved it open, hoping that such a new ship would mean the door made little sound. There was only a small creak in the end, one that would be lost among the other noises of a ship in water.

She descended the wooden ladder that led inside and blinked at the darkness that greeted her. She was glad, for if it meant she wouldn't know exactly how many rats might be already making their home among the barrels of flour, oats, salted beef, ale and other foodstuffs that would see the men through their journey. She felt her way to these barrels, her hands stretched outward, her feet stepping tentatively. Reaching her goal, she moved along the timber containers until she came to the far side of the ship. There, among cloth sacks and a large pile of rope, she cleared a small hiding place for herself. She sat down and curled her legs up against her chest. With luck she could remain hidden here until they'd sailed far down the coast, unable to send her back in one of the curraghs in disgrace.

.   .   .

IT WAS the retching that gave her away when they opened the hold on the second day. She had long since lost any desire to keep her presence hidden with the ship's constant rolling that left her stomach in such a miserable state. Worries over sufficient food and water had vanished after she'd emptied the contents of her stomach a few times, to be reduced to finding a position that provided the most comfort. Even the rats kept their distance, preferring to feast on the dustings of grain that scattered the floor.

The light that poured in from the open hatchway hurt her eyes. She felt so awful she closed them after a moment and it was only when her arm was grabbed and she heard an angry exclamation that she made herself open them again and saw the silhouette of a man looming over her. He'd spoken in Welsh, but she needed no translator to understand his query.

'I'm sorry,' she said in Latin.

After a few more expletives the man hauled her up, dragged her over to the ladder and up the steps. She stumbled along, trying to keep her footing, but it was mostly a lost cause. Out in the light she blinked hard and raised her free arm to shield her eyes. She could just make out her dark-headed captor, his face thunderous. He was only vaguely familiar, one of a number of men she'd seen around Hwyel.

She needed no introduction to the next face she saw. All kindness and compassion vanished when she stood before him, her feet fighting for purchase amid the rocking ship. The salt air stung her face, exacting a small price for the freshness that filled her lungs. She could only imagine the picture she presented—bedraggled hair, gown full of unmentionable stains and her face grimy. Despite her misery she was afraid.

'How is it you come to be on this ship, madam?' Madog's tone was clipped, anger simmering below the surface.

'I'm sorry, my lord, if this causes you great trouble, but I had no other choice.'

'No other choice? This is no choice. You shouldn't be here. You belong back in Gwynedd, safe with my brother.'

'I wasn't safe, my lord. That's the nub of it. That's why I had to come with you.'

'Safe? Of course it was safe. Why would you think otherwise?'

She searched her mind for the words she'd practiced before the ship had sailed, but they vanished in the face of her wretched state and the fury that confronted her now. 'I'm sorry. In truth I couldn't be separated from my brother once again.' It was feeble she knew, but it was all she could think of because it was the truth.

He scanned her face a moment and sighed, all emotion leaked out. Behind him men gathered, sporting expressions ranging from astonishment to anger.

'You must be rid of her, my lord Madog. She can't remain with us.'

It was the man who'd dragged her from the hold who had spoken, the scar that creased his brow a vivid red. His rage was apparent.

'It wasn't something we planned, I know Rhodri, but we must do what is right.'

'You aren't thinking of allowing her to stay here? A woman has no place aboard this ship.'

Madog gave him an even look. 'This is not the time to let your anger overrule what is right. I'll give some thought to the best possible course.'

Cormac came into view, his face awash with surprise and embarrassment. 'Aisling, how did you come to be here?'

She realized now her presence would cause him difficulties among his shipmates. She could only offer her apologies. 'I'm sorry, Cormac.' She lowered her head, suddenly very tired. Crumpling, she fell to the deck.

3

———————

The sun glared strong and hard. She shaded her eyes with her hands, staring out to the horizon. There was nothing. Not even a breath of wind. The wind that once had blown strong, sometimes stormy, tossing their ship like some small leaf on raging river, had disappeared these last few days, giving way to this hot, breathless haze that left the sails limp. Such weather was not in the tales she'd remembered from Brendan's journey. She counted the days that had passed in her mind, *lá amháin, lá a dó, lá a trí.* They had mounted, piled high and heavy like a stone cairn on her grave, but still there was no sign of the western lands.

'It won't be long, Aisling. We'll sight land soon, I'm sure.'

Those oft spoke phrases, chanted like holy words from avid apostles, were offered up to her and other doubters who viewed the empty horizons glumly, gazed at the thin gruel and drank from the half-filled cups in despair.

Aisling turned to face her brother and gave him a wan smile. His hair, usually tied back in a neat band, or braided in sections, hung loose and lank about his face. His skin was sallow, like hers, the dwindling rations taking their toll on everyone. She plucked at his stained tunic that gave off a slight sour smell and hoped his words were true. She didn't like to see Cormac looking so poorly.

'Have you heard something from one of the men?'

Cormac gave her a sheepish smile. 'Madog.'

Aisling forced herself to return the smile. 'Of course.'

'He's a good man.'

'I don't doubt it, but that doesn't mean he's always right.'

'You owe him much.'

She sighed. It was true. He'd made the decision to allow her to stay, rather than turn back and sail up along the coast once more, or land her somewhere on the Irish coast, far from her home. Some of the others felt she deserved such treatment or worse, especially Rhodri, the man who found her. He'd never stopped muttering whenever she came into view, casting scowls her way. Of late the muttering had grown to audible comments, words that blamed her for the cursed weather, the days drifting aimlessly on a vast ocean.

'You're right,' she said. 'I owe him much.' She patted her brother's hand. I am only cross from this heat.'

He nodded and gave a wan smile. 'We are all cross from the heat, and the endless days seemingly going nowhere.' He forced a smile. 'But it will soon be made right. Once we sight the western lands and go ashore.'

She refrained from pointing out the loosening teeth, the thinning hair and ravaged gums that were dogging many of the men. It was to no end, and she had opted to be a part of this journey, no matter the outcome. She lifted her braid to cool the back of her neck.

'I hope it will be as you say,' was all she said.

THERE WAS STILL no change in the weather a few days later as she sat on the deck mending a torn sail. With so little wind it seemed the best time to perform such a task, though the last storm they'd encountered had nearly made this sail fit only for scrubbing the deck. She would do her best though, and her dubious skill with the needle was better than any of the clumsy attempts Madog or any of the other men might make.

Here, too, she could avoid Rhodri, whose turn at the watch had recently finished and allowed him to find sleep. In the cramped quarters of the ship, it was hard to avoid anyone for any length of time, but she'd recognized and silently thanked Madog's efforts to keep Rhodri away from her.

She plied the needle, gathering up the frayed ends, and wove it into a semblance of unity. It was an interminable task, but somehow she found it soothing, taking her focus away from her grumbling stomach and the endless horizon in front of her.

'We're fortunate to have your many skills on this voyage.'

She looked up into the looming figure that blocked the sun, the features cast into shadow, but nonetheless unmistakable.

'My skills are not great, but I'm happy to apply them, my lord Madog.'

'But they are great. You've also worked wonders stretching the gruel over so many days.'

'Thank you. I appreciate your words.'

'They are truly meant.' He fell silent a moment, his face set. 'You must not mind the others.'

She nodded. She was grateful for his efforts to assure her that her presence was a help and not a curse, as some of the men believed, but she must convey the truth of their position.

She gave him a direct look. 'The situation is serious, my lord. There is little left. We've only a few days' provisions, and maybe a week's worth of ale. The cow's death has been a great blow.'

'I know the supplies are low, but you must believe that the land is there. I can feel it in the air. Its stillness. And if you close your eyes and listen hard, you can hear it speak to you in this stillness.'

She looked up at him, able now to discern the flushed face, the brilliant eyes that held hers. With a sigh she closed her eyes, knowing silence would greet her.

'I hear nothing, my lord.'

SHE FELT Rhodri's presence behind her before she saw him. There was something in the air, a tension that made her conscious of his proximity, something that she counted on in her daily negotiations of the ship and her various chores.

Here now, cooking the gruel in a pot that hung over the small metal box that housed the fire on deck, she could hardly avoid him when it came time for the men to come for the daily victuals, a task she carefully supervised in these days of strict rationing. What better way to ensure that she and Cormac were fed, and avoid Rhodri or any of the other twenty men taking an extra dip of the ladle or a larger chunk of bread that might mean the difference between life and death for Cormac?

With the back of her hand she wiped her brow, damp from the sun's heat and the fire that burned quietly underneath the pot. She took up the chipped bowl at her side, ladled a portion of the broth into it and handed it to Rhodri. He clamped a hand over her wrist.

'Give me more. The ladle wasn't full.'

She raised her eyes and frowned at him. 'That is today's measure. You're due no more than that.'

'I say you lie. I'm due a full ladle's worth of broth. I know Cynan had a full ladle's worth.'

'That was yesterday. Today Cynan will have the same measure as you. As will everyone else.'

Behind him three of the men shuffled closer.

'Is that true? You've given Cynan more than you give us?' It was Sion, one of the increasingly disgruntled group of men that Rhodri had collected.

'No, Cynan gets no favorable treatment. You all receive the same ration.'

The other two men exchanged glances. They were not convinced.

'I'm sure Cormac will get a full ladle's worth,' said Rhodri.

'Cormac will get the same as everyone else.' With her free hand she attempted to pry back his fingers from her wrist. He released her wrist, but not before he gave the inside of her arm a fierce pinch.

'It's your presence that has brought us to this state,' he said in a low voice. 'No woman should be aboard this ship.' He took the bowl from her and made his way below deck.

She watched his retreat, her eyes narrow. She turned to the other three men and began to serve them. 'Each and every person receives the same portion of gruel.'

'The weather's changing.'

Madog came up beside her where she stood at the prow, staring out into the darkening horizon. Above it, large thunderheads mushroomed, purple and bulbous. Directly overhead the sail cracked to attention, suddenly catching the sharp wind that gusted. It was hard to believe something that felt like such a blessing could be a bad portent, but the darkening sky looked less like a friend than the bright sun had.

'Will there be a storm?'

'I fear so. Very soon.' He wiped his brow of the sweat that gathered there. Her *léine* clung to her back under the wool gown and sweat trickled down between her breasts.

'Will it be a bad one?'

'I believe it will be.'

She nodded. The storms they'd suffered through before had been bad, but she'd never seen clouds of this shape and size beforehand.

Madog rested a hand on her shoulder. 'You should get below with your brother.'

His thin face was filled with concern, and something more. Was it fear? She turned to look at the dark billowing clouds once more and read their threat clearly. This would be no ordinary storm.

With another nod she made her way below to the row of rope hammocks that lined both sides, fighting to keep her balance as the ship began to rock, until she came to the one at the end, its makeshift curtain from a spare blanket affording her the only privacy on the ship. The ship heaved a bit and she grabbed the rope hammock to save herself from falling. Perhaps it was best if she tried to get a bit of rest before the storm worsened.

She climbed inside, the increasing sway of the ship making it impossible to do with any ease. Once inside, she saw the folly of her action when her stomach heaved with every pitch and roll of the ship. With great effort she managed to extricate herself, the condition of her stomach providing huge encouragement. She stumbled her way to the deck, seeking the air to restore her senses before she lost every last bit of her stomach contents.

In the open air, drops of rain slapped her face and the wind tore at her hair and clothes. She gulped the air, trying to settle her stomach and fighting to maintain her balance against the gusts that pushed at her. Around her, men ran across the decks, climbed ropes and fought to gather in the sails, paying little heed to her. She clung to one of the masts and tried to locate her brother through the wet hair that been loosed from its braid and now plastered her face. She saw him and shouted his name, but the wind tore it from her mouth as though she hadn't uttered a word.

A moment later large hands pried her fingers from around the mast and pulled her to the side of the ship. Through the driving rain she could see Rhodri, his dark hair whipping his face, his eyes furious. Frightened, she slipped and lost her balance, falling to the deck, but he dragged her upright. She tried to fight him, struggling against him as he hoisted her up to the rail, but his strength was greater than hers. With little time for even a scream, she fell over the side and plunged into the stormy waters.

She coughed and wheezed, her arms thrashing at the waves that pitched her around and threatened to shove her into the ship. Above her, she could hear shouting, but she hadn't the strength to call more than once. The thunder and crash of the waves and the storm's might made all attempts to cry for help futile. She could see the curraghs secured to the ship's sides swinging against it and straining their ties. A huge wave rolled the ship and threw her down into its trough, blocking her vision, but she could hear the splintering and shrieking of breaking timber. Planks and shattered boards rained down on her as she rose with the roiling sea. A curragh gone, broken from its ties. She was swept down again and shoved along with the pressure of a wave. Two of the planks knocked against each other and then slammed into her. Without thinking she grabbed at them and hauled herself up.

PART II

THE WESTERN LANDS

4

Smoke filled her nose; she couldn't breathe. Her mouth felt dry, her lips parched and her body was on fire, . She coughed and tried to open her eyes but they were sticky and wouldn't obey.

Her head was supported and lifted, and she heard words, but couldn't make out their meaning, though their tone was comforting. Her second effort to open her eyes was more successful and a face came into view, framed and cast into shadow once again by the strong light behind it. Was this the Ancient One, *An Seanduine*, the goddess her mother had spoken about so often?

Liquid passed her lips, a broth of some kind. She gulped it eagerly and coughed. Bile, tasting of the sea, filled her mouth and dribbled out. More soothing words and a gentle hand to wipe her chin gave her comfort once again. She eased her head back down.

Sometime later, she awoke to the sound of a crackling fire. The smell of the wood drifted over to her, a sharper, more fragrant scent than the kind she was used to. She opened her eyes and saw the canopy of stars overhead lighting up the night sky. There were stars here in this place. She traced their shapes and after much searching, identified *Arturus,* the pole star, in a different place, but keen to remind her of an earthly location.

She looked over to the fire on the other side and saw, reflected in its light, a man and woman, facing each other, in deep discussion, a discussion formed more with gestures and hand signs than any words.

They were a strange pair, both with long dark hair, the man's tied back, but the woman's hanging loose, shading most of her face. She could make out the man's high cheek bones and tilted almond-shaped eyes. They were animated at the moment, the man caught up in his discussion, his hands waving through the air as if conjuring something. It was then she noticed the finger, or rather the lack of it; an empty space in at the end of his hand where the smallest finger should have been. His gestures seemed to have more emphasis because of it. She watched him, mesmerized, having no idea of the meaning of all the gestures, but conscious of the woman's transfixed posture leaning towards him and nodding occasionally.

Whether it was her eyes that caught the light or the slight motion of her head, the woman glanced over at Aisling and noticed her stirring. She looked back at the man, motioned and with quick grace, rose and came by Aisling's side.

The woman bent over her, scanning her thoroughly, and then rested her hand on Aisling's forehead.

Aisling looked at the woman's face and recoiled. A swirling complex network of dots tattooed her chin down along her neck and the one shoulder that was bared. She'd never seen anything like it before and it unnerved her. Tales of her own ancestors' use of woad to paint threatening designs on their bodies before war came to her, but still she shuddered.

There was nothing but kindness reflected in the woman's eyes the few times they weren't averted from her gaze. Eventually, Aisling relaxed slightly and attempted a smile. The woman grinned widely, emphasizing several tooth gaps and a myriad of wrinkles around her eyes and mouth.

The woman nodded and spoke, the sounds and words so unfamiliar Aisling could only shake her head. Undaunted, the woman began gesturing to her, touching her forehead, her eyes, gesturing off to the distance and then pointing to her. Was she asking where she came from? Aisling could only imagine the meaning, but any attempt at answering the bundle of gestures seemed beyond her at the moment. She shook her head and tried to appear sorry.

The woman shrugged and gave a reassuring smile. She reached over and picked up a pottery bowl that sat near the fire, took up the spoon it contained and offered its contents to Aisling. She took a tentative sip. It was warm and tasty. She could detect something familiar in it, willow bark, perhaps. She sipped more of it and realized that she was hungry. The woman continued to offer her spoonfuls of broth and she took them gratefully. With great effort she managed to finish the bowl, but it tired her enough that she lay back down and closed her eyes.

It was light when she woke again; the stars had vanished, to be replaced by a searing sun halfway up the sky. She ran her hand across her brow, felt the beads of sweat there and shaded her eyes. Beside her the fire was out, its embers missing any trace of a glow. She could see no sign of the woman and found in her absence a sense of loss, a removal of some portion of the security she'd felt in her deep sleep.

She raised herself on her elbows, suddenly aware that she was only wearing her linen *léine*. She cast about looking for her dress but it was nowhere to be seen. Before her was a wide stretch of beach whose shoreline seemed some distance away, to disappear into an even wider expanse of sea and horizon line. The sun's glare created hazy rivers in the sand, a shimmer of lines and patterns that made judgment difficult. She looked to her left and saw the man a short distance away, in the shade of an odd tree, bent over a long narrow curragh carved from wood. With rough, light-colored bark, the tree bore branches and leaves that swayed heavily in the light breeze, to provide some cooling against the sun's strength. There was a smaller tree near where she lay, but its protective shadow had long since moved to the opposite side.

She watched the man rubbing the underside of his boat, eliminating the accumulated detritus from time spent in the water. Would she move to the small patch of shade of the nearby tree or did she have enough strength and courage to go to the cooler place in the deep shade where the man worked?

The heat won in the end, gave her the energy and the courage to rise up slowly, tug at her dirty, wrinkled linen shirt that only reached mid-thigh. She felt vulnerable, almost naked in the open air with so little on, though the fierce heat somehow made it seem less worrisome. With halting steps, she made her way over to the cooling shade. The man looked up, smiled and watched her progress. The distance wasn't far, but it was long enough for her, and by the time she arrived at his side, she found she was spent. Sensing her fatigue, he took her by her arms and eased her down on the tree trunk that lay behind him.

When she was safely settled he took a seat beside her. She pushed her hair back from her face and examined him carefully. Clad only in a leather breech clout, he had tattoos but they were confined to simple marks at his chin and an animal head on each of the backs of his hands. The silver bangles that circled his arms and wrists accentuated the dark tan of his muscled chest, arms, calves and bare feet.

He smiled at her and his face came alive. The dark hair hanging to his shoulders framed dark almond eyes that showed a depth, a caring that she initially found difficult to accept in someone so different to her. He reached over and lifted a large curl, long escaped from the semblance of braid that had survived her near drowning. He used the right hand, the one that was whole. He fingered the lock, rubbing it gently, his face full of puzzlement. After a few moments he tucked the lock back into her braid, a careful action given patient attention. With his forefinger he traced her brow, gently running the length of it. Her skin tingled as she allowed him this freedom and was surprised to find she wished for more.

His finger strayed down to her eyes, circling the left, across the bridge of her nose to the other eye, then down along her cheek to her mouth, following the contours of her lips, resting for a moment and then moving on. He cupped her chin in his palm, holding it there. She looked up into his eyes and, captured, she held her breath. Her lips were alive, responding to the memory of the light touch, until the enormity of her situation flooded her mind.

Everything came rushing back and a huge well of grief swept over her. A grief too much to contain, for all the loss that lay behind it. A sob rose up making her body heave, but the tears didn't come, just the uncontrollable moans that contorted her, bent her over with their power. The man lifted her up and encircled her in his arms, making soothing sounds while he gently stroked her hair and rocked her. He offered words she didn't understand, but their tone spoke enough and she allowed herself to be comforted.

She remained there, in his arms for some time while she waited for the tears. The tears didn't come, but eventually he picked her up, placed her directly under one of the trees and drew a light woven cover over her. He motioned towards his lips, indicating a drink and reached over beside the boat to pick up a worn leather bag. It was filled with water and she drank greedily, the full force of her grief and sun exposure giving her a tremendous thirst. When she'd had her fill she lay back again and closed her eyes. She could do no more for the moment.

This time when she woke, the woman was kneeling beside her, touching her arm. A strong breeze blew across her and under the darkening sky she could see the trees leaves about her bending against the wind's strength, creating a noise that competed with the crashing surf at the shoreline. The woman gestured for her to rise. With great care Aisling stood up and attempted a reassuring smile. The woman nodded and motioned for her to follow. Their progress was better than her previous journey from the fire, but with a strong wind at her back there was little enough gratification from the thought.

The woman led her along a sandy path among the trees until they came to a small hut of woven cane thatched with grass, sheltered from the wind by a band of thick mature trees and shrubby undergrowth. Aisling followed her inside the hut, ducking down as she passed through the entrance. The doorway, set in the opposite direction of the beach, provided enough light that she could find a seat on one of the small cane benches provided. The woman took a seat opposite and leaned over to pat her hand in reassurance. Aisling smiled back.

The hut could sleep two comfortably. Glancing around the hut she noted the cooking ware, a crude knife presumably for preparing food, and spoons, cups and bowls. Along one wall area were piles of baskets, some covered and stacked, woven in intricate designs, dyed colors and formed in shapes that produced clever results. Folded neatly beside one of the baskets was her dress.

Where was the man? Was this woman his wife? His mother? Their different appearances didn't seem to suggest it, but knowing nothing about them, or their customs, she'd no idea what to assume.

She allowed her speculation to extend beyond the hut, beyond the shoreline and out to sea, careful of any internal storm, as her host was careful of the storm brewing outside. Somehow she'd arrived here, to this shore of a land she knew nothing about. Was this the western land that Madog hoped for? Again she tried to recall the legend of St Brendan, told countless times by countless people at her own hearth and during celebrations elsewhere. The land of his tales told of floating ice larger than castles. Whatever Madog imagined, this was certainly not the land of Brendan's tales.

Were Madog and her brother here, now? Were they further up the coast surveying this land and wondering the same things as she? She prayed that it would be so. Prayed that the ship wasn't lost in the storm or crashed on some rock outcrop, dashing the ship and drowning all it contained. But then she'd been saved. Somehow. She could only hope for the same fate for them.

The woman took a scallop shell filled with a liquid and while rubbing two bits of stone, struck a flame that caught in the liquid. It provided a bit of light now the sky had darkened into night and allowed Aisling to see the woman's features once more. The woman pushed a basket over to her. It was filled with small dried fish. Aisling took one and chewed on it tentatively. It was salty, but she found that she had no trouble eating all of it. Aisling nodded her thanks and smiled. The woman took one for herself and bit into it.

Aisling pointed to herself. 'Aisling.' She looked over at the woman, an inquiring look on her face.

The woman smiled.

Aisling tried again only this time after she said her name she pointed to the woman.

The woman thought a moment and pointed to herself. 'Pakahle,' she said. Her voice was quiet, almost a whisper.

They sat together and ate in companionable silence until each had their fill. Aisling experienced no guilt about eating Pakahle's food. She seemed healthy. She wore a white mantle tied at the shoulder and another around her waist, under which were pendulous breasts and a generous stomach. She certainly hadn't gone without. Perhaps the man kept her well stocked, or perhaps she had her own skills.

She thought of the man, recalling his work on the boat. He might have seen Madog's ship or know if someone else had. Or he might be able to help her search.

Aisling leaned over and touched Pakahle's arm. She shaped out the man to the woman and opened her arms in question. Puzzled for only a moment, Pakahle smiled in understanding, shook her head and stroked the air to one side in unison. Aisling's heart sank and tears came to her eyes for a moment. The man had gone away in his boat. Would he return?

She made a motion to Pakahle to ask the question. Pakahle observed her gestures closely, cocked her head for a moment, then shrugged her shoulders and shook her head. Did that mean she didn't know? Or that she didn't understand the question? Aisling tried again, but the Pakahle frowned and shook her head.

Aisling attempted to suppress her frustration. She would make another effort again in the morning.

5

———

Though it was early morning, the sand already burned her feet, making her progress awkward and her steps tentative to minimize contact with the beach. She'd been afraid to walk too close to the cooler, wet shoreline where the unpredictable waves might come and knock her over. Her confidence around such energetic water had evaporated, at least for now. In fact her confidence and the remnants of any belief she'd possessed had vanished, swallowed in the churning ocean.

It was only out of a sense of duty, a minding of her obligations that she raised her hand to shade her eyes once again and scan the horizon for some shape she'd call a ship. The strain of such effort was beginning to tell, for she was making the slightest bit of haze into a sail. This was the fifth day she'd spent walking up the beach, each time venturing a little further, to search for signs of the ship, to return a little later to Pakahle in the hut. Pakahle seemed to understand her plight, from the bizarre gestures, drawings and growing bits of vocabulary Aisling had learned under Pakahle's instructions, and was happy to let her wander and return as she chose. There were little other improvements.

'The man will help you,' was Pakahle's constant refrain.

'When?' she'd gesture.

'When he returns,' came the reply.

'When will he return?'

'When he has finished his task.'

It was like a circular conversation with a young child. Always back to the original question. 'He will return when he returns,' ran through her head. In the meantime she was left to fret and worry and reassure herself that by walking the beach she was increasing her chances of finding her brother.

The heat on the soles of her feet proved too much and she edged her way to the wet sand, eyeing the waves with care. Just for a moment, she thought, until her feet had cooled. But the sheer joy of walking normally without pain won out and she continued along the shoreline and tried not to flinch when a small wave washed over her toes.

The sun still scorched her left side, penetrating her bedraggled *léine*, the weave so loose it let her skin burn on her shoulders and arms, in addition to her face and legs. A wool dress was an impossible thought in such unrelenting heat. Her right side was no better, since her return trip exposed it to the sun, like a side of beef turned on the spit. Her salt streaked-hair felt like straw in places and the ends were bleached almost white.

She took a little sip from the leather bag that hung at her hip. She'd carried it since the first day's excursion had left her lips dry and cracked. Pakahle had given it to her at the same time she tried to get Aisling to put a woven grass hat over her head and even attempted to drape a mantle of a strange fabric over her, but she'd refused, finding it too hot. The fabric, like the one clothing Pakahle, was woven from the inner bark of what she called 'mulberry.' A wondrous thought to weave from tree bark. Now she regretted her refusal of the exotic garment and hat. She could see such arrogance would get her into trouble here in this strange land.

She had long since passed the area she'd reached the previous day, but this time she was determined to stretch herself, convinced such an action would bring some reward. Or perhaps it was punishment. Punishment for not believing in its effectiveness, for giving up any thought to a good outcome for her situation. She could not fathom what she thought anymore.

She squinted out into the distance. There wasn't a cloud in sight, only a yawning horizon over a shimmering ocean. She frowned, wiped the sweat that trickled from her brow into her eyes and tried again, this time squinting harder, but still the same result. She looked away to the shoreline in front of her and realized the beach was narrowing into a small path that veered away from the shore into huge undergrowth tangled around tall trees. She halted uncertainly. Should she proceed further, explore that path? It would take her out of sight of the water and the horizon. She eased her burning shoulder and decided the risk was worth the time out of the sun's direct light.

As soon as the shade of the towering bushes and trees eclipsed her, she had no doubt about the wisdom of her choice. She blinked at the sudden darkening. After a short while she paused a moment and closed her eyes, drawing in the cool freshness that surrounded her and permeated the soles of her feet. She sank to her knees and then fell back, her head cushioned by a plant that grew in lush abandon. At her feet she disregarded the tickle of an insect crawling across her skin. Just a few moments, she thought. The rest will strengthen me.

It was the loud squawking of a bird that woke her. Startled, she bolted upright to a standing position, scanning the dense growth on either side of the narrow path. A disturbance among the plants near the path up ahead caught her attention, and a snake of more than respectable size slithered out and across the path. She froze. Cormac had pointed out one of these creatures to her in Wales and warned her to take care around them. Not all were harmless. She looked down at her bare feet. New swellings from recent bug bites marked them, and she fought the urge to bend down and scratch them. The sea must have washed off the grease and pinesap salve Pakahle had given her to prevent the bugs from biting.

She raised her eyes and watched the snake that seemed to pause, his forked tongue darting the air as if it was sniff, sniffing her. A tiny whimper escaped her. She held her breath and sweat gathered on her brow. And then the snake was gone, vanished into the undergrowth.

Aisling released her breath in one ragged exhale and remained motionless for a moment, unable to move in the aftermath of the sudden fright. With a shake she tried to gather up her wits and move forward. Was it too late? Perhaps she should return to Pakahle. She had no idea how much time had passed since she'd fallen asleep. She shivered slightly. The glare and heat of the sun held great appeal at the moment. She turned and began retracing her steps. Tomorrow was another day.

PAKAHLE POINTED to the squiggly line in the sand that Aisling had drawn as an aid to explain the snake's appearance and gave her own word for it. Aisling repeated it and the woman nodded. She pointed to the long green leaf that hung from the tree that sheltered them and indicated the snake drawing. Aisling gave her a puzzled look. Pakahle reached over and caught up the edge of the dress Aisling had donned against the cool evening, now faded to a pale mud brown, pointed to it and gave Aisling a questioning look. A moment later she pulled at the leaf again.

Aisling understood the question. Color. She pointed to her brown dress.

Pakahle nodded then frowned. 'Bad,' she stated in her own language and proceeded to make gestures that told Aisling the snake would bite. Were the green ones harmless? Aisling shivered at the memory of the previous day. Just as well she hadn't moved.

A short while later she began to retrace her steps, her pace rapid, the leather bag swinging at her hips. Pakahle had explained the snakes came from the river; they didn't stay on land all the time. The river. There was a river. How big was this river, could a ship navigate it and where did it go? She'd assumed the man had just travelled further down shore somewhere. Had he gone upriver? She could answer these questions best by finding the river. Pakahle's diagram, gestures and few words had led her to believe the river wasn't far from where she'd been yesterday.

When she arrived at the edge of the undergrowth she was breathing heavily, her *léine* thick with sweat and clinging to her back. Her calves ached from the days walking in the pliable sand. She stepped into the cool of the shade gratefully. For a moment she closed her eyes, allowing them to adjust to the sudden change of light. Once opened, she moved forward, but kept a wary eye out for any movement among the foliage.

The path continued for a good while, the tangled undergrowth bordering it and, at times, spilling over into it, nearly obscuring it. She was able to break through or step over the growth in such places, but the effort became tiring. Birds squawked loudly to one another and leaves rustled in the canopy above her. The trees, a strange variety of oaks, willows and others she couldn't identify nevertheless provided a welcome protection.

Just when she'd thought she'd sit down for a rest, the path came to an end, the tangled vines and bushes so thick they suggested a wall. For a moment Aisling stared at the greenery in disbelief. She looked around her hoping to spot something that she could use to hack at the vines and shrubs, but could see nothing. With a sigh she moved forward and began to use her hands, tearing, pulling and ripping at branches, leaves, and bits of vine, disregarding the sticky sap that gathered on her fingers and palms, or the small cuts that marked her skin.

After making some headway she pulled at a large vine that suddenly gave way and with it a large clump of branches and leaves. She stared at it and realized it formed some kind of screen, a screen that she'd been tearing at for some time, until she managed to pull on a key segment. Taking care this time, she lifted the remains of the screen and placed it behind her. When she turned front again she could see a path leading down through the trees and shrubs to a river.

The river was no bigger than the rivers that crisscrossed those near her home, decent in size, but not navigable for a ship as large as Madog's. For a moment she thought that might be a good thing. She could be certain they wouldn't have sailed upriver and out of her reach this way, but such a thought lasted only a brief moment, because she knew they could well have sailed on past her down the coast at any time during any of the nights since she'd washed up ashore.

She sat down and regarded the river below her, contemplating its significance until she remembered Pakahle's warnings about the snake. She jumped up and scanned the area carefully, wary of the slightest movement along the ground. Everything seemed still. She narrowed her eyes. Something about the shrub to her right didn't seem to fit. The leaves, yellowed at the edges, were dryer than the others that surrounded her. She moved over a little closer, reached and picked at it cautiously, careful should anything suspicious crawl or slither out from under it. It came away with such ease she fell back a few steps and saw she'd uncovered a small overturned boat. Placed neatly beside it was a short oar, flattened on one end. Like the man's boat, it was carved from a log, but it was much lighter.

She knelt down and ran her hand along the rough surface, marveling at its craftsmanship. Carefully she turned the boat upright, surprised by its light weight, and examined the interior.

It was dry as a bone and leakproof. Or it hadn't been used in a very long time. The shrubs that had covered it certainly had been there a while. But her detailed examination convinced her of its worth. She looked down at the water flowing below her. It might be worth trying it out, just for a small bit.

She grabbed up the oar and made her way carefully down to the river, dragging the boat after her. Just before she reached the river's edge she put the oar in the boat and eased it into the river without releasing it from her grip. The boat bobbed under the force of the current as she pondered how to get in it. Clutching a vine that hung from a tree overhead, she put one tentative foot inside and felt the boat shift around under the pressure. This craft was more precarious than a curragh. She eased in a little more, re-balancing herself forward on to the boat in degrees until she could feel secure enough to bring her other leg along behind. With both legs inside she knelt carefully in the boat's center and perched herself on the small seat. Her hand still clutched the small vine. Reluctantly she released it and took up the paddle and pushed off.

The current took hold of the boat and carried her downriver. Thankfully, her largely useless efforts at poling with the short oar weren't essential to her progress. She marveled at the boat's speed and could only attribute it to its light weight and the current's strength. She studied the river and could see little beneath the water line for the mud and shade from the trees that bordered the bank. She was reluctant to move away from the security of the riverbank, especially now its flow seemed to be increasing in strength. The speed began to worry her and she decided she'd gone far enough. It was time to turn back. With some degree of caution she dipped the paddle in and held it there while she attempted to reverse her course.

The boat turned suddenly and, caught in the current, bobbed wildly in an attempt to find its own equilibrium. Caught by surprise, she stabbed the water with the oar, trying to control the boat. The boat shifted violently, arguing with her efforts, and just as suddenly flipped and tossed her into the water. Plunging downward she flailed her arms, desperate to reach the surface. After a few moments the momentum of her actions carried her up until her head hit the air. She gasped for breath, filling her lungs as best she could and stroked the water around her while the current carried her along like a stray log.

The water continued to pull her downstream with no regard for the overhanging trees that dipped low the water, slapping at her face. She cursed each branch until she realized that it might play to her advantage. Gathering her strength she reached up and grabbed the next branch that loomed into range, hoping it would bear her weight and her grip would hold. Her first effort proved unsuccessful, but the next, a larger branch connected to a substantial tree on the bank, gave her a fighting chance. She gripped the branch with all she was worth, and then worked her way along it, closer to the bank, using the vines and leaves that clung to it to pull her across and speed her progress.

A short while later she lay on the bank, exhausted. She remained there, unmoving, her chest heaving, for some time. Thoughts of snakes and other unknown threats couldn't stir her.

When she recovered her breath enough to sit up, she surveyed her surroundings and cursed herself for a fool. The boat was gone and she'd no idea how far she was from her starting point upriver. Her hair, dress and *léine* would dry soon enough, but how was she to make it back upriver? There was no path; fighting her way through the tangled vines, bushes and trees seemed an impossible feat. The water was out of the question.

She sat there with dripping hair and clothes and contemplated her options while she scanned the ground on either side of her for suspicious movement. When she'd examined every possible bit of leaf, log and pile of dirt she considered afresh the possibility of attempting a tramp back upriver to the path opening. What other choice had she really? With a sigh she rose gingerly and cast around for a stick or something that might help her make her way through and perhaps alert a snake that she was coming. Surely with such a warning he would slither off away. It was a plausible assumption, she told herself.

She located a serviceable stick and with a few quick motions stripped it of its leaves and climbed up the bank a little before trying to work her way across. She winced at the assault on her bare feet. Without the path or beach to cushion her tender soles she knew this journey would be rough for them. Still, she ploughed on and tried to ignore the pain, parting and twisting through the tangled growth. The vines and branches pulled at her hair, loosening her braid until there were more strands hanging loose than caught up in its twist. With a swift motion she grabbed up most of it and shoved it down the back of her *léine*, out of harm's way, but the motion caught her off balance. Her weight shifted further and she fell against a small tree, her feet went from under her and she was sliding down the bank until she halted with a jerk at the river's edge.

Momentarily breathless and shaken at the close call, she closed her eyes for a bit and tried to collect herself. When she recovered her breath she turned around to see what it was that had halted her fall so abruptly and saw that her *léine* was caught on a tree branch, hiking it up around her thighs. She tugged it carefully in an effort to dislodge it from the branch, but it wouldn't shift. If she pulled too hard she could see it would create a deep tear. She worked her way up the bank, taking care not to slip back and put further stress on the fabric's tenuous strength.

She was just reaching up to the branch to pull it closer to her to unhook the *léine* when she heard the slap of a boat and a loud rollicking laugh below her. She looked down and saw the man sat in his carved wooden boat calmly plying the oar and looking up at her, his face creased with laughter.

Maybe it was the strain and fear from the plunge in the river, the threat of snakes and other, unknown, creatures, but she could only feel rage at the sound of his laughter. She turned back to the branch and, with swift tug, dislodged her *léine* with only a small tear from her lack of care.

Still laughing, the man disembarked onto the narrow embankment and lifted his canoe behind him, shoving it through some of the underbrush to beach it safely. He stood up and examined her. Aisling pulled herself to her full height and tried to ignore her bedraggled state. She greeted him slowly in the words Pakahle had given her. He raised his brow, the humor still present in his eyes, and greeted her in return.

'I am glad for the greeting,' he said. He went on to say more and it was only after fierce concentration on her part and pause for reflection that she realized he was thanking her for coming to meet him, but that next time she should pick a better spot for landing his boat.

She opened her mouth for a retort but could only gape and shake her head. He laughed again and she reddened. And then suddenly she could see the funny side of it and for a moment laughed too. It was a small connection.

The man picked up a lock of her damp hair, glanced at her gown, then looked around her and possibly asked her about her boat. Or lack of it. She shook her head and motioned that it was gone.

He grunted then picked up her hands, examining the scratches on the back and then the palms. 'Come,' he said. 'Are you afraid?'

'No, I have no fear,' she said.

He gave her a smile. 'Good.'

A few minutes later she was seated inside the boat in front of him while he stroked the water with his shortened oar in strong swift motions. They sped along, the overhanging branches and vines now a safe distance away in their course along the river's middle. She dozed a little, her exertions and mishaps taking their toll on her now that she was safe.

Sometime later the roar of the water awoke her and she opened her eyes to the largest expanse of river she'd ever seen. For a moment the fear she'd experienced in the small light-weight boat returned as she felt the swift current catch up the boat. A quick glance back to the man confidently stroking the water calmed her enough to resume her position, though her eyes remained open and alert. No amount of tiredness would stem the thought that she needed to be on her guard. Her *léine* and hair had nearly dried, so she must have slept for some time, though the breeze from the river might have contributed.

The water took them along and Aisling realized after a while that this river was not the same as the one she had capsized in. They had come in close to a bank that now rose high above them. She couldn't even see the other bank. The water's color, for so long a mud brown, had cleared to a fine turquoise. Somewhere along the way, while she slept, they'd left the other river and come to this larger one. Large enough for a ship. She bit her lip. Where did this river lead?

It wasn't long before she found out. With dramatic swiftness the river widened and the smell and taste of salt hung in the air. The water stretched out across the horizon, the distant waves shimmering under the sun's strength. The ocean.

6

———

She knew his name now. Caxna. Pakahle had told her after they arrived back from her mishap on the river. She'd hesitated when Aisling asked, but eventually said the name in a low careful voice out of Caxna's hearing. Knowing his name she could now stop thinking of him as 'the man.' Especially since he'd saved her life. Again. This last time was even more undignified than the first. She realized now how foolish she was to even attempt to use a curragh by herself in an unfamiliar river. Now the boat was gone and she'd barely escaped with her life.

She felt doubly bad about the loss of the curragh, since after recounting her tale to Pakahle she discovered that it had belonged to her. She'd no idea how she could make up such a loss to her, for the boat was an obvious connection to the communities Caxna told her were upriver. He'd explained all this on their journey along the coastline, the waves breaking gently against the curragh's side until they reached the stretch of beach that contained Pakahle's home.

Caxna handed her a bowl of broth taken from the earthen pot heated by stones removed from the fire Pakahle tended.

With the aid of drawings in the sand, Caxna began to explain the layout of the two rivers she'd travelled on and the location of the villages north along the main one. Necessity and these clear drawings helped her vocabulary expand even more, and with Caxna's patient tutoring, clear diction and gestures, she was able to understand much of what he said to her. At first she could only notice the finger, or the lack of it, as he used his hands to gesture or drew pictures in the sand, but eventually it was his mouth, and then his eyes that drew her attention, her struggle to understand stronger than her fascination with the finger's story.

'There are two villages up the big river.' He traced the stick along the line he'd drawn earlier and stopped at the first circle. 'The first village is small, only ten dwellings.' He counted the number off on his fingers so she could see the amount he meant. 'That village is on this side of the river.' He paused and looked at her. She nodded, indicating her understanding. 'The next village,' he continued, 'is further upriver on the other side. That has many dwellings.'

'You went to the big village? Is it far?' She took her time with the words, stopping on occasion when she needed to think of how to phrase them simply enough for her vocabulary.

He shook his head. 'That village is only a day's canoe ride away. I went many days' journey upriver.' He held up his hand and counted off five.

'Canoe?' She had an idea about his meaning but the word was unfamiliar. He pointed to his curragh, now leaning upturned against the trees. She nodded her understanding and considered his words. Five days. But it was upriver so the journey would be difficult. 'Is the river wide and deep far upriver?'

'Yes.'

There was no elaboration though she raised her brows in question. But it seemed that a ship might sail upriver at least as far as his own destination. 'Did you go to the big village?'

He nodded, this time not even bothering to utter a word. She sighed and felt compelled to ask the question that hovered over her.

'Did you see or hear about a very large and strange canoe?' She used the new word for curragh with hesitation. Was it the same as a ship, or would they use a different word? She decided to draw it on the sand and sketch in the sails and a mast to give him a more exact image. Pakahle peered over her shoulder, pointed and said something rapidly to Caxna.

Aisling turned around and looked at Pakahle. 'What? Have you seen a canoe like this?' She tried to keep the excitement from her voice.

Pakahle looked embarrassed for a moment, then shook her head.

'She said your picture looked very strange, like someone drying cloth in the wind,' Caxna said.

'Oh.' Aisling chided herself for jumping to conclusions, noting also the disappointment she felt. Disappointment she knew was more to do with her brother than anything else she might admit to.

She looked across at Caxna. 'Did you hear about a canoe?' It was an effort to keep her face neutral and steel herself for the answer she knew was to come.

After a brief glance at his eyes she looked away. She'd read her answer clearly in the compassion and pity she found there.

'Is your family on that canoe?' he asked.

She nodded, her eyes still focused on the drawings in the sand. Perhaps that was good news, she told herself. They might sail upriver or pass by the shoreline here. She studied the sand drawing more closely. There was a bay at the mouth of the river, an ideal place to anchor or shelter while they took stock. They might yet still come. She sucked her lip, counting the days since she'd been thrown overboard. Was it really plausible they'd find their way here if they hadn't done so yet?

'You saw no canoe anywhere?'

He shook his head slowly, as though reluctant to give her such an unwelcome answer.

'Will you go upriver again soon?' It was a small possibility, but maybe if she went with him she might see some trace or clue that might indicate they'd been in the area.

This time he shook his head firmly.

She frowned. 'Will you take me upriver?'

'I cannot. I must journey to another place that is far away.' He pointed down the coast in the opposite direction.

She glanced at the empty shoreline and tried to picture what might lie beyond. Another big village?

'Is it important? Can you do it later?'

'No, I must do it soon. It is very important.'

'What you must do?'

He gave her an odd look. With her limited language skill she knew she sounded rude and too forthright for anyone's idea of etiquette, but she had no choice. Still, she could make an effort. 'I am sorry for my poor words. Why do you go now?'

He gave her a considering look and glanced at Pakahle, who nodded. 'I am a trader. I must go to this place far away to trade for something very precious and important, to take a long journey upriver for a person for a special day. I cannot be late.'

'Oh.' She couldn't argue with that. His livelihood depended on goodwill with those he traded with. They wouldn't appreciate late delivery, she was certain. On the other hand, during his journey he might hear news of the ship. She brightened. Perhaps the ship had sailed further west, away from that bay. Others along the shore might have sighted them. Or they might actually be anchored just out to sea, out of reach of her walks but easily encountered if a boat was headed in that direction.

'I would like to go with you,' she said.

There was no doubt of the surprise on his face. He shook his head vigorously, his long hair working loose from its band. 'No,' he added for emphasis. 'No, it is too far and too dangerous.'

She wanted to laugh. It seemed farcical to consider danger in a large sense, in light of her predicament. She realized now that if she didn't find her ship her situation would be far more dangerous. Alone she was vulnerable to all. She needed to find them, not just for her own safety, but to reassure herself that her brother was well. What her plans were after that, she had no idea. Madog clearly had arrived at a land different to Brendan's but she had no notion what he'd make of it, if indeed he had arrived somewhere on these shores.

'I have known many dangers,' she told him.

He grinned at her. 'Falling out of canoes?'

She reddened and forced a smile. She would concede that point. 'There was much fighting in my land for a long time. I am strong, I work hard. I could help with the canoe, make your journey shorter.'

He only smiled this time, but there was laughter in his eyes. 'It is good of you to offer, but no. You know nothing of this land I go to. It is not a land for you.'

Not a land for her? She wondered at his meaning. 'What land is this? Different to here?' She gestured around her. 'If I go with you I can ask about my people.'

'You do not need to come. I will ask for you.' His eyes were kind and it was the kindness that caused tears to well in her eyes and nearly made her relent.

Beside her Pakahle nodded slowly. 'You must listen to Caxna. What he says is true. Where he goes is no place for you.'

She turned to look at Pakahle, distracted from her distress. 'Why? Why is it no place for me?'

'They are different. Their customs are different. They do not always like strangers,' Pakahle said.

'You have gone?' asked Aisling.

Pakahle shook her head. 'No, but this is what they say.'

They say. Aisling wondered who *they* were. *They* were sometimes a dubious source that often exaggerated things. And any difference would be expected. They were different. Different from her, from each other.

'I have been there,' Caxna said. She looked over at him, his dark eyes serious and his arms folded across his chest, the tattoos imprinted clearly on his skin. 'Their ways are unlike ours.'

'Of course. Your ways and my ways are different too,' she said suppressing a wry smile.

He nodded. 'Yes. I do not know your ways. Your people may not like strangers. But these people have bad ideas about some strangers.'

She puzzled over these statements for some time. Caxna had stopped periodically and explained to her some of the words he'd said and now she was becoming bogged down by new words in her need to win her point. 'I will help with the canoe, I will cook, I will stay with you and when we arrive at village I will hide and they will not see me.'

She had no idea now why she pressed so, there was as much possibility of finding her brother and the others by remaining here with Pakahle. There was something about him though, that made her feel safe and that thought drew her to him. She leaned forward and touched his arm, just above the tattoo, adding a plea with her eyes.

He regarded her hand for a moment and glanced across at Pakahle. Pakahle gave her head a slight shake. Caxna sighed deeply. 'No. I cannot do it.'

The disappointment hit her hard. For one moment she thought she could sense his indecision and his capitulation. She cast around for something to say to press her case successfully. The lack of words hampered her, she wasn't able to explain the finer points, or ask questions that might elicit information she could use to convince him to take her. She looked down at her bunched hands.

'When do you go?' she asked finally, her voice dull.

'Tomorrow. I need much time for this journey.'

'How many days before you are back?' Aisling asked.

He gave her a sympathetic look. 'Many many moons. Maybe three.' There was a hint of hopefulness in his tone that convinced Aisling of the optimistic nature of his estimate. Even so, three months seemed a long time to go without news. She bit her lip. She had until tomorrow to convince him to take her with him.

KNEELING in the canoe as comfortably as she could, her *léine* under her legs out of the way, she forced herself to maintain a calm demeanor, her ears pricked for any sign of Caxna emerging from the shrubs and trees. She'd been as quiet as possible when she left the hut in the early hours of the morning, leaving Pakahle and Caxna asleep on the floor mats. It hadn't taken as much effort as she'd thought to turn the canoe over and push it to the shoreline ready to depart. She'd loaded the packs he'd prepared the night before and positioned herself in the canoe. It was a feeble idea, but she could think of no other. He might agree if she was already in the canoe and she could only hope that he wouldn't forcibly remove her from it. She searched the interior for something to grip and tried to set aside the ridiculous image of a Caxna prying her fingers from the canoe.

'You do not understand "no"?'

Startled, Aisling looked up to see Caxna standing over her. Her breath caught. So silent and quick. She must never forget that.

She squared her shoulders, her jaw set. 'I have to go with you.'

He considered her carefully, taking in her posture, her lifted chin.

'You will do as I say,' he said.

She looked at him, her eyes narrowed. Was his tone a question? She took a gamble. 'I will do as you say.'

He nodded slowly. 'You will help me paddle. You will cook.'

'I will help you paddle and I will cook.'

He turned and retreated up the beach. 'You will start by fixing a meal before we leave,' he said over his shoulder.

She sat in the canoe for a moment, too stunned to move or speak. Her eye caught the oar in the boat. The paddle. Was there another? How did paddling work?

She sighed. She would find out soon. In the meantime she had a meal to prepare. She smiled for a moment and felt a small stir of excitement. Was it the prospect of actively seeking the ship? She looked over at the retreating figure. Or was it something else?

THE FINAL MEAL before their departure was not congenial. Pakahle, upon learning of Caxna's decision to take Aisling with him, spouted a tirade of words that Aisling could only generally understand.

'You are a fool,' she told him and added more words that reinforced that point. 'She will put you in danger as well as herself.' Pakahle added more words that Aisling could only imagine elaborated on how and why she would endanger them both.

Caxna let her speak her piece and tried to offer reassurance. 'I will take care. I know them and they know me. They want to trade. They need to trade with me. I will not let them see Aisling unless I have to.'

'These people are not fools. They will know you are hiding someone and they will want to know who it is.'

He nodded. 'You are right. I will not hide her. I will stain her skin with berries, give her a wig and call her my slave.'

Pakahle narrowed her eyes. 'Slave?' She looked over at Aisling and scanned her face and figure carefully. Aisling made an effort to return her scrutiny with a calm look.

'Her eyes, Caxna. The color, the shape.' Pakahle gestured to her own, tracing the differing appearance against her own.

'Who really looks at a slave?'

Pakahle regarded him dubiously.

'A slave must always look down.'

Pakahle took Aisling's hand and looked at her with concern. 'You have said yes to this?'

Aisling looked from Pakahle to Caxna. Was she willing to go that far? Had she any choice?

'She said she will do what I say.'

Aisling smiled wryly at Pakahle. 'Yes. I will do as he says.' She could only hope that such trust would prove the right decision.

Pakahle patted her arm. 'Then I will pray the spirits will look after you.'

7

———

Her arms screamed with pain, her hands burned and her back ached as the sweat poured from her brow, along the bridge of her nose to trickle down and drop from her chin. But still she kept on. Stroking the water, trying desperately to match the rhythm of the paddle behind her. She'd no idea how many hours they'd been at it, or how much distance they'd covered. In the vast space of time there had only been one stroke and then another, and the voice inside her pushing her onward, refusing to give up.

Caxna had fallen silent after the brief instruction on the correct way to paddle, his lacking finger causing him no impediment. In contrast, her hand, with its full complement, found it awkward, the paddle missing the water or plunging in too deeply. Caxna said nothing, no praise, no condemnation. Any initial attempt to engage him in conversation faded in the face of his monosyllabic retorts. In the end she was grateful for the silence, too breathless to talk, channeling all her efforts into each stroke of the water and maintaining her balance in a curragh that bounced along, the waves hitting the sides with a heavy slap.

She took little notice of the fish that teemed underneath, shoals of varieties she could neither recognize nor name. She did notice the sharks swimming in the distance, their dorsal fin the only evidence of their passing, and a procession of dolphins when their periodic leaping caught her attention. These were sights she saw rarely in her own land where the sea was a day's journey from her home.

She couldn't help but feel the sun burning through the cloth of her tunic and undershirt and scorching the back of her hands. She'd donned the dress over her *léine* before the journey began, but now she wished she hadn't. Sweat poured down her back and under her arms and her vigorous movement had caused a tear at one of the shoulders. The salve she'd applied to prevent the sun burning her had long since washed off her hands in the spray from the waves that butted the canoe and the sweat had rinsed her face free of it. The curious woven hat that Pakahle had given her provided some protection and she was glad Pakahle had insisted she take it, despite how foolish she felt wearing it.

Pakahle had thought of many things to ensure her comfort on the journey, packing little pots of salves and unguents and packets of herbs and plants with instructions too complex for Aisling to understand. She could only hope she wouldn't need them. Still, she appreciated Pakahle's concern and had hugged the woman before they departed. In response Pakahle had pressed Aisling to her, cushioning her face against her large breasts. Pakahle was like a mother hen and she would sorely miss her company.

Aisling noticed a trickle of blood seeping from her closed hand onto the paddle. She winced but felt no astonishment that the blisters formed long before had broken and now the skin was peeled raw and bleeding. She carried on and the blood trickled faster and thicker. She fought for a tighter grip on the paddle, but her hand slipped on the surface made slick from blood.

She had no idea how long before they'd stop and she'd really paid no attention to their course. Caxna's place in the canoe and his deft use of the paddle was instruction enough to relinquish any concern in that direction, so it was a surprise when she realized that they were heading inshore, bouncing heavily over the waves, against their swell and dip. She glanced up at the sky. The sun wasn't directly above but it wasn't close to the horizon either. There was still plenty of light remaining. She couldn't help but feel relief, though. She wasn't certain how much more she could endure.

When they were close enough to the shore, Caxna instructed her to jump out and help him drag the boat onto the beach. She tried to obey but her legs had a mind of their own, or rather no mind, because they followed no command and communicated no feeling. Caxna gave her a puzzled glance before jumping out onto the sand and pulling in the canoe with her inside it.

'I am sorry,' she said and gave him a helpless look. 'My legs do not seem to work.'

He stared down at her. She knew she looked pathetic with her reddened hands that still gripped the paddle, her dress stained and wet with saltwater, and her hair, long since freed from its braid hanging wet and loose about her. The state of her. She tried to square her shoulders, become the daughter of Medb, a child of the brave *Fianna* warriors, but the effort lasted only a moment before it collapsed in the pain of her shoulder.

She raised her eyes to him and for a moment tried to suppress the throbbing that seized her and thought she saw a look of admiration, but it was so fleeting she couldn't be sure. Without a word he leaned over and gave her his hand. She smiled wryly, took the hand and tried to rise again. This time the pain of a thousand pins jabbed her legs and she cried out in surprise.

'Careful,' Caxna said. 'Just stand still for a moment.'

She nodded and tried to remain upright while wave after wave of the needling pierced her legs. At some point she was able to lift her legs without too much effort and she stepped out of the canoe.

'It is from kneeling a long time without moving.'

She nodded again and released his hand. He noticed a smear of blood on his palm, raised a brow but made no comment. She resisted the urge to examine her hands. One step at a time.

'Go sit over there,' he said and pointed to a spot a small distance away shaded by trees. 'I will unload the canoe and make camp.'

She did as he said, walking with a slow stiff-legged gait and easing herself to the ground with a groan. Sand caked her right hand where she'd placed it on the beach to support her descent to the ground, the smeared blood providing the moisture to make it stick. She lay back, let her limbs go limp and closed her eyes.

It wasn't the shuffling of the packs placed on the sand near her, or the grating sound of the canoe being dragged that kept her from an exhausted sleep, it was the screaming agony of her shoulders, arms and back and the burning in her hands. Reluctantly she opened her eyes and tried to distract herself by watching Caxna pull out provisions and the small ceramic pots that Pakahle had given them.

'Hold out your hands,' he said.

She did as he asked and offered her hands, palms up. She winced at the sight of them. Rubbed raw to bleeding at the base of the thumbs and down along to the edge of her palm, they looked more like some freshly killed meat ready for cooking than her hands. Caxna stuck his fingers into the small pot beside him and grabbed a generous dollop of the salve it contained. He applied it gingerly, giving a care to the loose skin that hung from places on her palm. She felt his strong fingers work, tending each hand carefully, almost tenderly, covering every part of her fingers, thumb and palm, then the backs of her hands where the sun had burned them. Each motion was assured and she could feel it in every muscle, bone and tendon. His fingers, so strong and sure, seemed to count more than their required number, rather than less.

Though the salve stung at first, it quickly eased, and along with it the burning pain that had kept her hands on fire since the first blister had broken. But there was more than easing her discomfort. The feel of his fingers, the careful circular motion that pressed and probed in certain places, places that never seemed personal or private before, but under his fingers seemed the most intimate exchange possible.

She looked over at him, his dark head bowed in concentration and face hidden by the locks of hair that had long escaped from the top knot on the side of his head, the style he'd adopted for their journey. He'd told her so little about himself. Where was his home, really? How long had he been trading? It was strange not to know about a person. In her community such a thing would be virtually impossible, the network of relationships and connections were so strong. Here, now, though she was confronted with this virtual stranger caring for her in such a tender manner.

He looked up at her and, noting her scrutiny, gave a slight smile and placed her hands in her lap.

She returned his smile. 'Thank you. That is better.'

He nodded, reached over for one of the bowls and rose. 'I will return soon,' he said.

Before she could put any questions to him he strode away and disappeared into the trees. She sighed, lay back down and gazed at the sky. She'd never imagined such a vast sky, so blue. And a sun that shone with such fierceness each day without fail. If not for the storm the first night she was ashore she would almost believe it never rained here. The western lands. What was this place, who were these people, so different from her? She shook her head. They were certainly different from the tales of St Brendan that featured fierce beasts in the sea and great ice mountains.

A crunch in the shifting sand was all that announced Caxna's return a while later. She raised herself again, despite the pain that flared in her arms and back, and watched him curiously. He knelt beside her, stirring and blending some contents from one of the pots into the bowl. When it was fully mixed he looked over at her.

'You must take that off.' He pointed to her dress.

She looked down at the stained brown dress with its frayed hem and the rent in the arm and grimaced. Her impulse to shake her head wasn't from modesty but the seemingly impossible action of removing it. She gave him a woeful look. 'I cannot move.'

He grinned for a moment only, then nodded and set the bowl down. Slowly he helped her up to her feet, avoiding contact with her hands. Her back protested a little, but she managed in the end to stand with her arms at her side. That was the limit of her capability.

A groan escaped as he raised her arms to shoulder height and gently pulled her dress up over her head. She winced when the sleeves slid over her hands, the wool threads dragging at the bits of her skin. Caxna made no remark with each noise she emitted, but when the dress had cleared her head she saw the care he took with the removal of each sleeve. When the dress was completely clear of her, he gathered it up, placed it on the sand and moved towards her *léine*.

She folded her arms over her chest. 'No,' she said. Was it the thought of raising her arms again and enduring the pain in her hands, or was it the shadow of what might happen between them? Up to now he had made no advances, and in truth she'd given no thought to the possibility he might want to bed her when she'd pleaded with him to take her. She could only put it down to the security she felt when in his company. Now she questioned that feeling and was suddenly tense, on guard.

But Caxna seemed to accept her refusal and told her to lie down on her stomach. She glanced at the spot he pointed to and before she could imagine how best to make the journey to the position Caxna was firmly coaxing her body in a prone position. She took care her salved hands were clear of the beach, their stickiness certain to attract clinging grains. The warm sand molded itself to her contours, a cradling effect that seemed to provide some ease to her aches.

She felt his hands on her body immediately. He lifted her *léine* upwards, past her buttocks and back, to her shoulders, halting where it rucked under her arms. Tense, her legs firmly closed, she was ready to jump up at the slightest hint of any wandering hands.

'Do not worry, I will be gentle,' Caxna told her, his tone reassuring. He leaned down, gathered up her hair and placed it to one side.

For some reason those words brought a sob to her throat, until she felt the first touch of his hands on the base of her back. Coated with a different, stronger smelling salve, his fingers and palms worked deep into her flesh, kneading and pulling. Underneath all that firm touch she could sense calmness. Like a baby soothed by its mother, each fingertip spoke of comfort and care. Though she flinched and moaned when his fingers found all the knots and twists her back had created in the hours she struggled on the water, his fingers told her this was for the best. Her body relaxed and folded into his care as he eased his way up her back. She drifted off a little, hummed in her head the tune her mother had sung to her as a child and bathed in its comfort.

His hands moved outwards along the back of her ribcage, a spiraling motion that sent ripples to her spine and along up to her neck. She reveled in the gentle rhythms, feeling the ease throughout her body, down into her stomach. Slowly, his hands moved upwards, working into the shoulders and down in the shirtsleeves, one hand on either side, a parallel massage. She wasn't certain when it began, perhaps it was when he began to stroke her hair and gently knead her head, but it was as though she was floating, hovering just above the sand, light as a feather. There was no pain, no burning or ache, just a lightness that she felt all over, a sense of illumination in her mind and her heart. It was as though her soul had opened up and the sun came pouring in. In that shining light she could see herself, clothed in shades of rarest purple, her hair streaming free, hands lifted up to the sun.

WHEN SHE AWOKE, a deep crimson light was spreading overhead and ended in a fiery ball that was just at the horizon, casting the distant trees in deep shadow. Sunset and she was suddenly aware she hadn't eaten anything since the few bits of dried fish in the canoe hours before.

She looked around her. Caxna sat calmly beside her with one of the paddles in his hands, winding a small, flat root around its handle with meticulous care. Gingerly she sat up, on high alert for any signs of pain with each movement. To her surprise there were none. She rolled her shoulders tentatively. Still no pain.

Caxna looked up at her and grinned. 'You are awake.'

She gave him a brilliant smile. 'I am awake and I have no pain. It is ...' she searched for the word for "miracle," but she didn't know it. How to explain that in gestures and drawings? She shrugged. 'It is good,' she said.

He nodded. 'Pakahle has much knowledge about this.'

'Did she know I would feel bad?'

He gave her a wry grin. 'We both thought it might happen.'

She laughed. It was a good thing she hadn't known before

she started out, or she might never have had the courage to go through with it. But now, feeling better, she was glad she had. Nothing to come could be any worse than what she'd already experienced.

She looked down at her hands resting carefully on her linen shirt. They were still red raw, with bits of skin hanging loose, but the angry look had faded somewhat. She bit her lip. How would she handle the paddle tomorrow with her hands in this condition? She eyed her linen *léine* and sighed. It seemed the only solution.

With the edge of the fabric gripped firmly in her teeth she managed to tear first one strip and then another off the bottom of her shirt. It left just enough fabric to reach the top of her knee, but sure, what harm, she thought. Her hands needed it more. She took the first strip and wrapped it carefully around her right hand, crossing over and around the thumb to give it extra protection there. She did the same on her left hand. It was the best she could do to create makeshift bandages.

She waved her hands at Caxna. 'Is this good enough?'

He laughed. 'Yes,' he said. He took her hands in his and examined the wrapping. 'Yes, very good. This covering is soft, yet strong.' He fingered her sleeve. 'It's very fine quality. I have not seen anything like this.' He nodded to her wool dress. 'And that too.'

She looked at her sleeve, remembering when her mother had woven the cloth. 'Yes, my mother made it.' She indicated the dress. 'And that—animal ...hair?' Again she was stymied by the lack of word. How to describe sheep wool?

'An animal?' he asked.

She nodded. She made a baaing sound. Would that help?

He laughed. 'Yes,' he told her and named an animal after making a sound that seemed more like goat to her. She nodded all the same and made clipping and weaving motions.

He laughed again and handed her the paddle he'd been

working on. 'I have wound this root around the handle to help you grip it better and keep your hands from getting hurt.'

She took the paddle from him and examined his work. Caxna had placed each loop exactly beside the previous one, leaving no gaps. It spoke of time and effort, not to mention care and concern. She looked up and studied his face.

'I thank you. You are good to me.'

He shrugged. 'You must be fit for the journey. It is a long way.'

She nodded. 'You can paddle the canoe a long time.' She handed him the paddle.

He took the paddle from her. 'Yes.' It was a statement of fact, nothing more. His eyes revealed nothing.

'Have you been trader long?'

A flash of pain crossed his face and he studied the paddle. 'Many seasons,' he said.

'Do you like trading?'

'Yes and no.' He gave her a wry grin.

'Yes and no?'

'Yes and no.'

'What is the yes?'

'I like to see new places.'

'And what is the no?'

'I would rather go home.' His eyes returned to the paddle held across his lap.

'Can you not go home?'

He winced a little and raised his eyes to her. 'No. I cannot.'

For some reason she pressed him. 'Why?'

'I cannot. Yet.' He rose and went over to the packs and pulled out a parcel wrapped in leaves. 'Come, we will eat now.'

She sighed. There was more than a language limitation that had halted the conversation.

8

She lay still in the morning light for a moment, mentally checking her body for signs of an ache or a pain that might have returned in the night's chill. Caxna had brought out a mat to cover her against the cool air, explaining it was best to keep such sorely tried muscles warm. She'd accepted the offer gratefully, a mild peace offering for his earlier abruptness. She knew she'd been wrong to question him so persistently—her mother would have been appalled—but her situation stretched beyond any laws of hospitality or decorum. She would give it time, learn more of the language, and over the days she might learn more about where they were going and where he was from.

She pushed the mat back and rose slowly to her feet, still checking her pain. Caxna lay beside her, his eyes open, watching her move. She smiled down at him.

'I feel good,' she said.

'I hope you can say that at the end of this day.'

Her face fell and she nearly wailed until he started to laugh. 'That is a joke.'

He shook his head and continued to laugh, leaving her

confused. He stopped after a while, the look on her face a strong enough warning.

'You will be fine,' he said finally. He pointed to the water. 'There, go into the water. It will revive you, give you good health.'

She stared at him. Was he mad? Did he want her to catch a chill? Bathing the whole body in water was something to which a person didn't willingly commit himself. It was a daily habit that she'd noted both Pakahle and Caxna practiced upon rising, but up until now neither one had forced her to observe it.

She narrowed her eyes slightly. 'It is not my custom.'

His face remained impassive. 'It will become your custom on this journey.' There was no menace in his voice, it was mild enough, but something about him made her hesitate from further argument. She frowned, gave a sigh and made her way to the water. Her *léine* would remain in place; she wouldn't bathe without its protection. It would dry soon enough in this sun. When the water was up to her thighs she took a breath and sank to her knees, her arms over her head to protect her hands. Time enough for pain when she had the paddle in hand.

Behind her she heard the heavy splashing that signaled Caxna's entry into the water. She kept her face towards the horizon, determined to ignore his presence so close by. Overhead she could hear the cry of seagulls as they swooped and dived for their own morning meal. After a few moments she allowed the water's warmth to soothe her. In truth she'd no idea water could feel this warm, as though it had been heated to her requirements. She rose a bit and decided to walk further out, until she was submerged to her chest, the waves coming in and breaking gently over her in a slow rhythm. She closed her eyes and lost herself, tumbling into the safety of the sensation.

'Look out!'

She opened her eyes in time for a large wave to burst over her head, filling her mouth, nose and eyes with salt water. Sputtering and gasping for air, she lost her balance and plunged underwater and flailed her arms around her, as all the horror of the experience falling overboard came back in a rush.

Two strong hands pulled her up, out of the water, giving her time to get her feet firmly placed on the sandy sea floor. Her hair streamed down her face, obscuring her view, but the two hands and now an arm guided her back to the safety of land. There she pushed the hair out of her eyes and rid her mouth and nose of the saltwater that still remained there. Her bandages were a mess, sagging and coming away from the palms, all her earlier care a waste.

'Do not worry, the saltwater helps your hands. It is good. I will put on more salve before we begin our journey today.'

She looked up at him, fighting the tears of her earlier fears. His arm was still around her shoulders and for the moment she appreciated its comfort. She searched for the words for thanks, but could think of nothing. 'You are good to help me,' was the she could manage.

He looked away, his eyes cast down. 'It was nothing. I would not have you drown.' He added something after that and when she quizzed him she realized he meant it would be bad luck for her to drown. For whom? Certainly she would not be alive to experience the bad luck that would result. He could only mean himself.

She frowned a moment and studied him, trying to fathom the man before her. He was retying his breechclout around his waist, his wet skin glistening and his hair loose and dripping on his shoulders. Suddenly she was conscious of her own bedraggled state, the wet *léine* clinging to her body to reveal all her contours, her breasts, buttocks and thighs clearly visible through the fabric. She walked over to her dress, picked it up and struggled into it, disregarding the pain as her hands slid through the sleeves. She would have to use a different approach should she be required to bathe again.

· · ·

CAXNA PROVED to be right and wrong about her condition at the end of the day. While she could class herself as "fine," in that she could step out of the canoe and help set up camp, her arms still roared pain and her back ached. Despite these problems she did feel a sense of satisfaction that she'd managed another day's paddling. And this time it was nearly a full day. Her months of farm work since the servants had gone had at last produced something positive. There'd been no big words of praise from Caxna, but a smile and a nod had registered a deep note of pride inside her.

Now, settled on a small clearing at the ocean's edge, she examined her hands while Caxna went off to a small pool of fresh water he'd told her lay a short a distance away. That he knew the water's location meant that he'd been here before, a fact she added to her other meager bits of knowledge about him. She would have gone with him on the pretext of helping to carry the water so that she might question him further, but the state of her hands made such an offer a lie.

Though the linen wrapping had helped to protect her raw skin to some degree, it hadn't prevented the inevitable pressure and rubbing the paddling created. They were bleeding a bit and, before the blood dried in a crusted mess with her bandage, she carefully untied and removed the linen wrapping from both hands. With the bandages removed, she rose, made her way over to the water and, before she could lose her nerve, plunged her hands and the loose bandages in the water.

She couldn't help the small yelp of pain that escaped her, even though she knew the salt would sting terribly. He'd said the salt would help the healing. After a few moments, when the initial stinging eased, she picked up the bandages and began to rinse them. When the blood and dried salve were removed as much as possible, she drew out the bandages. They would dry quickly in this warm breeze and be ready to apply in the morning.

Satisfied, she resumed her place back at their small camp and laid out the bandages on her sleeping blanket. There was no fire. Like the day before, they hadn't bothered with a fire. Caxna said it was warm enough without and they had some dried fish, berries and other fruit to eat, so there was no need to cook any freshly caught fish, crabs, or clams they might dig up. She wondered if it was caution rather than practicality that drove the decision, or perhaps both. She cast her eyes around, searching the dense trees and undergrowth. Was it a human threat that would encourage Caxna to minimize their presence?

A rustle in the trees caused her to jump. Caxna appeared, his two drinking pouches hanging from his shoulders, full to dripping. Aisling breathed a sigh of relief and resolved to push her thoughts in a less imaginative direction. She leaned over and reached into one of the large leather pouches, untied the thongs that held its soft leather flap in place and removed the jar of salve. With quick deft motions she scooped out a small amount and applied it to each palm carefully. She decided to be sparing in its use for she didn't know if there would be more once it was gone and it had already proved to be a good healer for her skin. The angry red color on the back of her hands had faded to a lighter color and her palms were no longer a pulpy mess.

Pulling up her dress, she applied a little to the tops of her knees where it had burnt the day before. She lifted up her shirt a little and smiled at the big block of red between two great white sections of her calves and upper thighs.

'Your skin does not like the sun.'

Beside her Caxna smiled. He squatted down and touched her knee, his hand a warm brown color against her beet red. 'Your skin is hot there.' His touch was cool, his hands still wet from fetching the water, but still she flinched.

She pushed his hand away carefully, forced herself to look in his eyes and searched her mind for the words she'd need. She'd given much thought to how she might keep Caxna at a distance, prevent him from bedding her. 'I am not taken,' she said. 'I must not be taken.'

Caxna gave her a puzzled look. 'You are not taken?'

She pointed to him, then to herself and then to her womb, her face growing red.

His face cleared and he smiled. 'You have not been with a man?'

She nodded. 'I cannot. I am...a woman who sees.'

He considered her words, his eyes searching her face. She shifted her eyes away, uncomfortable under his close scrutiny, certain he would see through her deception.

'You are a shaman?' The word was unfamiliar, but she could only assume it was the right one. She nodded.

'But what does that have to do with being with a man? Is that the custom in your land?'

She nodded. He cocked his head to one side, as if the change in angle would improve the ability to read the truth of her word. His eyes gave away little, just a touch of humor and perhaps a little caution. He picked up a lock of her hair and fingered it. Dried out and tangled from the morning's dunking and the day's work under the blistering sun, it fell about her face like wisps of straw, the braid catching only half of it down her back.

'Your hair is like the sun. So bright.'

She read the change in subject as acceptance of her words. 'Many people in my land have hair like mine,' she told him.

A look of wonder crossed his face. 'You are not the only one?'

She shook her head. 'My brother has hair that looks like that.' She pointed to her dress. 'And my mother had hair that looked like that.' She indicated her red knees.

He gave her a skeptical look. 'Hair like blood?'

'Yes. She was beautiful.' She fought a sudden surge of tears. 'She was very beautiful.'

He gave her a doubtful nod. 'And where is your brother?'

'On the big canoe I seek.'

'Your mother too?'

'No, she is gone.'

'Your father?'

'Gone.' She couldn't search for more words if she tried, her throat was too tight with emotion.

'Where is your land?' Caxna asked after a moment.

She turned her head to face the wide expanse of ocean and slowly raised her hand and pointed. 'There. Across the water, far, far away.'

He followed her pointed finger and considered her words. 'Across the big water?' His eyes narrowed a little. 'Many moons' journey?'

She nodded. 'Many moons' journey.' Her eyes clouded with tears. Caxna placed a calming hand on her shoulder and she winced at the small sting of pain.

'Paddling?' he asked.

She turned to face him, gave a wry smile and nodded.

He moved over and pointed to the ground. 'Lie down,' he commanded.

And so it was, like the previous day, he applied the salve with hand so deft and magical, each motion probed the hidden nooks and crannies of the tiny knots that riddled her body until each muscle and tendon seem to float loosely through her and lift her up like a cloud in the sky to join the seagulls, gannets, sandpipers and other shore birds that flew along the coast that Caxna had pointed out to her during the journey. She glided away, soaring out on the water, catching the wind.

9

She leaned over and examined the back of her *léine*, the tell-tale red stain unmistakable against the white fabric. It was as she thought. The first grip of cramping had come when she was still paddling, the sun just beginning to find its way down toward the horizon and she'd uttered a mental thanks that this day she'd thought to wear her dress against the sun's burning rays. Though the sun had faded its color so much that it was on its way to matching her *léine*, it still covered the evidence that her shirt could not. Her monthly courses had come.

It was the first time she'd had her monthly course since the ship. She had dreaded its arrival and yet when the days had passed with no sign of them she repressed the worry that something might be wrong. It was here now and what little relief its appearance might bring was brief under the weight of wondering how she must manage it.

Aisling searched the shrubbery where she'd taken refuge the moment they'd come ashore for something that might serve as a clout. She didn't want to use any more of the linen from her *léine* or there would be nothing left of it. Though it had been eight or more days since she'd torn her hands so much, she still felt the need of the protecting cover of the linen strips. Despite salt treatments of the daily baths Caxna insisted upon and the regular administrations of the salve, the hands were still a little tender.

A good sized piece of dried moss caught her eye, caught against the clump of leaves at the base of the shrub. Dried and veiny, it was somewhat different to the moss she knew from home, but it might serve. She picked it up, rinsed it through with the water from her bag and patted it dry the best she could with her shirt. How much it would absorb, she had no real idea, she could only hope for the best.

When Caxna returned with the water he found her unpacking the provisions they would need for the night on the rocky sand. This shoreline was small and cramped. She'd little notion they would spend a comfortable night and unconsciously eased her shoulders at the thought. Though she was more accustomed to the daily rigors of paddling, it still took its toll on her. Caxna worked hard to alleviate the aches and pains with a massage, a gesture she found especially thoughtful and helped her growing trust of him. He'd spoken no more about her need to remain a maid and had made no move in that direction either and she was relieved.

Caxna indicated the sleeping blanket she'd just laid on the sand. 'I will ease the muscles for you now, before we eat.'

She nodded and removed her dress, an action she could easily manage now after a day's effort in the canoe. She took the familiar pose on her stomach and gave a brief grimace at the little stab of pain there. Willow, she must get out the willow bark that Pakahle had given her and make an infusion, if she could persuade him to make a fire. How could she manage that without telling him why? Would it matter if she told him?

'Why is there blood on your leg? Are you hurt?'

'Blood?' She raised her head and looked where he indicated.

On the upper part of thigh was a smear of blood. In her haste to make a clout and return to the camp she'd forgotten to ensure her thighs were wiped clean.

She blushed deep red. 'It is my ....' Again she didn't have the word for it. 'Blood time every moon.'

A blank look greeted her and then slow comprehension that turned to horror. 'You are having your moon time?' He jumped up and backed away. 'Why did you not say?'

'Say? Why should I say?'

He said a few words she didn't understand. He tried again. 'It is bad for anyone who touches or is touched by a woman in her moon time.'

'Bad?'

He said a few words again and she could only shake her head until with gestures and repetition she could gather that she was polluted and must not touch him.

'I am sorry. I did not know. It is not the custom in my land.'

He nodded, appearing calmer than his initial reaction of revulsion. 'I know you have different ways. But here, during your moon time, you must not touch me or anything I touch.'

She stared at him a moment. 'How is that possible?'

He cast a glance around the camp surveying everything. Since arriving she'd dug through one of the bags and removed the night's provisions, including the dried fish, dried fruit and the blankets.

He indicated the bag. 'You will eat the rest of the food in that bag and use the blankets. I will catch a fish and cook it for myself.'

'You will make a fire?' She was amazed to see what lengths this custom would drive him and realized how serious it was.

He pointed. 'I will make a fire over there and I will sleep there too. You will remain here.'

'You do not want a blanket?' She knew his answer. She'd touched them all.

He frowned at her. 'My ways might make no sense to you, or seem even funny, but they are the same everywhere here.'

'All the people here have these ways?'

'Yes. Some would have you go make a small dwelling and stay there for five days, until your time is done.'

She considered this. 'Do you want me to do that?'

He sighed. 'No, it will be enough if you stay separate at night and take care not to touch things.'

'But how will we manage in the canoe?'

He frowned. 'We will manage.'

SOMEHOW THEY DID MANAGE. It was awkward. She had to learn to get in and out of the canoe without his help, to touch only the same places on the canoe so that he could avoid them with care and to manage her bag of belongings and provisions without his help. Each day and night he plunged in the water, an extra dip against any pollution accidental contact might have given him. She was still required to submit herself to daily baths as well; no amount of protests on this point would move him. At the end of the day they camped separately, he with his back to her assuming his own idea of an isolated existence.

She found it somewhat amusing at first, but then the loneliness of the nights crept in and took hold and she was glad when the moss packed inside her revealed no further trace of blood. The thought of no longer spending nights at opposite ends of another lonely stretch of beach lifted her spirits. Officially she was acceptable to go among these people again, a fact she immediately shared with Caxna when she stepped from behind the bush she'd found to confirm her new status after they'd come ashore.

His answering smile to her news made her wonder if he'd felt the isolation just as keenly as she had. 'First you must bathe in the water,' he said. 'Take some of the soapwort I showed you from your pack. You must be properly cleansed. Take the paddle with you, too.'

She nodded and did as she was told. It was easier not to argue.

When she returned, paddle in hand, her hair washed and streaming down her back, the dry blanket wrapped around her, she settled in a place next to him where he was examining his own paddle for hairline cracks.

'Are we going to stop at a village or anywhere with people at any point?' she asked. She'd realized now how long it had been since either of them had encountered anyone.

'Yes. In a day or two, if the weather is good, we will stop at a village.'

She looked up at the cloudless sky. Not a leaf stirred in the dense wood behind them. 'If the weather is good?'

He nodded. 'Yes. Rain is coming.'

She gave him a doubtful look. 'Rain?'

'Yes. Tonight. Maybe tomorrow.' He rose and began to pick up the packs. 'We must move our things deep into the trees and make a shelter.'

Still doubtful, she nevertheless dressed quickly under her blanket and helped him gather up their things to follow him into the trees. He led her to a small clearing and placed the packs he carried on the ground. 'Wait here,' he said. 'I will get the canoe.'

'Shall I help?' she asked.

He paused, considering.

'My fair share,' she said. 'After all, am I not to be your slave?'

For a moment he looked bleak, but then his face cleared and he gave her a nod. 'Yes, alright.'

Sometime later, the canoe was safely wedged between two trees and a small low shelter was constructed out of woven branches covered with boughs and leaves to provide them with protection. From one of the bags he withdrew a long twined rope made of vine, wound it around his waist and tied off the end. He closed the pack and buried it along with all the other bundles in the sandy soil and lay branches on top. Noting these careful preparations made her wonder.

'This rain will be bad?' she asked.

He squinted up through the trees and frowned. 'Very bad.'

THE WIND HOWLED, a raging monster keen to show its strength. It pulled at the protective shelter around them, until with one final sharp blast the wind whipped the shelter away entirely, carried off like some stray feather. She clutched at Caxna who held her tightly to his chest while the rain pelted against them in horizontal sheets, drenching them in the space of a breath.

She hadn't so much as closed her eyes since dusk, when the first few drops fell on the shelter. It was when the wind grew so loud they couldn't speak that she grabbed Caxna's hand for comfort to stop herself from trembling. The sound of the wind drowned out everything. Caxna encircled her with his arms and then held on to the tree that bound him.

She huddled in tighter, her face turned into Caxna's wide chest, her hair plastered to her back, and tried to ignore the wind's insistent tugging. She felt Caxna reaching around his waist where he'd tied the rope and, with a few deft movements of one hand, wrap it around her and then around the tree to pull them in more closely. The raging wind made its own argument against shifting her position.

The violent storm continued unceasing, ripping at the two of them with such force she feared the tree wouldn't hold them; it would be carried off and she and Caxna with it. Suddenly she thought of her brother and the ship. Was it out in this horrible storm? Would they survive it if they were? At this moment it seemed she would never find them, the task too great, the land and ocean too vast. She thought about praying, thought of asking *An Seanduine* to protect them, to protect her, but she couldn't help but feel such an action was pointless now. An empty gesture that meant nothing. She would die or not, no matter how much or little she prayed. Perhaps it would be best if she ran back out to the water and let it finish off what it had begun many days before.

As if he read her mind Caxna tightened the rope around her and encircled her closer with his arm. She felt his chin press on her head and somehow she felt a bit of comfort.

THE DAMP LEAVES gave off a crisp clean smell as if washed to a pureness the singing and twittering birds recognized. She opened her eyes and looked up at the clear sky visible through the canopy of greenery above. Aisling sat up, brushed her straggly hair away from her face and studied her surroundings. Broken branches, leaves and other bits of debris were scattered around her. Trees with limbs missing or hanging precariously leaned in wearied relief. The thick, well-grounded tree that held herself and Caxna throughout the storm had several branches missing, but was still standing tall. She shuddered at the memory of the storm's power and gave the tree a pat of thanks and noticed the rope that had bound them in the night had become loose and unattached.

She scanned the area for a sign of Caxna. Though it seemed to still be morning, she could only guess. Hopefully he hadn't gone far. The thin layer of leaves and boughs that covered their buried bundles was still intact. Hungry, she began to unearth them herself so she could find the small sack of her remaining provisions. He'd already mentioned that they would have to supplement the dwindling dried fish with food they foraged or caught for themselves. The berries were out in abundance now and he'd also show her the edible roots and leaves. Hunting or fishing was a last resort because each required preparation and cooking.

She heard Caxna before she saw him. Crashing through the trees and shrubs, he emerged into their little clearing, his face thunderous.

'What is the matter?' Aisling asked.

'The canoe. It is gone.' He punched the tree beside her.

She was too shocked to reply for a moment. 'Gone? How? What happened?'

'It is gone. Carried away by the storm.' He dropped down into a crouch and put his head in his hands. 'All the planning, season after season of work, finished because I did not take enough care.' He clenched his hands and spoke again in a language she didn't understand, the words coming rapidly, the tone full of fury and self-loathing.

She reached out and put her hand on his arm in comfort. 'Is it truly that bad? Is there a village we can go to and ask to use a canoe?'

He raised his head, looked over at her and snorted. 'There is a village, but it is many days' walk.'

She gave him a bright smile. 'Let us go there. Everything will be fine.'

'No,' he said sharply and threw off her hand. 'Everything will not be fine. It will be too late by the time we get the canoe and resume our journey.'

'Too late for what? What is it you have to do?'

His face sagged, the anger replaced by resignation. 'I must be back in time to make an important trade in Etowah. To make a bargain.'

'A bargain?' She had no idea what he meant until he described it through drawings and a mime. A bargain of marriage.

'You are bringing something back from where we are going now to use in a trade for a marriage bargain? Your marriage?'

He nodded. 'I travel now to a place called Xicallanca where it is possible to trade for treasure so special not even The Great Sun of the grand city of Etowah would turn it down. But he gave me only three seasons to bring back this treasure to make the bargain for his daughter. After that she goes to another.'

She felt a slight pang on hearing his explanation. Somehow she'd never imagined that he had a woman waiting somewhere for him. A woman who lived in a great city. She had never been to Dubh Linn, or the place called London. The port of Wexford was the extent of her exposure to that kind of place and she'd found that daunting enough. To hear of large cities here was beyond imagining. If Etowah was indeed as grand as he said, the woman waiting for him was most certainly someone of refined taste and ability.

'You love her?' she asked.

He cocked his head for a moment and gave her a wan smile. 'This is not about love. I do this to save my people.'

'Your people?'

He straightened slightly. 'Yes. My family, my clan.'

'What happened to them?'

His eyes clouded. 'Another clan from across the water attacked them unawares. My clan lost their possessions and some, including my sister, were taken as slaves. All because I was not there.' His voice was bitter. 'I was away in my canoe, following my desire to explore new places. My family told me I should stay home, take up my duties as my uncle had taught them to me. And if I had done that then I would have been able to warn them.'

'How could you have warned them?'

'I am a shaman.'

That word again. She felt a chill down her spine. 'You are a seer?'

'Yes. I would journey to see the future and to heal others.'

She thought of what she'd told him of her own abilities.

Would he know that she was lying? But how could a journey give an insight into the future? Her own recent journey had given her no insight into the future and only reinforced her skepticism of the truth of his words.

'How do you journey to get visions? How far must you travel?'

He sighed. 'You can go as far as the stars, but it is not a question of how far. Other shamans show you how, if you are gifted.'

She marveled for a moment that here before her was someone who knew another method of vision seeking that was so different from the one in which she'd been brought up. But had he really seen visions?

'And you are gifted?' She searched his face for a clue to what marked him in this special way.

He shook his head and shrugged. 'I was. But no longer. It is not a path for me now, since I failed my family and clan. I was too busy paddling a canoe in some distant river. When I returned everything I held dear was gone. My uncle dead, my sister taken. I was so ashamed I left, told everyone I would not return until I could restore their possessions, their status and free those made slaves.' His eyes registered pain. 'I have been trading ever since, for many, many seasons, looking for opportunities and making connections to fulfill my promise. Now it is finished. My one chance is gone.'

'How? Can you use what you get from the place we are going to trade directly with the people who attacked you?'

He shook his head. 'I must have items they hold valuable. And men to persuade them of their value. The chief of Etowah promised me both if, in addition to all the goods I have in his warehouse, I could bring back something special from Xicallanca.'

'What special thing?'

He told her, but she didn't understand anything except that it was green stone set in gold he'd seen on his previous journey to Xicallanca. A jewel of some kind. An emerald perhaps? Any jewelry containing emerald and gold would be special.

She considered what he'd told her. 'Can you use your gifts to help?'

He shook his head. 'No I will not. I cannot.'

'Have you ever used your gifts?'

He looked at her, his eyes narrowed. 'I have. In the past.'

'You have, in truth?'

'You do not believe me?'

'I do not believe in the gift.' The words came out of her mouth before she could stop them. She looked away trying to hide her fear at her disclosure.

'You do not believe in the gift, yet you say that you are a seer.'

'I—I did not mean to say that.'

'You did not mean to say that you are a seer, or that you do not believe?'

She bit her lip and tears filled her eyes.

He put his hand under her chin, turned her face towards him and scanned her face. 'You do not believe?'

She lowered her eyes and shook her head. 'How can I? How can I believe when season after season, I climbed the hill with my mother, performed the rites, looked in the well and saw nothing?' He knew now, knew the falsehood she'd told him. She waited for his reaction.

He stroked her cheek with his crippled hand, each callused finger light on her skin. 'I cannot say why your rituals did not allow you to see, but my gift was true and I have seen in my journeying.'

She looked into his eyes, their color so deep she could lose herself in them, and for a moment she nearly believed again. 'The sight does not come. It never comes. Perhaps what you thought you saw was something else. Or it was a journey that you desired in a different manner.'

He shook his head and dropped his hand. 'I will not force you to believe me. It does not matter now in any case.'

He believed, yet still he said nothing about her disbelief and her desire to remain unbedded. She thought of his own sorrow then, a greater distraction for him at the moment. 'When must you be in Etowah?'

'By the spring season.'

By what she could determine it was now coming into the autumn. He'd said earlier that it would take them four months to return to Pakahle. 'How long will it take to go to Etowah?'

'Another two moons.'

Six months roughly. He probably was right. There really wouldn't be enough time now they would have to search for a new canoe, a prospect that was likely to take many days. She frowned.

'If I stayed here waiting for you, would you make faster time? Maybe someone could help carry the canoe back and speed the journey?'

He gave her a kind smile and shook his head. 'I cannot leave you here on your own.'

She knew he was right. She had no idea about the dangers around her and she wasn't certain she could even keep herself in food or fresh water. She rose, dusted herself off and gave him a bright smile.

'Then we should go now. All the paddling has made me stronger, so that we can make speed. We will get the goods you need for trade so you can reach Etowah in time.' She held out her hand to him. He looked up at her, his dark eyes catching the light. She saw the resignation there.

10

She wiped her brow with the back of her hand, a gesture that brought little relief in the sweltering heat. Though they'd hardly begun their journey inland, sweat ran in rivulets down her back, along her face and down her chest. She'd abandoned her wool dress long before, but even the light fabric of her *léine* seemed more than she could bear at the moment, plastered as it was to her back where the packed basket pressed against it. Caxna had fixed a woven strap that went around her forehead and enabled her to carry the basket with her hands free. It made for an easier journey in the general sense but the sweat and weight made her head ache. She wouldn't complain, though. Caxna had his own basket and it was much heavier. Though he'd left most of the goods buried where they'd spent the night, he'd retrieved a few to use in trade for the canoe.

Moss draped the trees around them like festive garlands, creating an eerie glow in the boggy water nearby. Even the bird-calls sounded strange, each exchange echoing slightly like a young boy learning his Latin phrases from the priest. Such a thought reminded her of her brother and she felt a pain in her heart. Where was he now? Safe with Madog? She nearly uttered a prayer to *An Seanduine* but repressed it in time. Such actions were so much a part of her life that it was sometimes difficult to remember their uselessness.

'Ho, Friend!'

Both Aisling and Caxna turned. A young man walked toward them, dark hair caught up in a side knot and clothed only in a breechclout like Caxna. His coppery skin was covered in a complicated pattern of dots and his forehead was slightly flattened.

Caxna smiled and walked to meet the man. 'You are a welcome sight, Friend. I never thought to see you here.'

The man gave him a punch on the arm and Caxna returned it. 'I have just come from a visit to my cousins, and caught sight of you from the path beyond.'

'You have cousins nearby?'

The man grinned. 'Everyone has cousins nearby.'

'I am glad to meet up with you, whatever your purpose.' He surveyed the area around him. 'Will we sit and visit, have a smoke?'

Aisling stood in stunned silence. He knew of their pressing need to make this journey as quickly as possible and now he wanted to stop and exchange news. This seemed to take hospitality too far. It was not for her to argue, she knew, and without a word she lowered her basket on to the ground and watched as the two sat down and started a fire.

The whole affair appeared leisurely to her, the men engaged in casual conversation, using a mix of the language she was learning and another. She had yet to discover the man's name, or he her own, and for a brief moment she considered leaning over and making the introduction herself. Their ways are different, she reminded herself.

They sat next to each other, their bare legs crossed. They had nothing on their feet and she could see the thick hardened soles that made them walk a forest floor or rocky path with impunity. Her own feet were scratched and sore, even from the short time she'd been forced to walk on them in places not covered by soft and forgiving sand. Caxna had promised her a pair of shoes —'moccasins' he called them—as soon as he was able to find the time to either make them or trade them. Such a skill was generally assigned to the women, so she would be better served if he could find a pair for her, rather than he make a crude pair with his sewing abilities.

When the fire was going strong Caxna pulled out two leather pouches. From one he withdrew a small bowl of dark stone. Around its base were two carved wolves. The other pouch contained dried herbs that he packed in the bowl, tamping it down with his finger. He took a small twig, lit it and put it to the bowl, while he sucked on the small stem that protruded from one end. Aisling watched in fascination as moments later he blew a cloud of smoke from his mouth. This process continued, him sucking in at the stem and blowing smoke, until after several puffs Caxna offered the bowl to the man who sat beside him. The man took it and with practiced ease repeated the same actions Caxna had used.

No words passed between the two men while they sucked the bowl and puffed out smoke passing it back and forth until Caxna broke the silence.

'Your family is well?' Caxna spoke in the language she could understand, a consideration that Aisling thought he might have made on her behalf. If so she was deeply grateful.

'They have good health. Your health is good?'

'My health is good. I am sorry I am late arriving to your home.'

The man nodded. 'My father thought something might have happened. I have been checking the villages on the way for news of you.'

Caxna glanced at her. 'I had a few delays. And yesterday I

lost my canoe in the storm. We were walking to the nearest village to get another canoe.'

'There are two of you now?'

'I have a slave now.' Caxna nodded his head toward Aisling.

'You? Keep a slave?' The man looked over and studied her for a moment. 'She is a strange looking slave.'

'She washed up out of the great water after falling out of a very large canoe full of people like her.'

The man grunted. 'She looks a bit thin to be of any use.'

Caxna smiled. 'She is stronger than you think.'

The man looked at her again. 'Odd hair color. And her skin is like that of a spirit ghost's.' The man then asked if she was something Aisling couldn't understand.

'No, she is not. She is from a land far away.'

The man glanced at her once more and shook his head. He wasn't convinced.

Aisling trudged behind the two men, the basket strapped once again against her head. The strange episode between Caxna and the one he'd said was called 'Midiwegi,' lingered in her mind and she tried to make sense of it. Caxna had seemed so calm then, untroubled by the loss of the canoe or the lack of time that had caused him such anguish a short while before. Though it was a relief when she realized they would be traveling in the man's canoe, it just seemed that Midiwegi's appearance was something more than a fortunate rescue.

Since Caxna spoke Midiwegi's language fairly well the two didn't always converse in trader language, something that left Aisling frustrated. She felt a strong need to know what the two talked about, for she was certain her future depended on it. Where were they going now? Was Midiwegi coming with them all the way to Xicallanca? Since Caxna had told Midiwegi that she was a slave he had treated her accordingly; speaking little, except to issue curt instructions. There was no opportunity for any extended conversation and she was only able to ask him a few short questions.

They arrived at Midiwegi's canoe by mid-day, stopping only briefly at their earlier camp to unearth the rest of the packs and baskets. Aisling helped them both to load the packs in Midiwegi's canoe without being told, though her feet and back were aching. The trek from the camp to this point on the beach had been more difficult, what with carrying the pack in her arms in addition to the basket on the tumpline. She was glad for the chance to sit.

She took up one of the paddles without thought and was about to step inside the canoe when Caxna laid a hand on her arm. 'You will not need to paddle the canoe.'

She gave him a surprised look, but released the paddle without a word. She wouldn't argue about something she was glad to avoid.

They placed her between the two of them, Caxna still paddling in the rear, and Midiwegi up at the prow. The two stroked the water with efficient skill, their experience and strength giving the canoe great speed. Aisling allowed herself to relax slightly and take in the scenery that passed. She noticed the beaches and trees showed evidence of the previous night's storm: fallen leaves, branches and broken shells scattered along the ground. Trees listed and limbs drooped drunkenly. The pungent odor of the ocean hung in the air from the casualties of sea life. In the distance, she could see a few dorsal fins protruding from the water, feeding on the hapless victims. It reminded Aisling that she could have just as easily been one of those floating dead on the water, serving as a food source for the sharks, or lying motionless on the shore.

It was when the last of the fading light had vanished that they finally pulled over to stop for the night. It was at Caxna's suggestion and Aisling felt that it was for her benefit. She had tried to limit her position shifts, but when her calves and feet started to complain in the shape of wild cramping and violent pain, she found it nearly impossible to stay still and Caxna could not help but notice. She was grateful and opened her mouth to thank him, but thought better of it.

She stumbled out of the canoe and tried to help them draw it up, but her legs collapsed under her, causing Midiwegi to give a derisory snort. 'You say she is strong?'

'It has been a long day,' said Caxna.

Aisling leaned over and rubbed her calves and flexed her feet, while the men unloaded the canoe and placed the packs and baskets on the beach. When the feeling had returned sufficiently, she dug out the drill board and stick to light the fire.

'No fire tonight,' Caxna said. He gave her a brief smile.

She repressed a sigh and nodded. She was glad even for his short smile. It seemed more important than ever in the face of Midiwegi's disdain. She returned the drill board and stick to the pack and set out some dried fruit and the remaining dried fish, then took a seat.

Midiwegi nodded to his small pack. 'There is some pemmican in there we can eat.' He looked over at her from his place on the sand, his face expectant.

She blinked, then rose and made her way over to his pack. Cautiously, she opened it and searched for something that looked like food. It was only the light of newly arrived stars that aided her hunt, so it was a little while before she located a small bundle containing what appeared to be dried strips of meat. She placed it on the blanket she'd laid out and hoped for the best. When no remark was made she concluded she'd guessed correctly.

The three of them ate without speaking, fatigue and reticence keeping Aisling silent. She was grateful when they'd finished and she could settle herself down for the night. Before she arranged her blanket she rose without a word and made her way to the nearest shrubs to relieve herself. She squatted down and lifted her gown out of the way, considering how she might arrange her morning dip out of Midiwegi's sight. She'd long since worked out she could bathe with her back turned, immersed in the water at the far end of their camp, out of close range of Caxna, but she didn't trust Midiwegi to keep his distance.

A hand came around and clutched her breast and a weight pressed against her chest. 'Maybe Caxna's slave is better at other things.'

She struggled to gain her balance only to fall forward on her face. Midiwegi thrust hard against her. 'You would have me take you from behind?'

'No,' she said. 'I would not have you take me at all!' She fought to release him and rise from the ground but he held her fast.

'She is my property and I would prefer if you did not touch her,' said Caxna. His voice had a dangerous edge.

Midiwegi released her and she was able to turn around to see the two of them. Caxna's face, visible in the light of the rising moon, held unmistakable anger. He held out a hand and helped her to her feet.

Midiwegi rose of his own accord and frowned. 'I see you do not like to share.' With a shrug he walked off, away from the camp to the far shoreline.

Aisling tugged her dress into place and looked up at Caxna. 'I am glad you came and stopped him.' She searched for the words of thanks and came up blank. How to express her gratitude? She took his hand and pressed a small kiss upon the back of it. 'You have helped me very much.'

Caxna withdrew his hand and shook his head. 'I am sorry he came to you. I should have told him before that you are not for the taking.'

'It is fine. You were in time.' She looked down, away from his scrutiny, and tried to push aside the memories. 'Where do we go now?'

'We still go to Xicallanca. But first we will go to Midiwegi's home. We will collect more trade goods and canoes.'

'Will he come with us to Xicallanca?' For some reason she wasn't able to say his name yet.

'Yes. It has been arranged.'

'This was planned before?'

'Yes.'

She considered his words, wondering how much had changed from the original proposal. Regardless of any changes, it seemed clear that Midiwegi or his family had some kind of influence over Caxna.

'Were there slaves where you come from?' she asked.

'Yes. Are there slaves in your land?'

She nodded. 'We had a few, but we always treated them with kindness. Something like that would have never happened.' It was a truth that held firmly in her family's household, but one that she knew would not hold in all the households of Leinster.

'Where is your homeland?' she asked. It was a question that had plagued her for some time. At this moment it seemed possible he might answer it in more depth.

'It is far, far north of here. Up many rivers and then west. To another big sea, many moon's travel.' He described the journey that held countless portages, waterfalls, rapids and other obstacles. There was so much new and strange about this land, about his culture. About him. She eyed him carefully while he made his explanation, examining his wide cheekbones, his tilted dark eyes and the long black hair, usually caught up in the top knot, but now framed his face and hung to his shoulders. In the moonlight his copper skin seemed darker, especially against the light colored fabric of his breechclout.

'Is it cold where you come from, do you wear more clothing

there?' She couldn't help the question. It seemed to pop out of her mouth before she knew it.

'It is colder there,' he said. 'We wear skins in the winter, sometimes with fur. We also have blankets we can use for warmth too. But in summer it is warm enough and we might wear as little as this.' He grinned. 'Or sometimes less.'

She blushed and was glad the cover of night hid some of her embarrassment. 'I see,' she managed to say. She fell silent and tried to clear her mind of the images he created there, reasoning that her own people used to go into battle clad in nothing but the woad painted on their skins and the weapons in their hands.

It was those thoughts that crowded her mind as she finally lay down to sleep after Caxna had walked her back to the camp. It was some time before she drifted off, and Midiwegi had still not joined them.

11

They pulled up alongside of the shore, Midiwegi's face alight with excitement. Aisling felt the sweat down the back of her *léine*, a steady drip that had begun when they'd set off that morning. After the first day in the canoe with Midiwegi, the heat had grown steadily worse, and as much as she might wish to wear her wool gown, the itchy unbearable heat it caused made it impossible. She swatted a fly listlessly and eased herself out of the canoe, noting the grubby sweat stains on her front where the *léine* rested against her breasts. It was nearly a perfect outline around their contours, but she was too hot to care. And since Caxna's encounter with Midiwegi the first night, Midiwegi had avoided even eye contact with her.

Children raced down to them and bobbed around Caxna and Midiwegi, pulling at their arms and hands and chattering loudly, naked as the day they were born. Aisling couldn't understand the questions and answers that flew around her, but she could see hear the laughter, and the pleasure on Caxna's face gave her heart a squeeze.

With deft motions Caxna divided up the bundles so that every one of the six or so children had something to carry, except the youngest one, a little girl who couldn't have been more than two years. He swooped her up in his arms and headed up the shore, the rest of the children following after him. With nothing left to bring, Aisling picked her way after them, at a loss, excluded.

They followed a path that eventually opened up to a huge wooden gated palisade. They passed through the gate to an expansive clearing covered in buildings of various sizes, all arranged around three different squares. The buildings were homes, row upon row, framed of cane, plastered with clay and thatched with palmetto leaves. In the center of the middle square was a large hearth surrounded by benches. People milled around its perimeter, outside the homes and in the doorways; women weaving baskets, drying fish on racks, or tanning hides, while the men lazed about and talked, or mended spears, bows and arrows.

Like Midiwegi, their foreheads seemed flattened, the hair gathered in the familiar side knot on the men and flowing loose on the women. Breechclouts or short cloth skirts covered most of the men, but not all. The women wore white mantles tied across their right shoulder, some covering the breasts, others only partially. Short cloth skirts, also in white, were worn underneath. It appeared a benign scene, and the smiles and the children's excited babble at Caxna and Midiwegi's appearance, did nothing to dispel that impression.

'I am come,' Midiwegi cried to the whole of the village.

An elderly man, a large folded length of multi-colored cloth draped across his shoulder, rose from the cane seat by a large building at the middle square's edge and made his way towards them. She could see traces of tattoos marking his weathered face and the exposed part of his chest.

'You are come. It is well,' the man said. He clasped Midiwegi's arm and squeezed it, then moved on to Caxna, repeating the words and the gesture.

Aisling had no expectations regarding her own welcome and so she wasn't surprised when he turned without so much as a glance and moved back through the groups of people that had gathered. Still, she found herself smarting, as if she'd been rebuked.

THE SENSE of exclusion hadn't dispelled by the evening, after a ragged-haired woman settled her with a bowl of food and a pointed finger to the far corner of the large hall, near the small sleeping platforms that lined the wall. Around her, men and women exchanged quips and laughter while they ate from the platters heaped with what she later learned were dishes consisting of variations of beans, squash, corn, partridge, rabbit, deer and other foodstuffs. Even before she passed through the wooden palisades and saw the rows of homes that were not much smaller than her own house, she knew this was not a small settlement, but a town, one that would nearly compete with Wexford. This structure, large enough to accommodate at least sixty, if not more, overflowed with people, and she knew more were sitting on benches outside and on the ground out in the square.

She had tried to communicate with the few women who paid her any notice when she first arrived, but blank looks were the only response she'd received. All she could do was watch the proceedings as the people began to gather. It appeared to be a joyful reunion, with Caxna the center of attention, seated as he was beside the elderly man who was doubtless the chief, or head of this large community. Several young men came up to Caxna at various times and exchanged greetings and a thump on the arm, before taking their place on one side, away from the women. He and Midiwegi had reappeared after being led away by some very motherly looking women and looked clean and refreshed in cloth wraps edged in stamped images.

A while later she saw Midiwegi gesture in her direction and then say a few words into Caxna's ear. Caxna glanced over at her, frowned and spoke back. Midiwegi grinned. Aisling flushed, not entirely convinced that Caxna's remarks about her were complimentary.

She set the bowl down, her appetite vanished, and turned her full attention to the women who moved about the hall serving the food. Their own dress was without decoration, their hair pulled back simply or hanging loose. They were quiet and attentive to their tasks and said little to the people they served. She could make no mistake, their rank was low, but still they ignored her. She looked down at her stained clothes and could appreciate that to them she might not seem of the highest rank either.

In contrast to the serving women's simple dress, an elaborately attired woman attended Caxna, Midiwegi, the elderly man and a few other men of advanced age. The mantle that draped itself across her curves was so light and finely woven it did little to disguise the generous breasts and hips that swayed seductively as she made her way among the group of men. A gold and jasper pendant hung from her neck and gold bracelets circled her arms.

She ladled a dark liquid into a Caxna's beaker, her long black hair falling forward to create curtain that shielded her face and caressed the back of Caxna's hand. From her place at the end of the room Aisling could read the appreciative response in his eyes. Next to him the elderly man smiled, an indulgent look on his face but Midiwegi regarded the pair carefully, frowning slightly. He muttered something to the elderly man who held up his hand, a gesture that silenced Midiwegi.

Aisling continued to observe this foursome for the rest of the evening, noting particularly each time the woman leaned over to fill Caxna's plate. Caxna, the woman and the elderly man all seemed to enjoy each other's company, but Midiwegi had grown sullen, sitting slightly apart from the three.

When the meal was nearly at an end, the woman took a seat among the other females dressed richly enough to denote a high rank. The woman ate her fill then while her companions chattered around her. Watching them, Aisling felt her eyes droop with tiredness and hoped that she soon might be told or shown where she was to sleep. It was late enough, darkness had settled long before and the stars were out in full, competing with the fires she could see lit in the square. The men appeared in no hurry to depart, though. One of the elderly men drew out the same object she'd seen Caxna and Midiwegi smoke that Caxna had told her was a pipe. A young man lit it for him and, after he drew it up and blew large cloud of smoke, he passed it slowly to the man next to him.

The pipe's arrival seemed to signal to the women and some of the men it was time to depart and they made their way to the hall door, the female slaves trailing after them. Aisling watched them filter through and wondered if she should follow. Her uncertainty was short lived. The richly attired woman who'd served Caxna during the meal approached her. Aisling rose and looked her in the eye.

'You are slave to Caxna.'

The words, spoken slowly and with difficulty, were not phrased as a question but still Aisling nodded. She noted the woman's proud bearing, the dark eyes that examined her now slowly. Aisling blushed, conscious of her stained and ragged *léine*, but tried to keep her gaze level with the woman's. The woman narrowed her eyes and anger flashed in them.

'You have not been slave long.'

'No.'

The woman gave a snort. 'You have much to learn. You will stay here, learn how to be slave when the men go.'

'When the men go?' Aisling looked over at Caxna, unable to

suppress her alarm. Surely the woman didn't mean she was to stay here while Caxna went on to Xicallanca. 'No, I cannot stay here. I must go with Caxna.'

The woman saw the direction of her look and gave a confident smile. 'You have no say. I tell you, you will stay here.' She lifted her hand and summoned one of the simply clad women. The woman came to her side immediately and nodded while a quick succession of words was said to her bowed head. When the instructions were complete the woman looked at Aisling, tugged her arm and led her to the door, following the other women that were trickling through it.

At that moment it became clear how much she was at the mercy of Caxna. And of these people who had no regard for her and knew only that she was a slave. She tried to calm herself, refuse the growing anxiety that threatened to overtake her. The woman led her along a path following the tide of people who walked ahead of them. They didn't travel far before the woman stopped and led her into a small building next to the hall. They entered and she could make out several small mats on the floor and baskets with blankets folded next to them. The woman pointed to one of the mats and spoke in her own language. Aisling pointed to herself, then to the mat and gave the woman a questioning look. The woman nodded.

Aisling sat down on the mat and sighed. Satisfied, the woman took one of the other mats for herself, lay down, her back to Aisling and gave all appearances of sleep. A few other women, obviously slaves, came in a short while later and with little more than a glance at Aisling, lay themselves down on the other mats, assuming a similar position. Aisling gave thought to her wool dress and her other small collection of ointments and pots that Pakahle had given her. She'd no idea where they were. She was certain that Caxna wouldn't be bringing them to her later tonight. He was very much engaged elsewhere. She wondered if he'd think to ask them about the ship, or if other things would cloud his thinking. Tears pricked her eyes and she fought off the wave of homesickness that seized her. She could only hope that she'd be reunited with her brother sometime soon; she still couldn't bring herself to have any faith in praying.

BRIGHTLY PAINTED men clad in breechclouts, fur tails and moccasins charged across the field in full tilt only to become a tangle of legs, arms and flailing sticks. Aisling watched this spectacle in fascination, a strange kind of war play, with opposing teams intent on winning. At either end of this long field were wooden poles with a cross bar and it seemed the teams aimed to get the deerskin ball to cross that boundary. The women and the remaining men wagered jewelry, fur pelts, finely crafted bowls and baskets. Beside her, Caxna and the elderly man shouted their appreciation for the players. Midiwegi was out on the field, one of the many men vying for the ball.

She'd been anxious when she awoke to an empty room and seen no sign of Caxna when she ventured outside. The sun had risen above the trees and she was certain that they had left without her. She'd made her way back to the hall and entered quietly, but could only see a handful of slaves performing tasks.

It was only when she'd heard the distant roar of a crowd that she felt some reassurance she hadn't been abandoned. Quickly she'd followed the sound to its source at the field. Caxna had seen her standing uncertainly at the end and had come over to her and led her back to his seat. The high ranking woman had been there, casting dark glances at her and Caxna, but he'd chosen to ignore them.

It was then he'd told her the woman, Mitiwohli, was Midiwegi's sister and the elderly man, Choola, was their father and the chief of the village. She had sat silently for a while, watching the men run around the field as she tried to create some order out of all the questions that crowded her mind. Caxna had seemed oblivious to her turmoil, caught up in the enjoyment of the game. Now she marveled anew that he could seem so concerned and driven to reach Xicallanca as quickly as possible one moment and then casually relaxed about it at other times.

'We are not departing today, then?' she asked finally, her voice quiet.

Caxna drew his eyes away from the field reluctantly and looked at her. 'No. Today we prepare.' He looked back at the field.

'Prepare, how?'

He sighed and shifted slightly to give her his full regard. 'It is customary here to fast before venturing out on an important journey.' He gestured to the men playing. 'This is a holy thing. Special. The ball is the sun and it goes across the sky.' He frowned. 'Do you understand?'

She considered. 'I think so.' She could hear the doubt in her voice.

He gave her a close look. 'Do you not have holy rituals for special times that all believe will ensure the best outcome?'

'Yes. There are special rituals that are followed at certain times and they believe it will help.'

'They believe? You do not believe?'

'I believe nothing, not anymore.'

He put an arm on her shoulder. 'That is a fearful thing. A person is lost without the holy ones, the spirits. And you risk their anger.'

'If I do not believe, how can I risk their anger?'

He gave her a puzzled look, shook his head and turned his attention back to the field. She resisted the desire to tug on his arm, get him to tell her in all that he deemed holy what his plans were and how she now figured in them. Before she could get his attention once again, Mitiwohli leaned forward and spoke in Caxna's ear.

Caxna glanced at Aisling and then turned to Mitiwohli. 'No, she will remain with me.'

Mitiwohli leaned forward and spoke again, louder but in her own language so Aisling couldn't understand her exact words, but she'd no doubt about the meaning. Despite what she might have said to persuade Caxna to change his mind, he shook his head and repeated his previous statement. She pouted at him and rose after a few moments, to take herself to another place at the field's edge.

'She wanted me to stay here while you went to Xicallanca?'

Caxna gave her a sympathetic look. 'She told you this?'

Aisling nodded. 'Yes, last night.'

'It is not for her to say.'

'She thinks that I am a slave.'

'It is still not for her to say.'

She thought about his reply, wondering what power he had over her in their view. 'Did you happen to ask anyone if they have seen sign of my brother and the others?'

'I did ask them. I am sorry, they have not seen or heard anything of them.' She nodded and swallowed, trying hard to set aside the sorrow that filled her on hearing those words.

PART III

XICALLANCA

12

'It is a farewell ceremony,' Caxna said.

Aisling nodded and pulled in a little closer behind him, feeling a cool breeze at her neck. The air had signaled a slight change, though at home the breeze would have brought with it the seeping damp of mid-autumn by now. She could barely allow herself to consider the time that had passed since she'd left her home in Leinster, that air filled with spring promise. A summer she'd seen only from a ship's deck; rolling waves instead of verdant fields and forests.

She looked at the group assembled before the canoe: Choola, Mitiwohli and the elders. Midiwcgi stood next to Caxna and the two faced the growing number of people that crowded the shoreline. Behind them, three canoes were loaded with packs and ready for launching. Caxna had brought her down to the shore, groggy and barely awake after collecting her from the sleeping quarters. The ball game had gone on all night and into the morning, the whooping and hollering continuous, making any attempts at covert napping at her place by the field impossible. She'd dragged herself to her bed and it seemed barely closed her eyes when Caxna had come to get her. The others around her now her seemed no worse for wear, even Midiwegi and the other ball players. They stood silently, waiting for Choola's signal that the ceremony would begin.

Choola lifted his hand to the gathered crowd and intoned a short speech. Mitiwohli stepped forward with a bowl, dipped her finger into it and placed a yellow mark on Midiwegi's forehead. She moved to Caxna and repeated the gesture. Choola nodded solemnly and put his hand first on his son's shoulder and then on Caxna's. With his other hand he gestured back to his daughter and said a few words to Caxna, a big grin on his face. Caxna nodded, smiled and put his own hand on top of Choola's.

Aisling felt a deep sense of unease at his actions. It was a disquiet that she couldn't fully explain to herself. She only knew that this journey had much more at stake for herself, and it seemed, for Caxna, than she first thought.

The paddling was left to the slaves, all men. They were from another village, another clan, captured during raids many years before. Unlike Choola's people, with their unflattened heads and lack of tattoos, they seemed indifferent to her and Midiwegi and Caxna. Aisling noted they loaded the goods with alacrity, speaking little to one another and reminded herself she must follow their example and say little. She thought again of the slaves back home, taken during raids across the waters or far from home. Her mother's servant had been one, joining the household when her mother arrived newly wed, though her father on principle didn't keep slaves. Áine had seemed part of the family and all were sad at her death.

It came as a surprise to Aisling that they would travel in not one, but three canoes, the packs enlarged and multiplied through Choola's generosity, or so Caxna explained. She eyed them dubiously, wondering what price such generosity would require. Caxna seemed light-hearted and she could not quibble with the reason; their journey speed had increased under the extra manpower and the larger number of trade goods made chances of success better. Like any trading place, richer and more plentiful trade goods improved a person's status so they had access to better markets and prospective buyers.

Caxna explained this to her as they made their way along the coast, with him sitting directly behind her in the middle of the lead canoe, while Midiwegi travelled in one of the canoes that followed. Endless trees, chestnut, cypress and the intermittent oak gave way to shrubs and coniferous trees with grudging needles that she didn't recognize and Caxna hadn't identified. Occasionally a shoreline stretched wide and silky smooth, its pristine condition marred only by the sandpipers, seagulls and other shorebirds that plundered it for hidden food.

The water still teemed with life; gar, bass, trout and other fish. Caxna used the opportunity to drag a fishing line, and his foresight brought huge rewards that flopped and bounced in the canoe, until he silenced their thrashing with a deft stroke of his obsidian knife, slicing them open to remove the guts. Each time he intoned a few words and then heaved the pieces into the water, back to their source.

'A blessing?' she asked, twisting around to see him and forgetting all she had resolved about speaking.

'Of sorts. I have no wish to offend the gar spirit or the bass spirit. I am thanking them for the life they offered so that when the need is there, they will offer more.'

She considered this view. 'There are fish spirits?'

'Of course. And animal spirits. Each type of animal and fish has its own. I am kin to the wolf spirit. I would not eat wolf because it would be like eating one of my own.'

He explained it to her as though it were the simplest thing in the world and not his odd belief, part of the strange world he inhabited. But she inhabited it now and she could only feel confusion. It was different to growing up with the Christian faith. That faith was woven into the fabric of her homeland, but she was part of the weft, the thread that ran in the opposite direction, over and under the warp of Christianity. Her mother had set her on that path, while her father and grandmother ensured that Cormac followed their faith. Though she'd attended the mass under her late grandmother's watchful eye when the priest came to visit, her father hadn't been so strict. Even on the ship, when the others observed the Christian rituals, she'd begged off, unable to show even a modicum of pretense, despite the undercurrent of tension such actions caused.

What could she believe now? This man, as well as his beliefs, was so different to her. He, a former holy man, had refused his role not because he had ceased believing, but because he deemed himself no longer worthy of the gift.

'Do you not have spirits like ours?'

She paused, wondering how to explain. 'No, not the same as yours. We have the gods, the goddesses, the holy ones that have been part of the land since memory began. And then there is the newer one, the one that came later and has as his intercessor, Jesus. Many of my people believe in that god and that one alone.'

'But you do not?'

'I do not. It was the goddess Anu and *An Seanduine*, The Ancient One...' She trailed off, unable to voice exactly how they fit into her world then and no longer did.

'Have you stopped acknowledging their presence, put them from your life?'

She shook her head. 'They never came. I called and called, asked for visions, asked for protection. I called, and my father died. I called and the cattle were stolen, and the lands taken. They never showed me the way, never gave any protection. They have given me only loss and pain, failing me utterly.'

'How does that show you they are not there? And are you certain the failure belongs to them?'

'How could I be the one that failed? What have I done? Tell me, what have I done?' Her words broke off into a soft wail that revealed more than she wanted. She covered her face with her hand and turned back around, unwilling to show her tears to anyone, especially him.

She felt a hand on her shoulder, the hand that was itself incomplete, a demonstration of failure. 'There are those who fail only in that they are too ready to turn away from themselves and their true calling. Your own path may yet be revealed.'

She swallowed her tears and nodded, her back still turned to him. 'And you have found your true path as a trader? You are happy with that?'

The hand withdrew. 'My path is to restore my people to what they were before—noble people of great wealth.' There was an iron determination in his voice. He would never be swayed.

'So, you will return to the north.'

'I will, when I have secured my allies and all is prepared.'

There was no mistaking his conviction and she had no doubt he would do all that was in his power to accomplish this aim.

DAYS BECAME weeks and the journey continued, sped along by the slaves who toiled for hours on end, paddling the canoes, while Aisling prepared the food they, Caxna and Midiwegi, provided. She was conscious of Caxna's watchful protection, providing privacy when necessary, stopping when her moon time came and exiling her at the far end of the camp. Not one of the slaves cast her looks that made her anxious, for they mostly ignored her. They knew little of the trader language and conversed among themselves.

From Caxna she learned about the birds that flew overhead, the fish that swam around them and they sometimes caught, or the animals snared or shot in brief forays in the time they went ashore for the night. Sometimes he pointed out the stars, where some believed that the sky people lived, the original beings that created the people below. It was part of Midiwegi's people's story, he told her. He spoke usually in a low voice and she resisted the urge to turn and face him, knowing that he would rather not call attention to his words that she knew were meant to give her comfort, to take her mind off the long journey and her loss. Midiwegi, in contrast, seemed to regard her as nothing more important than the cook who prepared the meal day after day.

Caxna also told her something of the people of Xicallanca, once part of a great people, with towns so large you couldn't see their end in one day and great buildings of stone that nearly touched the sky. But the buildings had tumbled down in many places or been swallowed by vines, bushes, shrubs and other plants that came from the surrounding forests, though still a center for trade of the most exotic and varied goods.

The terrain had changed quite a bit in the days and weeks since they'd departed Midiwegi's home. The water was still the strange shade of blue that was not quite green, yet so clear she could nearly see to the bottom. The sea life had become more prolific though, and if possible more brilliant in their colors, while the bird calls were more shrill and varied; occasional flashes of bright markings showing their presence in the trees.

THE MORNING SUN WOKE HER, its blinding light finding her easily through the sparse shrubs that separated her from the beach. Overhead the branches and leaves were already dry, the night air cleared long ago of the drenching rain. She wasn't certain when the rain had stopped, but it seemed to have lasted half the night as she struggled to remain still and dry away from the drips at the edge of the shelter.

Now the trees and leaves appeared to be nearly bone dry.

She sat up cautiously, noting that Caxna and Midiwegi stirred slightly. If she crept to the water's edge now, before the others rose, she might be able to take a short morning swim to refresh herself. She pulled her *léine* down as far as she could, then leaned down to nip one of the long frayed edges with her teeth. Caxna had told her the night before there was a mantle and skirt in the pack for her, put there on Mitiwohli's instructions. Perhaps she would don them afterwards.

Her luck held and she was able to forage through the designated leather pack and retrieve the mantle and skirt before anyone awoke. She made her way to the water's edge and ran into the surf, thankful that its noise would cover her splashes. This time she allowed no lingering, it was a quick dousing, raising her hair out of the water to avoid extra salt accumulation. Since she'd been travelling her hair had become lighter and more like straw. It was only when she was able to wash it thoroughly in fresh water that it lost its dryness and she hadn't had any opportunity for many days. She could only comb it with her fingers now, as she had all the other days.

She left the combing until she'd changed out of her wet *léine*, taking up the skirt first, wrapping it tightly around her waist and securing it with some firm tucking. She longed for her brooch to ensure it would not slip, but the rough woven cloth seemed to grip well. The mantle proved simpler, coming up under her left arm to tie at her right shoulder. She adjusted it to cover the full extent of her chest, as much for protection against the sun as for her modesty.

'It suits you well.'

She whipped around to see Caxna a short distance away. 'Thank you,' she said, resisting the urge to tug at the skirt.

'Your other clothes are not what they were. It is time you had something better.'

She nodded and glanced down at herself, noting the large length of bare legs, arms and shoulder. It was strange without the weight of her *léine* and wool dress. 'I am not accustomed to showing this much skin. It is cold where I come from.'

'Your skin is so pale, I can tell that it does not see the sun. It never grows so hot that you must wear less?'

'It would never be this hot.'

'But it is hot here and these clothes are for such weather. You will feel more comfortable.'

She took a deep breath and nodded. 'Yes, I hope so.'

'Before we set off today, you must put this on.' He held out a cloth-wrapped bundle.

She looked down at the bundle. 'What is it?'

He gave a wry grin. 'A wig. And some berry juice to stain your skin.'

'Must I?'

He sighed. She could detect no anger and she was glad for his patience. She was trying to understand.

'Yes. For your own protection. As a woman, a strange looking woman, with no connection, no kin, no power or authority of any kind can be taken and used at will in such a place as we are going to.

'Used at will?'

He gave her a wan smile. 'That would be the least of it. You could be beaten, taken as a slave, killed for a whim. Or killed for a sacrifice.'

'Killed for a sacrifice?'

He nodded. It was no joke. 'Xicallanca is a very big city, with many merchants coming to trade from many areas. In these places people trade in all types of goods. Further north of there is a place that often sacrifices people. With your hair the color of the sun and your pale skin you would be something that they would covet, I think.'

She stared at the bundle for a moment, aware of Midiwegi's eyes on her. After giving Caxna a brief nod she set the bundle on the ground and withdrew the wig. She held it up on her fist, noting the natural fall of the various strands. A good piece of craftsmanship and surely not for any serving woman or slave. Could it be, she wondered? Would Midiwegi's sister surrender something so well made to use for her?

Carefully, she wrapped her hair close around her head and pulled the wig over it. The hair fell a little unevenly, but the effect didn't seem to be too bad. She cast around, looking for a pool of water but could see none. That would have to wait for another time. She looked over at Caxna. His eyes widened and he broke out in a smile that soon erupted into laughter.

'You're right to laugh, Brother,' Midiwegi said. 'But it will have to do.'

She looked over at Midiwegi and saw the calculating look on his face. He eyed her up and down, lingering a little too long at her legs and then her chest. Was she suddenly more appealing to him with her dark hair? She looked down at the pot containing the berry juice.

'She looks fine,' Caxna said. 'The wig will serve.' He gave her a reassuring smile and she matched it with a feeble one.

'There's nothing I can do to improve it,' she said.

'Perhaps she would be better without the wig,' said Midiwegi. 'She might be a good bargaining tool.'

'No.' Caxna's reply was immediate. 'I mean that we would do well not to have her attracting attention that may cause problems with our trade.'

'It wouldn't cause problems, I am certain. I know they would find her hair color very special. And her skin. It is so pink. Many of the nobles would surely give much for that kind of woman. That could be used to our advantage.'

Caxna shook his head and reached for the pot of berry juice and handed it to Aisling. 'Go on, rub this along your skin.'

She took the pot, removed the cork stopper and dipped her finger inside. Carefully she wiped her finger along the back of her hand, where it left a dark brown stain.

'Not that heavy. Spread it thinly over your body.'

She looked at him, understanding his intent, but determined not to follow his instructions here, under Midiwegi's careful scrutiny. With as much dignity as she could muster she turned and walked up the beach to the lush growth beyond.

13

———

Bright sun bounced off the bleached limestone buildings and streets. Aisling blinked hard against it, despite the curtain of her new hair, and lowered head. She could feel the heat from the buildings they passed and from the many bodies that jostled her, crowding her in, as she followed Caxna and Midiwegi at a respectful distance, a basket of goods strapped to her head with a tumpline. Behind her the slaves carried the other packs, lumbering under the heavy weight.

Refuse gathered in gutters beside the street they walked, overpowering the scent of the sea that had colored her days up until now. The noise and the odors made her head ache and the jumble of people overwhelmed her, making her self-conscious of her near naked appearance with nothing on her feet.

Men and women in all manner of dress passed her, all with a purpose, some sumptuously clothed and adorned with gold and silver and colored stones of all shades glowing against their copper skin. These people usually trailed a host of servants or slaves whose clothes and hair were arranged in simpler styles. Other men of more moderate dress, eyes calculating or searching, were accompanied by only a few men carrying baskets strapped to their heads as she did. She supposed they were slaves too.

She glanced at one man's arm where a gold band encrusted with green stones wound its way upwards. Fascinated, she examined him more closely and gasped when she saw not only was his head flattened and elongated, but his eyes were crossed. For a moment she forgot herself, her mouth open, her eyes staring openly, until she collided with Midiwegi.

He turned and caught her eyes. 'Take care, you clumsy woman,' he said in an angry tone. 'And keep your head down!'

Abashed, she immediately lowered her head and muttered an apology. She berated herself for being so foolish. Caxna had warned her that she must call no attention to herself; it was dangerous if it were known that she was here, and all she could do was gape like an idiot. She pulled a larger lock of hair to block her face and hoped that no one had seen her.

After a few moments she couldn't help but notice on the street they now walked people who entered or emerged from the buildings they passed, their clothes worn but well made. And like the people's garments and adornments, the stone from which the buildings were fashioned showed deep cracks and damage in many places and sported faded designs and wall paintings whose tones of blue, yellow, black and green must have once added more dazzle to this busy place.

They turned down another street, and she could see weeds and vines climbing eagerly in many areas, finding purchase on the bits of rubble that gathered at the base of some of the smaller buildings and tumbled down walls along this street. Caxna stopped halfway along and hailed someone inside. A man emerged, pushing aside the leather curtain, his dark face weathered like a dried apple, his black hair threaded with grey. The dyed green mantle he wore showed no decoration, but it was finely made and a gold brooch fastened it at the shoulder.

Aisling straightened for a moment, released the tump line and set the basket down, grateful for the respite.

'Welcome, friend,' the man said. 'You have come. I was thinking circumstances had changed your mind.'

'I am come, Rest-house Keeper,' Caxna said. 'I had some unplanned delays.'

The man smiled and bowed, looking beyond Caxna to the others. He raised his brow. 'The delay has seemed only to increase your prosperity. You are here now and that is all that matters. I will have your rooms available in a short while. The market is full of tradesmen today and there is a festival tomorrow, so I am very busy. If you come back when the sun is fully overhead they will be ready for you and your people.'

'Of course,' said Caxna. He eyed the man. 'My assistant and I will leave our goods here with the slaves for now and perhaps have a look at what the market has to offer.'

'Very well,' the man replied. He held aside the leather curtain for the slaves to pass through with their goods. Aisling looked up at Caxna, wondering if she should follow, but he shook his head. She breathed a sigh of relief. She had no desire to quit Caxna's side in this strange place. In the days since departing Choola's town she had come to learn nothing more than the slaves' names; it seemed impossible for her to communicate with them beyond a few gestures and smiles. That made her feel more vulnerable, especially with her new appearance.

She looked down at the basket that rested at her feet, and then to Caxna and Midiwegi, who were already making their way down the street, and made a decision. Quickly she hefted the basket back up and replaced the tumpline at her forehead. This might make her more invisible in the marketplace, just one of a huge number of slaves who toted their master's goods.

Aisling followed the pair through a labyrinth of streets, then up countless treacherous worn and broken steps, so that her legs ached with the effort to maintain her balance and the weight of the basket at her back. Caxna slowed when her ragged breath communicated her distress to him, while Midiwegi muttered unintelligibly and cast her scornful glances.

When the three reached the top, Aisling paused to rest her legs and catch her breath. The square was expansive and edged with buildings while in its middle rose another staircase, leading to a further building on the top. Around the square were scattered reed mats of all sizes and colors laden with more wares than Aisling had ever seen assembled. Earthenware pots of all sizes and shapes, painted bright red, orange and yellow, crowded against baskets of wicker, reed and other materials and held anything from vegetables to grains. Stacks of fabric were side by side layers of mats. Merchants hovered over their wares, some shouting in a language Aisling couldn't understand, while others pulled out a selection of goods to wave in tempting gestures to potential customers. Near her, strong smells of fish and various meats warred with the spices and herbs from the stall opposite. The color, noise and smells seemed to run riot through the square and for a moment it made Aisling dizzy.

'I think the best thing might be to leave you two over by the chocolate stall so Aisling can rest. It is out of the way and only high born and servants visit that stall, buying for their masters. I will make my way around the market and assess the level and quality of the trade.'

'Leave me with her?' Midiwegi gave her a scornful look.

'Yes. I think that is the safest way. You can watch out for her.'

'Why am I just your assistant? I am certain my father would want me to be your partner.'

'You are my assistant because they have never met you and they trust me. If they learn you are a partner they would wonder at my abilities and worth.' He nodded grimly. 'You must follow my lead or you could endanger everything.'

Midiwegi scowled, but followed Caxna over to the designated stall. Aisling set down her basket again with relief and looked at Caxna uncertainly. She wasn't comfortable remaining alone with Midiwegi, but she understood his reasoning. After his brief farewell she watched the last sight of his dark head above the masses of people, fighting the panic that suddenly seized her after the crowd swallowed him. She felt so vulnerable without his assuring presence.

Beside her Midiwegi muttered his own lament, shifting from one foot to the other, surveying the stalls and people. A few moments later he turned to her.

'Wait here, I will be back in a moment.'

Before she could say a word, he took off like a flash, vanishing in the opposite direction to Caxna. She stood aghast and helpless, the laden basket at her feet, and scanned the market desperately, hoping to catch sight of Caxna. The sun beat down upon her, altering her vision, while wave after wave of haze rose up from the stone paving, distorting the view. She stepped back a little to the welcoming shade of the building that was near the stall. Her sight cleared but still she could see no sign of either Caxna or Midiwegi.

She looked at the man in the stall selling the strange mixture called chocolate. He was tending to a customer, a lady, weighty with jewelry, wearing a filmy skirt and mantle over a darker colored undergarment. Her hair was elaborately arranged high on top of her head, exaggerating the elongated flattened forehead. Beside her stood a younger, simpler dressed woman holding bundles wrapped in cloth, most likely her maid.

Aisling was as curious about chocolate as she was about the lady buying it. The vendor, a slip of a man with a beaky nose, had a large covered basket from which he took a handful of beans, ground them with a mortar and pestle and mixed them with some other powders, before stirring in water heated in a pot over a small fire. Then he poured the mixture into a cup and whisked it up with a splayed stick, until a frothy film appeared. He offered the cup to the lady with a smile.

She took the cup, her face impassive, and sniffed it. After a considered pause she sipped the liquid tentatively. Her eyes narrowed for a moment and she shook her head before returning the cup to him. His smile disappeared and he opened his mouth to speak, but she held her hand up and said words Aisling didn't need a translation to understand: she would not pay. The vendor's face clouded and he said something in return that contained a pleading note. The woman turned her back before he could finish and walked away, her maid giving the vendor a quick sympathetic glance before scuttling off to her mistress. The merchant muttered what could only be a curse, helpless to do much more in the face of the woman's obvious wealth and status.

Aisling couldn't help but feel sorry for the man. The woman certainly seemed hard to please. She thought of some of the women she'd seen at the market back in Leinster. Though smaller and much less exotic, she'd witnessed one or two similar incidents. Some things were common everywhere.

She was so caught in her reverie she didn't notice the tall man emerge in haste from the building she leaned upon. It wasn't until he bumped her basket and knocked it against her leg that she looked over at him. He scowled down at her and said something to her in a biting tone.

Startled, she looked up at him. Richly dressed, his dark hair was twisted up in a knot at the back of his head and gold studs pierced both ears. His dark eyes glittered. It was only a brief moment that she looked before she quickly lowered her head. 'I —I am sorry,' she said. 'I do not understand.'

He stopped and considered her. She shrank back to the wall and kept her head and eyes as low as she dared. It was then she noticed the dagger slipped in the straps of his calf high sandals.

'What have we here?' he said, switching to the trader language.

He came closer and lifted a lock of her dark hair. 'Such fine hair for a slave.' He fingered her mantle, sliding his hand down along her arm. She shivered under his touch and jerked away.

'Come, come, no need to be modest. We both know slaves have large appetites.'

She looked down at her basket, wondering if there was something in it that might help her. She could hardly snatch up her basket and make a run for it.

'Young merchant warrior, would you care for a cup of chocolate?' said the vendor from the stall.

The merchant warrior gave him a cursory glance, his thick lips frowning in disdain. 'Keep out of this, old man. I want none of your chocolate.'

'No harm meant, young man. I thought with your good taste you would appreciate something as fine as my own cacao beans, grown in my farm where the soil is sweet as honey.'

Aisling took her chance and reached down for the knife, but the man was too quick for her. He grabbed her hand before she got halfway and brought it up behind her back.

'Hold, now my beauty. There is no cause to be rude.' He shoved her arm further behind her back and she winced. 'See what rudeness can bring?' He pushed her up against the wall.

'My master will be back shortly,' she said, cursing the quiver in her voice.

'Your master obviously cares little enough for you to leave you here with your basket.' He looked down at them, the cloth coverings giving no indication of its contents. 'And little enough for what it holds.'

He leaned down and started to pull back one of the cloths. She could see the sinewy strength of his large arms that bore truth to the vendor's description. He was a warrior.

'Stop,' she said. 'You must not.' She felt herself flushing under her stained skin.

He paused at her remark and gave her a puzzled look. 'You

talk much for a slave.' He raised a hand to her chin. 'Look at me, girl. Let me see your face.'

She kept her head down under the touch of his fingers that began to press on her chin.

'It is not proper.' It was all she could think to say.

'Let me taste those lips, girl, so I can see if they are indeed the lips of a slave.'

Should she let him? Without further thought she raised her knee with a jerk and aimed between his legs. He grunted at the impact and keeled over, clutching his groin.

'Remove your hands from my slave.'

Caxna grabbed the man by the shoulder and pulled him away from Aisling.

'This is my property and I would ask that you respect that.'

The man lifted his head and gave Caxna a furious look. 'Your slave has caused me injury and should be punished.' He eyed Caxna up and down, straightening with great effort. 'Someone like that deserves to have his property taken off him.'

'It is you who sought to cause her an injury.' Though Caxna was taller than the man, and well muscled from paddling, she doubted he had the warrior skills this man did.

'It is fine, Master. I am unharmed.'

The two men looked at her. Caxna nodded. 'I will take no offence then, if you will not.'

The man narrowed his eyes. 'I will leave it. This time. If an apology is offered.'

'I will offer an apology on that condition then.'

The man nodded, gave Aisling a disdainful look and walked off.

Aisling hugged herself close. It was likely his pride that kept him from making more of the incident. She'd been lucky, but the encounter gave her no confidence about their prospects here.

'Would the kind merchant care for a cup of chocolate?' The

old vendor came over to them. 'I am sorry for what happened. I did try to distract him, but he would have none of it.'

'I thank you, Chocolate Seller. Do you know that man at all?' Caxna said.

'Everyone knows that man. He is Chaak, one of the Putun warrior merchants. He is not a man to anger lightly.'

Caxna nodded and accepted the man's offer of a cup of chocolate. After taking a sip he passed the cup to Aisling for a taste. Even the wondrous burst of rich flavor did little to dispel the growing sense of foreboding she felt.

14

She was still feeling shaken when they arrived at their rooms in the rest-house, with the tumpline around her head and the basket at her back, stumbling behind a tight-lipped Caxna and a sullen Midiwegi. The rest-house keeper apologized for the delay and showed them the three rooms that were to be their own. It was an interlinked affair on the ground floor that allowed them access to a small courtyard at the back. There, in the little shed against the wall, she was to make their meals. Too upset to do more than nod, she relieved herself of the basket and made her way to the shed, fighting tears. It was all too much.

There was little enough in the shed: three large stones, a small bench with a few ceramic pots and bowls covered in modest designs of muted colors. She picked one up, the tears spilling down her face, and saw nothing of its shape and size. Her thoughts were only of her brother. She sat on the bench, shifting aside the pots and bowls and allowed her grief a few moments. Dry, heaving sobs took her, contorting her body. All the fear and all the strain of the past months expressed themselves physically. Would she ever be able to return to her land, her home? Here, in this strange place, with all these buildings and people so different to her own kind, it didn't seem possible.

She felt herself lifted up from the chest and arms enfold her with the kind familiar touch, reminiscent of the time on beach those many months before when grief first overtook her. Aisling settled into the embrace, feeling all at once that, rather than privacy, she needed the comfort of someone who understood exile, understood the loss of family and land through war and events beyond personal control. It struck her that Caxna, too, was someone trying to regain something of what he'd lost, trying to find the means to go home.

A hand stroked her hair slowly, establishing a rhythm that added to the comfort his arms provided. She lifted her head and looked into Caxna's eyes and saw a well of compassion and understanding. He brushed a stray lock from her face and his fingers followed the contour of her cheek, along her jaw, to rest by her mouth. She closed her eyes and felt his lips brush hers for a moment only, a space so brief that the sigh that escaped her had still to finish when his lips were gone. She felt their absence, and before she could open her eyes and ask for more, he'd released her with a pat to her shoulders, took her hand and drew her across the courtyard and inside.

'I have sent Midiwegi out with three of the slaves to get some provisions for cooking,' he said to her. 'In the meantime I want to check a few of the trade goods.' He knelt down by the two baskets. 'Come, help me unpack them.'

She nodded dumbly and knelt down before one of the baskets. Carefully, she brought out each item and laid it on the blanket he had unfolded for the purpose. When they were both finished the pieces were arrayed on the floor side by side. They were strange and beautiful to her, she who had seen only a finely crafted comb, some gold coins and a gold brooch in her home growing up. Her time among Hwyel's fine ladies and men had been brief and their valuables of jeweled and gold necklaces and earrings were of a different sort than what she saw before her.

From one of the baskets came piles of cloth dyed varying shades of yellow, green, and red, or a mixture of these colors. She fingered the cloth, its light weight and smooth texture like nothing she'd ever seen. She imagined it next to her skin.

'It is very fine, is it not?' said Caxna. 'I am hoping that I will not have to part with all of it, for Choola said I may have any remainder.' He reached over and pulled out a bundle wrapped in plain white cloth. He unfolded its layers to reveal a fabric in a shade of deepest purple. She'd never seen anything like it, the color so rich, the fabric so soft. She ran her hand over it, wondering what it might be like to wear a gown fashioned from it.

'This cloth is rare even here, because of its color,' Caxna said. 'The dye is difficult to obtain. No one in Etowah has seen such cloth, or such a color, and it would be highly valued. It would make a fitting gift for a chief's daughter.'

She frowned at the reminder of the true purpose of these items. They were a means to an end. But still, she couldn't help but view them in wonder and curiosity.

Besides the cloth there were also varying sizes of conch shells and pearlescent shells that, like a sunset, reflected subtle hues of blue, purple and even a pale red. Caxna removed leather bags from the baskets that contained pendants and highly polished ropes of carved jasper beads and the curiously sculpted and polished pipes used in smoking. He examined the contents of the bags and the objects for chips or cracks until he was satisfied everything was unharmed. Next to the bags he placed another cloth-wrapped bundle, removed the covering and placed the objects on the blanket. Copper gorgets, beaten flat, with intricate swirls and patterns etched in them, glinted in the light that came in through the courtyard doorway.

'They are very fine,' Aisling said. She could imagine them around the necks of any fine nobleman or lady.

'My uncle crafted them.'

She nodded, aware now that the price of surrendering these fine pieces was higher than she first imagined.

'They will surely bring enough,' she said.

'I hope so,' he said. 'They are unusual for goods traded here.' He sighed and pulled out one more object, again wrapped in a plain cloth. When he unfolded it and laid two objects beside the copper gorgets, she could only gasp. The first object was a gorget of highly polished gold, the edges scalloped and punched with tiny holes in intricate patterns accented by etched designs, its center inlaid with highly polished seed pearls.

She fingered the workmanship and looked up at him. 'Your uncle?'

He nodded and gave a grim smile. 'His last piece. It was in my possession when they were attacked. My uncle made them for the potlatch, the celebration for my naming.'

'You would give it up?'

Pain crossed his face. 'If I have to.'

She looked at the gorgets. These pieces were his last connection to his home, his family and his past. She could only imagine what it would cost him to part with it. 'Let's hope that only one of the gorgets will be enough.'

SHE LOOKED at the pot of stew that rested on top of three large stones in between which hot coals nestled. It seemed impossible that she would sit in front of this hot fire against the fading light and still find the energy to cook in this sweltering heat. She took up the wooden spoon and stirred the mixture. Caxna had obtained some meat, beans, squash and cornmeal and some seeds to flavor the stew and the *keehel wah*.

She held the spoon to her lips and took a tentative bite. It didn't look like much, but the taste was acceptable. Beside her she had a pot of something Caxna called 'tamales'. Different, she thought, but she would eat it.

She tugged at the wig, fighting the itch at the center of her scalp, and wiped her hand across her brow to remove the beads of sweat that gathered there. It was always hot, even under the palm thatch that covered the little shed she was in. The stone in the courtyard still radiated the heat gathered from its day-long exposure to the sun. With a weary sigh she gave the stew a final stir, grabbed up the small bowls beside her and began to dish up the stew.

When she had the bowls filled she took up two of them and approached the door. She could hear their voices, kept deliberately low, but both tinged with unmistakable anger. When she entered the room the talking ceased abruptly. It didn't matter that their faces were unreadable after the bright light of the outdoors; she knew the argument was something to do with her.

She placed the bowls down on the mat and returned to the shed for the pots of beans and squash and the *keehel wah*. She put a gourd of water and earthenware cups next to the bowls and took a seat next to Caxna. The slaves, ranged around the room, looked on, their faces expressionless until Midiwegi instructed them to eat in the courtyard.

'The water for drinking is down at the end of this street,' said Caxna when they left. 'There is enough here for tonight, but you will have to go there tomorrow for more.'

She looked over at Caxna and realized he was talking to her. She nodded. What else was she supposed to do? Would she have to stay behind and do other tasks while they traded, or would she go with them and carry things? She glanced over at Midiwegi and caught a smug smile. Suddenly she decided she wouldn't ask. Let him take on the whole burden of explaining what she was to do and when. Why should she make it any easier for him?

She reached for a bowl and Midiwegi's hand shot out to restrain her. 'You will wait until we are finished, like any other slave.'

Anger rose inside her. She looked over at Caxna.

'No,' he said firmly.

'Yes. She must. She is a slave. That is what she must be. At all times. What if someone should come in unexpectedly and see her eating with us?'

Caxna regarded Midiwegi, his eyes narrowed. After a moment he grimaced. 'You make a good point, it is true. But you are posing as my assistant and as such you would eat after I am finished.' He reached for a bowl of stew.

Midiwegi reddened visibly and pursed his mouth. 'If you insist.' He rose. 'While you eat, then, I will take a walk and pretend I am on an errand for my employer.' He walked over to the curtain that hung across the door to the corridor and the outside door. 'She will have to wait until I return to eat.' He flung the curtain back and vanished through the opening.

Aisling bit her lip, dismayed at the scene. As much as she disliked Midiwegi she knew it did her no favors if she caused trouble. 'I am sorry,' she said.

'Do not worry. His father does not pay him the attention he believes he is owed and it makes him too aware of the regard he believe others must pay him.'

She gathered her legs next to her and put her arms around her knees. 'Still, I do not like to cause trouble, but I am unaccustomed to behaving like a slave and I am unfamiliar with the ways they follow here.'

He gave her a reassuring smile and gestured to the meal. 'Eat some food. Forget what he said.'

She tucked into the corn cakes, followed Caxna's example and dipped them into the bowl of beans, scooping a bit of the mixture up like a spoon. It wasn't bad and it certainly filled her empty stomach. Suddenly she felt a little better, her hunger abated and the room's relative shade and coolness making her less edgy.

'Will you trade your goods tomorrow?' she asked.

'Some of them. We'll go to the marketplace, see what prices we can get and what we can trade for the cloth and the other goods. The rest-house keeper's brother is arranging for a private meeting with one of the noblemen he knows for the jewelry pieces.'

'Can I go with you to the market?' The sights and sounds of the market held infinite interest to her compared to remaining behind in these small rooms. Besides, she felt secure with him.

He looked at her and sighed. 'I think it might be safer for you to remain here.' He frowned. 'Though Midiwegi pointed out that it would be better for me to continue to be seen with slaves.'

'I promise I will remain silent, keep my head down and stay with you at all times.'

She could see he was considering and pressed her advantage. 'Please. I am sure nothing will happen. I would be under your care, a safer place surely. If someone should come here and see me without your protection it might prove awkward.'

He frowned. 'That is true. I guess that is the best course.'

'And will you ask after the ship for me?' she whispered. 'Please?'

A flicker crossed his eyes. He nodded. 'Of course.'

They ate the remainder of the meal in silence. Midiwegi returned eventually, his point made. Caxna rose and Midiwegi took his seat. Aisling offered the bowls to him in an attempt at humility. 'I will clean up when you're finished.'

His eyes narrowed. 'You have eaten?'

She flushed red. 'N-n-no. I just find that the heat is too much. I am not hungry. I prefer to wait until the cool of the early morning.'

He nodded and reached for his bowl.

Much later, as she lay on her mat, in the small room with the other slaves, Aisling allowed herself to recall the touch of Caxna's lips on hers. What lay behind that kiss, she wondered? She ran her finger along her mouth, savoring the arousing tingle, thinking of his lips and hers. Her reaction was one she'd never have expected, one that stirred something inside her and made her wish for more. He was only across the room, a short distance. Would he welcome her? She sighed, knowing that she was only playing games with her imagination, that she would never cross that floor, to the room next door, pass the sleeping figure of Midiwegi, lay her naked body beside Caxna and take him in her arms.

15

It was still early enough in the morning to tolerate the heat when Caxna, Midiwegi and Aisling and two of the slaves left the rest-house laden with their goods and made their way to the market. Caxna, his hair pulled neatly back from his face and tied in a knot high on his head, had donned a finely woven mantle and skirt dyed a subtle shade of green with yellow threading along the border. His sandals were new and Aisling couldn't help but notice how the high backs emphasized his muscular calves. It was difficult not to admire the full effect, even against the obviously handsome features of Midiwegi, a fact his simple mantle and skirt of yellow only reinforced. Maybe it was Caxna's height, so striking among these people of shorter stature. Whatever it was, it made Aisling feel a sense of pride and hope that it showed him as a man of business, someone to be respected. He would surely make some good trades this day.

They approached the market and Aisling could feel a small breeze coming from the sea that cooled her neck and left a slight tang of salt on her lips, reminding her of the long days she'd spent tasting it. Her surroundings now couldn't have been more different, though. And this day the market seemed busier than the day before, more people crowding around more stalls, buying more goods.

With the other slaves trailing behind her, she followed Caxna and Midiwegi over to the section where fabrics, rugs and other textiles were sold, the colors and materials a riot of variety that was difficult to take in. They stopped by one particular stall piled high with folded lengths of fabric. Shaded by the overhanging cloth draped across wooden posts, Aisling was better able to view the range of colors and quality the stall displayed. She could see they were of similar type to the lengths the slaves held in their baskets. Midiwegi glared at her and she lowered her eyes.

The stall keeper was dressed well enough, his hands dark against the light cloth he smoothed as he responded to Caxna's greeting.

'You seem a man of discerning taste,' the stall keeper said. 'Can I interest you in my latest lengths just in for the festival today?'

'The festival?' Caxna said.

The man examined him closely. 'I see you are a stranger to these parts and will not have known that today is the festival for the scribes. Though there are not as many as there used to be, we are still proud to say that there a number here in Xicallanca.'

Caxna nodded. 'Thank you, good friend, for telling me of this special occasion. I did not know and I look forward to whatever festivities may unfold.'

'It will be a good one. The scribes are still important in this city. After the ceremony, there will be a ball game. It will not be as grand as were held in times past, but our temple is still whole and the ball court not destroyed or damaged like the ones further inland are.'

'A ball game?' Midiwegi's face showed keen interest.

The man grinned. 'I know you will enjoy it.' He pushed a

finely woven length of green and red cloth towards him. 'This would be a fine length to purchase to celebrate such an auspicious occasion.'

'Actually, good friend, I was hoping to interest you in some of my own goods,' said Caxna. He pulled a selection of his cloths and unfolded them. Aisling noted the purple cloth wasn't among those he offered.

And so they began to bargain. It was a session even her father would have admired, he who could force gold from the most miserly of men. In the end, the stall keeper took it all, for as Caxna reminded him, he had decided that he would allow him to be the buyer, rather than his fellow stall keeper across from him, because he seemed more honest and generous.

'You will make me honest, generous and poor,' the man said at the end of the bargaining. He handed over a pouch of carefully counted cacao beans, the currency as well as the source of the chocolate she'd sipped the day before.

Caxna smiled at the joke and bade the man a good day's trade. The morning continued with equal success. She watched Caxna negotiate with admiration, his deft use of persuasion and flattery subtle and creative. Any doubts over the success of his plans evaporated when he brought the trade to a close and came away with another weighty bag of cacao beans.

With a lighter heart she followed Caxna and Midiwegi around the market, listening to Caxna's comments on the quality of goods they saw at the various stalls. This city was like nothing she'd ever imagined, and she could only guess what a marvel of learning and ability they must have. Pots of all sizes and shapes with designs in shades of ochre, rust, darkest grey, gold, and all colors of the sea were stacked and lined along blankets in stalls. Sunset and autumn worked their way into the rugs displayed in random fashion tempting passers-by to stop and examine them. She thought of her own home. It seemed so rough in comparison.

They moved to another section of the market where a cacophony of clucking, warbling, and other noises came from an assortment of birds in all sizes and shapes in cages and baskets. It wasn't far from the birds that Caxna stopped to examine a stall with wares laid out in all their glory. The blues, golds, emerald greens she'd seen moments earlier on the bird were laid out in piles as individual plumes for sale. These feathers were also gathered into finely sewn mantles and it was one of these Caxna picked up, a covetous smile on his face. The feathers were soft, beautifully arranged for harmony of color and size. It was flamboyant, but there was no doubt the wearer would convey a sense of power and wealth.

Caxna pointed to the mantle, his face arranged in a neutral expression. 'How much would you want for one of your mantles? Say, for instance, this one?'

The vendor regarded Caxna carefully and then noted the mantle in his hand. 'That is one of my finest, and so I would have to ask a price worthy of it.'

Caxna nodded. 'I can see that the workmanship is fine, as it is in your other mantles.'

The man named a price and Aisling caught her breath. It was nearly all the cacao beans they had. Caxna appeared to consider it for a moment. 'Perhaps that would be fair for this mantle. But I have seen one similar for a lower price at your fellow vendor nearby.' He put the mantle down and began to walk away. It was all the man needed to conclude the sale at a more reasonable price.

Aisling was stunned. They'd come away with the mantle and at least a third of their cacao beans left. Would he buy something else? Or save the beans to take with him? With a private smile at his clever bargaining she followed the two men back into the growing crowd which now pressed more closely against her. It seemed impossible that there were more people here than before the purchase of the mantle, but it was true. She glanced around and saw everyone was heading in one direction. Caxna stopped and asked one of the food vendors its cause.

'The ceremony is about to begin.' The man pointed to the end of the market square where stone steps rose to an imposing platform containing a group of richly clad men. Colorful feather mantles draped their shoulders and their hair was arranged elaborately on their head. They weren't close enough to see the ceremony clearly, but as the crowd fell silent Aisling could hear voice tones that were unmistakably ritualistic.

Caxna motioned her closer. 'Stay at my side,' he muttered. 'I do not want us to get separated.' She nodded and drew towards him as the crowd became more intense.

Up on the stone platform men filed out from a stone building. Perhaps it was their sacred building and they were the holy men, thought Aisling. She craned her neck for a better view, risking raising her head with all eyes fixed forward. One of the holy men lifted a smoking pot to the heavens as he intoned words loudly. He spoke for some time, his speech interrupted only when the men lined up before him murmured a response. The crowd remained silent, watching intently. Aisling could make nothing out of the words and there was little enough in the actions, but something compelled her to keep watching.

It was when the priest vanished into the building briefly and emerged with a small child painted blue that she began to hold her breath. The men gathered around the child, blocking the specatators' view. She could only hear the priest intoning once again, louder this time and see something grasped in his raised hand. The hand disappeared, but a few moments later appeared again, this time clutching something that dripped down his arm. The crowd roared its approval.

Caxna grabbed her hand and started pulling her away.

'What is it, what are they doing?' she asked. She knew really, she just couldn't believe her eyes; that they would cut out the heart of a small child.

'We will leave. I did not know there would be this kind of ceremony here still. We must go back to the rest-house.' He motioned to Midiwegi and the two slaves. Midiwegi gave one last look at the spectacle and followed them.

THEY MISSED THE BALL GAME, something she wasn't sorry about since she could only imagine what form it might have taken. Back in their rooms, after the game, she laid out a plate of some dried fruit and some kind of poultry meat they'd bought in the market afterwards. On their return, they found the rest-house keeper's brother had left word that he'd arranged for Caxna to meet with the head scribe and his wife tonight to view the wares he had in his possession.

'It is a big honor,' the rest-house keeper had told him. 'You are invited to the feast for the scribes afterward, too. It is possible that if they have no interest in your wares, one of the other scribes might be.'

Caxna thanked the man profusely and it helped alleviate the pall that hung over the group since they'd witnessing the horrifying episode at the market. The images still pressed in on her when she was least aware, even as she sat picking at the small bowl of fruit she ate on her own in the courtyard. After a few moments she gave up and went inside and found Caxna putting together a small bundle of goods.

'There are a few other things I need to do,' he said. For a brief moment he caught Aisling's eye. 'It might be a good idea to look for a finer mantle to wear tonight. I also want to get a sense of the worth of my jewelry pieces and inquire after a merchant I know and see if he still has that green stone necklace.'

'Shall I come with you?' Midiwegi asked.

'No. It is better that I go alone. The two of you can stay here. If anyone comes asking for me, you can say I will return soon.'

'Are you expecting someone?'

'No. But I will be making inquiries,' he said. 'For the merchant.'

Midiwegi nodded and appeared to be satisfied.

Aisling rose and gathered up the remnants of the meal. She worked slowly, trying to comprehend the morning's events and Caxna's recent conversation. She was no clearer in her mind when all was completed. Were the words he'd spoken earlier in fact a message that he was asking about the ship? In some ways she hoped that there was no news here of her ship. This was not the place she would wish her brother to encounter and she had no desire to remain here any longer than was necessary.

16

Caxna returned just as the rest-house keeper's brother arrived, deferring any opportunity Aisling might have seized to question Caxna about his time in the market. Though very short, the merchant was well dressed, his mantle of finely woven cloth dyed an alarming shade of green, his arms and neck heavily adorned with jeweled bands and necklaces. One particular pendant hung prominently and its leather medallion was stamped with tiny images.

'It is good to see you back in the city, my friend,' the man said. He gave a broad smile. Like many of the other well-dressed people in the city, his eyes were slightly crossed, a feature the people thought was attractive, though his head was of normal proportions. Were it not for the conversation's content and the fact that she and Midiwegi were beneath notice, the crossed eyes would have made it impossible to be certain whom he was addressing.

'Welcome, welcome. I am glad you were able to see me. Can I offer you some refreshment?' Caxna asked. He indicated a place on the floor mats and the two took seats while they exchanged pleasantries.

Aisling scurried to the water jug and poured some into two of their three cups. She wasn't certain if that was what Caxna meant by refreshment, but she wanted to appear to be busy so that she wouldn't be dismissed into the next room. As it was, Midiwegi took the two cups from her and waved her away.

She moved to the edge of the room and watched the merchant lay out a dark cloth and then unwrap and place on it a fine piece of jewelry. Though she was hardly experienced in viewing high quality green jewels it took no expert to appreciate that the craftsmanship in this piece was of the best to be found. It was a gold necklace wrought in such a delicate manner that it could appear almost as a spider's web, capturing not insects, but tiny green gems that circled a larger version at its base.

Aisling stared at it, marveling at the beauty of such work and the skill of its maker, and just for a moment, how it might look around her own neck. With a sigh she let the image go, for she knew whose neck it was intended for. But with such a necklace even she might be able to get her own land and holdings restored.

'There,' said the merchant. 'You see? It is just as marvelous as you remembered, isn't it?'

'It is indeed, it is indeed,' Caxna said. 'But, the price must be right.'

For a few minutes more they bargained back and forth until finally Caxna held up his hand. 'I can see that you are not coming into my price range as much as I had hoped.' He paused.

'Are you giving up so easily?' the merchant asked.

'Not giving up, no. What I will do is talk again with you in two days' time. By that point I will know what my own trades might bring and what I would be willing to pay for this piece. For now, though, I would have you enjoy my feeble hospitality.'

The man gave a gracious nod and sipped his drink. 'I understand, my friend. A piece such as this is not meant for the ordinary person. You must have a particular customer in mind to make it worth your while.' He smiled, his eyes searching Caxna's.

Caxna gave him a noncommittal nod and ate a spoonful of stew. After a suitably hospitable interval, the merchant departed. Aisling hoped he wasn't disappointed. Perhaps the trade with the prominent scribe might make this purchase possible.

Caxna seemed to possess this hope as he turned his attention to his preparations for the visit to the noble scribe's house. He went to the bathing rooms at the end of the road and returned with his hair wet and hanging loose, his body shiny with oil. From the basket he removed a bundle and unrolled it. He donned bracelets, a gorget, and a nose ring one by one, his appearance gradually changing under the layers of silver. On his head he placed a circlet banded in fur and then across his shoulders draped a woven and sewn blanket emblazoned with stylized wolves and eagles in black and red. This was no Xicallanca manner of dressing, no matter that he wore the sandals and waist wrap common here. His hair, dress and manner all spoke of a man from foreign parts. A man of wealth and importance.

Midiwegi did his own amount of preening, his hair pulled back into a knot, his mantle and wrap of good cloth edged in a bold pattern. He even added his earrings and a simple bangle around his arm. A well-dressed assistant reflected on the wealth and status of the employer. What about her though? Would she remain behind with the other slaves? Aisling wondered about the mantle and skirt she wore, the small stains and soiling it had acquired through cooking and other labors. It was with some relief that she saw Caxna hold out a clean set of clothes to her and told her it was safer if she stayed with them.

It didn't take her long to change, but when she appeared again Caxna and Midiwegi were at the door, ready to go. Midiwegi handed Aisling a leather bag, which she slung across her body. Aisling could only guess that it contained the fine pieces

Caxna wanted to sell. She followed the two silently, through the door to the corridor and out into the street, reminding herself to keep her head bowed.

They made their way quickly, down one street and onto the next, retracing their steps toward the market, until they veered along a street that was a little wider, the stones, a little smoother and evenly placed. They climbed several sets of steps, until they opened out onto a wide terrace fronting an impressively carved stone building. Murals decorated either side, depicting elaborately dressed figures in various poses, each possessing an elongated forehead made more prominent against an exaggerated nose.

The leather door swung open and a servant appeared carrying a basket. She started at the sight of Caxna, Midiwegi and Aisling approaching.

'Greetings,' Caxna said in a friendly but firm manner. 'I have come to see your master and mistress on business. She is expecting us.'

The woman gave him a puzzled look, shook her head and said something in her own language. She held a hand to signal him to wait and disappeared back inside. A short while later she returned with a man by her side. The man nodded to Caxna.

'You have business with the master?' he asked, his manner polite.

Caxna nodded and explained his visit. The servant seemed satisfied and ushered them through the entrance to small hall within, leaving the woman behind to resume her errand. Once inside Aisling blinked at the darkened room after the strong light of the outdoors.

'If you will wait here, I will confer with my mistress a moment,' the servant said.

Caxna nodded and they watched the man depart, swallowed into another part of this grand house of which only another, bigger hall, lit with torches, was visible. Aisling could see the tension in Caxna's face, evident now even in the dim light of the hall. There was much riding on this transaction; his future, and to a certain extent hers.

She regarded Caxna once more and as if in response to her thoughts, he looked at her and gave her a wan smile. She sighed and her eyes slid over to Midiwegi. Why had he chosen to accompany Caxna on this journey? She could see no key reason he might have to do so. There was no real profit in it for him, other than ensuring that his father's goods were traded well and the profit shared as he'd designated. Exactly what had Choola to gain from helping Caxna? She cast her mind back to the visit to his village and Midiwegi's sister, who'd made her own preference for Caxna clear. She might have persuaded her father to help Caxna, but why would she do that if it was to enable him to marry another? She considered Caxna again. Had he told Midiwegi and his family the full truth? What was the full truth? She was in no position to know for certain that he'd told her everything. She sighed. There was no point at this moment puzzling over something she couldn't solve now. All she knew was that she must take care.

Midiwegi shuffled his feet and glanced at Caxna. 'Do you think there is a problem?'

Caxna shook his head, but Aisling could see he was worried. 'I think not. It is possible that they are engaged in something else at the moment. I am certain they will see us when they are free.'

More time passed and Aisling could feel the tension from them both. She peered through to the next room, willing someone to emerge who might explain the delay. After what seemed an interminable period of waiting, filled with more shuffling feet and several frustrated sighs from Midiwegi, the servant appeared once more and with a flick of the head, indicated they should follow him.

Whisked through several spacious rooms that opened onto a

central courtyard, the group finally arrived at a large room alive with brightly painted murals and cooled by the breeze from the courtyard. Pillars were dotted around, granting the room its large space and providing an airy quality. Thick pallets and cushions covered in rich woven fabrics provided a sense of intimacy in several areas. Against the walls, various painted and carved chests supported vases, figures and other finely crafted objects.

Such wealthy furnishings would have captured Aisling's attention were it not for the woman reclining on the central pallet, just out of the sun's direct light, but placed perfectly to catch the breeze coming through the courtyard opening. The woman possessed the now familiar elongated and flattened forehead and the slightly crossed eyes, all of which seemed emphasized by the elaborately worked gold hoops and rings that covered her nose and ears, and the large intricate folds of oiled hair on top of her head. Her ankles also showed gold chains, revealed when she unfolded her legs from under her mantle.

Though the mantle and the skirt beneath it were long, the cloth, of the palest gold color, was so fine, so transparent, that Aisling was left in no doubt of the woman's large full breasts and russet brown areolas. The woman's eyes slid over Caxna, taking in every bit of him. She gestured to her servant and spoke briefly to him in her language.

'My mistress apologizes, but she does not speak your language and has asked me to remain and translate for you.'

'Your mistress does not need words to explain her appreciation for fine things,' Caxna said. 'But I thank you for assisting in my humble visit. I am Caxna, a merchant from far beyond this kingdom, come to offer your mistress an opportunity to own some items that will show her beauty to its best advantage and add to her very fine collection.'

After the servant translated, the woman gave a considering nod and spoke, her tone sultry.

'My mistress says her beauty can stand on its own, without adornment, if she so chooses.' The servant's tone was neutral, his face betraying nothing.

There was something in the pitch of her voice that made Aisling lift her head and examine the women carefully. Recognition hit her like a blow. She was the difficult woman at the chocolate stall. Quickly she lowered her head, then realized a woman like that would have never noticed her in the market, and she would never notice her here now. But would a woman like that wish to purchase Caxna's goods? She looked at her, the flashing gold, the haughty smile and the revealing clothes. Caxna might need to trade more than his goods to complete this transaction successfully. And for a moment she wished that Caxna would refuse, should the woman make the offer.

'Yes, of course,' Caxna said, his tone soothing. 'I meant nothing but that. Your beauty requires no adornment, and no jewelry would ever rival it. I merely thought that these pieces would add to the beauty of your collection.'

The woman allowed herself a lazy smile at his response and gestured for him to continue. Midiwegi removed the leather bag from Aisling's shoulders and carefully unwrapped the bundles it contained, one at a time, and laid the pieces out on the cloth. Though she had seen them before, Aisling caught her breath again in the face of the fine craftsmanship. The woman leaned forward, examining them carefully from her seat on the pallet. She pointed to a piece, one of the gorgets, and Midiwegi lifted the necklace from its place on the cloth and brought it to the woman, kneeling beside her. She lifted it with one hand from his palms, laid it across her other arm for a moment and then shook her head. She rattled a few words to the servant and waved Midiwegi away.

'My mistress says that the etching is too clumsy for her tastes.'

Caxna paled, taking the unjust insult without a word. The

woman leaned forward again, her eyes moving across to the other gorget, the final piece, the one Aisling knew was too delicate, too subtle for a woman with such a heavy mouth and nose and enough gold rings and bangles to frighten the gods with the noise. The woman gestured to Midiwegi, pointed to the jewelry and he obeyed, laying the necklace in the woman's open palms when he knelt by her side once more. She held up the gorget to the sun and the light caught its rays, bending and multiplying the light, catching the shimmer of the seed pearls. She spoke to the servant. He nodded and she spoke again, directing her gaze at Caxna.

'My mistress says that she will consider this piece.'

'I am glad that it pleases her.'

'You may leave it with her and she will let you know if she will have it and what price she is prepared to pay.'

Caxna forced a smile. 'I can understand your mistress's desire to keep the necklace to examine it at her leisure, but I must insist that she can examine the piece only in my presence.'

The servant translated and the woman leaned forward, her breasts pressing against the cloth, her eyes and mouth full of invitation. She gestured to Caxna to come closer. Midiwegi stood back and Caxna moved to her side, the smile still pasted on his face. She reached out and caressed his thigh and further up his leg, and murmured a few words.

'My mistress invites you to stay for some refreshment. She is hosting guests for her husband later, but she is prepared to entertain you for a short while.'

Caxna nodded, the smile fading somewhat under the strain of the hand that had now wandered even further. 'Tell your mistress I am honored.'

The servant relayed the message, then bowed and left the room. So caught up in the scene playing out before her, Aisling was startled when the woman looked to her and gestured her and Midiwegi into the courtyard. With great reluctance Aisling followed Midiwegi to stand in the blazing sun while Caxna was left to persuade the woman of the necklace's worth with tactics that had nothing to do with the skill or quality of the work. It was laughable to be told to go, when she could see the woman from here, pulling Caxna down onto the pallet, his blanket sliding off, her hands leaving no bit of him unexplored. Midiwegi pushed her behind him and craned his neck to see, impeding her own view. She was glad of it and put her hands over her ears, wishing all at once to block it all out.

Midiwegi gasped. Aisling caught a glimpse of the woman, her arms encasing Caxna, her lips on his. At the entrance at the far end of the room, a man strode in, the servant following quickly behind, babbling words in an apologetic tone. Heavy lidded, the woman lifted her head and looked over at him, her mantle shoved aside, baring her breasts. She gestured to the man to sit while she released Caxna and reassembled her clothes. The man remained standing, his face dark and thunderous, an anger made even more evident by his height and muscular frame. Aisling moved closer and was horrified to see that it was the man who had accosted her in the market, Chaak.

In a manner worthy of any queen, the woman regarded Chaak. She murmured a few words and leaned across to pat his arm. On the other side of her pallet, Caxna rearranged his own clothing, his hair no longer immaculate, his face flushed. He picked up his blanket from the floor and draped it around his shoulders.

The woman reached across him to the floor where the gorget had fallen during their embrace. She lifted it up and held it out to Chaak, touching his fingers with her own in the exchange, holding them for a moment, her look seductive. She brought her fingers to her mouth and kissed them.

Chaak flushed, his eyes glinting, the anger transforming into lust. He glanced over at Caxna and for a moment Aisling could only feel fear as the recognition registered on his face. He looked down at the necklace in his hands, fingered the filigree work and the gems one by one. The woman spoke a few words, a question. She cocked her head.

'Where did you get this piece?' Chaak said to Caxna. Caxna rose and moved away from the woman.

'It is my piece. I brought it with me from my home, far away.'

The man's eyes narrowed. 'Liar. You did not bring this with you. You stole it.'

'I did not steal it. I am no thief.'

'I say you stole it. This piece is mine. I brought it back with me on my last sea journey to the islands.'

Caxna glanced at the woman who watched the exchange with detached interest.

'I repeat,' Caxna said. 'The piece is mine. I brought it with me. My assistant will verify this truth.' Caxna turned to Midiwegi and motioned him forward. Aisling hung back, reluctant to remind him of their previous encounter, but Midiwegi grabbed her hand and pulled her along with him.

'An assistant,' Chaak said. 'No one will credit the word of an assistant.' He cast a disdainful glance over Midiwegi. Behind him Aisling kept her head down, praying he would give her no notice.

The woman rose, sat beside Chaak and rested her hand on Chaak's arm, posing a question. Chaak laid his hand on top of hers and rubbed it, his eyes calculating. He murmured an answer, ran his fingers along her arm, caressing it lightly then brushed them against her breast, playing with the nipple under the cloth. She leaned forward and planted a kiss behind his ear and smiled. He handed her the necklace and slid his hand under her skirt. She gave a throaty laugh and pushed his hand deeper between her legs. Chaak grinned and plied his finger for a few moments before withdrawing it. He said a few words to her, his hand clasping hers, the necklace still clutched between her fingers. She looked at him, then glanced across at Caxna, who stood speechless before this display. The woman turned back to Chaak and nodded, an amused smile on her face.

Chaak turned to Caxna. 'Mistress Ix Chei has agreed that the piece belongs to me and you are a thief. You will be taken away at once and imprisoned.'

'What?' Caxna said in disbelief. 'No, that is not possible. It is not true. I am no thief.' He turned to Ix Chei. 'Please, mistress, you must believe me. The piece is mine, I did not steal it.'

Ix Chei gave a small smile, then shouted, and the servant came rushing through the door. When she pointed to Caxna and gave an order the servant looked bewildered. Ix Chei barked out her order again and the servant took Caxna's arm, his reluctance obvious.

Caxna pulled away. 'No there is a mistake, I tell you the piece is mine.'

The servant took his arm more firmly. 'It is no use resisting. The mistress has made up her mind. We will have to send for the guards.' Caxna pulled on the man, broke his grasp again, but the servant shouted and others came to assist him. Caxna was led away protesting and resisting his captors.

Aisling viewed the events with increasing fear and horror, shrinking behind Midiwegi as much as she dared. As if galvanized by the last sight of Caxna, Midiwegi rushed forward, snatched up the pieces left on the cloth, stashed them in the leather bag and rushed out with Aisling in his wake. She followed him back through the spacious rooms, back to the large hall and the small hall, amazed that no one heeded their passage. It wasn't until they reached the bottom of the labyrinth of streets that Midiwegi slowed down and Aisling could catch her breath, though the horror remained acute.

17

'What will we do?' Aisling followed Midiwegi inside the rest-house, her voice breathless from the hurried journey. Midiwegi had successfully led them back through the maze of streets, his pace brisk but not noticeably fast. She had done her best to keep up, but any effort to keep her eyes averted was lost in her distress and desire to return to the relative safety of their rooms and question Midiwegi about what means they would use to secure Caxna's release.

As soon as Midiwegi reached their rooms he ordered the slaves to pack their belongings. Aisling repeated the question.

'You will help pack the rest of these things, instead of wasting time standing around.'

She knelt down beside him and began folding up a length of cloth piled in the corner. 'We must help Caxna.'

'We will leave this place as quickly and quietly as we can,' said Midiwegi.

'Leave?' Had she understood him correctly? 'Leave Caxna here?'

He paused and looked at her a moment. 'Do you believe

there is something we can do? I am an assistant in their eyes. And you—you are a slave.'

'But there must be someone we can approach.' She sought for the word that meant 'judge', but found she had no knowledge of any. 'Is there a person who listens to explanations of wrongdoing and then decides whose cause is just?'

He gave her a hard look. 'They have such persons. They are the people in power. And who do you think they are? Recall whose house we were in when Caxna was taken.'

She blinked at him, remembering. 'A scribe's house?'

'The head scribe's house. One of the most powerful people here.'

'His wife wanted the necklace.'

He nodded. 'And who do you think they will believe? His wife, her lover Chaak or you, a slave, you stupid girl?'

She drew herself up. 'I am not stupid, it was that I did not know all the details. Is there someone else we might approach for help? The rest-house keeper or his brother?'

Midiwegi snorted. 'Why would either one risk his livelihood and perhaps his life to come to the aid of someone who is not from this community and is not influential?'

She paused to consider. Her ignorance of this place, these people, was such that she couldn't fathom any other alternative at the moment, but that didn't mean with some careful thought or discussion some kind of possibility might be uncovered. She couldn't just leave Caxna here. She relied on him, relied on his skill and his knowledge of the waterways that would help her find her brother. There was no question, she needed him. She moved closer to Midiwegi and placed a firm hand on his arm.

'I can see that there is no one we can ask for help, but let us think a moment. There must be something we can do.'

He shook off her hand. 'There is nothing to consider. The longer we linger here, the more likely we, too, might be taken.'

'Could we go somewhere else for aid? Would your father help, or someone he knows?

'There is no time. Can you not see? Caxna will be dead tomorrow, and it is likely we could be joining him if we do not leave this place. Though we are insignificant, we are the only two who might challenge Chaak's version of events.'

'Dead, tomorrow? They will kill him?'

'Dead, I am certain, with all the other prisoners. To celebrate the feast of the scribes. And what better way to honor the head scribe, but a sacrifice of a thief who dared to shame him and his wife by trying to sell stolen goods?'

She took a deep breath, trying to absorb his words. 'Sacrifice? They will sacrifice him in the same manner they sacrificed the child today?' She shuddered and willed away the image that formed in her mind. Caxna must not meet his end as a sacrifice, for something so wrong and deceitful as Chaak's lie. A lie brought on by Caxna rescuing her from Chaak's notice. If not for that, Chaak might have overlooked Caxna and just been content for Caxna to surrender the necklace.

She thought of the necklace. She'd never seen such beautiful and unique workmanship. Worthy only as a gift for the gods, really. Wearing something like that, she could almost believe again that she would have no trouble seeing the visions in the water. Even *An Seanduine* would come to her, inhabit her body, if only for a chance to wear, to feel a piece as beautiful as the necklace. If only she could have a vision, a vision that would put the fear of *An Seanduine* in these people, especially in Chaak. Her thoughts descended into the familiar abyss of self-doubt, disbelief and failure, a path so worn and easy, its pace was rapid.

'Hurry up, girl, or I will leave you behind to your fate,' said Midiwegi.

It was then a small idea formed in her mind, an idea so ludicrous she couldn't put it aside, and the more she considered it the more she could think there was no alternative.

'Wait,' Aisling said. 'There is a possibility.'

He paused and looked at her, his eyes narrowed. 'What possibility?'

She composed herself, gathered in all her training and skill and gave him a direct look. 'In my homeland I am a woman of power. Spiritual power.'

'You have a spirit helper?' His look was skeptical.

She nodded. 'I am a priestess for a goddess, a strong spirit helper of great authority. She will hear me, I assure you, if I summon her.'

'You tell me that you have the ear of a strong spirit helper, yet you are here, a slave on these shores?'

'I am not a slave.' She lifted her chin. 'I was sent here to Caxna to help him and his people. We chose to let you think I was a slave.'

He gave her a puzzled look. 'Why were you sent here to help Caxna? What has your spirit helper to do with him?'

'He and his people are favored by the goddess and she seeks to restore him and his people to their proper position.'

'She sent you to help.'

'Yes.' She took a deep breath. 'I was given the vision back in my homeland and then I was sent here.' She had taken the first step. If she could convince him, she might be able to go through with it and convince others.

'So how do you propose to help Caxna now?' His tone held a measure of respect, but there was caution in his eyes.

'I will summon the goddess and she will help us.'

He nodded slowly, his acceptance growing.

'I will need some things, first. Copal, incense and something gold. The Lady likes gold.'

He examined her carefully, weighing the options. He nodded again, the gesture firm this time. 'We will try this, then. I will go to the market and get the copal and incense.' He pointed to one of the baskets, a slave bent over it, packing. 'There are pieces fashioned from gold in the yellow bundle in there. I will be back shortly.'

She watched his departure, marveling at the respect that had crept into his tone. It gave her some bit of confidence that she might be able to carry out the plan that had formed in her mind. The slave stopped the packing and moved out of the way. She motioned to him and the others to go to the shed, where earlier she had left bowls of beans, squash and cold tamales ready in anticipation of their return from the scribe's house.

After their departure, their faces a jumble of puzzlement and curiosity, she took a deep breath and knelt down by one of the baskets. Carefully, she unpacked the lengths of cloth that moments before the slave had placed in there, until she came to the one she remembered from the previous day. The white cloth bundle. She unfolded it and removed the special fabric that it had protected. The purple cloth shimmered deeply against her pale skin. She moved her hand across it, its weave so smooth and close it was like the water's surface. Carefully she unfolded it, removed her servant's garb with a few swift movements and draped the cloth around her body, folding and tucking to create something as graceful and elegant as she could manage.

A few fumblings among Midiwegi's basket and she found the gold arm bands, bangles, nose rings and earrings he'd mentioned wrapped in a dark piece of cloth. She had no memory of seeing these pieces. Had Midiwegi bought them here or were they among things he'd had with him to trade? It was a puzzle she must leave for later, she decided, and slipped on the arm bands and bangles. She picked up one of the nose rings and a pair of earrings. She would have to leave them, there were no holes in her ears or nose to oblige. Besides, she thought grimly, her spirit helper didn't require it. They might serve another use, though.

She removed her wig and, for a moment, scratched her head in relief. Her hair was damp with sweat and was not at its best, but it would have to do. She unwound it from its twist at the back of her head and it tumbled down. She drew her fingers through it, released some of the tangles and hoped the glare of the torches would give strength to its color.

Taking up the gold rings, she deftly braided them in scattered places through her hair and nodded in satisfaction when she'd finished. It wasn't something she'd ever seen before, but it would certainly add to the effect. From inside the basket, she picked up the mantle of feathers Caxna had purchased earlier and considered its use. It certainly had possibilities. She laid it aside and dug out a kohl stick and a large length of dark cloth which she thought would serve as a cloak. The kohl stick she used around her eyes as she had seen the women here do. Her feet peeked out from the draped fabric and for only a brief moment she considered searching for better sandals until she realized that bare feet would be best.

She moved closer to the light at the doorway to examine the rest of her appearance, wondering if there was more to be done. The cloth, whispering quality when she moved, molded itself around her figure, straightening her spine and lifting her chin. She closed her eyes, absorbed the changes the dress, the gold and the feel her hair at her back created in her. She cast her mind to the prayers, the rituals that had been so much a part of her life. The sun heated her arm and she drew that energy in, used it to bring her to a different sense of herself and her surroundings. She'd no idea what would happen, how successful she would be, but she made an effort to push these fears aside.

'I hope this will meet your requirements.'

Aisling blinked a moment and turned to Midiwegi who knelt just inside the room, his head bowed, offering her a small parcel. She took it without a word, opened it and gave a brief nod. After a moment's pause, she filled a large bowl with water, took the copal from its wrapping and placed it in another, smaller bowl.

'Would you get me an ember from the fire?' she asked Midiwegi.

Once he'd returned, she lit the copal with it and waited the few moments while it caught, its small tendrils of smoke rising slowly upwards. The pungent odor soon reached her nose and she inhaled deeply, taking in the small subtleties of scent that followed. She allowed them to soothe her further, raise her above all that cluttered the room; the fears, the desires, the confusion. It was only her and the words, and the words became her hopes, her hopes became her strength. She could see what she must do. She lingered with these thoughts, allowed herself the luxury of a few extra moments of peace and assurance before she opened her eyes and faced Midiwegi.

'We must wait until dark,' she told him. 'Then She will come.'

Midiwegi lifted his head and nodded slowly, still kneeling.

WHEN THE SUN HAD DISAPPEARED, Aisling rose. She smoothed the cloth. It shimmered against the dim light of the single flame from the wick floating in the oil-filled shell Midiwegi had lit some time before. She leaned forward to douse it and her hair fell forward, nearly touching the floor. It felt good to have it loose and now, under such freedom, it had nearly dried of its sweat and returned to its familiar golden shade. By the time she reached the temple it should be completely dry.

She took a deep breath and tried to calm the turmoil within her. There was so much at stake and she knew she must do everything she could to convince them she was *An Seanduine*. Her disbelief, her lack of visions and inability to feel or contact the Lady, she must now put aside and do her best to create the idea that she could do all these things. She raised her eyes and intoned a prayer before taking up the black cloth and wrapping it around her, covering her head.

What had Caxna said about this color? Black was the color for death.

Midiwegi led her silently back through the warren of streets, now filled with leering shadows and an occasional torch born by a slave escorting groups of drunken men. Aisling and Midiwegi drew themselves closer to the wall as one particularly large group passed in the same direction. The streets had taken on such a vastly different character it was difficult to believe it was the same place.

'It is the festival,' Midiwegi said, as if he read her thoughts. 'Everyone is celebrating.'

Aisling nodded, drew her wrap tighter, and the pair moved on. The stone-paved street was still warm under her feet, still retaining the sun's strength. Midiwegi quickened his pace and she matched it as the crowds thickened. She tried to focus the prayers, repeating them over and over, taking comfort and strength in the words. She reached out to *An Seanduine*, to Bríd, to her mother, to anyone that might help her here tonight. So focused were her thoughts that when Midiwegi drew up beside the temple steps, she nearly collided with him.

He pointed to the top. 'See, they are assembled on the plaza.'

She looked where he pointed and saw within the semi-circle of light created by the torches fixed to the temple walls a group of men dressed in white robes. Their chanting, a rising hum, left her in no doubt that there was some ceremony underway. She became conscious of the crowds around her, mostly men, laughing and jostling each other as they craned their necks to view the scene above. Though the night was warm, she shivered.

Aisling straightened and turned to Midiwegi. 'Leave us now.' She spoke quietly but in a deeper, authoritative tone. 'Go collect our things and wait for us at the canoe.'

Midiwegi nodded and without any argument, disappeared into the crowd. She gathered the skirt of her gown and began her ascent, counting the steps as she went and keeping her thoughts centered on the approaching confrontation. She must be strong, project her thoughts, her voice, her whole being on this group of men. This group of priests and scribes. How powerful were they? Would they see through her? Would they take any notice to a woman, even a goddess? She shook her head. It was no use allowing such thoughts to enter her mind now. She would go through with this, no matter what the consequences.

A few steps away from the top, the circle of men came into clear view. Behind them she could make out several people gathered at the side, their hands and feet bound, while in the circle's center, a man lay stretched out on a large stone, three priests bent over him. She scanned his face desperately, hoping she wouldn't recognize the features. A moment later she breathed a sigh of relief. It wasn't Caxna.

The man was naked, except for a small breechclout, and his skin was painted a vibrant shade of blue. She paused and watched him struggle as the two priests held him down, one for his arms and the other, his feet. The third priest clutched a blade in his hand and raised it above the man's heart. Though Aisling closed her eyes, she knew all too well from the events earlier that day what would follow. The man screamed out in agony and then was silent.

She looked over at the rest of the prisoners, examining each one carefully. She need not have paid such attention—she recognized him instantly, despite the ragged hair that hung loose in his face and about his shoulders. His head was bowed and his shoulders drooped with fatigue under the blue of his painted skin. He was bound and linked to the other men and women that surrounded him. Her faint hope that she might secure his release without being noticed disappeared. There was no escaping what she now must do. She allowed the cloth to slide from her head and tied the feather mantle around it so that it encased her head like a crown.

She stepped onto the plaza and made her way to the circle of men. When she arrived at their sides she halted, tossed the cloth onto the ground and raised her hands.

'*An Seanduine* speaks!' she said in Irish. Though she knew they didn't understand her words, she hoped that her tone and actions would be all that was needed. She would speak her language, the language of the goddess, and hope it would all come right.

The men turned and faced her, their expressions a mixture of annoyance, puzzlement and curiosity. She stepped forward, into the circle. The man on the table lay groaning, his chest ripped apart, his life's blood draining rapidly. She tore her eyes from the sight and focused on the head priest, the knife held in one hand, blood coating the other.

She gestured upwards. 'I am sent from above with a message.' She turned slowly around, her arms still raised, her long gold hair swirling out, catching the light. A gasp or two and a stifled cry among the scribes gave her courage to continue. And suddenly it came to her, her own image swathed in purple that she'd seen all those months before on the beach. Was this a prophecy fulfilled? Her heart soared under the power of it and she circled once more, intoning the prayers to *An Seanduine*. She would carry this through now, because surely she had the blessing of the gods.

She stopped when she faced the group of prisoners once more and lowered her arms and pointed to Caxna. He'd raised his head and looked at her, recognition, surprise and fear flashing across his face.

'Release that man now,' she said. 'He is marked for us. He must carry out his destiny far from this place.' She walked over to Caxna slowly, allowing the skirt of her dress to trail after her, her hair cascading around her, and hoping the flickering torch-light showed the brightly colored feathers effectively.

The men permitted her to move to Caxna's side where she

motioned to one of the guards nearby and pointed to Caxna's bound hands. 'Release him.' Her meaning was clear.

The guard looked first at the priests, and then to her, uncertainty and fear written on his face. She stared at him, allowing all the mounting anger and frustration to show. He moved to obey her until the priest shouted. The guard halted. She turned to face the priest, her eyes flashing the anger that welled up inside her.

'Who dares to speak against the word of *An Seanduine?*'

She walked a few steps towards the priest, reluctant to move too far from Caxna. She'd seen the desperate shake of Caxna's head. He didn't like what she was doing.

The priest gestured and spoke to the guard, who came forward and grabbed her, holding both her hands behind her back. For a moment she panicked, and a small cry escaped her, but she held onto her anger, let it surge through her once again to reinforce her will. With a firm tug she broke the man's grasp and stepped away from him. The priest watched her, his eyes narrowed. She raised her hands above her and shouted to the heavens.

'Oh Lady, stay with me now. Give me your strength, your courage to bring the message to these men.' She intoned the prayer, the special invocation she'd used so often in the past as she stared into the sacred pool. She turned, once, twice, three times, and each time she marked it with a cry to *An Seanduine.*

Throughout her ritual she was aware of the stillness around her, all eyes focused on her actions. If she could hold them like this while she secured Caxna's release, she might have a chance.

She moved back to Caxna, continuing her intonation, until she arrived at his side. She looked at the guard and pointed to Caxna's bound feet.

'I say let him go now,' she said. Her voice rang out, echoing off the temple wall.

The guard moved without hesitation and knelt at Caxna's

feet. His hands were shaking so much it took longer than Aisling would have liked for him to work the bonds free. When he'd finished, she pointed at his wrists. This time he acted more quickly. She allowed herself a moment's satisfaction before taking up Caxna's hand and leading him out to the center, where the dead man lay in stillness on the stone slab, his skin grey.

'He is not for you,' she said in a loud clear voice. 'He is for *An Seanduine*. So sayeth the goddess.' She looked around, her eyes locking with the priest's. 'He is mine,' she said in trader language. She stilled the violent tremble that threatened seized her momentarily. Had it been a mistake to use the trader language?

The priest's eyes narrowed, showing understanding. Before any objection might be raised, she turned, led Caxna to the steps and began her descent, her breath held. She lifted her head high and resisted the desire to rush down, making each step she took appear regal, without worry. Behind her, some of the men followed. A figure emerged below and made his way towards her, his face catching only a flash of the torch light from above.

She quickened her steps just a bit and Caxna followed suit, his hand now firm in her grasp. His short intake of breath came only moments after she recognized the man hastening towards them. Chaak.

'Where are you going with him?' he shouted. 'Take him back, he is to be sacrificed.'

She paused on the step, trying to keep some distance from him and reduce the possibility he might recognize her. The light was uncertain, but the men descending behind her had torches with them. She drew herself up as tall as she could and projected her voice with all the force she could muster.

'I speak for *An Seanduine*, the goddess. This man is not for your people. He is for *An Seanduine*.' She spoke again in Irish, not wishing to give anything to chance that he might recognize a familiar intonation or word that would give her away.

Chaak stared at her a moment, then regarded the men behind her. 'Is she a priestess?' he asked in trader language.

One of the men spoke. 'She appears to be. The priest has heard her goddess speaking through her. She demanded this man be released. We know not why exactly but it seems that her gods and spirits have need of him.'

Chaak turned his gaze back to Aisling, his face skeptical. She lifted her chin slightly then continued her descent, towing Caxna behind her. She swept past Chaak with all the dignity she could muster and prayed he would not make any further objection. She didn't get far before she heard his challenge.

'How do we know what she is? She could be a trickster, a witch.' He rushed down and grabbed a lock of her hair. 'Hair this color is not natural.' He pointed to her arm. 'Skin as light as this—she is like a ghost.'

'Exactly, Merchant. And not for you to meddle with. You must leave such matters to us.'

Aisling turned to face him. She looked him directly in the eye. 'Release me now.'

Chaak returned her gaze, a glint of uncertainty in his eyes. A moment later he lowered them and let go of her arm.

Suppressing her relief, she resumed her descent and felt Caxna squeeze her hand in support. In what seemed an interminable time, she reached the bottom of the stairs where the crowd parted for her, creating a path away from the market area, back into the tangle of streets.

'Turn left at the end here,' Caxna said, his voice soft.

'We must make our way back to the canoe,' she replied.

'Yes, I know. This way will take us there quicker.'

The street was dark except for the light from the torches back in the market. They quickened their pace, Caxna coming alongside Aisling.

'No,' she said quietly. 'You must let me lead you.'

Behind them the noise of the crowd rose and the street was

suddenly alive with men. She dared to glance behind and saw that some of the scribes and the priests from the temple were making their way down the street, Chaak in the lead.

'Go to the right,' said Caxna softly.

'What?'

'Just do as I say.'

Without further word she turned right at the end of the street, trying to keep her pace steady. She made her way past a few houses.

'Go to the right again at the gap,' he said.

She complied and tried to feel her way along the dark, narrow street. With a quick tug he pulled her into an alcove, a tight squeeze, but deep enough for the two of them. His breath was on her face, a slow release, heavy with tension. In the distance shouts sounded as the crowd made their way along the large street they'd left moments before. She couldn't make out their words, but she could imagine their anger, fear and curiosity.

After what seemed like ages, the noise subsided and Caxna took a tentative look into the street. 'Wait here a moment,' he said and disappeared into the darkness.

She suppressed the panic that rose inside her and reached up to smooth her hair. The feathered mantle that had once stood tall and proud on her head drooped, some of its feathers broken. She removed it and quickly plaited her hair loosely, minding the gold rings that hung there. Rearranging the cloth wrapping, she draped it over her head.

Caxna reappeared at her side. 'Come now, quickly.'

He grabbed her hand and they strode out into the night, dodging down streets. She followed him blindly, trusting that he would find the way.

18

The relief she felt when she sighted Midiwegi and the slaves by the loaded canoes was overwhelming. It was only then that she acknowledged that she'd thought he would have left her and Caxna, saving himself and gaining the trade goods at the same time. Perhaps she had misjudged him. He did possess honorable qualities, but more likely he was fearful of her power with the goddess. She straightened the cloth that wrapped her body, tidying up the folds, but refrained from pulling off the black length that covered her hair. No use in increasing their chance of pursuit in any small way just to support the image she'd created in Midiwegi's mind.

When she and Caxna reached the canoe, Midiwegi was already pushing off, paddles in readiness. They splashed into the shallows and Caxna helped her in before taking the rear seat and taking up a paddle. With quick, adept strokes he took command of her canoe, and with the slaves pushing hard on their paddles, they soon were further along the coast, far from their point of departure. No one said a word, each person too intent on the desire to create as much distance they could from the threat behind.

Dawn was breaking when the group slackened the pace, as if consenting to an unspoken agreement that it was now safe to slow. Aisling's heart had recovered its normal rate, but she still felt a lingering sense of dread that left her shaken. It was only when they slowed that she began to notice her surroundings, her mind before caught up only in the count of the paddle strokes, the growing number providing her greater assurance against the horror of the day before.

'Over there is good,' Caxna said behind her. Midiwegi nodded and the canoes headed toward the shore, to a small stretch of sand.

'We're stopping?' she asked.

'It's safe now and we must rest.'

She knew he was right, but she couldn't help the surge of fear she felt.

'And I must think,' he added in a low voice.

Think. That was something she resisted. She wasn't ready to face what lay behind its consequences for the future. Of course it was worse for Caxna, she knew that, but for the moment she just wanted to feel safe and perhaps enjoy the feel of the sand between her toes.

When they were close to shore, Aisling lifted her skirts against the shallow water, stepped out of the canoe and made her way up the beach. The salt water had stained the cloth in several places, one of the prices for the rapid pace. The thought crossed her mind that she could remove the marks with some fresh spring water, but she knew the cloth could never regain its original beauty. Still, she would change out of it and fold it away so that perhaps something of it could be salvaged. A shorter length, some clever needlework, something. She wouldn't give up yet.

She started to unload the pack that contained her clothes and thought of food. 'Will I light a fire and cook something?'

'No,' Caxna said. 'We will have some pemmican and some

water if there is any left. Then you should try and get some rest. The slaves will keep watch.'

'Keep watch? You think we are still in danger?'

'I am just taking care, that is all.'

Caxna lifted out the pack containing the pemmican. Aisling took it from him and set it on the sand, next to the bundle that held her clothes. She would change before she did anything else. With a quick word she scooped up the bundle and headed for the bushes.

By the time she returned, dressed in her old wrap and mantle, making her way quietly on the sand, Caxna and Midi-wegi were seated chewing on the pemmican, the leather water bags beside them, deep in discussion. She held back when she caught their words.

'Who is she? What more do you know of her than what you said when I first saw you with her?'

'No more than what I said.'

'You did not know that she had a spirit helper? A powerful one, as strong as the Hero Twins of my people?'

'No, I did not know that.'

'If not for that spirit helper who came to her, no—that she summoned—you would be dead, Brother.'

'I know, and for that I am grateful.'

'You may owe her gratitude, but I would also have a care. Someone with that much power is to be watched carefully, especially since she is not one of us.'

'One of us?'

'You know my meaning. She is not of our land, our people.'

'No, she is not one of my people, but then, I am not one of your people.'

'Ah, but my father and sister would have it so. They would love to have the prestige of a trader such as you in their midst. My sister would be certain to become a clan mother and it would ensure my father's position as council leader continued unchallenged.'

'Surely your own trade journeys would do that.'

'Whatever I trade, it never seems enough for my father.'

Though she was curious about Midiwegi's revealing statement, Aisling felt it best that she make herself known now the conversation had shifted away from her. With as much noise as possible she made her way to Caxna and handed him the purple cloth, now neatly folded.

'I am sorry that I wore your beautiful cloth, but I had no other garb that would have suited. Even sadder, it is not the same as it was, and I can only hope that I might be able to fashion it into some garment that would disguise its recent use, or at least cut it to two usable lengths.'

'There is no need to be sorry. The use of this cloth is nothing against the fact that you saved my life wearing it.' He looked up at her, his eyes intense and searching. 'It took great courage to do that and I shall forever be in your debt, because of it.'

'You have no need to thank me. I am just glad all that is behind us now.'

He fingered the cloth and gave a wry smile. 'Its condition is of no consequence. I doubt that I gathered enough strange and exotic goods to bargain for the marriage.'

She had feared this might be the case, and for a moment she felt a flicker of relief, but pushed it away. Surely it was too soon to give up. 'Are you certain that with all the goods you have there is nothing among them that would ensure the marriage?'

He shook his head. 'No, I am not certain, but it is a reasonable guess.'

'If it is not certain, we should still try.'

'There is another path,' Midiwegi said. 'My father might give you enough trade goods to make up for the lack of the necklace and whatever else you were hoping to use.'

'What would he want in return?' Caxna asked.

'I am not sure, but I could persuade him that you would be able to bring many canoe loads of trade goods from Etowah and places further north if your bargain is successful. Would you be willing to do that?'

'I would. But what of your sister's plans?'

'My father's wishes would override anything my sister wants.'

Caxna gave a slight smile. 'I thank you for your words on this, Brother. I will give them some thought.' He looked up again at Aisling. 'For now, you should get some sleep. As will I.' He lay back onto the sand shifted around a bit for more comfort and then closed his eyes.

Aisling looked over at Midiwegi, who stared out to sea, his eyes hooded. As if sensing her scrutiny, he looked up at her and narrowed his eyes. She returned his gaze, her eyes frankly appraising. After a few moments, he nodded slightly and returned to watching the water.

It was an acknowledgement, she knew, but what was he acknowledging? Her power? That he'd underestimated her as an opponent? What did he have to gain from helping Caxna? What did she gain for that matter? A chance to ask for word or sight of her brother, so that she might find him and go back to her land? She forced herself to admit that after all these months it seemed unlikely it would ever happen. What was to become of her if she didn't find her brother and the others? She followed Midiwegi's gaze and looked out to sea. It appeared vast and unending.

SHE AWOKE SUDDENLY, pulled out of her dream by the fear. She shook her head, trying to remember what she'd dreamt but all she could recall was blood. Taking a deep breath, she reminded herself that it was probably nothing and rather than any kind of vision, it was more likely the after effects of her time in Xicallanca.

She sat up carefully and looked around her. The sun was just beginning to appear in the east, over the trees that bordered the short beach. At a guess she'd been asleep for a few hours. Across from her, Midiwegi lay unmoving and the slaves were in a deep sleep. She could see no sign of Caxna. For a moment she panicked. Had he gone, left the two of them to fend for themselves? She caught sight of the canoes, still resting on the beach and berated herself for such a thought. It was an action she would credit Midiwegi with, but not Caxna.

'You are awake,' Caxna said, his voice soft.

She turned and saw him behind her, squatting over the contents of a pack scattered around his feet.

'Lost something?' she asked, keeping her own voice quiet.

'No, just retrieving it.' He held up a silver disk. 'Perhaps if I had kept this with me when I went to bargain for the necklace I would not have had such bad fortune.'

'Is that a talisman? May I see it?'

He rose, made his way over and sat down close beside her, crossing his legs, his knee touching her leg. His thigh, bared as usual, was well muscled, she noticed, an indication of the strenuous life he led, paddling, portaging and walking.

He placed the silver disk in the palm of her hand. At its edge was a small hole, where a chain might fit through it. Though rubbed to a soft sheen, she could still see three linked circles engraved on it. She held it up to the light to determine if there was something else etched on its surface. Was there a word? Letters? She turned the disk over. The other side was smooth, containing only a blurred reflection of her blue eyes.

'Did your uncle make this?'

Caxna shook his head. 'It has been in my clan for all memory. It is custom to present it to the clan shaman, so it was given to me. I had it with me as well as the gorgets that summer. My uncle made the gorgets for the potlatch celebration when I was named.'

'Named?'

'I was given a new name, a name of power, worthy of a shaman of great stature, of a great clan. A hero from the past.'

'You were not called Caxna at birth?'

'No, like everyone I was given a child's name at birth, to fool the spirits, make them think we are unworthy of notice. It is only later we are given a great name, a name that carries power and promise.'

'What did the Caxna of the past do?'

'That was not the name given me. I am unworthy of a great name. I was never worthy.'

For a few moments, until he turned away the pain of this revelation was visible in his eyes. She reached out to touch his arm, but then thought better of it. 'There is still time for you to take up that name again,' she said.

He turned back to look at her and his eyes softened. 'That is kind of you to say. I owe you much already.'

He reached out and cupped her chin, looking at her intently, and for a brief moment she thought to close her eyes and offer her mouth. The moment passed and he dropped his hand from her chin. 'Your spirits were powerful this night past.'

'My spirits?'

'They filled you with power, it was there all around you.'

'You saw?'

He narrowed his eyes, taking in her hair and face and down along her body. 'I saw great power. Surrounding you, filling you.'

'I was not certain.' She leaned over, touched his hand. 'I had a vision of it. Before, that first time on the beach when you tended to my aches and pains.'

He nodded. 'Such things are known to happen at those times with one who is gifted.'

Her breath caught in her throat and for a short few moments she looked at him in wonder, wanting it desperately to be true.

Had she really had a vision and was it really the presence of *An Seanduine* that had filled her at the temple?

Caxna rose and went over to one of the packs and returned with a gold bangle. He handed it to her, but she could only stare at it.

'I would give you much more, but it is what I have to give freely. It may become useful to barter for information or passage to join your people, should you find them.'

She nodded, confused at her response to this offering of thanks. Why did his words rankle so? That he would give her a bangle only because it might be useful, rather than to adorn her? Or that he thought of her as not of his people like Midiwegi did? Or that he wanted her to find her people and would even give her something to barter with to ensure that end? But that was what she wanted. It was, of course.

'My brother is the only one on that ship who is of "my people." The rest are not from my family or my clan. They are of a different people. Like the difference you and Midiwegi share.'

He nodded, considering her words. 'You would still search for them, because your brother is with them?'

She paused, then rushed out an acknowledgement. 'Of course.'

'Then we must do what we can to see that you find them.'

'Yes,' she said. She looked down at the bangle in her hand and handed it back to him. 'There is no need to thank me. You must keep all the goods you have for Etowah.'

He pressed it back into her hands. 'There is every need. I would not like it if you did not accept this.'

She looked down at the bangle and something compelled her to fold her fingers around it. 'I will keep it then. But only if you promise that if you find you need it, you will ask.'

He nodded and grinned. 'It is a bargain, then.'

She smiled. 'A bargain, then.'

PART IV

ETOWAH

19

In some ways it was as if they were still making their way towards Xicallanca and all that had happened there had never occurred. It was the routine, the slaves paddling, she fixing the meals, and all the other tasks they had each done before, that created this feeling. The coastline was on her left for the most part, of course. Midiwegi was more wary of her, acknowledging her presence through respectful nods when she alighted from the canoe, or uttering a few words of acknowledgement when she gave him his meal. There were no more leers, no more surreptitious squeezes and pinches taking her unawares. She was no longer a slave.

Had Caxna changed in his behavior toward her? There were times when she felt that he wanted to say more than the bit of praise he gave her at her improved skill with the obsidian knife, or any one of a hundred different pleasantries they exchanged. Then there were also the times his hand lingered longer when he passed her something, or helped her from the canoe. It was something she thought about, but it was possible her perceptions stemmed from her wishful imagination.

As each paddle stroke brought her closer to Pakahle's home,

the place she began the journey, her thoughts turned to her brother. Where was he now? Had Madog kept him safe? She would describe him as a good man but it didn't seem to be the same quality of good she felt Caxna possessed. Or was her judgment poor? Caxna had allowed her to journey with him, protecting her and to some cost in time and trouble. If she had not met with Chaak in the market and angered him, the terrible events that followed might never have happened. Yet Caxna didn't blame her for that. He still wanted to help her find Cormac. Would Madog have been so generous? He did allow her to remain on board, she couldn't dispute that, but that might have been because it was easier, kept him from losing time returning her to shore. Somehow, she felt that Caxna's decisions came at a deeper cost. This was a man who had lost everything —his name, his clan, his standing and now restoring it all rode on this trade. Though he had spoken of nothing more than the ordinary since that first rest stop, she was increasingly aware of his loss.

These thoughts ebbed and flowed in her mind like the tides pushing the waves that swept in and out of the shoreline. She hardly noticed the teeming fish, the dolphins playing, or even the few sharks that drew near to the canoes on occasion. It was only when they stopped to camp at the end of one of the countless days that she was jolted from the reverie that had formed the days and nights since they'd departed Xicallanca, when Midiwegi mentioned that they would arrive at his home place sometime the next morning.

She paused after his remark, the fireboard in her hand. What would another visit to Choola and his people bring? She looked down at her stained mantle and skirt and sighed. She was in no fit state to see anyone.

'Perhaps Mitiwohli will give you another mantle and skirt.'

She looked up and saw Caxna regarding her stained clothes. 'Perhaps,' she said, her voice skeptical. Midiwegi's sister would more likely prefer her in clothes more ragged and stained than the ones she had on.

'Have you thought what you will do there?' she asked in a low voice.

He glanced over at Midiwegi, who sat on the beach fashioning a new arrow. For all appearances he was engrossed in his task. Days before he and Caxna had gone duck hunting, but some of Midiwegi's arrows had found shrubs instead, crushing and ripping the feathers on the arrow shafts.

'I will visit with Choola's people and complete my obligations from the Xicallanca trade,' he said quietly.

'Is there enough time to journey there to meet with the chief?'

He gave a wan smile. 'There is time enough. I did not stay in Xicallanca as long as I thought I might.'

'So you will go on to Etowah?'

'I will see what unfolds. There will be news of your brother, I am certain, long before that. Pakahle will know.'

She lowered her head and fought the sudden tears that came to her eyes. 'I fear that soon I will have to accept that I will never find my people,' she said in a voice barely a whisper.

'Can you not ask your spirit helpers to find them?' asked Midiwegi. He looked up from his task, his eyes narrowed and speculative.

She stiffened and bit back a sharp retort. She took a deep breath and gave him a cool look. 'There is no help from that quarter.' She hoped that remark would keep him quiet.

Beside her Caxna gave her arm a slight squeeze. She turned and saw the sympathy in his eyes and quickly looked away again. It would do no good to have tears flood her eyes.

Mitiwohli was no less attractive than Aisling remembered, despite her slightly flattened head. Her skin was still a smooth polished bronze, her dark eyes thickly lashed. Her hair was loose, thick and lustrous, falling down to her waist. She wore a mantle edged with an intricate design and a skirt that shaped itself around her curving hips. A few gold bangles adorned her wrists and neck. It was if she knew they were arriving.

She appeared at her father's side when Aisling, Caxna and the others approached the hall, Midiwegi shouting a greeting. Mitiwohli gave Caxna a particularly warm welcome. He acknowledged it with a nod and put his hand on Aisling's shoulder. Mitiwohli frowned.

'I would introduce you formally to my companion, who is in fact a holy woman, though I brought her here in the guise of a slave. I would ask you all now to welcome her as befitting her status.'

'Of course,' said Choola. He bowed to Aisling. 'But why the ruse in the first place?'

'It was for her protection. From those who might have disliked such a woman among them, a powerful stranger from a distant land.' He smiled widely. 'But it is no longer necessary, we are now among friends and far from the lands near Xicallanca.'

Mitiwohli eyed her skeptically, but gave a nod. 'We will of course welcome her with all courtesy.'

LATER, once the bundles and packs were removed from the canoes, Caxna had guided her to the large hall where Choola sat among the elders. She had no role in the festive preparations, but now she was allowed a prominent position.

Aisling tried to hide her discomfort sitting among these men she didn't know, speaking a language foreign to her ears. If not for Caxna by her side, she could almost wish herself working among the women gutting fish or the strange 'opossum' Caxna had caught on their journey. She pulled her mantle closer around her, grateful for the warmth of the hall. She would have to don her wool tunic and *léine* again, no matter their state. She looked enviously at Choola's fur mantle and those of the other elders. She'd noticed it had grown cooler in the past few days, the winter season starting to bite. The mild weather in the journey to Xicallanca had allowed her to ignore the real passage of time, but here, the breezes were anything but summery. Though not as cold as the winters back home, she could no longer put aside the fact that they were deep into winter.

The aromas from the cooking fires outside wafted into the hall and her stomach growled. To distract herself she watched Midiwegi hanging on to the elders' words, nodding periodically and commenting. Their faces betrayed no furrowed brows, their voices contained no joyful animation; the news was not extreme. She sighed. In truth she hadn't expected to hear any news of the ship. And perhaps it was time she faced the probable truth that the terrible storm had taken the ship and all those who sailed in it.

And it was that thought that filled her with fear, a fear that overwhelmed the grief at the loss of home and family, the loss of 'her people.' Here she would have no people. Wherever she went she would be mistrusted, distanced, clearly 'not of their people.' She wouldn't allow herself to think of Caxna and how he might regard her, but she did consider Pakahle. Pakahle lived alone, rarely left her surroundings to visit other communities, and only infrequently received others, so perhaps she wouldn't mind someone living with her who was not of her people. Aisling allowed herself to take comfort from this thought.

Mitiwohli appeared next to Caxna and squeezed herself between Aisling and him. She had changed into a different mantle and skirt, one edged with larger, more elaborate designs in gold and green. Where the previous one had set off the creamy bronze skin and the midnight color of her hair, this tunic seemed to create subtle shades of red in her hair and suggest amber flecks in her eyes. Her fox fur piece, draped carelessly over only one shoulder, only emphasized the effect.

She gave Caxna a beatific smile. 'You are comfortable?' she asked him. 'Refreshment is on the way.'

Caxna gave her an amused look. 'I am comfortable, thank you.'

Mitiwohli turned to regard Aisling, her eyes taking in the ragged, grimy clothes and the bedraggled hair that hung loosely braided down her back. No, she was not an imposing sight and Mitiwohli's calculating eyes registered that.

'Do you require anything...I am sorry, I do not remember your name.'

Aisling met the challenge in her eyes. 'I am called Aisling. It means 'One Who Has Visions' in my language.' Whether or not she was worthy of such a name, this one would never know that.

'Aisling.' Mitiwohli struggled with the pronunciation. Whether it was deliberate or not, Aisling couldn't say.

'You will find it easier once you get used to hearing it,' Caxna said. There was humor in his eyes that left no doubt he was enjoying this exchange. Aisling gave him a slight frown.

'Her language, I would think, is very foreign,' Mitiwohli said. 'So different to our languages, even the language of trade. And one that must come with some very strange customs and eating habits. Do you have any that I should know about? Any special food you require? We do want to make all strangers here feel they are welcome.'

Aisling allowed herself a sardonic look but refrained from mentioning that on her previous visit she'd had no experience of any sort of generous welcome. But then she wasn't perceived as a stranger, just a slave.

'During the many moons since I have come, Caxna has assisted me in learning the customs and habits here and I have grown comfortable with them, so no, I require nothing different or special in terms of food or otherwise.'

Her answer was impulsive and for a moment she regretted it. Perhaps she should make a fuss and request special attention, if only to emphasize her power. Then she saw the appreciative look on Caxna's face and the responsive glow that rose inside her convinced her that any show of power or authority might hinder Caxna's cause. She didn't want to do that.

Mitiwohli formed a smile that gave up past the mouth. 'Do not hesitate to say if there is anything we might do for your comfort.'

'Aisling could use help with another mantle and skirt. Her own, as you can see, is worn and not much comfort against the cold air.'

Midiwegi's sister's eyes narrowed, all attempts at a smile gone. 'I am sure we can find something to replace what you are wearing.' She turned to Caxna, her face once again assembled into patient kindness. 'I can see that you too are governed by a great consideration for strangers,' she said.

'I am no different from any other trader,' he said. 'But Aisling is not a stranger to me.'

Women appeared bearing platters and bowls of food, leaving aside any further talk. They set the various dishes in on the floor in front of the men, so that each person had a selection of plates of food available to him. The women passed out cups of black drink for the men. After the one sip Caxna provided from his cup, she decided to keep to the water she'd been handed, ignoring his laughter at the face she made.

'Well I guess that is one custom you are not comfortable with,' he said.

'No, and I doubt I shall ever be comfortable with that drink.'

'It is for the men,' Mitiwohli said. 'My brother likes it very much.'

'I bet he does,' Aisling muttered.

She looked over at Midiwegi and watched him fill his bowl full of beans, squash, choice bits of venison cooked in some type of herbs, some slices of duck, and bread made from maize. He watched the men near him, listening still to their conversation, oblivious to her presence and Caxna's. He had paid them scant notice since they had come to the hall and sat among the elders. His whole attention had been for the elders and his father, taking a seat next to his father with self-conscious importance. Did he really intend to help Caxna? She wished she could understand what they were saying, though Caxna didn't seem concerned. Or was it just a deception? She turned to study him as he reached to fill his own bowl with the selections of meat, beans and squash from the platters near them. Under her careful scrutiny she detected tiny lines of tension around his eyes and in the set of his mouth. He was concerned.

She felt reassured in some strange way. It meant that he really was still thinking of going to Etowah. That he had hopes he might make a bargain there. To make that marriage contract. It was what he wanted, she knew. Above all things, he desired to help his clan regain all that they had lost. His sense of guilt and responsibility would allow nothing less. It was a quality she had come to recognize in him, a sense of honor and obligation to do what he thought right. Caxna hadn't given up, despite all the passing seasons that had turned into years.

'Do we want to expose ourselves to the danger of losing so much of our very best trade goods? Our clan has already given him much and he has not profited us or himself.'

'Profit is not always made in one season. Sometimes we must let it age, like a very fine deerskin, working in more fat, softening it, until it becomes supple, and only then can you fashion it into the finest of tunics.'

'Yes, but who is to say he will not fall to the same sort of misfortune he had before? He will be dealing with powerful people in Etowah too.'

It was Choola who'd responded to the protest of the grey-haired woman, her face as weathered as an old walnut. Despite

Choola's reply others still looked doubtful or resistant. Two men and another woman had spoken of their worries, their manner of address respectful but insistent. This old woman's tone possessed more of a challenge.

The discussion, spoken in trader language, had followed Midiwegi's tale of their travels and his request to assist Caxna further. Aisling had listened to Midiwegi recount the tale with interest, wondering initially how he would cast himself, if he would twist some aspect and, most importantly, how he would present her part in it. Her first observation was that Midiwegi neglected to mention he was posing as Caxna's assistant and he inferred that all the trading and bartering were completed in partnership with Caxna. Caxna held his peace, and even when she caught his eye, he remained impassive.

He had also omitted the incident with Chaak in the market plaza, and the events that led to Caxna's seizure were glossed into a brief statement about the arranged meeting and Chaak arriving when the woman was examining the necklace.

'It was unfortunate that the lady who would trade with us coveted the necklace and the merchant coveted her. He was a powerful merchant, well known in the city and the lady was the wife of the head scribe,' Midiwegi said. 'We could not challenge their word when they accused Caxna of theft.' He glanced at Aisling. 'At my request Aisling agreed to call on her spirit helpers for assistance.'

'You knew of her spirit helpers?' asked Choola.

Midiwegi's face faltered for a brief moment. 'She had mentioned something of them in a discussion with Caxna.'

Midiwegi's father nodded. The other elders murmured among themselves. Aisling worked to keep her face expressionless. If Caxna felt there was nothing to be gained by correcting him, then she would follow his example.

'One of her spirit helpers, a strong and powerful one, came and made them release Caxna. Her voice rang out strong and loud among those priests and they cowered at the sight of her.'

Aisling stifled the laughter that suddenly filled her. At least Midiwegi wasn't taking the credit himself for Caxna's release. If only she had that power to summon the Lady, *An Seanduine*.

It was a thought she had now, again, in the face of the objections of this grey-haired clan mother who cast such doubt on the success of Caxna's proposal.

'We will be meeting with people who know Caxna,' Midiwegi said. 'They have dealt with him before and trust him. Is that not so, Caxna?'

'That is so, my friend. I have traded with Etowah nobles for many seasons now and I know the kind of goods they desire. I can also promise you that they would look with favor upon trade in cured fish from the sea, abalone shells, pearls and the needles and awls you make from stingray spines,' he said. 'I assure you that I will work to form a permanent trade link for you there. And if my own plans are successful, you will gain much from it.'

He surveyed the faces around him, his eyes stopping for a moment at each one. 'I understand this is a risk for all of you. That there is much to lose should I fail. Should Midiwegi and I fail. You have no obligation to help me make this marriage contract so that I might restore my honor and my clan's honor.'

'You are not lacking in honor,' Mitiwohli said. Except for a few murmurs of disbelief during the tale, she'd remained quiet throughout the proceedings. 'We all regard you as a person worthy of great trust and as such you would be more than welcome to remain here and set up your trade. My father has spoken of that.' She glanced at her father, her face tense.

Her father gave her a tired glance then looked at Caxna. 'While it is true we trust you and would welcome you among us, I understand your desire to help your clan in any way possible. That the manner in which you wish to achieve this brings possibilities of great power and status to us as well.'

Caxna nodded. 'I am happy to share this with you and your people.'

The other elders smiled at him. Aisling could admire the way the chief had deflected the focus from the possibilities of trade loss to Caxna's thoughtfulness at including the village in his plans.

'There is much status to be gained,' Choola said. 'We would do well to take part in Caxna's plan.'

Some of the elders nodded, others appeared undecided, but no one looked to object to the plan, except for the grey-haired clan mother whose head was lowered, her eyes closed, as if she'd drifted off. Mitiwohli coughed quietly and the woman opened her eyes and looked around, confused for a moment. She found Mitiwohli's face. Mitiwohli gave an almost imperceptible nod.

'My niece proved a worthy clan member when she pointed out that we would be happy to make a place here for you,' she said, her voice frail. 'You say you would restore your clan's honor and that is a commendable aim. But there are other paths to such an aim. A path that could be found here, among us.'

Aisling stole a look at Caxna, aware that all eyes were on him now. How would he respond to this request? Could his clan be restored through remaining here? She looked around and saw the answer in the thatched roof, the clay walls and the bare floor. She saw the fine skirts and mantles the men and women wore, the gold bangles around some of their wrists and the occasional gold ring through the ear.

'I am most grateful for your words,' Caxna said. 'They warm my heart and though I can say it makes me pause, I could not in all honor accept. I must follow this path that has been laid for me by my own spirit helper. It is not an easy path, but it is one from which I dare not stray. I would not seek to anger the spirits in this way and by doing as they ask I will also bring benefit to your people.'

The old woman shifted in her place, glanced at Mitiwohli and gave a slight shrug. She nodded at Caxna.

'It is settled then,' said Choola. 'We will assist Caxna. We will decide tomorrow the terms and the actual trade goods to send with him, after we review our requirements and what goods we might want from them.'

The rest of the elders murmured their assent. It was done. Caxna would get his help in return for establishing trade links with Etowah.

20

Aisling fingered the hide tunic she wore, noticing the wear at the waist, where a braided belt cinched it in. The back also showed a polished buff in some places, rubbed to the shape of the wearer when they sat. Mitiwohli probably did a lot of sitting, she thought caustically, though she knew such a garment would only do for a slave. Underneath it she wore her undershirt, cautious about the hide against her skin. Despite the shirt, the fit was loose, her own figure not near as full as the former wearer's; her hips more narrow, her breasts sitting higher and smaller. She had no fat to spare, not after months of paddling, hauling goods and water, and preparing meals.

At least her hair was clean now. At one of the slave women's suggestions, made in gestures she only half understood, she'd allowed herself the luxury of immersing herself in the small pool of water and scrubbed her hair with the soapy plant offered to her. It hung around her now in long curling tendrils, the winter sun still strong enough to enable it to dry quickly. She tossed it over her shoulder and examined the state of her callused hands. No amount of scrubbing would soften them in one try.

'Are your hands paining you? I am certain Mitiwohli will have some ointment you can put on them.' Caxna's tone was light and teasing.

'Oh, I think Pakahle's ointments would have more effect than anything Mitiwohli might want to give me. I have no need of any ointment though. My hands are fine.'

He took her left hand in his and examined it. He traced along the palm, his finger moving over the hardened mounds of skin, down along each finger one at a time. The skin of his finger was far from smooth, but she minded that not at all, welcomed it in fact, and the tingle it spread throughout her body. She sank into that feeling for a moment, closed her eyes and surrendered.

'Your hair is like polished gold,' he said. She opened her eyes and he dropped her hand, raising his own to her head. He ran his hand along the side of her head, his fingers entwining in its locks and catching them up. 'So soft.' His eyes found hers. 'You are remarkable, you know.'

'Remarkable?'

He nodded. 'I have never known anyone like you.' He brushed a lock of her hair from her cheek. 'I owe you much for all you have done.'

'I have not done that much.'

'You have. And I will never know how to repay you for it.'

'I am not asking for payment.'

'Nevertheless I would make it up to you some day. If my plans come to good, I will be in a position to then.'

'There is no obligation.'

He nodded. 'You could remain here, you know. They respect you and they would look after you.'

She eyed him skeptically and shook her head. 'There is no place for me here. For many reasons. No, I will journey back to

Pakahle's with you, if you do not mind. I know it is a feeble hope, but there might be some word of my canoe.' She refrained from saying, 'my people.' She couldn't use that term to him.

'You will come with me to Pakahle's?' He smiled at her. 'I can say that I am glad to hear that. I think Pakahle would give you a generous welcome. I know she will have missed you.'

'I have missed her, too.' She realized it was true. She thought of the old woman with great warmth, remembering how Pakahle fussed over her.

'You do not mind that Midiwegi will bear us company?'

'I know that he is coming along on the journey.' She grinned. 'You certainly need someone of his trading skill for such an enterprise.'

For a few moments they shared the humor with an exchange of laughter. 'So you have settled the details over the trade goods?' she asked eventually.

'We have. We should be leaving a little later today. That is what I came to tell you. Pack up your belongings. They are already gathering the trade goods down on the beach. There will be no slaves this time, though, but they are providing us with a different, bigger canoe. Do you think you could manage to help us paddling the canoe?'

She held up her hands to him. 'What do you think? Are they still hardened enough?'

He took both hands in his own and smoothed his thumbs along the calluses. 'If they pain you again, I will rub Pakahle's ointment on them.'

THE CANOE WAS LARGER than she expected, the dugout sections polished to a shine and the outside carved in swirling designs at the prow. It was already afloat in the shallow sea water, the packs and bundles distributed along it for the best possible weight balance. Though it was large, it would ride the waves a little easier and be less likely to find itself tossed around a rough sea. There would be fewer days when they might have to wait onshore for a rough sea to subside and so make better time.

Aisling approached the waiting group, her own small bundle in her arms. It only contained the wool tunic she'd had on when she arrived and the freshly laundered skirt and mantle along with a few personal items for her monthly courses. The bangle Caxna had given her was still around her wrist and for a brief moment she wondered if she should remove it and put it in her bundle since she would be paddling all day. When she caught sight of Mitiwohli she decided against it. Let her have something more to think about after she'd gone.

She walked past the village members and the elders standing on the shore and waded out to the canoe where Caxna and Midiwegi stood. Caxna helped her into the canoe and turned to face the people. Mitiwohli broke away and walked up to him, her fringed tunic swaying with the motion of her ample hips.

She placed her hand on his arm. 'I would give you this talisman before you go. To help you and to have you know that I wish you well.' She placed an object in his hand and folded his fingers around it. Aisling couldn't make out what it was, but Midiwegi's eyes widened.

'I thank you for this thought and your desire to wish me well in this path.' Caxna squeezed her hand and turned to the rest of the group. 'I am glad for your blessing and hope that I will prove worthy of your trust.'

'Go with our blessing and may it keep you and my son safe,' Choola said. 'We look forward to your return.'

Caxna and Midiwegi pushed the canoe further into the water and climbed in. The journey had begun.

·   ·   ·

THE SUN WAS STILL a distance from the horizon when Caxna signaled they would break and head for shore. As they made their way in, Aisling was pleased to note that though her arms ached and her hands felt a slight burn, after a while she had matched the pace Caxna and Midiwegi set. It had meant that her view was for the most part confined to the area just immediately around Midiwegi's back and head. There was no time for meandering glances at the passing shore and out to sea, but she did find a slight thrill at the canoe's swiftness.

Her deerskin tunic, lacking the fine stitching at the arm holes, hadn't restrained her or torn at the seam as her wool tunic had. If the shirt she wore underneath ripped further, it wouldn't show, and with the fish spine needle she now possessed, she had some hopes of keeping it mended and perhaps even making her wool tunic wearable.

They paddled around a small peninsula and headed into a lagoon that she could see provided decent shelter when winds were strong. When they neared the shore, she stepped out of the canoe with the two men and helped them pull it up along the beach, the heavy packs, bundles and laden baskets it contained making the canoe weighty. The beach was larger than the small clearings Caxna usually preferred, but with the larger canoe perhaps he felt it was preferable. When she spotted the other canoes upended in a cluster at the far side of the beach she was surprised.

'You have been here before?' she asked Caxna.

He nodded. 'These people are relations of Midiwegi's.'

She looked over at Midiwegi. His face was devoid of any expression, joy or otherwise. 'Are they close relations?'

'They are relations, but it has been some time since I have seen them. This is their winter home. They have a summer camp further along the shore.'

'How nice for you that we are able to visit them now,' she

said. It was a pleasantry that came to her automatically and when his eyes darkened she couldn't help but wonder exactly how enthusiastic he was.

Even as Aisling finished speaking, three men appeared from the trees and began to make their way along the beach towards her, Caxna and Midiwegi. Their hair was twisted and pinned to the sides of their head in the same manner as Midiwegi's and they possessed the same flattened head and stature. After a moment they clearly recognized both men and shouted out greetings. When they drew alongside, there was much back slapping and arm punching that reminded Aisling of Cormac greeting his friends and she felt a momentary pang.

They spoke in a mixture of their own language and trader language so Aisling could only understand the gist of the torrent of questions that issued from them, until Caxna interrupted and introduced Aisling to them as a travelling companion.

'She seeks news of a large wind-borne canoe containing her relations,' Caxna added. 'Have you seen or heard of anything of that sort?'

'A wind-borne canoe?' the tallest man asked. He wore several strands of shell necklaces. 'How is that possible?'

'They have cloth attached to tall poles,' Caxna said.

The men exchanged doubtful looks. 'We have heard or seen nothing of that manner,' the tall man said. 'And we have no news of strangers who might be related to your companion.'

Midiwegi cast a speculative glance at Aisling. 'I am afraid we can only stay for one night,' he said. 'But we will gladly tell you of our journeys in that time. Before that we must unload and stow our belongings for the night.'

'You may leave them here, if you wish,' said the tall man.

Caxna looked at Midiwegi, considering the proposition. Midiwegi shrugged.

'We will only bring the packs further up the shore, away from the water's edge,' Caxna said.

With the three men helping, the packs and bundles were quickly removed and carried to an agreed spot at the base of an outcropping of bushes. When everything was arranged there to Caxna's satisfaction, he caught up a small bundle and began to head in the direction where the men first appeared, over towards the other canoes.

'The way is through here,' the tall man said. He gestured in the opposite direction where there was a small opening cleared. With a brief glance over his shoulder, Caxna retraced his steps and followed the men and Aisling along the path, Midiwegi bringing up the rear.

AISLING STOOD at the door of the small house that provided her sleeping quarters for the night. Above, the sky was cloaked in stars. She could smell the salt in the air, reminding her she was still close to the ocean. These moments she could treasure, see the beauty in the sky, savor the taste of the salt sea, something she had grown to love in the past months.

Inside, the steady rhythm of soft snores assured her she wasn't disturbing her hospitable companion, an old widow who had lately married off her son to a young girl of another clan. It wasn't the snoring that had kept her from her sleep, but a niggling feeling that she couldn't rid herself of since observing Caxna's guarded behavior once they arrived at the community. The small bundle he'd removed from the canoe he'd later passed to her before she retired for the night. The careful manner with which he selected the food, taking from only those dishes that had been sampled by others first. He'd also encouraged Midiwegi to recount the tale of their journey, a telling that had all the flamboyance of the previous one and perhaps with even more emphasis on the role Midiwegi played and his trading abilities. As before, Caxna said nothing, only smiled when they later teased him about his unfortunate capture.

Why had Caxna wanted to stop here with Midiwegi's relations? It had been his idea, not Midiwegi's, and that seemed more puzzling to Aisling. They could have paddled on for a good while, covering more distance, drawn that much closer to Pakahle's home. It wasn't that he had thought she'd tired of the paddling, her arms too weak to go further, she knew that.

Out of the corner of her eye she noticed a movement. A figure slipped quietly past one of the houses, skirted the neatly hoed patch of field and disappeared down a path. Caxna. Even in the dim light of the stars she couldn't mistake his shape, his gait. She slipped through the door and followed in his wake.

It was only because the path she took was so worn, and the trees and bushes that surrounded it were bare enough in this season to let the starlight through, that she was able to make her way without mishap. She was so focused on avoiding stumbling or alerting Caxna in any way that it took her by surprise when the path emptied out onto the beach, by the cluster of canoes. At the far end she could see their stowed belongings. She pulled back onto the path when she saw Caxna stoop down by the canoes and run his hand along the side of one of them.

She watched his hand move along to the prow, his fingers tracing the carving there, finding the grooves that created its shape. She looked closer and gasped. It was his canoe, the one lost in the storm. How had it come to be here?

Caxna turned and stared in her direction. He gestured to the canoe. 'You may as well come and see for yourself.'

She moved out of the shelter of the trees and bushes toward him. 'There can be no mistake, it is your canoe.'

'No, there is no mistake,' he said.

She placed her hand on its smooth surface, noting for the first time how sure and deft the carvings were that shaped the prow, the swirling figures unerringly portrayed; the eagle's eye, the raven's beak, a round orb caught up in it. So different from the canoes that surrounded it.

She fingered the orb, so perfectly shaped, so well polished. She placed her hand over it, the shape fitting perfectly in her hand.

'That is the sun,' he said.

'The sun?'

'What you cover with your hand is the sun.'

She looked at the orb held tightly in the raven's beak. 'Why does he hold it in his beak?'

'He brought the sun to my people, so that we would no longer live in darkness. He stole it from Creator Nascakiyiel, who kept it locked in a cedar box, away from everyone.'

She regarded the raven and the orb clutched so tightly in his beak. The sun. Their god, this Creator Nascakiyiel had kept the sun from his people. It seemed a terrible act, to keep people forever in the dark, and it served to remind her that she could never fathom the ways and reasons of the ancient ones.

'Is Raven your spirit helper?' she asked.

'Raven is Raven. He will do as he wishes. Sometimes he will choose to help, and other times,' he shrugged, 'he will not.'

That sounded about right to her. There was nothing definite, nothing to be sure of when you invoked their assistance, just hope. She sighed.

'Do you have the bundle I gave you?'

She bit her lip, guilt taking hold. 'I am sorry, I saw you head down the path and just followed you without thinking.'

'You must go back, then. I would not want anyone to come across it and think it was their own.'

She gave him a puzzled look. 'I assure you I left the widow sound asleep and the bundle tucked under my sleeping rug.' She put her hand on his arm. 'What is the matter? How did your canoe come to be here?'

His eyes were remote, expressionless. 'I am not certain how the canoe found its way to this shore. As for the rest I am only trying to take extra care. I would not want to lose anything of great value by accident. There has been enough of that.'

She searched his face for some further clue as to his suspicions but found no help there.

'Go back to the widow. Get some sleep.'

'Where are you going?'

'I think I will sleep here, near our belongings.'

She nodded. It would do no good to press him further, she could see that. She would have to wait until the morning to see if he would take up the issue of his canoe.

SHE WAS AWAKE LONG before the widow stirred in her bed. When the pink dawn light had disappeared and she began to hear the stirrings of fires and footsteps on paths she rose and dressed, careful to tuck Caxna's small bundle inside her tunic. She could appreciate the advantage of the loose fitting deerskin now. Behind her she could hear the widow stirring and quickly left, making her way to the path she used the night before. It was rude to disappear without a word of thanks to the old woman, but she wanted to ensure that Caxna had passed the night without any further event.

She hadn't even reached the path when Caxna emerged from it, unharmed. She greeted him and he stopped. 'Did you sleep well?' she asked.

'Nothing disturbed me.' He gave her a reassuring smile.

She nodded. Suddenly she wanted to quit this mire of intrigue and resume their journey and see Pakahle. 'Will we leave soon? Shall I see if Midiwegi is ready?'

'We will eat something first and give our thanks to our hosts.'

His tone was ordinary, but still she found she didn't like the words he'd uttered. Was there an underlying intent in them?

It was later, as they sat together in the tall man's house finishing the last morsels of smoked fish offered to them that she knew for certain that Caxna would never relinquish a canoe carved with the spirit of his people. A people who valued the light, a helper that risked the wrath of the Creator god to bring them that light. She knew this because when she saw him talking with Midiwegi's relations his bearing was straighter than theirs, his face bore no hint of softness and his eyes didn't waiver from their faces. She watched him take in each one, the tall man's narrow-set eyes, the sulky set of Midiwegi's mouth, the chin that betrayed a hint of softness.

'When I walked along the beach this morning to check that the tide I could not fail to notice that my fortunes had increased through your good people's presence.'

Aisling lowered her eyes for a moment, knowing this was no innocent remark of thanks.

'We are only too glad to offer you our hospitality,' the tall man said. 'And in return you provided us with a good night's entertainment.'

'It is not that I speak of, though I am grateful for the hospitality,' Caxna said. 'No I speak of the canoe you have in your midst. In some great play of the spirits who took my canoe in a storm, it seems they have arranged it so that it washed up on your shore, so that now, all these moons later, I can reclaim it on my return journey.'

The tall man forced a smile. 'That was good fortune indeed. But are you certain it is your canoe?' He narrowed his eyes a hint of menace there.

Caxna gave him a direct look. 'I am certain.'

The tall man considered him for a moment, weighing possibilities. The men around him shifted, hands drifted to the knives at their bowls. A moment later the tall man's face cleared.

'Well then it is only right that you should have it back,' he said.

Aisling looked at Midiwegi. For only a moment, anger flashed across his face and then it was gone, replaced by a smile that didn't reach his eyes. For herself, she was relieved. The relief was for the safe return of the canoe without a disastrous confrontation, but the questions about its appearance still lingered, as did the feeling that there was something amiss with this intended trade journey.

21

There was no escaping the fact that her arms screamed in pain now. Days of fighting the choppy waves in unsettled seas, trying to maintain Midiwegi's pace while he muttered behind her, had taken their toll. Ahead, in his own canoe, Caxna paddled strongly, seemingly unaffected by the effort needed to keep his canoe under tight control with only his strategically placed bundles and packs maintaining some sort of ballast. But then he would be used to it, all his journeys trading along the coast and along rivers, season after season.

Since they had left Midiwegi's relations she had long given up trying to fathom the man up ahead. She'd reviewed the events countless times. Had Caxna known the canoe would be there? Is that why he wanted her to paddle, to ease her in so that when he recovered his canoe she would be able to help with Midiwegi's? It might have been the pains in her back and the aching arms that made her resent this foresight were it so, but he could have at least explained that to her. Asked for her help. Did he still think her untrustworthy? In all their exchanges up to now, had he told her the truth?

Her thoughts had followed darker and darker avenues as the

days wore on, and their tenor wasn't improved by Caxna's seeming disregard for the distant attitude with which she chose to treat him. It was if they were as much strangers as they were on the first few days of their initial journey, after they left Pakahle's. At times it made her want to cry, but she knew deep down it was just the fatigue speaking. She resolved that this night she would find the ointment Caxna used to relieve the aches and pains all those months ago. Perhaps that would help her manage some sleep, rather than be kept awake from the stabbing pain that seized her when she shifted position, as it had the last few nights.

She sighed with relief when she saw Caxna head in towards shore. It wasn't a large clearing, and she could see little signs of driftwood that might be used for a fire, which meant she would have to go collecting further afield, among the trees. She would use different muscles at least. Behind her, Midiwegi muttered a bit more. Since the scene on the shore with his relations Midiwegi had been at times overly friendly and helpful, and other times distant and sullen. She didn't know which she preferred, but the distant and sullen seemed truthful at least. Tonight would be the more honest of demeanors.

Later, the wood gathered and her drill board set ready to start the fire, she used her frustration to work the stick. Caxna had remained silent at her initial attempts at conversation and Midiwegi had proved just as uncooperative, beyond handing her the two bass he'd caught while she'd been gathering the wood.

With the fire caught, she began to gut and scale the fish, her fingers working with deft quickness after months of practice. Who would have thought she would be able to prepare fish so well? Back home it had been a rare occasion when they would have fish this large, and from the sea. One of the slaves or servants would have prepared it under her mother's supervision. She looked at her hands, red and callused, nails torn and skin cracked in places under the ravages of the salt water. These were servant's hands. Her mother would have been appalled at their state.

Any satisfaction she'd felt earlier vanished under these thoughts. She thrust a peeled wooden stick through the body of one of the fish. 'How long before we arrive at Pakahle's?' She'd promised herself she wouldn't ask this question to avoid exerting any more pressure on Caxna's determination to make the journey quickly, but that resolve had vanished.

Caxna turned his gaze from the horizon and focused on her. 'We will be there soon. One sleep, maybe two.'

She grunted, glad to have some idea. She eased her back.

'Your back is paining you?' Caxna asked her.

She gave him a dark look. 'My back, my arms and even my neck a little.'

'There is still some salve left in the packs.'

'Yes, I know. I will apply some after we have a meal.'

Caxna nodded and returned to his view at the sea.

When the three of them had eaten their fill, she searched through the packs for the salve as she had promised she would and located the jar in the third small pack. She lifted it out and Caxna took it from her.

'I will rub it on for you. Give me your arm.'

She searched his face, puzzled over the offer. There was no animosity, no teasing evident, nothing she could detect but a glimmer of kindness and somehow she found that annoying. She felt the ache in her back and arms and with a sigh held out her right arm. Caxna scooped up some of the salve and began to massage it into her skin, his skillful fingers pressing and rubbing in all the right places.

'Are you certain that is meant to help aches? The odor is enough to drive a bear away.' Midiwegi rose from his place. 'I think I will go for a walk. If you two want to assault your nose in that manner, that is up to you. I, for one, prefer to smell odors like that only if I have to.'

Aisling sniffed. Was the odor really that bad? In truth she hadn't noticed it was so terrible and perhaps in the sweat and exhaustion of the previous times she was in no fit state to be offended by it. Even now, though she could smell a faint trace of something unpleasant, it didn't seem to be that remarkable.

'I think he just preferred not to be present when I rub the ointment on your back.'

She considered that possibility as she watched his fingers work up her arm, enjoying the relief. Midiwegi was the man who hadn't hesitated in placing his hands on various places on her body or trying to take sexual pleasure, though that had been before they left Xicallanca.

'Why would he mind that?'

'Perhaps he thinks you have nothing on under the tunic. And a woman with such power as you have, he would not want to offend you or your spirit helpers with his glances.' Caxna gave a wry grin. 'He would of course not be able to resist looking your way, so he removes himself from the temptation.'

'I have little, if any, power, you know that.'

'He does not think that.' He placed her arm at her side, scooped up more salve and took her other arm. 'And neither do I.'

She gave him a puzzled look. 'You think I have power? I have only had one experience that might have been a vision and nothing since. All those times in the past I performed all the rituals and then—nothing.'

'Is that what you think is the source of your power? Visions that you require at an appointed time? We cannot control such things.'

'I know that visions cannot be controlled,' she said, her tone frustrated and angry. 'But I also know that if you open yourself up in the right situation the Lady will come. My mother taught me the rituals, showed me the kinds of places she comes.'

Caxna smiled. 'Sometimes when we think we have all the

skill and the desire to bring about what should happen, still the time is not right.'

She narrowed her eyes. 'What about you? Could you not apply such views to your own situation?' she said, thinking of Xicallanca.

His face darkened. 'If you mean being with my clan, the time was right. I was just not ready. If I had been there with them I would not now be wandering through distant lands to find the wealth to restore my clan.' He gave a bitter laugh. 'You might say my desire to travel was granted, for I have done nothing but travel for many, many seasons.' He slapped her arm lightly and placed it at her side. 'Now lay on your front.'

She said nothing, her mind taken with his last words and, without thinking, she removed the belt around her tunic, lifted the tunic up over her head and laid herself on the sand, taking care not to aggravate her back. The salve felt cold at first until the heat of Caxna's hands migrated to the salve, then to her skin and eventually to her aching muscles. His fingers seemed to know the exact location of the soreness and worked it well, eliciting groans of pain and relief from her.

As she relaxed into the massage, her mind turned again to his last statement. It was true that he wouldn't be here if he had been with his clan at the time of the attack, but didn't he realize he most likely would be with his disgraced clan as a slave, or even dead? Or perhaps he did realize that. But he too was a vision seeker. And from what he'd told her, he'd actually seen visions in the past. He described it as journeying. Was it the same?

'Have you ever seen the future when you journeyed for your people?' She tried to remember the words he'd used. 'The spirit journeys you mentioned?

'The future is always there to see during the journey. It is whether we are able to see it.'

She suppressed a snort. 'You certainly have all the words of a vision seeker.'

'My uncle taught me well,' he said in a neutral tone.

'If your uncle taught you that, who is to say that you would have been able to have prevented the fate of your clan if you couldn't see it before you left them and went on your travels, why would it have been any different if you stayed?'

He sighed. 'I might have, though. It is something I will never know.' His fingers began to knead her back with greater force. 'And that possibility is a burden that drives me even more to do what I can to restore my people to their home. Can you not understand that?'

'Yes,' she said. A wave of sadness rose up and threatened to overwhelm her.

HER EYES SQUINTED against the sun as she tried to make out the shapes on the shoreline. Was Pakahle on the beach waiting for them? Had she seen them approaching in their canoes? She fought the urge to cry out to her, so strong was the need to be quit of the bouncing canoe, the strain of the paddling and the incessant view of Midiwegi's back.

Caxna's estimate had been right, and after one more night of camping, Aisling could look forward to a cozy meal and chat at Pakahle's fireside. She realized now how much she valued the comfort of Pakahle's presence; how warm and friendly Pakahle had been to her, a stranger from a different people. The months since she'd left Pakahle's had shown her that.

As they drew closer to the shore she could see Pakahle emerge from the trees and come toward them. She held her hand up in greeting and Aisling couldn't resist the urge to return the gesture, breaking the rhythm of the paddling and causing Midiwegi to look back at her. Caxna reached the shore first and jumped out to drag his canoe up along the beach with Pakahle's assistance. Her face was flushed with pleasure and her smile lit her eyes.

As soon as the water was ankle-deep, Aisling jumped out, making the canoe rock precariously for a moment. Midiwegi followed, steadied the canoe and began to pull it in. With his canoe safely onshore Caxna supported Midiwegi's efforts and Aisling, feeling guilty from her hasty exit from the canoe, leaned down to lend her help. The canoe was soon drawn up beside the other one and Aisling was able to turn to Pakahle, who drew her into a warm embrace.

'Welcome, child. I am so happy to see you safe,' Pakahle said.

Aisling gave her an affectionate squeeze. 'And I am so happy to be here.'

Pakahle pulled back and regarded Caxna, whose face was filled with pleasure. Beside him stood Midiwegi, his expression guarded.

'I am glad to see you safe, too,' said Pakahle. 'And you have brought a companion.' She gave Caxna a questioning look.

'Yes,' said Caxna. He made the introductions, explaining his tribe and name. 'He is a trader also and will accompany me to Etowah.'

Pakahle nodded. 'You will first want to rest and refresh yourselves before you turn your mind to Etowah. Come, I will make you a fine meal now and you can tell me of your journey.' She gestured for them to go ahead of her.

Caxna cast a glance down at the packs in the canoe. Pakahle noted his glance. 'They will keep for now. First rest a while and have something to eat.'

'I do not have the time for a long visit,' Caxna said.

She cast her eye over him. 'You have time to eat and rest. You will get nowhere if you have not the strength or energy,' she said. Her tone brooked no argument.

He gave a wry grin and made his way up the shoreline and the others followed suit, Pakahle bringing up the rear.

True to her promise Pakahle gave them a meal nearly worthy of a feast. Aisling, not realizing the extent of her hunger, ate with enthusiasm as well as gratitude that she had no hand in preparing the meal. She also appreciated the warmth of Pakahle's house, the clay walls and thatched roof a luxury after the weeks camping in the open.

She could see from the pleasure on both Caxna and Midiwegi's faces that they too enjoyed this respite from the constant travelling and were grateful for the warmth of Pakahle's fire. And for a moment she could allow herself to relish this feeling of shared delight, and once Caxna had briefly recounted the tale of their journey, the few words of general conversation related to game and fish stocks that they exchanged and what else Caxna might need for traveling. Caxna even mentioned the use of Pakahle's salve on Aisling.

'She has learned to paddle well,' said Pakahle with a proud smile. She lifted Aisling's left hand and examined it, tracing her thumb along the calluses. 'She had much practice, I see.'

Caxna grinned. 'I have no doubt she could handle a small canoe herself, now, though she would have to learn how to rub the salve on her joints.'

Aisling gave a shy smile of pleasure at his praise. 'I am sure the need for the salve has gone,' she said. She flexed her back. 'My back and arms no longer ache.'

Caxna gave Midiwegi a sideways glance. 'Midiwegi will be grateful for that.'

Midiwegi grimaced slightly. 'We are here now, so there is no cause for any more aching limbs.' He gave Aisling a wary look.

Pakahle looked over at Aisling. 'You are not going upriver with Caxna?'

'I—I have not decided.'

'But you will of course, when I tell you what I heard from my brother's son.' Pakahle leaned across and put her hand on Aisling's arm. 'Several moons back, not long after you left, a strange large canoe with white cloth tied to its poles was sighted at the mouth of the river. It sounded like the one you seek.'

For a moment Aisling could neither think nor speak from the shock of the words she'd been wishing for, hoping for all these many months. Could it be true? Had they sighted the Madog's ship? 'They survived,' she murmured.

'That was just after we left?' Caxna said. He reached for her hand, squeezed it and studied her face. 'And they are still there?'

Aisling, feeling his gaze, avoided his eyes and focused on Pakahle. 'My nephew did say that some smaller canoes were seen going upriver, while the big one remains floating at the river's mouth,' Pakahle said.

'They went upriver?' Aisling repeated.

Pakahle nodded. 'So my nephew heard.'

Aisling fought through the turmoil of her thoughts. Was there anyone left aboard ship? Should she go there first, or would it be better to go upriver and search for the small boats where her brother was more likely to be? There was no question she would join Caxna now. She had no alternative but to go with him to find her brother and the others.

'I must go with you now, Caxna. You will take me, won't you?' she asked him before her nerve failed, before she thought of other possibilities. She had to find her brother as quickly as she could now and assure herself that he was well, that no mishap had befallen him in the storm or since. She would do whatever he might request in return for that help. She'd seen the desire in his eyes, unspoken, an offer that had never been unattractive, but one that she had as yet to acknowledge.

Caxna answered her query with a nod, his eyes full of questions. 'Of course you would want to search upriver for your people. You may come with us, as far as necessary, but the journey will take at least one moon.'

'I will not delay you. If we sight my people you only need stop as long as it takes for me to reach them, though I am certain my brother would like to find some way to repay you for your kindness. As would I.' She gave him a tentative smile, avoiding the questions that remained in his eyes. Why did he have questions? Didn't she make it clear she must find her brother? Wasn't he committed to his own path, one that had no place for her in it?

'Is it wise to come with us?' Midiwegi asked. His eyes had narrowed, his look wary. 'You might find that your people had gone up a different fork of the river than the one we must take.' He looked at Pakahle. 'You must have a canoe. Could you not take her, Old Woman? You should know the way.'

Why didn't Midiwegi want her to go with them? Perhaps it was as he said, that he thought she might cause delays, but something told her it was more. Since Caxna found his canoe she'd thought much on his behavior and found it wanting on many occasions and a little strange on others.

'I would do nothing to delay Caxna's journey,' she said. 'But if both Pakahle and Caxna prefer I find another way, I will.'

Pakahle gave Midiwegi a direct look. 'As you say, I am an old woman. A woman who stays here by the fire in the winter time.' She patted Aisling's hand. 'But if it is necessary I will take you to my brother's place and ask that he find someone to paddle you upriver. It will take a few days, though.'

'Thank you for your kind offer,' Aisling said. She gave Caxna a pleading look.

'I have already said I you may come with us. I have not changed my mind.' He glanced at Midiwegi. 'Midiwegi will appreciate your help paddling his canoe.'

'You will still take both canoes?' she asked.

'Yes. I do not know when, or if, I will ever be back here. Since Midiwegi is representing his clans for the trading he can return to his home with the details about the arrangements if we are successful. I will have to remain there. And later I will be going home.'

Pakahle nodded, her face sad but full of understanding. Aisling felt an ache in her heart. Would she ever return here? She thought of all that Pakahle had done for her. She could never make it up to her and what could she do in appreciation? There must be something.

It was later, after all the goods had been taken ashore, the supplies checked and restocked, ready for the next day when they would depart, that Pakahle sought out Aisling and spoke of her leaving.

'It is not easy to say goodbye,' Pakahle said. She touched Aisling on the cheek. 'You are like a daughter to me. And now after many moons away, you have returned, only to leave again.'

'I am sorry,' Aisling said. 'I would that I had more time to be with you. If only to thank you for all you have done for me.' She gave Pakahle a hug. 'You were so kind and good. You healed me from more than just a near drowning. You shared your hearth, your food and your good nature which made a very difficult time for me easier to bear.'

'There is nothing to thank me for. The spirits meant for me to be here to help you. You know this.'

Aisling gave her a puzzled look. 'I do?'

Pakahle nodded and took Aisling's hands. 'And now you must look after him. Your spirit helper commands it.'

'Look after him?' Whom did she mean?

'Many spirits pull on him, try to claim him for their own. Always it is this way with him. But he is for you.'

'I do not understand. Who is for me?'

Pakahle squeezed her hands and looked deeply into her eyes. 'You know, my daughter, you know.'

22

They portaged the canoes, the packs and baskets to a small river, a morning's distance from Pakahle's. Caxna explained this route would be an easier method to join the larger river that would take them up to Etowah than by attempting to enter the river's mouth, where they would have to fight currents where it joined the sea. This strategy meant that they had to take the journey to the branch river in stages, Caxna and Midiwegi carrying the first canoe, and she taking some of the packs. They would place the canoe and packs at a certain point and then return for the remaining canoe and more packs, and on the third trip collect the rest. It was a tedious business and it left Aisling sweaty, hot and somewhat impatient.

She was glad when they finally launched the canoes. Finally, they would make progress. She felt new energy at the thought and thrust her paddle in with force and sensed the canoe's gathering speed, until she realized the direction they headed.

'We are going downriver?' she asked Midiwegi. He sat in his accustomed spot at the prow of the canoe.

'We are. This river flows into the larger one. It is not the other way around.'

'So we are going backwards now?'

'In a sense, though we are now headed in an easterly direction. We have no choice. It is the way of the river.'

She nearly groaned at the thought of all those hours spent portaging, most of it now gone to waste, as they had to some degree doubled back. She gritted her teeth. There was no help for it, but the thought of it was still frustrating. She set her mind to paddling faster and stronger, to bring the journey down this river to a quicker end so that they could begin to make their way upwards and closer to finding her brother.

Though her mind became increasingly fogged with fatigue she couldn't help but notice the overhanging trees, their branches draped in moss like necklaces. Bird calls echoed in the distance, but the river was nearly still at points, a mist rising off it, carrying the sounds of the birds' twitters and whoops and their paddles parting the water.

By the time they stopped for the night she was exhausted. Her emotions and physical strength had been pushed to the limit and she could hardly find the mental processes to put a meal together for the three of them. She stumbled over to the packs with some of the provisions and withdrew the tools to make a fire.

Caxna took the drill board and pouch from her. 'Here, I will do that for you. You go and collect some dry moss and make wood shavings. Midiwegi, why don't you gather some firewood?'

Midiwegi nodded and headed off into the dense thicket that surrounded their campsite. The mist was forming into a heavy fog and for a moment Aisling wondered if Midiwegi might get lost until she realized he would be used to these conditions. She busied herself closer to camp, taking some moss from a dry patch underneath a fallen tree that had settled nearby and then collecting some sticks for kindling, selecting a suitable one for Caxna to peel back with his knife and make shavings. He took it from her with thanks and began the task of setting the fire.

Under his expert hands it caught with the first efforts and soon the two of them were feeding the small flame. Aisling added a bigger stick and a small spark shot off and landed on her tunic. Before she could act Caxna was beating the spot.

She gave a nervous laugh. 'Thanks. I would prefer not to be tonight's meal.'

'No.' Caxna gave a wry smile. 'I don't think you have enough meat on you to satisfy Midiwegi's appetite.'

She laughed again, though this time the laugh was more genuine. 'I think Midiwegi likes his portions more tender, too.' She gave a small sniff. 'And I think my seasoning would not be to his taste.'

Caxna took her hand and touched her arm with his other hand. 'I have noticed some very tender parts over these moons since you arrived. Though now, I will say some of them are not so tender.'

He ran his finger along her palm, tracing the calluses in the same manner he'd done before and it was all she could do not to snatch her hand from him, denying the strong response she felt to such a touch. She resolved she would only allow a few moments of this pleasure, to savor the touch of his finger, and then she would break it. But then he was lifting her hand and laying the back of it against his cheek.

'This part, I am glad to say, remains tender,' he said. He leaned forward and cupped her chin. She raised her eyes to his and saw only the flames of the fire reflected. He ran a finger over her lips. 'And your mouth,' he said. He leaned down and kissed her. For a moment she sank into the kiss, felt the softness of his lips and the response that came alive inside her. She marveled at it, such a kiss as nothing she'd had from anyone else. For a moment she thought she could do what he asked, what she thought he wanted from her. To couple for the night, or two nights, to enjoy his company and pretend that they would part all the better for such a night's pleasure. But it was only a moment, and the moment passed because she couldn't bear to think Caxna would take her only for temporary pleasure. She pulled back.

He released her and sighed. 'No, you are right. As much as I might wish it, it is not the right choice. For either of us.' He knelt down by the fire and threw on more sticks, his head turned away.

She choked on his words but nodded nevertheless. 'Not the right choice,' she echoed.

She watched Caxna feed the fire in silence until Midiwegi returned, his arms filled with firewood. The silence continued while she laid out the provisions for the meal, deciding on the smoked venison and dried berries, because anything else seemed like too much effort. Her body ached all over and she fought fatigue with every motion, but it was her heart that felt heaviest. Was it his rejection? But she was the one that had pulled from his kiss. Or was it that he seemed only to regret that they would not spend a night's coupling?

She tried to shake these thoughts from her head. This was not a path she should even follow, for it would go nowhere. Her attraction to Caxna, for she could not deny that it was there, was merely rooted in her loneliness and his kind manner and the protection he'd given her over these many months. Caxna was a good man, a man anyone would admire; a man many women did admire, in fact. She thought of Midiwegi's sister and the scribe's wife at Xicallanca. She sniffed at the thought of Xicallanca. There was no doubt that scribe's wife was not shy about her attraction.

She regarded Midiwegi, who was wolfing down the venison, his fingers filled with the juice of the berries he'd smeared on the meat to enhance the flavor. Though Midiwegi was well favored and his build muscular, his manner, which could at times be ingratiating or condescending, she found less than appealing. She had no doubt, given the chance, he would cheat at any game, be it dice or *fidchil*. Or whatever games he might play here.

'Have you engaged in trade for your clan much?' she asked Midiwegi.

Midiwegi gave her a puzzled look. 'Why do you ask such a question?'

She shrugged. Why did she ask it? Some inner feeling, something about him made her want to know more. 'I ask for no reason in particular. I just wondered.'

He straightened, his chest broadening. 'My father has entrusted me with a few trade opportunities. I accompanied Caxna on a previous journey. And I have traded with a few other clans near to my home.'

She nodded. 'You enjoy it, then?'

This time he was the one who shrugged. 'My father thinks it an important pursuit that will bring us much status and wealth.'

'And has it so far?'

Midiwegi glanced at Caxna. 'There are some among my clan who have made good trades. My father particularly admires Caxna's achievements in the seasons since he visited us first.'

Despite the words Aisling could detect no admiration in Midiwegi's tone, though she was immediately distracted by the implication of his statement. She looked at Caxna, the first direct look since their encounter earlier.

'What achievements?' she asked Midiwegi.

'He means that I arrived first with just a canoe and a few pots of herbs, salves and ointments, smoked meats from the north, some painted bowls and one obsidian knife. I traded these goods with them for their fine baskets, shell necklaces, and other goods that I left and traded on further down the coast for better, larger goods. I continued to improve the amount and quality of the goods over the seasons.'

'You had good luck,' Midiwegi said.

'No, I asked questions and listened to the answers. Wherever

I went, I found what people valued and remembered where others had it in plenty. I was willing to travel to areas that required portaging or walking long distances. I would track large game in rough weather and I knew where to locate it.' Caxna explained his success in an ordinary tone, with no trace of pride or derision.

Despite the neutral tone Midiwegi's face darkened. 'The spirits favored you, too, I think.'

'If they did I am glad of it. It has not always been the case.'

Midiwegi raised his brow a fraction but let the matter drop, though Aisling could see there was something about Caxna's success that festered within Midiwegi. She had noted the manner in which he garnered the scant praise from his father and could only imagine his desire to win more of it. Was he looking for more status within his own clan too? His aunt was a clan mother and clearly had influence. Aisling sighed. It was difficult enough to unravel the clan politics of her own people, she found it nigh impossible with a people of which she had no real knowledge.

THEY FOLLOWED the river's winding path, passed trees, bare of their leaves, shrubs clinging to the sides of rocky outcrops that on occasion towered above them, and sloping hillocks full of wild grasses. All the while Aisling kept close watch for curraghs tied up or in motion, smoking fires, anything that might indicate the presence of her brother and the others. They passed only one canoeist, travelling downriver close to the other side of the riverbank, quite a distance away. He raised his hand in greeting but didn't stop.

As they progressed upriver, signs of heavy frost began to appear, especially in the early morning hours. The air held its chill longer and it took more paddle strokes before she felt sufficiently warmed. The days continued to erode away and still

there was no sign of the ship members or the end of their journey. She watched Caxna paddling, cleaning the canoe or skinning some meat when camped. His manner to her since they'd
kissed had been courteous, but she keenly felt the distance he
worked to maintain between them.

THE DAYS MOUNTED. Occasionally Midiwegi and Caxna paddled
through the night while she attempted to doze in the canoe. The
weather had become milder and the birds more insistent. Spring
was in the air already.

Eventually they halted at one small village visible through
the bare trees from the river's edge. Though the day was far from
over, Caxna had decided to bring them here.

When they disembarked near the worn slope that held a
sprinkling of canoes, she could see that it was only a collection
of a few houses, the thatch of branches and pine boughs
covering the roofs ragged and old. The man who eventually
greeted them wore a grease-stained hide tunic with leggings
underneath and a mangy fox fur draped over his shoulders, the
eyes and teeth of it lost long ago. A few old women and some
young children, equally poorly dressed, hung back a short
distance.

'You are come,' he said. He pronounced the words of the
trader language slowly, his wizened features belying the twinkle
that appeared in his eyes. 'We have food here just prepared that
we are happy to share.'

Caxna smiled. 'I am come. We will gladly share what food
we have, if that helps.' He glanced behind the old man. 'Your
young men are out hunting?'

'They are,' the old man said, a rueful look in his eye. 'As you
can see we are not a large band, but we still must eat before the
planting time.'

On Caxna's instructions he and Midiwegi unloaded the

packs and baskets, then hefted the canoes upside down over top of them, a quick and easy method to hide and protect their belongings from the elements and prying eyes.

When they arrived at the chief's house among the small cluster of buildings that comprised the settlement, Aisling noted the spread of food on the woven mat on the floor. Portions of dried fish, a few bowls of squash and a few other items were laid out. It wasn't a huge feast, but with the smoked meat and berries they had brought it would be enough.

The chief motioned for them to sit and he followed suit. The two older women who had entered with the chief took seats behind him. They both wore hide tunics; one with ragged fringe accompanied by leggings and the other with moccasins that reached nearly to her knees, sparsely beaded.

Despite what their appearance might suggest, the food was well seasoned with wild herbs and a tracing of something else she couldn't put a name to. In a climate such as this one, it seemed herbs still grew at this time of year, an advantage she could taste in the food she now savored. She'd had no time to forage for herbs that might or might not be like the ones she knew from home, but she could clearly taste the thyme in the squash.

'You are travelling far?' the chief finally asked after they ate their fill. He was the only one that ever spoke directly to them and, after he'd translated a few comments to the women, Aisling realized the others didn't speak the trader language.

'We are travelling to Etowah.'

The chief nodded. 'And you have come far already.'

Caxna smiled. 'We have travelled far. It is a tale I will gladly share.'

'I would like to hear such a tale. Winter is not quite over and it will keep us through the next one.'

Caxna relayed the tale of their travels to Xicallanca, describing the wonders of the many buildings, the richness of the markets and the many people it contained. He said nothing of the sacrifices, or even the ball game, and made little of the trading he sought. He avoided any mention of the arrest and the events that followed that. But still it made for a tale the chief appreciated.

'Is that where you met your companions, in this place called Xicallanca?' asked the chief.

'I am not from Xicallanca,' said Midiwegi, his tone somewhat curt. 'I am Caddo.'

The chief nodded and looked at Aisling. 'But she is not from either one of your clans.'

Caxna laughed. 'No my companion is from across the big water. She was separated from her people during a large storm. She fell from the large canoe with white cloth attached to upright poles that carried her and her people during the storm.'

'I have heard tell of this large canoe.'

Aisling caught her breath. 'You have?' She wasn't certain if it was custom for women to speak but the question came out before she could think.

The chief looked at her and gave a slight smile. 'One of my clan met another man on the river during the harvest moon, before the season of frost, and he told him of the large canoe with white cloth attached to upright poles at the mouth of the river.'

'Did he say anything more? Did they see people on the canoe?' She could hear the anxiety in her voice.

The chief shook his head. 'That is all I know. Perhaps when it is warmer and there are more people on the river we will hear more.'

The brief surge of hope receded. She was really no further enlightened than she had been earlier.

'Have you seen a group of strange canoes pass here?' Caxna asked.

Aisling was grateful that he brought up the topic with the

chief. He'd spoken little to her since they had kissed, and had kept his distance whenever they stopped for the night. His manner towards her still left her distraught and anxious. Now it seemed he had given some thought to her predicament and was trying to help. Or did he just want to relinquish responsibility for her as soon as possible? In any case she was grateful he'd laid the question before the chief. She had wanted to herself but wasn't certain it was wise for her to do so.

'Before the frosts there were many groups of strangers passing,' the chief said. Some, like you, on their way to Etowah, others on hunting trips before the snows settled in up north.'

'But none with people that looked like me?' Aisling asked.

His eyes were sympathetic. 'I cannot say that I have seen or heard of anyone that looked like you. But before the frost sets in, the women are often away gathering berries and harvesting the corn, squash and beans and the men are hunting, trapping, fishing or checking weirs. It is possible we did not see them if they passed.'

She tried to take the comfort that he offered in his final words, but she could see that she still had no certainty about anything, except that the ship was anchored at the mouth of the river. For all she knew they were lost at sea and someone else found the ship and sailed it there.

Caxna laid a hand on her arm. 'The river splits soon. We will be taking the branch going east,' he said. 'It is possible that your people may have taken the other route heading northeast. Do you want to remain with us, or see if you might find someone to take you in the other direction?'

'I am sure one of my nephews would take you,' the chief said. 'I will ask when they return from hunting. You are welcome to remain here until that time.'

For a moment all she could feel was a surge of panic. How could she make such a choice? She had no certainty of the outcome of either option. There was no clue to show her where the others might likely be. What must she do? She nearly closed her eyes to intone a prayer asking for guidance. She looked at Caxna; there was sympathy there. Sympathy and something more.

She sighed, still uncertain. 'I will go with you,' she told him.

23

She saw the watchtowers first. Rising up above the huge array of nut trees, their buds already in evidence. She later found that the trees formed a semi-circle around Etowah on its perch at the edge of the river. 'The trees keep flaming arrows from falling into the city in the event of an attack,' Caxna told her.

She'd only asked him the name of the trees. He'd told her that and more; that the city was bigger than she'd ever imagined, ruled by a chief who was descended from the sun. The city contained a large temple mound, which supported countless buildings. It also had a plaza filled with a market bazaar, stick-ball fields and ceremonial areas. He told her many more things and they all crowded in her mind, until it was too much to take in at once.

Homes had dotted the riverbank for some time as they had approached the city, leaving little doubt the community was large and Caxna's details certainly reinforced that. But nothing prepared her for the sight of it. Or the awe it inspired.

They had banked their canoes just east of Etowah, where other clusters of river craft were beached. Caxna arranged for men to help unload the packs and baskets. And now they carried them up to Etowah, following behind her, Midiwegi and Caxna, one nearly bumping into her as her pace slowed to a crawl when they approached the city.

She hardly noticed the houses that sprawled at the city's outskirts, or the moat they crossed to the wooden palisades. Her eyes were drawn instead to the distant mound which rose so high it seemed to touch the sky, its breadth as wide as three of the fields from home. A mountain made by people, shifting more earth than she could ever imagine in a lifetime. It somehow was more impressive than anything she'd seen at Xicallanca. From the entrance she could make out the outlines of some of the buildings the mound supported, and that amazed her even more.

Once inside the palisade, she could see rows and rows of straw thatched houses that encircled the mound, some revealing a trace of the woven branches underneath the painted gold clay that plastered them. Caxna led them through the maze of houses and she thought of Xicallanca, its rows of streets containing crumbling and deteriorating buildings. There was no sense of decay here.

People teemed about her, some even stopping to look curiously at their little procession. The men wore their hair in topknots on their heads, some with feather plumes or fur bands. A few men had ears pierced with rings and wore elaborately etched copper gorgets on oiled bare chests, and copper bracelets on their wrists. Tattoos were evident too; swirling designs on calves and chests where they dared brave the cool weather. Women wore kirtles wrapped around their waists and grey fur mantles on their shoulders.

They seemed to have walked ages before Caxna finally halted at a substantial house painted with angular designs. A woman opened the woven mat door at his hailing. Dressed in a simple hide tunic cinched at the waist, she gave a puzzled look when Caxna first spoke to her in trader language. It was only after he switched to her own that her face cleared and she moved out of the way to usher them in the door. The bearers deposited the goods just inside the door and took themselves off.

'They need no form of payment?' she asked Caxna in a whisper.

'No, they are from the bearers' guild and are paid by the city's merchants.'

She nodded, wondering what a guild might be, until a man appeared, his arms open in welcome.

'You are welcome, my friend,' he said. It has been many many moons.'

'Too many moons and yet here I am to ask you for your help once again.' Caxna turned to Midiwegi and Aisling and introduced them. 'I am fortunate to have among my friends, this man, Chewakla, the master potter of Etowah.'

'You praise me too much, Caxna,' Chewakla said.

Like some of the men on the street, he was tattooed and wore a gorget against a bare chest. He also sported a breechcloth and moccasins; nothing more was necessary against the warmth in the house, which became immediately apparent when he drew them through another doorway to a large hall.

The high roof pitch, window and bright colored mats made the room seem larger than it was, but it was still capable of fitting many more people than the handful of women she saw moving about at the far end. In one corner, by a window, an older woman weaving at a backstrap loom nodded to them. Beside her, two other women sewing beads looked up and smiled as a young girl with a wooden doll clutched in her hand waved it in their faces. In the hall's center another woman placed wood on the substantial fire that heated the house.

Nearer the fire's center sat two men, one quite a bit older and the other barely into manhood. It was to this group that Chewakla ushered them and made introductions.

'My father, Patofa. He is the one that has made me a master at my craft. Beside him is my son, Oconee.'

The two men nodded at them and Patofa greeted Caxna. His grey hair scraped back off his face into the familiar topknot, Patofa's face revealed dark eyes still keen and sharp. Above his brow was a small arrow-shaped scar. The son's face was unmarked except for the line of dots tattooed at his chin and cheeks.

Aisling settled herself on a bench between Caxna and Midiwegi, conscious of her grease-stained tunic and worn moccasins. In such garb they would think she was fit only to stoke the fire, like the servant who was making her way to them with some bowls of food. It couldn't be helped, she thought. She straightened her back. Clothes were not the only way to convey importance.

They exchanged a few words as the woman laid out the food. Midiwegi described his own home place and how he came to know Caxna, his respectful tone bordering on ingratiating. 'My people are related to the Caddo; my father is the snake clan and my mother the turtle. We live near the big water, where the days are very hot in summer. The turtle clan is known for its fine basket work and my mother and my sisters are both highly skilled. My uncle and his uncle before him have traded in these goods along many paths south. I recognize some of the patterns we have in your floor mats, which are very fine.' He indicated an elaborate decorated pot that stood in the corner. 'Caxna speaks correctly about your skill. That is your own making?'

Chewakla looked across at the pot and gave a nod of appreciation. 'Yes, it is my work.' He grinned at Caxna. 'Your skill is worthy of praise, too, my friend.'

Caxna shrugged off the compliment. 'What news is there?'

he asked in a pleasant voice. 'Is The Great Sun still keeping the nobles in line?'

Chewakla frowned for a moment. 'Yes, our leader still manages to prevent them from quarrelling with each other too much. Though lately he seems to favor Tuscalusa and his family far too much for anyone's comfort.'

'Tuscalusa? He has two sons, does he not? Both warriors?'

'He does, though one is not a warrior. The warrior is very skilled at stick ball and chunkey. Not an easy game to play. All the women admire him.'

'All the women?' asked Caxna in a soft tone.

'All the women,' Chewakla said. 'Including The Great Sun's daughter, or so the Great Sun would have us think.'

Caxna gave a small sigh. 'There is little I can do to compete with that. No matter how rare my trade goods are.'

Chewakla leaned forward and rested a hand on Caxna's shoulder. 'I would not give up so easily. There are other nobles who would do much to see Tuscalusa's favor wane. I will talk to one of them tomorrow. He has a great interest in trade and would do much to bring in more high quality goods. Anything you brought back from your travels, he would approve. And he has The Great Sun's ear.'

Caxna smiled at him. 'I glad for your help.'

Chewakla turned to Aisling and gave her a friendly and curious look. 'We have heard from our Caddo friend, but we have not allowed you to tell us of yourself. Have you come far?'

She flushed under his gaze, suddenly unsure what to say about herself. How should she begin? Though Caxna had introduced her as an equal, in her shabby tunic and worn moccasins she felt a far cry from the woman who had confronted the priests in Xicallanca.

'I have travelled a great distance,' she said. That much she was certain about. How much detail should she add, though?

Should she begin at the start, in Ireland? Or at the moment she washed ashore here? She looked at Caxna for guidance.

'Are you of the people that were here not so long ago? You have the same fair skin and light colored hair.'

Aisling's breath caught and for a moment she could think of nothing. All explanations fled from her mind and a multitude of questions rushed in to replace them. 'You saw my people? Here? Were they well?' She blurted out the questions disregarding how impolite they might sound, so strong was her need to know.

'I saw them up on the plaza once, meeting with The Great Sun. There were many watching the discussion, so I was not able to get a close view. But they appeared well enough. And I glimpsed some of them at the market on a few occasions.'

'They were well.' She repeated that phrase as if to counter all the times she'd thought she would never find them, that they were lost at sea. Even the early reports she'd doubted to a certain extent. It wasn't until she had the first real tangible evidence they were alive that she understood how much she had believed it impossible to ever find them again.

'You say "were?" They are no longer here?' Caxna asked.

Chewakla shook his head. 'No, they left several moons ago.' He glanced at Aisling. 'They were sent away.'

'Sent away?' Fear flickered inside her.

Chewakla regarded her carefully. 'They did not know our language and only one had some knowledge of trader language, so they were naturally unfamiliar with our customs. Some things, though, are clear no matter what the language. One among the group did not heed the warning that all contact between men and women was forbidden during the time of the Green Corn Ceremony.'

Caxna sucked in his breath. 'That is a serious violation indeed.'

'How, what happened?' Aisling looked from Caxna to

Chewakla, gauging their expressions; Caxna's concerned and Chewakla's full of compassion.

'It is a sacred time, when we give thanks to the ancestors for our harvest and cleanse and purify our homes and ourselves, ready for the sowing of the next harvest in the spring. It is a very important ritual and all honor it most carefully, for fear of polluting the cleansing and angering the ancestors. Men and women do not come together at that time, but this man, one of your people, chose to violate that rule. He took one of our young women, forcibly. You must understand that is a terrible shame for any of our people to live with.'

'What happened?' she asked in a whisper, though she knew the answer.

'She took her life.'

Aisling set down her bowl, feeling physically sick, the bile rising to her throat. She was certain the man who would do such a thing could only be Rhodri. And now he had thrust Cormac and the others into danger through his reckless behavior.

'Where were they sent?' she asked finally, when she could get her emotions under control.

'They were given a piece of land on their own, west of here, where they will not contaminate the Etowah people. In return The Great Sun requires only that they send tribute every harvest moon.'

'Tribute?' she asked.

'I am not certain of the exact nature of the tribute, but it would normally be a portion of the harvest—skins, baskets, pots. Things of that kind.'

She nodded and wondered just how much they understood about these obligations and what would happen if they didn't meet them. Would they even know how to reap a harvest, find the game here, let alone fashion baskets and pots?

'Would you be able to find out the details of the tribute?'

Chewakla gave her kind smile. 'I will see what Ichisi says, he will know. He is the man I told you about. He lives up on the mound and is close to The Great Sun.' He looked over at Caxna. 'And I will ask him about your matter as well. I am certain he will be able to set up a meeting with The Great Sun for you.'

'I can only hope that your efforts on my behalf will prove successful and so that I might repay you in kind,' Caxna said.

Chewakla clapped Caxna on the shoulder. 'You have nothing to worry about. You were more than generous to me in the past. I owe my prosperous trade with the various towns in the south to your efforts.' He looked at Midiwegi. 'And now you bring me more trade possibilities.'

Midiwegi, who had remained curiously silent up until now, seized the opening. 'I am certain my people would find your pots the highest quality and would be very interested in establishing a trade link.'

Chewakla nodded. 'I am glad to hear it. We will talk more on it. Now we must leave these heavy matters and enjoy ourselves.' He motioned his young son to stand. Oconee reached behind him and clutched a small wooden flute in his hand. With feline grace he rose and began to play a soft air. Aisling's thoughts eventually turned to Cormac. He'd played the flute a little when they were young, wiling away the evening winter hours by fire. It was a sound that always sent her thoughts adrift, it helped soothe her when she was troubled and somehow it paved the way to a solution.

Now she followed the path the music took her and all she could see was danger. She felt it in the fear that now gripped her stomach and the restless energy in her mind. She looked again at Caxna. His eyes were on Midiwegi, his face full of enjoyment, but feeling her gaze he returned it, his eyes questioning. The fear didn't lessen. What was it she feared?

24

———

'I am sorry, but I cannot take you,' he said. 'Someone will, though. I will ask.'

Aisling's heart sank at Caxna's words. She picked at the worn hide tunic, noting the additional small hole from some stray spark from a camp fire. Somehow she had counted on his agreement, even though it made no sense, given that he had his own problems to attend to. Even now he expected to hear at any moment if Chewakla had been successful in arranging a meeting with Etowah's leader, The Great Sun. Such a peculiar title, though when she'd remarked on its strange nature to Caxna he had narrowed his eyes and asked what name her people gave to their leader?

'King,' she said simply.

'And what does king mean?' His tone held only a hint of mockery. 'The sun is supremely powerful, connects us to all things, it brings light, gives life to every living beings; without the sun all would die.'

'Are you saying their leader is the sun?'

'The Great Sun is of the sun, and in many ways, for Etowah, it is one and the same.'

'And it is not true for you?'

Caxna shrugged. 'I am not certain what is true for me, anymore. If you mean do my people share the beliefs in The Great Sun, no they do not. They are a far, far distance from here. Where the snows come heavy in the winter season, the summers cooler and the rain is so soft and fine that it hangs on the trees and in your hair.' Caxna gave a small sigh. 'My people have headmen, chiefs. And clan elders whose sage advice is heeded.'

She thought of the truth of her birth and the ties that bound her to her family. It had been this thought that prompted her to ask Caxna to take her to her brother and the others. She must let them know the danger they were in, the details of the tribute and the price of failure.

She looked at him now and nodded. 'I understand. It was silly of me to ask. I know your own matters take precedence and you need to stay here for that.'

He returned her gaze, his eyes filled with compassion. Suddenly she was conscious of the room's small size and their close proximity as they stood by the narrow window that looked out on the house beside them. It was only a short distance away and she could see in the window facing them a woman pouring water into a bowl. The moment she'd entered this room where Caxna and Midiwegi were to sleep, she'd been conscious of the window, as if it were alive, gaping at her. Perhaps it was because the room held only enough space for the two platform beds, a small woven mat and a chest covered with piles of fur and brightly colored blankets. She was no longer a slave here, but a guest, and custom meant she slept with the other women.

She bit her lip. 'Would you at least allow me to come with you when you meet the Great Sun so that I might explain my people's mistake and perhaps help him understand they did not intend for it to happen?'

'You know that person did not intend to take that woman against her will?' He narrowed his eyes.

She shifted uncomfortably under his gaze. 'I am sure he did not fully understand the serious nature of his offense.' The irony that she should defend Rhodri's actions didn't escape her.

'Is it not a serious offence among your people when a man takes a woman by force?'

'No. I mean yes, it is a serious offence, but the man alone would be punished.'

Caxna snorted. 'But is not the clan responsible for the behavior of one of their members?'

She thought about that and struggled with an answer that would explain the complex relationship she had with Madog and his men and could only conclude that, as much as she might wish otherwise, Madog was responsible for Rhodri.

'Can you also not see that to exile the one would mean sure death for him, whereas if the whole group is sent away together, the man will live and have the support of his group to make the reparation?'

For a moment she allowed herself the thought of Rhodri exiled on his own and felt satisfaction. 'You are right,' she said. 'I had not considered that. But I still feel I ought to apologize and see if I can help. I can at least find out more about the tribute owed and make sure they understand it.'

He gazed at her for a long moment, his expression unreadable. She knew that it was asking much that she accompany him. Her very presence might adversely affect his proposals to The Great Sun. That he even gave it thought filled her with gratitude. Perhaps in return she could plead his case to The Great Sun. Help him secure the daughter for his bride. Despite the pang it caused her, she resolved to do whatever she could to help him.

His gaze moved along her body and he frowned. 'If you come we will have to find you something better to wear. You could never appear in front of The Great Sun dressed like that.'

She smiled at him, understanding that he was telling her he would take her with him when he met with The Great Sun.

MIDIWEGI WASN'T HAPPY. The scowl on his face and the manner in which he held his body told Aisling everything. His words confirmed it.

'Is it wise to have her come with us?' He cast Aisling a sideways glance. Caxna hadn't waited long to inform Midiwegi of the new plan. It was still morning, though Chewakla had left some time ago for his pottery workshop and to try and make the arrangements for the meeting. The women of the house were busy at their tasks and Caxna, Midiwegi and Aisling discussed the latest turn of events in Caxna and Midiwegi's room.

'It will not harm anything. It might help us.' Caxna gave him a patient smile.

'How could it help us? Her people have been banished.'

'I have done nothing wrong, though,' Aisling said. 'I am willing to risk The Great Sun's displeasure.'

Caxna nodded. 'Aisling knows the trader language, and if she can provide a suitable explanation for her people's behavior to The Great Sun and the other nobles there is potential for us to be involved in another important trade link with The Great Sun.'

'Another important trade link? What do you mean?'

Caxna cast a glance at Aisling. 'It is possible that Aisling's people would want to trade with your band. They have many items that would be of use to your people and the people of Etowah. They also have men among them who have the skills to make such things like large canoes for long journeys. That would be useful for trade. If Aisling can smooth the way between her people and Etowah, many good things can come of it.'

Midiwegi considered his words and Aisling held her tongue, not daring to utter any contradictions. She wouldn't mention that the 'canoe' in which she'd crossed the ocean had been built by others than Madog and his men. With the exception of Madog, the men had little understanding about navigation and only the handful of men who manned the ship knew how to sail her. These men possibly knew something of sheep and other elements of farming.

One skill Madog's men all shared, though, was that they knew how to fight. Their weapons and approach to warfare were certainly different to any of the people she'd encountered so far. The bows and arrows both peoples might use, but she had yet to see a sword, a knife not fashioned from obsidian, or anything else made of forged metal. The ship's iron cooking pots might hold some interest too; so far she'd only seen pottery cooking containers in this land.

'I can appreciate that her presence might have some beneficial effects,' Midiwegi said in a reluctant tone. 'Though it might also have the opposite result.'

'I will take responsibility for the consequences,' Caxna said. 'I have more to lose if I am wrong.'

Midiwegi gave a thoughtful nod. 'Yes there is that to consider.'

'Good, it is settled. She will come with us,' Caxna said.

Midiwegi frowned. 'That is presuming a meeting will be set up.'

'It will. But in the meantime we must make our preparations.'

'I, for one, intend to have a look at the city,' Midiwegi said. 'It is so large, it would take many days before a person could see all of it.'

'I would not mind that either,' Aisling said. She looked at Caxna. 'Can you show us?'

'I need your help with a matter first.'

'I will go on my own, then,' Midiwegi said. He nodded to the two of them and left.

'Wait here,' Caxna said. He gave her a crooked smile and vanished through the doorway before Aisling could question him.

She moved over to the window again, the light strong now as the sun rose in the sky. The chill present earlier in the morning had vanished and she could feel the warmth growing in the room. The window across from her was empty, the woman no longer visible. The rest of the wall was blank, except for the angular designs painted on them.

The city here, like Xicallanca, was bigger than anything she knew in her own homeland, or that of Madog's. So many people in one place, it was more than she could grasp. Each, it seemed, had their own skills that they plied exclusively to anything else. There were no crops growing by the houses, or sheep and cattle grazing. Though they might still obtain their meat by hunting, still she observed no hens, even in the small courtyard. Not even an herb garden. She could only suppose that like Xicallanca, all these items were purchased in the market. It was a marvel that she still found difficult to comprehend.

It was only when she felt Caxna's hand on her shoulder that she realized he'd returned. 'There is not much to be seen through that window,' he said.

She turned to him and gave him a rueful smile. 'I see more than you might think.'

He held a bundle out to her and she detected a twinkle in his eye. Behind him Chewakla's wife clutched something under her arms, her face tentative. Aisling took the bundle, puzzled, and unfolded it carefully. When she caught her first glimpse of the deep purple color she halted, only too aware of the generosity of the gift. She looked up at Caxna in disbelief.

'You cannot mean to give this to me.' She folded the dark

cloth back into place and held it back out to him. 'No, it is too much.'

He pushed the bundle back to her. 'I do mean it. It is yours to fashion into a garment worthy of a lady of visions. A garment that will impress and show all the people who you are.'

Her eyes filled with tears. 'Do not mock me,' she said softly. She'd seen no visions at all in the months since they'd left Xicallanca and she wasn't even certain that the daydream she'd had before was a vision. She glanced briefly at Chewakla's wife, who looked at Aisling curiously. Could this woman understand their words?

'I do not mock you,' he said. 'I would never mock you in this way.' There was something more than kindness in his voice. Firm, decisive, all these elements were present, but it was the trace of passion that made her look up at him and seek his eyes. And there she read something that didn't seem possible, something that promised her much more than either of them could ever allow.

Chewakla's wife held out her own package and Aisling tore her eyes away from Caxna's.

'For you,' the woman said. She motioned again.

Aisling set down the cloth and took the other package from the woman. 'I thank you.' She smiled at her and quickly removed the soft hide wrapping and uncovered a pair of honey-colored moccasins embroidered with tiny shells and quills to form an intricate flower pattern on their tops.

'They are beautiful,' Aisling said. 'They are yours?'

The woman gave Caxna a puzzled glance. He said a few words in her language and she looked at Aisling and nodded.

'Chewakla's wife has only a few words in trader language. She is happy for you to wear these moccasins when we have the meeting. They are the moccasins given to her for the day she married Chewakla.'

'They are her wedding moccasins? I could not take them, they are too special.'

'She says it is a special occasion for you and so you must accept them.'

'Tell her I promise I will take every care with them and return them as soon as the meeting is over.'

Caxna nodded and relayed her words. His pace was not rapid-fire as she'd heard the others of Etowah speak, but she couldn't help but admire his skill with the language. She knew herself what a good teacher he was. Not just in languages, either.

The woman spoke once more to Caxna, exchanged a nod with Aisling and then left.

'She says you must excuse her but she has tasks to attend to,' Caxna said.

'And I guess I have my own task to attend to.' She shook out the cloth. 'Viewing the city will have to wait until another time.'

'Do you need anything more to help you fashion something from the cloth?'

She looked up at him and felt the tears fill her eyes once again. On impulse, she gave him a quick kiss on the mouth. 'I do not know how I can ever thank you for this,' she said.

Startled, he said nothing for a moment. 'You have already thanked me in many ways,' he said. He smiled at her, but behind the smile she could detect a hint of sadness. The passion was gone, as if chased away by what she could only imagine had been evident in her own face. The impossibility of it all.

25

She tugged the tunic in place, praying that her stitches would hold. The coarse needle and thick thread she'd created from the fringes of the fabric were not the finest of tools to make her garment, but still, she was pleased with the result. Under her arms, the seams held without revealing the stitching, and the lacing at the back allowed her to don the gown with greater ease, like the gowns of the Welsh women. Chewakla's wife had helped her put it on, so that the gown fell along her hips and across her bust in comely curves. And now, freshly laced in, standing in the small room, Chewakla's wife nodded her satisfaction, an action that gave Aisling more confidence than she cared to admit.

Chewakla's wife lifted a lock of Aisling's hair. 'Color. Very pretty. Like sun.'

'Thank you.' Aisling looked at the woman's hair, for a moment trying to gauge whether she might try a hairstyle customary to Etowah. Now it was a damp clean tangle. 'Your hair is lovely too.' She touched a lock and smiled.

The woman gave a small bow. From a pouch at her side, she removed a wooden comb, polished smooth against any possibility of snagging hair. She offered it to Aisling, a question on her face. Aisling nodded and the woman motioned for Aisling to sit on one of the chests.

The woman took the comb to her hair and with deft, sure motions began her work. It had been some time since Aisling had been able to comb her hair with anything other than her fingers and she braced herself for the inevitable battle with tangles. Under the woman's ministrations, though, the hair seemed to take little coaxing before it made its way through in long, smooth strokes and Aisling began to enjoy the whole process. It was almost with some regret that she felt Chewakla's wife tap her on the shoulder, signaling she was done. She moved to the front of Aisling and surveyed her work, her face intense. Aisling lifted her hands to examine the results and felt the strange twisted coils on either side of her ears. It felt good to her and when she saw the satisfied smile on Chewakla's wife's face she knew she could be pleased with the results.

The woman held up her finger, pointed to the door and disappeared through it. A moment later she returned with a wide bowl filled with water. She gave the bowl to Aisling and pointed to the window.

'Look,' she said.

Aisling nodded and took the bowl over to the window where the light was best. She looked down inside, waiting for the water to still and form her reflection. It took only a moment for the familiar features to take shape: the nose, the mouth and her eyes, now curious and searching. And then the hair, the soft mounds twisted at either side of her head, like oversized snail shells. She turned her head slightly, trying to see more; the head of the wooden hairpin tucked into the second ring of the coil and the other along the bottom, its dark color evident against her fair hair.

The water moved, stirred by an undetectable breath of air, and for a moment her image was replaced by another, or so it seemed. The moment was so brief, though, she couldn't be sure and when she blinked, all that she could recall was the color that flashed across it. Rust-red, the color of blood. She blinked again and saw it again. Blood. Blood soaking grass. She caught her breath, blinked again and it was gone. Her panicked face was the only image she could see. What was it? A vision. What did it mean? She bit her lip, suddenly wishing she'd seen nothing at all, for deep down she knew it spoke of nothing good.

'That cloth has not gone to waste,' said Caxna.

She turned from the window, the bowl in her hands still held up to the light, and saw the admiration in his eyes. She pushed aside her misgivings and gave a shy smile.

'I am glad you like it.' She set the bowl down, rose and turned slowly so he could see the gown in full. 'Do you think it suitable?'

His eyes lingered over her figure, the expression remote. 'Oh, very suitable. I am sure you will be admired by every nobleman there.'

'Thank you. Is the hair acceptable? They will not be offended?' She touched the coil at her right ear and smiled at the woman. 'I have Chewakla's wife to thank for it.'

'Yes. It is as though your hair mirrors the sun. A wise choice, I think.'

'I had not thought of that.' She nodded, pleased. 'You look very fine, too.' She noted the blanket around his shoulders. It was the one he'd worn to the scribe's house. And on his head, the same fur band.

'It is important that I do my clan honor when I meet with The Sun.'

'You have not let them down, I am certain.' She could see the appreciation in the eyes of Chewakla's wife and knew this for a true statement. He would be admired.

·   ·   ·

THE PRESS of people in the chamber seemed to close around her even more as she struggled to follow Caxna, Midiwegi, Chewakla and his son through the crowd to the front of the room. They were all finely dressed; the men's hair swept up in carefully oiled topknots and encircled in fur bands or feathers, the women's hair loose and flowing or coiled into elaborate styles. Shell and pearl necklaces adorned the necks of both the men and the women, some in multiple ropes piled against each other like the ridges of a mountain. Those without the necklaces displayed their wealth in the gold hoops at their ears and the gold bands around their arms and wrists. A few even wore gemstones in their ears, noses or below their mouth.

It was as if the adornment alone was enough to convey their wealth, for each person seemed to try and outdo the next with the choice of clothes. Woven fabrics unfamiliar to Aisling were dyed shades of red, yellow and green and formed into kirtles and tunics to wear with feather or fur mantles. The effect, over-all, was one worthy of any high king's hall. And like the people at any high king's hall, these attendants milled around, talking among themselves in clusters, some individuals casting the occasional sideways glance at other groups of people. Strategies, negotiations, alliances, these were the topics present, she was certain, as they would be back home.

Nobles, Caxna had called them. Or that was the meaning she'd understood when he explained Etowah's hierarchies. Like the nobles that existed among her own and Madog's people, she supposed. They were the privileged group who, unlike the arti-sans, the farmers, the servants and then the slaves, had no need to labor to live. They owned farms and workshops and employed people to work them. Their reward for such owner-ship was to live here, up on the mound, among the clouds.

A land in clouds was what it seemed as she climbed the narrow flights of steps that ascended the large hill created by these people's ancestors, in a time beyond memory. Though

Xicallanca's temple steps rose high above the city, climbing them hadn't conveyed this sense of ascending high into the sky, reaching upward. Perhaps because most times in Xicallanca she'd kept her tell-tale eyes lowered, so she was never able to fully appreciate its size and grandeur, as she was here in Etowah.

Now these nobles crowded around this chamber outside the large hall, waiting on The Great Sun, many casting curious glances her way. He was later than usual this day, for he'd been unwell the previous night, as Chewakla discovered when he inquired. Not a good omen, Aisling thought, but there was no help for it.

Aisling straightened her dress, conscious of the growing number of people staring at her. She assumed she was the object of their curiosity, though Caxna's blanket certainly made a colorful and unusual display. She resisted the urge to run a finger along the eagle's head outlined on it, just a hair's breadth away from her. He glanced at her and gave her a reassuring smile.

'It will not be long now,' he said.

As if summoned, a man appeared at the doorway and announced something in the Etowah language. People surged forward, pushing Aisling, Caxna and the others along with them into the great hall.

The hall was large enough to accommodate everyone in comfort and the numerous windows it contained increased the sense of space. A fire at its center offset the small breeze coming from them. At the head of the hall was a wooden chest occupied by an older man, his greying hair pulled up into an elaborate knot and adorned with a crown of feathers and fur. A long, heavy mantle of bear fur draped his shoulders and lap, and rabbit fur encased his calves. Even from the far end of the hall, Aisling could see the heavy gold rings in his ears. She could only imagine what riches lay under the mantle.

Beside him stood a group of men and women whose dress

and stiff and haughty posture left her in no doubt they were closely related to him. A middle-aged man approached him and gestured as he spoke towards the back of the hall, where they stood.

Aisling glanced at Caxna. He watched the man carefully and leaned towards Chewakla and said a few words. Chewakla's whole demeanor spoke of tension, from the set line of his jaw to his stiff back. His son seemed unworried, his eyes roaming the room curiously. Caxna appeared unruffled, but she noticed the expression of his eyes, where laughter seemed always near to the surface, but now appeared remote, unapproachable. Midiwegi appeared to be the only one who didn't conceal the strain. His frowning face and darting glances had anxiety writ large upon them.

For once, Aisling could sympathize with Midiwegi, and resisted the temptation to bite her lip and made her fingers relax. She gave Caxna a bright smile.

As it turned out there were a few people who went before them, insistent petitioners who brought others with them to vouch for their honesty, or the importance of their request, or perhaps something entirely different. Aisling could only guess as she watched these groups stand before The Great Sun and present their case. She saw the king hear the requests, his face betraying impatience for the most part, as each petitioner knelt before him in obeisance. A quick wave and a man was removed by attendants who hastily appeared; a nod and another man knelt down and kissed his feet. Whimsy, or cool decision making? Aisling couldn't tell.

She felt no more enlightened when their turn arrived. They were summoned from the back, an attendant announcing Chewakla's name, followed by Caxna's. The group made their way to the front, the clusters of people parting to allow their passage.

Chewakla and Midiwegi knelt before The Great Sun, bowing

low. Caxna and Midiwegi followed suit. Aisling took a place beside Caxna and assumed the position, too, careful not to trip on her skirt. She was keenly aware of The Great Sun's gaze, his impatience vanished in the light of the unusual display she knew they made. He gestured for them to stand.

Caxna rose with fluid grace and adjusted his mantle. He spoke a few words of greeting in the Etowah language. The Great Sun gave him a speculative look and nodded.

'I am honored to come before you on this day, Great Sun. I am Caxna, a Tlingit from the far north of here,' he said, switching to trader language. 'My people are nobles of a mighty clan.' His voice was loud and firm, his bearing speaking his pride and lineage.

'Yes, I remember you,' said The Great Sun. He spoke the trader language with deliberation, his pronunciation careful. 'You came before me just after the last Spring Planting Ceremony. You are the trader from the northern icelands.'

'I am,' Caxna said. 'I have come, as I said I would, bringing many goods, strange and wonderful, from places far away. They will delight you and show you how much rich trade I can achieve in a short time. Trade that can only benefit you and Etowah, enhance your standing and bring items to you that are truly worthy of The Great Sun.'

The Great Sun gave him a considering look. 'If that is so, I would see such items as you have amassed in your travels.' He looked at Aisling, who stood just back of Caxna and to his left. 'Is she among those items you speak of?'

A flush crept up Aisling's neck and face. Chin lifted a fraction, she made a small step forward and ignored the warning that flashed in Caxna's eyes.

'I am not, Great Sun,' she said. 'But I can vouch for the beauty of Caxna's goods.'

'Then who are you and what links have you to this man that you can come here before me and vouch for him?'

A thousand deliberations crowded her mind. Should she broach her own request now, before Caxna had made his? If he looked unfavorably upon her it could affect the outcome of Caxna's petition.

'I am Aisling of the Uí Bairriche, a Gael from across the great water.'

'You are very like those men who were here before the Green Corn Ceremony. Are they your people?'

'They are. I was separated from them in a terrible storm and I have been seeking them ever since. I met Caxna and he took me on his travels to help me find them.' She glanced at Caxna, helpless in the face of the probing questions. It seemed too late to retreat now.

The Great Sun frowned. 'As I have said, your people came before the Green Corn Ceremony. We gave them every welcome. Did we not, Hirrihigua?'

A young man stepped forward from the groups of nobles behind Aisling and approached The Great Sun. Like the others in the hall, his bearing was proud, but perhaps due to his youth or the muscular physique evident under his feathered mantle, breechclout and leggings, there was more than a touch of arrogance present.

He gave Aisling a hooded look, his eyes roving every curve of her figure. 'As you say, Great Sun, we gave them every welcome.' His words were difficult at first to comprehend, his thick accent and sometimes awkward pronunciation affecting Aisling's ability to understand him.

'They did not seem to value this welcome,' he added. He gave Aisling a direct look. Though he was only her height, with his arms crossed against his broad chest he appeared intimidating. 'They committed a terrible offense against the people of Etowah, against The Great Sun himself.'

'I am sorry to hear of the offense they committed,' Aisling said. 'I would seek to apologize for them and explain that the actions of one man, while deplorable, are not the actions or nature of the other men.'

'The actions of one man are the actions of the group,' Hirrihigua said.

She glanced at The Great Sun, who followed the exchange with great interest. 'I understand the action was terrible. My people, though, have little understanding of your language or the trader language. I am sure that once they know the serious nature of this offense they would be more than willing to apologize and try and make it up to The Great Sun and the people of Etowah.'

'They have said their words, but the one who is dead cannot hear them any longer.'

'The one who is dead?' Aisling could guess who his cousin was.

'My relation, the one who is dead, took her life after such a dishonor.'

Aisling nodded. 'That is indeed a terrible and I am sorry for your troubles. What is the custom in this awful situation? I would be glad to help explain to my people what you require in reparation.'

Hirrihigua cupped her chin for a moment, pulling it to the right, and then the left. He moved to her hair, touching the soft roll coiled at her left side and then fingered the rich purple fabric at her sleeve. 'She was to marry me.' He dropped his hand. 'And now I have no wife.'

Another man stepped forward. Unlike Hirrihigua he was slender, his feather mantle drooping along sloping shoulders, but he had the same hawk nose. 'As my brother says, he is in need of a wife, and I am in need of a sister-in-law.'

Aisling worked to maintain her composure in the face of the unexpected direction of the conversation.

'A wife is needed, and a daughter, and a sister.' said The

Great Sun. He looked across at an older couple who nodded. 'Her family agree.'

'A wife is needed,' Aisling echoed softly, her lips dry. 'Did you not ask them for a tribute? Perhaps that would be better for the people of Etowah.'

'You ask what the custom is and I tell you now. A wife, daughter and sister are needed. Before, your people had no woman to give. And now you have said you will help.' He smiled widely. 'Hirrihigua needs a wife. You will be that wife. Her parents have no daughter, you will be that daughter. I will be generous, though and allow your people to remain where they are and reduce what I will require in tribute.'

Aisling could barely hear the murmurs of discussion these remarks provoked. She found she had no breath, no heartbeat. There was only a denial, a rejection that rose from somewhere inside and filled her head, threatening to burst from her mouth. 'May I go and talk to my brother, my people?' she said finally, her voice just above a whisper. 'Explain this change in circumstances?'

'That is only fair,' said The Great Sun. 'Itaba and Hirrihigua will take you so that the two can meet your family. Itaba will negotiate the reduced tribute.'

'I would ask that I might be married after the visit, so that my brother could be present for the ceremony.'

'No,' Hirrihigua said. He gave her a dark look. 'We will have the ceremony soon, before we go.'

'We can wait, Brother. What is the rush? Are you afraid she will not be pleased to marry you and will run away? Let her have her brother come to the ceremony and see that we are Etowah, great and powerful. We do not fear their sticks or mantles of metal. At least I think, my warrior brother, you do not fear them.'

Hirrihigua turned to Itaba and gave him a sardonic look. 'No, Brother, I do not fear them.'

'Enough,' said The Great Sun. 'We will do as you request, and let your brother come to the ceremony.' A smile formed on his face, beneficent, self-satisfied. 'You may kiss my feet.'

Aisling stumbled forward and did as he asked, her mind numb. She rose and took her place behind Caxna, lowered her head and prayed for a shift in attention.

'We will have something to eat before we hear more of your petition, Trader Caxna.'

Caxna nodded and knelt with the other three men as The Great Sun retreated from the hall. Aisling could only stare after his retreating back, all thought of kneeling impossible under the weight of the events that had just occurred.

26

———

Caxna led her outside, away from the others, before the brothers could claim her or any member of the dead woman's family. He'd pushed her in front of him, through the groups of milling people, and out into the bright, late winter light. She shivered against the cool breeze that blew across the treetops and scattered the few clouds above her.

'How did this happen? I never meant to do anything but help Cormac.'

Caxna put a hand on her shoulder, a comforting gesture, but she could feel no comfort. She could only feel horror.

'We will find a way out of this, Aisling.' She looked up at him and saw the empathy, and somehow that made her more afraid. 'How could I be a wife to that man? How is that even possible?'

'These are exceptional circumstances.' He squeezed her shoulder. 'I will talk to Chewakla. I will try and find out what The Great Sun wanted as tribute before this and perhaps we can find a proposal that would be more attractive.'

She gave him a wan smile and nodded. 'Thank you. I am grateful that you are willing to help me.'

'I will aid you in any way I can,' he said, his voice soft. His eyes searched hers. 'I would not have any harm come to you, you do know that.'

She allowed him to see the fear, pain and the hint of despair that crowded her mind. 'You would not, I know. But there may be nothing you can do in this case.'

'I will try. I promise you that.' He took up her hand and clasped it hard.

She nodded and looked down at the hand he held. 'Will I have to go with that woman's family...or the two brothers, now?'

'I will try my best to see that you can remain with us until you are to journey to your brother. I am not certain they will allow it, but we will see.'

'And after that? On the journey?' She forced herself to voice the words.

'The Great Sun has decreed they must accompany you. No one can counter that but he, so it is him we must convince to have it otherwise.'

She nodded. The journey would not be pleasant, she was certain, and the question she wanted to ask, but couldn't, hung between them. Even if he did accompany her, there was no certainty that she wouldn't be expected to keep Hirrihigua's bed warm. And she had no idea what services a sister-in-law was expected to perform. As much as she might try, she could not keep the fear and revulsion from her thoughts. She swallowed hard and glanced up at Caxna and saw in his eyes that he'd read every thought and emotion that played across her face.

Midiwegi approached them, his face a study in anger. He nodded to her and drew Caxna aside and spoke in a low voice. She could catch some of the words but she understood none of them since he spoke in his own language. Caxna calmly replied in kind, only a few words in the trader language interspersed, but that made no difference to her. It was the dark looks cast her way that left her in no doubt she was the cause of Midiwegi's anger. A few moments later, he left, hardly appeased by the words Caxna spoke.

Catching her concerned look, he shrugged. 'Midiwegi worries too much,' he said.

THE GOODS WERE PILED at The Great Sun's feet, great lengths of cloth providing splashes of lavish color, bowls, baskets, jars of honey, multi-colored feather mantles, large conch shells. There was also a bundle containing the valuable incense copal, and cochineal for dyes. It was the mat directly under the Great Sun's gaze that attracted the most attention. Here Caxna had laid out his most treasured items. The finely crafted gorgets.

'This is very impressive, Trader Caxna,' said The Great Sun. 'You have indeed found some unique items to share with us.'

'These are but a sampling of items I have in my warehouse here.'

'Including the jewelry?'

Caxna frowned. 'These are all my jewelry pieces, but they are unique.'

The Great Sun leaned down a picked up one of the gorgets and examined it carefully. 'And where does this come from?'

'It is from my own homeland, Great Sun.'

'I see. And you know this skilled craftsman?'

'I do. It was my uncle.'

'Was?'

'He is no longer alive.'

'Oh?' There was mild curiosity in his voice.

'He was killed in a war between my clan and another.'

'Ah, a warrior too.' The Great Sun gave an appreciative nod. 'But so sad. And is this the clan from which you seek to reclaim your clan's honor?'

'It is, Great Sun.'

'And you are asking me, The Great Sun of the Etowah People, to accept these gifts in return for marriage to my daughter and support for your efforts against this clan?'

'Yes, that is what I propose and hope you will accept. As your son-in-law I would also work to expand your wealth and status through establishing many new trade links. Including those with my own people.'

The Great Sun turned the gorget in his hand. 'I see. Are there any other craftsmen who can create this kind of fine work?'

Caxna lowered his gaze. 'I am skilled in it,' he said in a low voice.

'Are you? Well that is interesting. A trader and a craftsman. Yet you are not a warrior?'

Caxna was not pleased with this line of questioning. There was something about the stillness of his posture that convinced Aisling of this. She stood between Midiwegi and Chewakla, buffering herself on either side from any immediate approach of the two brothers.

'My people can be warriors and possess other skills as well.'

'You are a man of many talents, then.' He turned to the young woman standing to the right of him and took up her hand. Gold glittered at her ears, around her neck and at her wrist and arms. Her black hair was oiled and piled in elaborate folds on her head, a style that only seemed to emphasize the length and breadth of her nose.

'Would you find such a man to your liking, Daughter?' The Great Sun asked her.

She replied in the language of Etowah, her voice containing a hint of haughtiness, but no disdain. Her eyes wandered beyond Caxna and fixed on Oconee who stood at his father's side, behind Caxna. A blink, then two and she leaned down to her father and added something more in a low voice. Her father nodded.

'She says, for a man of so many virtues and goods, she wonders that you are not back among your people already.'

Caxna flushed. 'It is true I have been separated from my people for some time, but I have let no opportunity slip away in my efforts to acquire the wealth and status I held before.'

The woman raised her brow slightly and gave a small smile. She spoke again to her father. He replied, his voice firm, and she spoke once more, a hint of contrition in her voice.

'I have told my daughter that your proposal is worthy of full consideration. You have proven your worth and kept your promise that you would put before me great wealth. I will send someone to your warehouse to review the goods and see the tallies. And then we will talk again.' The Great Sun nodded. Caxna's audience was over. He made his obeisance and when the Chewakla and Oconee made to follow The Great Sun spoke again.

'I want you and your son to stay, Chewakla. I would have him play his flute for me a moment.' Oconee and Chewakla halted, a pleased look on their faces.

Chewakla bowed. 'My son would be honored.'

Caxna, Midiwegi and Aisling reached no further than the small outer room before Hirrihigua, Itaba and the dead woman's parents caught up with them. Aisling drew herself up against Caxna.

It was of course to Itaba the parents looked to voice their wishes, the man who used his wit as his weapon, and to great effect. He spoke to Aisling directly. 'Your parents have not given permission for their daughter to leave.'

'I—I was returning to Chewakla's home. I did not realize that

I would be required to meet my people's obligation so soon.' She looked up at Caxna for help.

'She has belongings at Chewakla's still and she will of course need to give thanks to Chewakla and his family formally for their hospitality. That is a sacred duty among her people.'

Itaba narrowed his eyes, but translated the replies to the couple. They glanced at Aisling and she saw the sadness in the woman's eyes. She knew about loss, too.

'I promise, I will come soon, but I would like to fulfill my obligations to Chewakla and his family.'

Hirrihigua stepped forward. 'We can allow you to complete this duty, but tomorrow we will leave to take you west to your people.'

'Tomorrow?' Itaba said. He looked down at the couple. The man shrugged, but the woman, the mother who had lost her daughter, looked pained and gave her head a small shake. Her husband said a few words to her, looked over at Itaba and nodded.

'Tomorrow we will take you west,' Itaba said.

Aisling watched them leave, uncertain whether she should feel relief she wouldn't have to go with them at this moment, or fear that her reprieve was only until tomorrow.

THE STARS WERE SPRINKLED like dust across the night sky, an endless array of tiny beacons of light. There was no moon, so Aisling was free to count their numbers, as if by such a feat she might spend the rest of her days in safety. She shivered, not from the freshness of the air as she stood at the window, but the thoughts of what tomorrow might bring. She'd told herself she'd come to Caxna's room to bid him farewell, but she knew the real reason was that she hoped he could give her some comfort about her future.

He stood beside her now, both of them silently staring out of the window, so much hanging between them. She made her decision.

'Caxna.'

He put a finger to her lips. 'I am sorry I was not able to do more today. But there is still time. While you are gone, I will see if Chewakla can help me persuade The Great Sun to take a different course.' He spoke softly into her ear, his tone so gentle despite the words. She could almost feel his lips there, and for a moment she allowed her thoughts to take a different direction.

The moment left and she turned her attention to his words. She held out no great hope for Caxna's success. Perhaps if he did become The Great Sun's son-in-law there might be more hope for her. That could take some time, though, and she didn't have that kind of time.

'I will hope that you have success,' she whispered.

He took her hand. 'It is possible that he might wish to couple with you in the meantime. But I will try and come to you before that.' For a moment all she felt was the pressure of his hand on hers, until slowly the words sank in.

'How long is the journey?' she asked.

'I do not know, perhaps ten sleeps. They have not yet told me where your people are. I am trying to find out.'

'Thank you,' she said. She closed her fingers around his hand and pulled it to her cheek. 'Thank you for everything.' Tears filled her eyes with the realization that this moment might be the last opportunity to be alone with Caxna, that after tomorrow she might never see him again. She felt suddenly bereft. 'What will I do without you at my side?'

He shushed her with a comforting noise. 'You will be fine. Remember you are the woman who confronted the priests of Xicallanca.'

The tears spilled over, frustration and loss giving them force. It was not the fear of being alone again that prompted her remark, it was the pain that she would no longer have his company. And that his company would be replaced by two men that inspired only revulsion in her, one of whom was to be her companion for the rest of her life, if she fulfilled her obligation.

'What would happen if I ran away, failed to return here with Hirrihigua and Itaba?'

'They would kill your people. For the people of Etowah it would be a loss of honor and others would then think them easy prey.'

She nodded. It was what she expected and she had no doubt that a city such as this could amass a force that would easily eradicate every last one of the men, including Madog and her brother. She would meet her obligation.

She gazed up at Caxna, his eyes full of sorrow and regret, and scanned the familiar territory of his face, drinking in each contour, committing them to memory. In this dim light she filled in the details, the faint tattoos on his chin, those on his hands, to the missing finger on his left hand, the one she held. She raised the hand to her mouth, kissed the empty space and pulled the hand down to rest against her breast.

'Will you do one last thing for me?' she whispered. 'Will you initiate me in the ways between men and women? I would much rather you, than anyone else do that.'

He removed his hand from her breast and placed it under her chin. 'You would have me do this? Why? I will do my best to persuade The Great Sun on a different course.'

She knew doubts over the success of his plan had no part in making the request, but a trust of a different sort that kept her from saying any of the words that had plagued her mind for some time now. How could she speak of her love to a man she had no idea about beyond what she'd observed since she'd met him? How did he, of a people far away from here and even further away from her kind, regard a strange woman from another land and people? But she could at least ask him for one night of lovemaking.

'It may be that the plan will work, but I ask you all the same,' she said. 'Please.' She paused a moment. 'Midiwegi will not return?'

If there was a nod or shake of the head she didn't see it, she only felt his hand along her neck, then his finger tracing the line of her collar bone and slipping inside the *léine* opening to touch the tip of her breast. She slid off her dress and shirt, anxious to feel more of his caresses, to offer the full expanse of her naked flesh to him. He took her into his arms, kissing her deeply, his hands following the contours of her back, her waist and buttocks. He pulled her down to the bedding and removed his own breechclout and laid his aroused body against hers.

Life among farm animals had taught her much about the physical act, but it had not prepared her for her body's response to Caxna's deft lovemaking. Her mother had never left her in doubt there would be pain, but it was short lived and lost among the rush of desire, stifled cries and subsequent bliss. His lingering kiss when all was over left her joyful, and in some ways, content.

'Thank you,' she said. 'It was all I could have hoped for.'

'You have no regrets?'

She gave his cheek a quick kiss. 'None.'

He sat up and handed her the dress and *léine*.

She put a hand on his arm. 'Please, can I remain a while? Unless Midiwegi returns soon.'

'He has found his pleasure elsewhere, but still it is not safe. It is better if no one sees you leave.'

'It is not light yet.' She leaned over and kissed him. This time he allowed her to and then pulled her to rest her head against his shoulder.

'The stars are still there in the sky dancing a song. There is still much of that song left to hear,' she said.

She kissed his chest, tasting the salt, inhaling his scent, allowing all her senses to absorb every part of him, and it was soon they were singing their own song. For Aisling, the song was bittersweet and when the first hint of dawn appeared, she allowed herself a moment to cling to him before they exchanged one last kiss and she slipped out the door.

PART V

REUNION

27

She pulled the fur mantle around her shoulders against the chill air. Though there were two canoes to handle, paddling no longer provided the energy to keep her warm since Itaba and Hirrihigua had servants enough to perform this task for them. Or were they slaves? She could not be certain, since the brothers' blatant disdain for anyone below their rank gave her no clue. The fur mantle had been the parting gift of the dead woman's mother, thrust in her hands with a shrill few words in their language when she arrived with Itaba's escort at the canoes' launching area.

In truth the mother seemed a good woman and one that she might persuade herself to warm to eventually. She glanced just ahead of her, at Hirrihigua's back. It would not be the case with him, or his brother, she had no doubt of that. Nothing they could do would change the desire she felt that grew as the distance between her and Caxna increased.

She fingered the silver medallion she held in her hand, as if by that motion she might conjure him now. He'd given it to her in a stolen moment in the hall when only Chewakla's mother was present. He'd pulled her aside and pressed it in her hand when she appeared to await Itaba's escort, her bundle in her arms.

'I give this to you. So you will not forget my promise to help.'

She stared at the medallion that filled her palm, the faint workings still strong enough to show skilled craftwork. 'This holds great value, I cannot take this.'

'It holds more value than you know. It belonged to my uncle and then his uncle, and the uncle before that, back as far as time of The Three Women Going Under, and before that. But now I give it to you, so that you know I will see you soon.'

'You do not need to give me something as precious as this to show me you intend to keep your promise. No words even need to be spoken.'

'Keep this all the same and remember me as someone who holds such a trust sacred.' He touched her hair briefly and gave a wry smile. 'Oh woman of the hair of sun and powerful spirit helpers. May they keep you safe on your journey.'

The tears came again, as she knew they would come in the days ahead. This time she would fight them, hold them back, if only that she might see him more clearly and take one last kiss. She glanced over at Chewakla's mother, who stared at them with open curiosity, and made a decision. With her hand around his head she pulled him down to receive the kiss, a long and lingering one that awakened the barely sleeping desire from the night before. He allowed it for a moment only before breaking off and removing her hand, a rueful look on his face.

'They will be here for you soon,' he said. It might have been wishful thinking, or a misunderstanding of the trader language they always used, but the word, 'beloved' seemed to slip out just before he turned from her and left the hall.

She contemplated the word now as she slipped the cord that held the medallion around her neck. She thought then of her brother and how much she had seen since last she talked to Cormac. How much she had changed. She was no longer the young girl striving to be the seer her mother thought was her destiny. The visions, if they had come, were few, and what was she to do with them? She was past hoping she might save her family or her land with them. She thought then of the blood-soaked grass that she'd seen in the bowl at Chewakla's home. Did that mean something for Cormac? Was he in danger? She bit her lip, trying to fathom how she might use this piece of sight, if indeed that's what it was.

She looked over at the brothers, their faces fixed firmly ahead. Were their people the danger? Would this journey put her brother at risk? This journey would give more than enough problems to her, so who knew what would happen when they arrived at their destination. And after that? Would she be tied to this brother for life? Perhaps he would tire of her, especially when he came to realize she was not the key to great wealth or status. Then she might find a home with her new 'mother' and 'father.'

But even now it was possible she carried a child, a child they would want and think might be theirs. She smiled at that irony. Would Caxna achieve his aim and marry The Great Sun's daughter? It seemed a possibility. If it failed he might be willing to take her as his wife, providing she did manage to disentangle herself from Itaba and Hirrihigua. She permitted herself to entertain the thought for a few moments and solved the problem of his clan's dishonor by imagining Madog and the others could help. After a moment she sighed. Such thinking was too full of wishes and contained little that was probable.

There was no stop for refreshment midday; pemmican and a leather flask of water that Hirrihigua passed her provided the only refreshment. Perhaps it was because that refreshment was so brief that they halted for the night well before the sun had set, pulling over to a suitable embankment.

Once the canoes were safely stowed on the riverside, Aisling was free to observe the servants set up the camp and she began to contemplate what might happen this night. What should she do? She made her way over to the young man tending the newly lit fire and offered her help with the meal. His hair hung short and loose around his shoulders and the few tattoos he displayed on his bare chest were few and faint. At her question he gave her a quizzical look then glanced at Itaba.

'Leave it,' Itaba said. 'He does not understand you in any case.'

'Come sit over here.' Hirrihigua waved her over to his side, near his brother, who'd made himself comfortable on a small mat laid out for him.

Her heart filled with resignation, she knelt in the proffered place and arranged the hide tunic carefully over her legs. For once she was grateful for the unappealing state of the hateful garment that she'd chosen with deliberate care that morning not just for its practicality, but for its grease stains and worn areas. As it was, Hirrihigua put his hand on her and it was all she could do to refrain from slapping it away. Itaba reached across and removed Hirrihigua's hand, a move that puzzled Aisling.

'We need to settle a matter between us first,' Itaba said.

Hirrihigua gave him a puzzled look. 'I do not understand.'

Itaba spoke in their language and glanced at Aisling. Hirrihigua retorted, his tone disdainful. Itaba spoke again, his words initially full of anger. After a moment he paused, spoke a few words and nodded. There was no mistaking the triumph on Hirrihigua's face as he uttered what could only be agreement and there was no mistaking the agreement concerned her.

Itaba turned to her. 'We have decided that the best arrangement to ensure your compliance to the obligation would be for you to spend nights with Hirrihigua on the journey when he wishes it and then later, once we are back at Etowah you will return to your parents until you are wed.'

Though she'd suspected the nature of the discussion, the blunt words Itaba spoke nevertheless sent a shock through her.

She swallowed and nodded, knowing that seeming compliance would be a better ally than open resistance. An idea began to form in her mind and she gathered her courage. Would she be able to go through with it?

She barely tasted the meal that was served first to Itaba and Hirrihigua and then her. Hirrihigua's hand constantly found its way to her knee and under the tunic despite her efforts to tug it down as low as possible. Itaba watched with narrowed eyes each time his hand strayed near her and she knew that Hirrihigua's seeming eagerness was in part a tool to taunt his brother.

Finally she made an excuse to go to her bundle and there she withdrew a packet of herbs Chewakla's wife had passed to her. 'For moon time,' she'd said. Had she known? Now she took the herbs and asked the brothers if she might brew the tea.

'It is for my moon time,' she said.

Hirrihigua jumped up and backed away from her. 'You have started your moon time?'

She nodded calmly. 'Yes, just as we pulled up on the bank. I felt it as I stepped ashore.'

Hirrihigua looked down at the cup in his hand and threw it on the ground. 'Why did you not say so before? Are you trying to pollute us?'

'I do not understand. Why would you need to know?'

Itaba stood. 'Please remove yourself from this area at once. Take one of the furs and move over to the edge of the campsite and keep your distance. One of the slaves will take you a bundle of food and place it near you. Please do not touch him. From now on, until your moon time is finished in five days' time, you will see to your food yourself.'

'I am sorry, I did not know.'

Itaba gave her a skeptical look. 'Whether you knew or not, it is done now. My brother and I as well as the slaves are polluted and we will have to purify ourselves.'

'I understand, now. I will go to the edge of the campsite, as you wish.'

She gathered up her bundle, taking care not to touch anything that wasn't hers. 'May I have a fur?' she asked.

Itaba gave her a disdainful look. 'I will send something to you with one of the slaves.'

She nodded and made her way over to the far end of the campsite and arranged her belongs there. When the area was as comfortable as she could make it she rooted in her bundle for her moss pads. Under Itaba's keen eyes it was best to make an effort at realism. Rising, she moved over to the nearest large bush and put the pad in place. Somehow she must manage to put blood on it, just to be safe. She had a bit of time to contemplate that problem and time to see just how much distance they intended to maintain.

All evening, from her place of exile, she watched as the servants dig a pit and then cut striplings from nearby trees, working with expert speed and skill to create a small rounded hut over the pit, layering the structure with boughs and bark to make an almost airtight enclosure. When the structure was complete they lit a fire inside it. After a while Itaba and Hirrihigua disappeared inside and the slaves followed suit. It was well after dark by the time they emerged, naked, sweating and silent.

28

The dank odor of wet fur overcame her need to cover herself against the cool breeze so she kept the mantle low on her shoulders. A fine mist of rain hung in the air, coating the fur, her hair and forming fine droplets on the edge of her nose. The day was as miserable as she felt and she took no satisfaction from the fact that both Itaba and Hirrihigua continued to keep their distance, to the point where the two sat together in the other canoe. It was left to the slaves to endure the risk of possible pollution by paddling her canoe.

The two brothers had debated how to handle the situation the first thing that morning, with Itaba in favor of staying at the campsite for the five days of her moon cycle, while she remained in isolation in the small hut they'd built the night before. Hirrihigua was against such a delay, arguing that she posed little risk as long as she kept her distance. They had conducted the discussion in trader language and she could only guess they were keen to make her aware of her gross transgression and keep the servants in ignorance.

They had not yet spoken to her directly, as if by communicating with her they might in some way be contaminated. She was astonished at how meticulous they were about the taboo, more so than Midiwegi and especially Caxna. Or was it that Caxna no longer held any belief in the spirits and gods that governed such thinking?

Thinking of Caxna led her to wonder at the length of time he'd spent travelling across many lands, meeting different people to try and restore his clan. And the risks he'd taken. Risks both financial and physical. Was it all for his clan, or was it for a deeper need to redeem himself?

Who was she to question his motivation, though, she who put on and off obligation like a well-worn cloak? The land was gone, her father and mother, too, and there was nothing she could do about it. She needed no vision to see that truth. Her best hope to ensure that her brother remained alive was to marry Hirrihigua, a decision born of love and not from a sense of obligation or need to redeem herself. She must be content with that.

For the moment though, she would continue with the charade of her menses. She'd been lucky that she was able to burn the moss pad in the fire out of sight of the others, but she could not guarantee that she could continue to do that. She must try and snare a small animal, a rabbit perhaps, so that she could soak some pads in blood. In her wet state, though, sitting in the canoe, it was difficult to turn her mind to such problems. Later seemed a better time for working out strategies like that.

THE RAIN HAD STOPPED, leaving her hair and clothes damp and uncomfortable, so that even as she mustered a large smile before she left the campsite to go on her declared hunt for a small rabbit or wild fowl, she only wished to crawl inside her fur and dry off.

She trudged through the undergrowth, a small bow in hand, mindful of the dripping branches that threatened to whip her face and arms and almost wished she could say her menses had finished early. Four days remained and then Hirrihigua was free to take her. But she would grow used to it, surely. How would she manage that?

Her long braid caught on a bush unnoticed until it tugged her back towards its thorny prison. She bent down to unloose it, trying to untwine the fine hairs, but her eyes, blurred by tears, could not make out the means to secure her release.

'Aisling.'

She looked up at the sound of the familiar voice and winced as a thorn pricked her finger. She blinked at the image before her.

'Caxna.'

He moved toward her and picked up a section of the braid, following it where it was caught on the thorn bush. 'You are a captive then.' His tone was light, worthy of any banter that they had exchanged in the past.

'I am indeed captive. And my captor has strong defenses.' She matched his tone, but her eyes betrayed her true feelings and the tears that now came in full only emphasized the emotion they showed.

He leaned over and worked at the braid, unwrapping the fine hairs from around the thorn until finally, it was released. 'There, I have secured your freedom.'

'I am grateful to you.' She brushed the tears from her eyes and put her braid down over her shoulder so it trailed down her back.

Caxna brushed a hair from her face. 'I am sorry I did not reach you sooner. I hope the time was not too oppressive for you.'

'I managed, despite the fact Hirrihigua wanted to take me to his bed.' She grimaced.

Caxna's face darkened. 'How did you manage?'

'I told them it was my moon time.' She delivered the words

in a neutral tone but couldn't help the smile that flashed for a brief moment. 'They were none too happy, though, and went to quite a lot of trouble to purify themselves.'

'You told them that?' He chuckled. 'That is the resourceful woman I remember from Xicallanca.'

She drank in the praise, knowing she needed the strength it gave her. She had no illusions about the success of Caxna's mission, regardless of his presence. 'This gives me some time, I know.'

'Time?'

'To consider how I might grow accustomed to him.'

He lifted his hand and cupped her chin. 'And do you think you might grow accustomed to him?' His voice held an edge and it nearly undid her.

'I—I can only hope I might.'

As much as she tried, she failed to keep her voice calm and her face expressionless. Caxna wasn't fooled. He took her in his arms and she was grateful for the comfort they provided. Stroking her hair he murmured soothing words that helped to push back the tears and eventually ease her mind.

After a few moments she pulled away and wiped her eyes. 'I am sorry, the journey has been difficult and so much has happened. I think it came upon me then.'

'You have no need to be sorry. I only wish that you had not endured so much.'

She gave him a wan smile. 'You have come a good distance at great speed to have caught up with us. What news do you bring? Is there some change in The Great Sun's plan?'

She tried to push aside the tiny bit of hope that flickered inside and recalled that he had approached her without honoring the taboo the brothers would have expected. A moment later, his face told her much before he even spoke. Whatever news he had, it would not change her situation in her favor.

'I came to let you know that I spoke with Chewakla and he said there was no possibility The Great Sun would change his mind. Even so, I did approach him again, and asked him to consider a different agreement that included an offer of more goods. I am afraid he refused.'

'Nothing has changed.'

'No, nothing has changed.' His voice was low and she tried to take comfort in the trace of regret she detected.

'And what of your own plans? Has he accepted your offer?' She made every attempt to keep her tone steady and assured herself that the decision over his offer to The Great Sun would have no effect on her future.

Caxna looked away. 'He has said nothing definite yet, but he has given me hope he will. But I think his daughter might be interested in someone else and he is giving that some consideration.'

She remembered the daughter's keen interest in Chewakla's son and wondered if that might be the focus of her attention. 'Will he tell you soon?'

'I do not know. It could be soon, or after the next moon. Midiwegi is this moment meeting with him to add his own assurances and promises of trade to my own.'

She nodded, though she made her own conclusions about Midiwegi and the nature of his arguments, knowing he would put himself in the best light and Caxna in the shade.

'It must cost you much to come and tell me this.'

He took her hand, his eyes an insistent plea. 'You had to know as soon as possible what the outcome was. I discovered where your people are located and followed your trail, catching up with you just before you stopped for the evening. Later, I saw you leave the campsite and took the opportunity to meet you alone. There are steps you need to take.'

'What steps?' This time she couldn't hide the bitterness that filled her words. She sought to pull herself back, retreat into a place that would allow her to accept what she must do.

'When you reach your people you must convince them to take you and return to their ship and sail away from this land. Go back to your home or somewhere far from these people.'

'Go back?'

She had been so intent on her duty, her sense of obligation, she hadn't considered that Madog could be persuaded to leave. What had made all of them remain in such threatening conditions? She realized how much she didn't know about their situation since she'd been so maliciously tossed overboard. She looked at Caxna, saw the concern in his face and searched for something else.

'You would have us leave?'

'I can think of no other way to keep you safe and save your people.' He lifted his hand to her face. 'I promised I would do all I can to help.'

She nodded. 'Could we go to your people? I would think my brother and Madog would feel indebted to you and want to help you with your own desire to restore your clan's honor.'

Such a feeble plan. She knew it as soon as she uttered the words, but she could think of no other alternative that would keep him in her life. Would he understand that was what she sought? She looked up at him and saw the struggle on his face.

'Would that truly be a possibility? You cannot say this with certainty, as I cannot say with certainty that The Great Sun will accept my offer, but it has a stronger chance of succeeding. I have worked countless moons for this opportunity. I must see it through.'

'You must, of course,' she said. She'd heard the pain in his voice and now felt no anger, only sorrow. It was a growing tide within her, rising higher with every moment she stood next to him. 'Go now. Return to Etowah and I hope with all my heart that you have success. I will pray for it.' She lifted his hand, kissed the empty place belonging to his third finger and turned to go.

Caxna folded his fingers around her hand and pulled her back. 'Come with me now. I will keep you safe until you reach your people. My canoe is nearby.'

She sensed the impulse of his offer and would have none of it. 'But should you not return to Etowah as soon as possible? And what of Itaba and Hirrihigua? They will be very angry when they discover I am missing and they will surely pursue us.'

'They will, but my speed will be greater than theirs and we will be able to reach your people first.'

'This action will only endanger your own plans.'

'I think not. No one knows I am here and I will be able to slip away once you are safely delivered to your people.' His tone was more decisive now and he took her more firmly by the hand. 'Come now, we must not delay.'

Before she could protest they were plunging through the trees, heading towards the bank where his canoe was pulled halfway up from the water. He gave it a great shove and helped her in. She could hardly think except to be grateful she had slipped the medallion around her neck as comfort that morning, feeling it safe to wear this token during the length of the moon time taboo. The rest of her belongings, her worn woolen dress, shirt, even the beautiful gown of the purple cloth, were all left behind. None of it mattered, though, not when she thought of the hours she would spend with Caxna, the renewed possibility that something might happen to make it all come right.

She took up the spare paddle and with fresh energy joined Caxna in paddling, feeling her strokes find the rhythm that matched his and savoring the enjoyment of the familiar motion.

THEY PADDLED through the night and she worked hard to match Caxna's unceasing efforts to create as much distance as possible between them and the inevitable pursuit. She could detect no sounds that indicated they were followed, but she knew that meant nothing. It was sometime around dawn that Caxna slowed and they stopped for a rest. She used the opportunity to relieve herself, remove the offending pad and swallow some pemmican he'd brought for the journey.

'How much further is it?

'Another day, maybe less if we press on.'

And what then, she wondered. Would she be able to persuade Madog to leave? There was so much she didn't know. She glanced at Caxna. She realized now he risked so much more than discovery by the brothers. How would Madog and the others receive Caxna? Would they be hostile? How would Madog view someone like Caxna, or her brother, after their experiences in Etowah and wherever else they might be? She resolved that no harm must come to him, no matter what happened.

At her insistence the stop was brief and they resumed their journey once more. It was only as the sun faded that she allowed the exhaustion to overtake her and she signaled to Caxna the need to stop. He nodded and they moved to the nearest bank, drew up the canoe and created a small makeshift camp.

'Just for a few hours,' she mumbled, nearly too tired to speak. She took in some food, drank deeply from the flask and lay back on the bank. Caxna drew out a fur from the canoe and put it over her. Almost before he tucked it around her, she was asleep.

She awoke suddenly and sat up. Caxna was packing up their belongings and the moon was low in the sky. She had no idea how long she'd been asleep.

'I am sorry,' she said. 'I did not mean to sleep so much.'

'It is fine. The moon has only just appeared.'

She rose and brushed herself down, conscious of Caxna's scrutiny. Her hair was tangled and filled with dried sweat and the hide tunic had gathered more stains in the past few days. Hardly a becoming picture. Her vanity disappeared when she glanced at him and saw the naked desire flicker in his eyes, but then it was gone, hidden underneath a careful expression. She resisted the urge to go to him, kiss him full on the lips and once more beg him to take her. That was the past. She must think now of what lay ahead.

The journey resumed in much the same pattern as it had begun, silent except for the frequent splash of the synchronized paddle strokes that moved them closer and closer to reunion with her brother and to Madog.

29

———————

The roar of the nearby falls made conversation impossible, but even so, she could hardly have been able to speak. They had come back almost to the point at the river fork where many days before she had made her choice to remain with Caxna. This time Caxna took the other river fork, travelling the way she would have gone if she had chosen to ask that village leader to escort her there. All the possibilities crowded in on her, so that she didn't actually see the stone walls that rose up on the rock bluffs high above them until Caxna tapped her shoulder and pointed.

Even at the extreme height above the trees on the plateau overlooking the river, the stone walls seemed out of place, strange and awkward in this region of the land that had no buildings fashioned in such a manner. The shape and nature of the buildings were familiar to her, though, seen in her land and in Madog's home.

She stared at the edifice, wondered that they could have missed it, that no one had mentioned its construction and all the other hows and whys that came to her. Caxna shouted to her and she turned to him. He indicated that they would need to retreat, go down the main river a distance until they could find a place to draw up the canoe and then walk to their destination. She nodded and followed his direction, once again paddling with the current.

When they did stop she was calmer, and the sense of near despair at the path her life had taken was balanced against the hopeful possibilities a reunion with her brother and Madog might create. They stowed the canoe safely, wedged in amongst some small trees. Caxna took the precaution of covering it with dead leaves and some small branches he cut.

He led her up along the rocky cliff, squeezing through narrow passages and ascending the slippery facades at a brisk enough pace, his sense of direction seemingly unerring. Sometimes he held her hand to assist her through tricky passages, or helped her through difficult sections as they climbed the steeply curving embankment. Neither spoke a word. Aisling valued the silence that allowed her time to gather her thoughts and decide how she might convince Madog and the others of the danger of their situation. For it struck her now that Caxna had deliberately placed her at a point where she would not be able to do anything but leave with her people. They were all in danger from The Great Sun's anger and most assuredly Itaba and Hirrihigua's anger. Perhaps there was still a chance she might persuade Caxna to come with them, show them another place they might settle, convince him that he must finally live a life that wasn't imprisoned by an obligation that overruled all. An obligation that reminded him of his loss of faith in himself.

She heard the sounds of hammering and chiseling before she could see anything. They had found a path that led in the direction of the noise. Caxna halted a moment later and held a hand up.

'Stay here. I will go and see what is happening, first.'

'No, it is fine, I am certain. I know what it is.'

He looked at her intently for a moment and then nodded.

They continued on the path, Caxna still in the lead with Aisling following close behind. Now that the reunion she had looked for so long was close at hand, she felt a flutter in her stomach. She looked down at her moccasins and hide tunic and wondered what they would make of her. She'd tidied her hair into one long braid, secured at the end with a small length of rawhide, but that didn't disguise the dirt and sweat that clung to her scalp and kept her scratching her head periodically. Hardly the impression she wanted to make, but she had no choice in the matter.

The path flattened out into a very large clearing. Just ahead men labored over a deep trench. Beyond them others worked at building a defensive wall of stone and mortar. Even to Aisling's eyes, it seemed impressive.

A familiar figure near the trench caught her eye. 'Cormac!'

The figure looked up and stared at her for one long moment before he began to move in her direction, his face lit with joy. 'Aisling!'

She ran to him, threw herself in his arms and hugged and kissed him, the wonder of finding him safe overtaking everything else. She murmured the old endearments, the words spilling out of her in Irish.

'I thought you dead,' he said when she finally released him. He smiled at her.

'Well, you can see, Brother, that I am not. But I thought the same fate had befallen you.' She pulled back and allowed herself to examine him and saw the growth of beard, the longer hair. All the traces of childhood were gone from his flesh and even his eyes. Hardened muscles were evident under his worn tunic and the youthful innocence she remembered in those bluest of eyes had disappeared.

His face darkened a moment. 'Did you encounter a guard as you approached here?

She glanced at Caxna and shook her head. 'No, we saw no guard.'

He frowned and shouted across at one of the men. 'Cynan, go check on Owain.' The man dropped his pick and went off in the direction she and Caxna had just come. The situation resolved, Cormac turned to her once again.

'You are well?' he asked. He lifted her braid and touched her tunic. 'It would seem you have your own tale to tell.' He raised his brow in question and though she heard the hint of mockery in his voice and the cynicism in his look, she refused to acknowledge it.

'I am well. As you say, I have a tale to tell.' She gave him a bright smile and turned to Caxna, who stood a small distance away. 'I would have you meet Caxna, who is a large part of the tale and the reason I am able to be here now to share it.' She spoke these words in Irish and motioned Caxna to come forward.

Caxna moved toward them and nodded to Cormac.

'I am indebted to you, Caxna, if you have indeed done half of what my sister says.'

Aisling relayed his words to Caxna, explaining that he was her brother. 'Tell him there is no debt. You have more than paid any debts that might have been owed,' Caxna replied.

Cormac glanced at Aisling and to her consternation she flushed. 'There is no need to translate,' he said in trader language. 'I am able to understand.' He turned to Caxna. 'I am glad to hear there is no debt, though I would still thank you for escorting her here.'

Aisling looked around her at the men who stood nearby and was surprised to see a few native faces among the familiar ones. She saw no sign of Madog, or Rhodri for that matter.

'Is Madog well?' she asked Cormac in Irish.

'He is. I'll take you to him. He's in the keep.'

'The keep?'

'Well, we call it that, but it's really a small stone building.'

She looked beyond him, past the deep trench and half built

stone wall and across the open grass to the building he indicated and could see the justification for the description. The keep was rectangular, with stone walls barely more than a man's height and a steeply pitched roof thatched with tightly stacked grass and boughs. The windows were narrow, barely wide enough to let light in. Again she was struck by how out of place it seemed here, though she had no doubt it was a good defensive structure.

Cormac led her forward and she grabbed Caxna's hand, all at once needing the comfort of it as they passed the men who paused to regard her with curious expressions. Only a few raised their hand or called out a greeting and to those few she gave a smile or a shy nod. In the light of such an uncertain reception from them and the nearly guarded one of her brother, she had no idea what to expect from Madog.

They entered the keep and she blinked her eyes against the sudden dark, trying to make out the figures within. The room was just large enough to fit the twenty men from the ship at the rude table that stood in its center. A door at back indicated another room beyond. Near it, looking out another window at the rear, stood Madog, alone. From the feeble light that poured in through the narrow opening, she could see that he'd aged. The grey that streaked his once black hair and his drawn face told her much. What story did her appearance tell?

She moved toward him. 'Madog.'

He turned, his face questioning. 'Who are you?'

She reached the window and let the full extent of its light fall upon her.

'Aisling!'

He moved to her and took her face into his hands. 'Is it really you? We thought you'd been lost to the storm.' He spoke in Welsh initially, but switched to Irish.

'Yes, it's me, not a ghost.' She gave a wan smile.

He dropped his hands and searched her face. 'You have no idea how much joy this brings me, how much this restores my hope that all will come to good. I have long prayed for a sign, something that would sustain me to help the others.'

She was overwhelmed by his response that told her much and expected much, and through it all she was conscious of Caxna's presence at the door beside Cormac. What could she say?

Madog regarded her carefully now, taking in her ragged state, his face darkening slightly. 'You are sound and whole?' he asked.

'I am,' she said. The simple response was sufficient for the moment. She would save the fuller story for a later time.

He fingered her tunic. 'You have been among these natives for a good while?'

'I have.' She moved back over to Caxna and pulled him forward, avoiding his wary and speculative looks. 'I have this man to thank for my safe return,' she said.

Madog eyes narrowed and he glanced at Caxna. 'A native?'

'Caxna is a noble man of the Tlingit people who live far to the north and west of here. He has helped me over these many months as I tried to find you.'

He gave Caxna a curt nod. 'Did he? That was very good of him. I think I have a trinket or two left that we might give him in thanks.' He nodded and smiled again.

'A trinket? Caxna is not a man you give a "trinket" to.' Her voice was patient and calm. She wanted him to understand. 'His service to me was beyond any mere payment. He saved me many times and helped me in so many ways, at great personal cost. Later I will explain it in full and I'm sure you'll understand.'

'I'm sure I'll see it more clearly after that.' He lifted her tunic again, the distaste evident. 'In the meantime I know you will want to refresh yourself and don some more comfortable clothes. Cormac has your things here in a chest.'

'Thank you. I know Caxna would appreciate the opportunity, too.'

She translated briefly to Caxna what she'd just said and he nodded agreement.

'You speak his language?'

'I speak the trader language, the language in common use among those who travel among different peoples.'

He gave a tired sigh. 'Yes, I did learn a few words of that language and a bit of the others, but have failed to go much beyond that. Cormac seems to be adept at it, though.'

Cormac moved towards them. 'If I had only known as much of the language last summer as I do now,' he said in a bitter tone.

'I am not certain it would have made a difference,' Madog said.

'It might have. And we wouldn't be here, exiled and forced to fend for ourselves.'

'It is done,' said Madog, his tone firm. 'Now why don't you show Aisling and the native where to refresh themselves?' He turned to Aisling. 'We will speak in full later.'

'HE IS YOUR LEADER?'

They were alone. Cormac had led them through several rooms to a small one that contained the chest and then went in search of someone to bring water and food. He'd told Caxna he would unearth some garments for him when he returned and show him a path to the river where he might bathe.

Aisling nodded to Caxna. 'He is a nobleman. Cormac was living in his brother's household and when my mother died, I left my people to bring Cormac home.'

'That man is not one of your people?'

'No, among all these men here, only Cormac is one of my people, as I mentioned before. My land is across the sea from Madog's land.'

'Were you to wed him?'

'What? No.' Her response was emphatic and a part of her

laughed at the woman that might have thought of such a match. That woman seemed alien to her now.

'I think you might wed him. He would like to protect you. I am certain you will have no trouble convincing him to take all of you back to the large canoe and leave.'

'You are wrong. Madog feels an obligation to protect me, but only as he does all others under his care. I am not sure I will be able to convince him to leave, but I will try.'

'You must.'

She looked at him, standing there in the half-light, his eyes dark with worry. 'I know that we are in danger from Etowah and that at this very minute Hirrihigua and Itaba could be making their way there to recruit men to come and destroy us all, but there are other possibilities, too.'

'This is the most likely possibility.'

'Then come with us. Please.' She moved next to him her arms at his shoulders. 'I know how much you risk being here and how little the chances are that it will not become known that you assisted me.'

He looked down at her, the pain, frustration and something more revealed in his eyes. She lifted her hands and drew him down to her, kissing him full and deeply, leaving him in no doubt that her feelings were engaged anywhere else. For a moment he surrendered to her, pulled her into an embrace and allowed her to press against him. But it was a moment only and then he pulled away.

'I cannot. As much as I might want to, you know I cannot.'

'But why? You cannot continue to live a life in order only to fill an impossible obligation.'

'Impossible it may be, but I must at least attempt it.'

'You have done more than anyone would. Can you not see that?' She saw the pain in his eyes and her heart went out to him.

'I have not done enough, not yet.'

'Please, Caxna. Please come with me.' Tears choked her words but still she continued. 'I need you, do you not see that? Have I not shown you how much you mean to me? I love you.'

'You must not say that. You have your people. They will give you all the care you need, now.'

'I do not want that. I want you, by my side.' Her voice, hoarse with emotion, was barely a whisper. 'Can we go away, just the two of us?'

A pained look crossed his face. 'No, it is better that you remain in the safety of your people. That is best for you.' He moved to the chest. 'Your things are in here, ready for you. I will be gone as soon as I have some food and water. Before long, you will forget me.'

'No. I will not.'

Cormac entered, cutting off the conversation. Two native women followed him, carrying bowls.

'If you wish for more food, the women will get it for you.'

'You have native women living here?'

Cormac shrugged. 'Not just women. We offer all of them protection from other bands who threaten them. Some of our men enjoy the women's company.'

She looked at the two women who offered them the food. Dressed in plain hide tunics and their dark hair hanging loose about their shoulders, they were both comely. One had a rounded belly, visible evidence of someone's enjoyment. The woman bore no trace of being forced, she seemed well fed and there was nothing cowed about her demeanor. A common enough situation among any fortified holding where warriors must be idle for lengths of time. Had Cormac taken his pleasure with any of them? He was clearly a man now, in every other way, so she could only assume that he was a man in this way, too.

'Madog would like to talk to you in more depth, when you've eaten,' Cormac said. 'I do as well.' He smiled, an action that almost reached his eyes.

She took his hand. 'I would hear your tale, too.'

He patted her shoulder. 'You shall.'

The question that lurked in the back of her mind suddenly formed into words that she nearly spoke, but managed to change at the last moment. 'Have you suffered any losses among the group since I saw you last?'

'There are eighteen of us now. Two succumbed to fever, one drowned.'

'I'm sorry to hear that. Were any of them close kin to Madog?'

'They are all kin to Madog. He took it hard.' He glanced at Caxna. 'What of Caxna? Will he be remaining with us?'

She looked at Caxna, his eyes full of question at the mention of his name. She realized she'd spoken in Irish and now she switched to the language he understood.

'Caxna says he must go, but I am hoping that Madog will persuade him to remain once he hears our tale.'

Cormac nodded. 'I must go now and check on the work progress. I'll return shortly and wait with Madog.' He gave her hand a reassuring squeeze, nodded to Caxna and left.

Caxna took a second bowl of food one of the women offered and drank deep from the cup by his side. 'I will be gone from here before you relay your tale.'

'Please stay with me while I tell it. They might have questions for me that I cannot answer. It will not take much longer.' She tried to keep her voice calm, knowing that any bit of emotional display would only make his resolve stronger. After a few moments' consideration, he nodded.

'I will stay while you relay all that has happened. But I will leave as soon as the discussion is finished.'

'Thank you,' she said. She could only hope in that time she would think of something that would change his mind.

30

She saw Rhodri first, standing by Madog, who seemed not to have stirred from his place by the window. Rhodri's stance, still arrogant, had an added air of authority as he leaned slightly towards Madog and spoke to him in a low voice. He looked up when he saw her enter and his eyes darkened. There had been little change there.

She fiddled with her braid, trying to find calm. As Madog had promised, she'd found her other dress and *léine* in the chest and had slipped them on after a brief wash of her face and hands, offering Caxna the same opportunity. He'd refused the offer of clothes, giving her an odd look, but sluiced his face while she turned her back and put on her shirt and gown.

The moccasins had remained and she wondered what Madog made of her attire now as she greeted him, Cormac and then Rhodri. A few of the other men had joined them, too, and Madog motioned for everyone to be seated at the table. Benches scraped across the hard earthen floor. Aisling took the place next to her brother and indicated for Caxna to sit on her other side, at the end. He followed her direction, and once beside her, she allowed herself the small pleasure of that comfort.

Madog sat at the head. She noted his distant manner, the careful way he eyed her as if she might be tainted. He spoke coolly. 'Take your time, but you must tell us in full what has befallen you since you were lost from the ship.'

She couldn't resist a glance at Rhodri. Where to begin the tale? Should she mention how she ended up in the ocean, left to drown? She gathered her thoughts and decided there was too much she didn't know, too much to uncover about their own event since she'd seen them last.

'I was fortunate that the storm washed me ashore, somewhere near where the ship is now at anchor. Caxna and a woman named Pakahle rescued me and nursed me back to health.' She told them of Caxna's background, his talent as a merchant and the wealth he'd accumulated over the years visiting distant places, experiences that led her to ask him to take her on his journey in the hope she might find them.

'The storm blew us further south, but then we retraced our steps. You must have just missed us,' Cormac said.

She looked at him and nodded. 'I realize that now.'

'But that was nearly a year ago. How far did you travel, how many places did you visit?' asked Madog.

She looked at Caxna, aware that he'd been studying her carefully since she began the explanation, as if by close scrutiny of her words he might make some sense of them. On impulse she told him briefly what had been said until now. He nodded, his face neutral.

'You never told me how it was you came to be in the water, when I found you washed up on the shore,' he said in a quiet voice.

'It is complicated,' she said, glancing at Rhodri. Had he understood the exchange? She had no idea how much Madog understood or how many beside Cormac spoke the language.

Caxna nodded and made no further comment, his face thoughtful.

'I was just explaining to Caxna what we've been discussing.' She took a breath. 'We left Pakahle and journeyed along the shore for many many days, stopping only to rest for the night.'

'Was it just the two of you?' asked Cormac. 'In a canoe?'

'Yes, we traveled in a canoe. Caxna taught me to paddle. He was on his own, with only a small amount of goods so that he could cover the distance—'

Madog cut across her. 'How long did you two travel alone?'

She cursed the betraying flush that she knew was spreading across her face. 'We were alone for only a short time. Then another trader and his slaves joined us.'

'All men? No noblewomen or even one humbly born?'

She straightened, sensing the rising hostility from Madog and even Cormac.

'Caxna behaved honorably. And no one else troubled me.' There was no need for them to know anything more.

'What is it? What are they saying?' asked Caxna, his voice tense.

'Nothing,' she said. 'There is no cause for concern.'

'Have you dishonored my sister?' Cormac asked.

Caxna frowned. 'Do they say I have dishonored her?'

'You have done nothing and I told them so,' she said.

'Is this true, Tlingit?' Cormac demanded.

She'd had enough. 'Why are you questioning him?' she said in Irish. 'You question my honor and his when I've heard there are those among you who dishonored a woman in Etowah.'

'How do you know what happened in Etowah?' asked Rhodri.

'We've just come from there. I'd heard that you were seen there and so I accompanied Caxna and the other trader. I found out what happened when I arrived and met with The Great Sun to see if I could find a way to make amends.'

'Etowah? You've been to Etowah?' asked Madog. 'How did

you leave things there? Are they still demanding that ridiculous tribute?'

She flushed deeply and reached for Caxna's hand under the table.

'You met with their leader, this "Great Sun?"' asked Madog.

She bit her lip. Caxna saw her distress and squeezed her hand. She took some reassurance from the gesture. 'I tried to explain to The Great Sun that you didn't mean to offend him or his people in any way. That it was a mistake born of ignorance.'

Cormac gave Rhodri a dark look. 'And what did he say?' he asked.

'He was not persuaded.'

Caxna tugged her hand. 'Have you explained about the agreement with The Great Sun and Hirrihigua?'

'What agreement?' Cormac demanded in the trader language.

Caxna leaned over and looked at Cormac. 'She agreed to replace the woman who killed herself and marry Hirrihigua, a noble of Etowah.'

Cormac translated the information to Madog, the fury evident in his voice.

'Why did you do this?' asked Madog. 'Why give yourself to a native, a creature that has no understanding of our niceties?'

She glared at Rhodri. 'Niceties? What niceties did he possess when he violated that woman?' The word came out as bitter as it tasted on her tongue. She took a deep breath. It would do no good to give in to her anger. 'I was drawn into the agreement when I was trying to persuade The Great Sun to release you from your tribute. A tribute that I understood was impossible to meet.'

'We have no need to meet anyone's tribute,' said Madog.

'That isn't true. Don't you understand how much authority The Great Sun has? He is all-powerful, he carries more sway than the High King of Ireland or the King of Gwynedd and can command a force that would easily overpower all of you.'

'We have made a great defensive fort here,' said Cormac.

'It is not enough,' said Aisling.

'Tell your leader that you must leave as soon as possible,' Caxna told her. It will not be long before Hirrihigua is here.'

'Why?' asked Cormac. 'Why must we leave now? Is she still bound to Hirrihigua?'

'She is. I took her from him and his brother two days ago. They were on their way here to meet you and tell you of the agreement.'

'You rescued her? Why?' asked Cormac.

Caxna glanced at Aisling, who closed her eyes, waiting to hear the words. 'I thought she would be safer back with you. But you must leave immediately. You do not have much time before the full wrath of The Great Sun will descend.'

'Is there anything we can do to alter this?' Cormac asked.

'No.'

'Yes, there is,' Aisling said in a firm voice. 'I could go back to Hirrihigua.'

'No,' said Caxna.

'No,' said Cormac. 'I won't let you, my sister, make such a sacrifice. I'm sure the others will agree.'

He turned to Madog and translated the conversation into Welsh.

'Of course not. I would never let a woman keep such an agreement,' said Madog when Cormac had finished. There was no comment from the other men, except Rhodri.

'They exaggerate, both of them,' said Rhodri. 'I'm sure it's not as bad as they say. Why don't we send someone to The Great Sun and explain the situation? Surely he would make Hirrihigua behave and we can remain here. Set up our own trade links. Maybe even this boyo here—Caxna? Maybe he could help.'

'No,' said Madog, his face filled with anger and bitterness.

'We mustn't allow them any more opportunities to cause us more damage. I've had enough of it, their double tongues, the strange food, the oppressive heat and cursed biting bugs in summer. Enough, I say! It's time to return home.'

'Return?' said Rhodri in disbelief. 'There are riches to be made here, Madog, if only you would give it a chance. It's too soon to leave, we've only just begun to explore the treasures this land holds.'

'You have done a fine job exploring women, already,' Cormac said. 'While I feel there is much that could be done here, and in other circumstances I wouldn't be anxious to leave, I have to agree with Madog.'

Rhodri looked at the two men beside him and spoke in Welsh, clearly asking their views.

The two men shifted uncomfortably. The one with the ruddier face spoke for a few moments.

'See?' said Rhodri. 'He wants to stay. He's not ready to give up the comfort of his Appalache woman that's been warming his bed. We can find some solution to this.'

'No,' said Madog. 'It's decided. We'll leave as soon as possible.' He stood. 'Despite what you've been through, you belong here with us.'

Aisling looked up at him, her hand still clutching Caxna's. 'Can we take Caxna with us? He has knowledge of these waters and he could assist our escape from here.'

Madog gave Caxna a brief glance and shrugged. 'You may be right. He can at least guide us to our ship. We'll see after that. There might be a use for him on board.'

A man entered the room in a rush and spoke in rapid Welsh. Aisling saw the looks of concern. 'What is it? What did he say?'

'A native man approaches. He is nearing the last rock passage and the guard wants to know if he should let him pass,' said Cormac.

Aisling gave Caxna a fearful glance and translated the words for him. 'Hirrihigua?' she asked.

'Ask what he looks like,' Caxna told her.

'Is the man tall or short? Well-muscled, or thin?' Cormac asked the messenger.

After the man had spoken, Cormac gave the description to Caxna. 'He is short, not particularly well muscled. He carries no bow, wears his hair in a simple topknot. And his forehead is flattened.'

'Midiwegi?' Aisling said to Caxna. What was he doing here?

Caxna frowned. 'Yes.' He looked at Cormac. 'It is fine. He is a friend, the trader who accompanied me to Etowah.'

Cormac nodded and gave the order to allow Midiwegi to pass through unharmed.

By the time Midiwegi reached them and entered the room smiling and seemingly at ease, Madog was seated and fully apprised of the approaching visitor. After requesting some food and drink, he indicated Midiwegi take a seat at the end of the table opposite him. Aisling watched him as he carefully arranged himself on the bench, shifting his weight from the bench edge to the middle, clearly finding its uneven surface uncomfortable against his breechclout. The dark circles under his eyes told her what she suspected. He had not paddled leisurely here, but had spent day and night in the canoe. Had he encountered Hirrihigua and Itaba?

He nodded to Caxna. 'I have come, Brother, to save you from yourself.'

Caxna narrowed his eyes. 'I assure you, I have no need of saving.'

Midiwegi gestured toward Aisling. 'You cannot see what you have done?' His voice was mild, but there was an edge to it. 'By taking her from the brothers you have endangered yourself and the goal you have worked so long to achieve.'

'I understand the situation. There was no need for you to come.' He narrowed his eyes. 'How is it you knew I was here?'

'When I found you had left I had no doubt where you were heading. I followed on as fast as I could, in the hope I could convince you to return before any real harm had been done.' He leaned toward Caxna. 'We are nearly there. The Great Sun has all but agreed to the trade we have proposed. And your marriage.'

'You have met with him?'

'No, but Chewakla has, and he tells me that The Great Sun is in favor of such trade links.'

'What does he say?' Madog asked Cormac. He'd been following the exchange between the two men with intense concentration, glancing only briefly at Aisling when Midiwegi had mentioned the word 'marriage.'

Cormac translated the gist of the conversation, but there was no mention of the marriage contract, leaving Aisling to wonder if he had understood all that had transpired. There was one detail that Midiwegi still hadn't addressed.

'How did you know that Caxna was here with me?'

Midiwegi turned to her, his eyes telling her nothing. 'I had no certain knowledge. I just assumed that he would go where you were. Chewakla told me where your people were located.'

She studied him a few moments longer, but could discern nothing more and had to accept that his words were truth. 'Did you encounter Itaba and Hirrihigua at all?'

He shook his head. 'I passed them a good while ago when they rested. I took care to disguise my canoe with branches and leaves and floated by. Thankfully the river is high and the current strong this time of year, so that most sounds go undetected.'

'And you are alone?' Caxna asked.

Midiwegi nodded. 'Chewakla gave me the loan of a small canoe so that I could make good speed.' He held out his hands, his eyes full of innocence. 'What are all these questions? I wanted only to convince you to return with me. Now I ask that you bring her back, give her to Hirrihigua, while things can still be repaired.'

'No,' said Cormac. 'She will not return with either of you. Aisling stays here, with us, where she belongs.'

Midiwegi regarded Cormac with baleful eyes. 'How does this concern you?'

'She is my sister, and I say she remains here with us.'

Midiwegi gave a slight nod. 'I see. But your sister has made an agreement with The Great Sun and she must honor it. To do otherwise invites harsh consequences, probably death for her and all of you.' He looked around.

'Can we change the agreement? Offer something else?' asked Cormac. He turned to Madog and explained Midiwegi's words.

'Ask if we can offer some of our cooking tools, farm tools, or even one of our swords. They don't seem to have anything like that here.'

Cormac added Madog's question to his own but Midiwegi shook his head. 'You have no other woman with you so there is nothing you could offer that would change his mind.'

Cormac explained Midiwegi's answer. 'Then we must leave as soon as we can make ready,' said Madog.

'Where will we go?' Rhodri asked.

'Back home, to Gwynedd,' said Madog. 'The succession is bound to be settled by now and we can live there in peace again.'

'But there might be riches here, at another place.' Rhodri looked at Aisling. 'That place you described, Xicallanca? We could go there. That sounds like a place that would offer many opportunities for wealth.'

Aisling paled, remembering their hasty exit. 'I don't think it would be a good place, but Caxna might know of others.'

'Ask him,' said Rhodri.

'No,' said Madog. 'We return home, it's the safest course of action. There's no danger they would pursue us there, but we have no guarantee they wouldn't be able to do so if we remain anywhere in this Godforsaken land.'

Madog rose. 'We have much to do. Rhodri, see to it that all the men understand the situation. Cormac, can you tell the natives and organize the packing?' He nodded to Cormac. 'And see that the two native men have a place for the night and enough provisions for their return journey.'

'I will,' said Cormac. He turned to Midiwegi and Caxna. 'You may stay in one of the rooms here. I am afraid that we have only the floor to offer you, but I can provide you with some extra furs.'

'We will not stay the night,' said Caxna. 'As soon as Midiwegi is ready, we will be on our way.'

'Let me at least get you some provisions for your journey,' said Cormac. 'It is the least we can do.'

'We can surely have time for such a generous offer,' Midiwegi said.

'Of course,' Caxna said in a reluctant tone.

Aisling watched the full exchange, searching for some thread of possibility, some hope she might seize and use to convince Caxna to remain with them. Would he consider a journey to a new land, to Gwynedd or Ireland? What would these lands offer him? She had only moments to discover an answer.

31

———

S he stood beside him, in the near darkness of the early evening. There were no stars yet, just a heavy dusk that gave her a reassuring cover for her emotions. She leaned upon the stone wall, the cold of its northern exposure seeping into her after only a few moments. That she'd managed to persuade him to come here, away from the eyes of everyone so that she could bid him farewell gave her a small amount of hope.

Underneath her woolen dress and *léine* she could feel the medallion against her breasts, the promise it spoke of as cold as it felt there now.

'Madog has told me to give you his thanks for bringing me safely here and asks if there is anything you want. He would have you come with us, if you wish it.'

He gave her a grim smile. 'Tell him I regret that I cannot. I must return to Etowah.'

'What is there for you now in Etowah?'

'There is my clan obligation.'

'Still? You have hope that The Great Sun will give you what you ask?'

'Midiwegi has said nothing that made me think any differ-ent. The Great Sun has no idea that it was I who took you from Itaba and Hirrihigua. If I can return now, there should be no reason for it to be otherwise, and in the meantime you will be safely gone from here.'

'Who is to say Midiwegi speaks the truth? What is to say that Itaba and Hirrihigua did not return immediately to Etowah and they are not now on their way with canoes full of warriors? You would encounter them on your return.'

'But they would not know of my involvement, and you will be gone before they reach here. Your brother knows the danger. As does your leader, I think.' He finally turned to her, took her hand. 'You belong with them. And I belong here. Your brother and Madog know this.'

'No. No they have not said that at all. They would have you come if you wish it. We could be together then.' She failed to keep the pleading tone out of her voice and clutched his hand tight, trying to convey her need in every way possible.

He put a finger to her lips. 'I would choose this if I could. If everything was different.'

He leaned down and kissed her. She took in his kiss, locking him into an embrace and poured all her desire into her mouth, her hands and the body she held against his. For a moment he consented to it, drew her in closer, ran his hand along her back, but it was a moment only that left no time for even a flicker of hope and joy to rise inside her. He pulled away.

'It is easier for our parting if we do not follow this course.'

She moved to his side and took his hand and kissed it. 'I cannot help my feelings. I cannot bear the thought that this will be the last time we are together.'

'We must bear it. We have no choice.'

'You have a choice, but you will not see.' Her voice was choked, but she no longer cared. What did it matter that he saw her distress? He would be gone soon and it seemed nothing would convince him. She reached inside her tunic, withdrew the medallion and removed it from around her neck.

'I will return this to you now. There is no need for it to remain in my keeping. You have fulfilled your promise to me. Now you can complete your obligation to your clan.'

Caxna looked down at the medallion in her hand and folded her fingers over it. 'No, I would have you keep it.' He took her face in his hands, leaned down and kissed her, full and deep. 'I give you my most precious thing and my heart. Know that you have both in your possession, even though my body is not present.'

He turned then and left her there to fall back against the wall, feeling all the coldness seep into her once again.

SHE HAD no idea how long she'd been there. The passing time meant nothing to her any more. That her dress and shirt grew damp as a light rain began to fall seemed not to matter; she was aware of nothing but the emptiness she felt.

A hand pressed against her mouth and another seized her arm and shoved her forward. 'Don't make a sound.'

She recognized Rhodri's voice and started to struggle, but that only made him grip her harder, and when she opened her mouth to bite his hand he thrust a rag inside it. He quickly tied her hands behind her and pushed her forward again, shoving her to the side of the keep, ducking quietly past the guard and creeping to the trench. He dragged her down inside it and pulled her along its bottom while she tried not to stumble over the piles of dirt and broken rubble thrown there.

They reached the far end at the edge of the tree line and pushed her up to the top and along into the trees. She stumbled, losing her footing on the path slick with the rain that fell steadily now. He righted her with a sharp jerk on her arm.

Her mind whirled with questions and she struggled to

answer them. He would solve nothing with her death, he must know that. Had he a mind to take her to Etowah himself? To search for Itaba and Hirrihigua? It seemed too farfetched, but she could sense the desperation in him and knew it was possible he had no mind to be sensible. If only he would release her, let her speak, she would tell him that she would willingly go to Hirrihigua, leave them free to stay and make a life here or return to Gwynedd. Remaining behind was the only chance she had that she might see Caxna again, if only that they might both still live in Etowah. There would be some hope then they might one day be together.

Rhodri pushed her towards the first rock passage and a figure loomed out from behind it and moved towards them. There was little light from above, the stars hidden under a cloak of thickened cloud and heavy rain. It wasn't until the figure was nearly upon them that she recognized Midiwegi's shape. She drew in her breath sharply and choked for a moment on the rag that gagged her mouth.

'Here is the woman,' Rhodri said, his words slow and simple in the trader language.

'Good, you have her bound and gagged,' Midiwegi replied.

Rhodri released her and Midiwegi gripped her other arm firmly. 'We will part here. I will see to it that she is returned to the brothers.'

'You give your word?' Rhodri asked. 'We will have no more trouble from Etowah?'

'You will have no more trouble from Etowah.'

Satisfied, Rhodri nodded. 'Good. If I hear that it is not true, I will come and kill you.'

Aisling heard a shout from behind. She turned and saw Caxna running towards them.

'Release her, now!' he said. Moments later he was upon them, pulling her from Midiwegi's grasp and shoving her behind him.

Rhodri drew a knife from his side and moved toward Caxna. 'Hand her back or you will have me to deal with,' he said.

'No,' Caxna said. He moved tentatively to Rhodri, circling him with caution.

Rhodri lunged at him and Caxna moved aside and so they began a slow dance, Rhodri with his knife seeking Caxna's flesh and Caxna circling in and then out with each of Rhodri's attempts to wound, as he tried to disarm him. The rain had stopped and a feeble moon cast some light on the scene. Aisling watched in helpless frustration and fear, her arms still tightly bound, her mouth full of the rag that made all but the most muted of sounds possible. Midiwegi moved to grab her arm again and she wrested herself away, resisting his grasp until she stumbled and fell.

Caxna used the distraction to grab Rhodri's hand and the two struggled, a will of strength, each fighting to gain the upper hand. Rhodri slipped, lost his footing in the sodden grass and the two tumbled to the ground, Caxna's hand still fixed around Rhodri's. Rhodri strived to free it, the knife still clutched in his hand, and Caxna pulled it down. The pair continued to fight for control, rolling and tossing.

Midiwegi picked Aisling up and slapped her, jarring loose the rag from her mouth. She shoved all her weight on him, straining to release her bonds. They fell against each other and she pushed her knee in his groin. He released her immediately, groaning at the pain. She turned and saw Rhodri roll on top of Caxna, who'd finally grabbed the knife from Rhodri. Caxna plunged the knife in deep in his lower chest and pushed upward, hitting home. Rhodri grunted and collapsed on Caxna.

It took only a moment, a moment that would play in her mind for the rest of her days. Midiwegi swept past her, another knife in his hands while Caxna fought to disentangle himself from Rhodri. The knife aimed for Caxna's throat, but Caxna managed to knock his hand a little, blunting the blow.

'No!' she screamed. She staggered to his side, her hands still bound and helpless. The blood poured from his neck onto the wet ground, spreading out on the grass, coating it red. Rhodri's dead body lay still on top of him, pinning him down. She saw the flicker of life in his eyes. 'No! You cannot die. You have your obligation to the clan. You have to live.'

Midiwegi pulled her away. 'We must go. Itaba and Hirrihigua await us.'

She struggled against him, twisting to see Caxna, but he gripped her harder and pushed her forward, down through the rock passage. There she saw a guard lying still, his throat cut. She stumbled and he grabbed her arm again, pulling her down the rock face to descend slowly towards the river. Her mind reeled against what had just passed, denying the death of her hopes.

The two canoes were waiting in the water, just down along from where Caxna and she had stowed his. Hirrihigua stood impatient on the shore and Itaba sat in one of the canoes, the slaves around him holding their paddles in readiness.

'Good, you are here,' Hirrihigua said when they neared him. He took Aisling from Midiwegi. 'Was there any trouble from Caxna or anyone else?'

A hailstorm of arrows rained down on the canoes, some finding purchase in arms, chests and thighs. A slave slumped over and a moment later Itaba clutched his neck, an arrow embedded in his throat. Midiwegi turned in time for the second flight of arrows to strike him down. Hirrihigua dropped to the ground and crawled to a tree, dragging Aisling with him. She resisted, pulling back on his hand with all her weight, until he released her and she ran up towards the fort path. She had run near where the dead man lay when Cormac met her, a bow in his hand, ready to shoot off the next arrow. Behind him was a line of the men with their bows primed and ready.

'Have you seen Caxna? Is he alright?' She scanned the men with him.

'I don't know. I'll find out later, when this is finished. You'd best go back to the keep,' he told her after quickly releasing her bonds.

She nodded, barely giving him time to finish his words before she rushed past him, back through the line of armed men and up along the rocky path to the last passage. When she slipped through the opening to the grass slope beyond, she could see the two figures lying on the ground, a coupling that made no sense at all.

Once by their side, she knelt down and rolled Rhodri's body away from Caxna so that she might see him better. The bleeding had stopped. The rain had washed the blood from his neck, but it still pooled on the cold wet grass. She recalled her vision, for there was no doubt that's what it had been. What good was such a gift now? With a wail she lay down beside Caxna, put her hand along his waist and nestled her head into his chest. It was at that moment she heard the faint flutter of a heartbeat.

32

___

She searched the men who trickled up the side of the hill for her brother, but in the end she grabbed the first man who answered her call.

'Please,' she said in Latin, her tone desperate. 'Help me carry him inside to the keep.'

She leaned over and tried to lift Caxna and heard a soft moan. Though it caused her pain to think of his suffering, she felt reassured. He was still alive.

'I will take him,' said Cormac, who came up beside the man. He shouted to a few others and, with the four of them together taking a limb and supporting the torso, they hoisted Caxna and made their way up the hill. Despite their progress, it wasn't quick enough for Aisling. In the starlight she could see dark stains making a trail on the grass.

'Please hurry,' she said. 'He's bleeding again.'

In what seemed an interminable time, they finally arrived at the keep, where Madog was busy giving orders to the newly arrived men while behind him, others shoved belongings into small chests and sacks.

He eyed them, his brow knitted in concern. 'Are there any more casualties?' he asked Cormac.

'Can we speak of this later? We need to tend to Caxna's wounds now,' said Aisling, her tone brisk. She ushered them over to the fire and asked for a bowl of water, a cloth and a needle.

When Caxna had been safely deposited on the earthen floor by the fire, she took the time to examine him while she awaited the water. Blood trickled from the gaping wound. The cut was clean and deep enough, but as wide as she first feared. She pressed her hand to it to try and stem the flow of blood. His eyes fluttered for a moment.

Cormac handed her the bowl of water and cloth. She glanced up and saw Madog standing behind him.

'We need to quit this place as soon as possible,' he said.

'But not until I see to Caxna,' she said. She took up the cloth and began to clean the wound.

'You're not thinking of taking him with us?'

She stared at Madog, the cloth poised midair. 'You're not suggesting I leave him here, are you?'

Madog glanced down at Caxna. 'He's in no fit state to travel, not now or in the immediate future. We can't afford to wait for his recovery.'

She stiffened. 'Then you'll leave us behind and I'll stay with him until he is fit to travel.'

'I will do no such thing. I can't leave you here.'

'We have a bit more time, my lord,' said Cormac. 'The brothers are dead and so Etowah will not suspect anything is amiss for at least a fortnight.'

Madog frowned. 'That might be true, but with this man and his friend gone from Etowah, wouldn't they suspect something was amiss?'

Aisling bit her lip, knowing there was truth in his words.

'Can we delay at least for a day or so? Once I've stitched his wound, he might improve enough.'

Madog glanced at Caxna and gave her a dubious look. 'We'll wait, then.'

SHE WIPED Caxna's brow one more time, willing the fever to abate. It was the second day since he'd been wounded and she'd had high hopes for his recovery initially, until this fever had taken hold in the early hours of the morning. He still hadn't regained consciousness since he'd been wounded, and the flush that filled his face and body she'd first seen as a welcome sign, until the beads of sweat appeared on his brow. He stirred restlessly.

'Shhh,' she said to calm him. She took up the small bowl of willow bark tea and encouraged him to sip it.

Madog appeared at her side. 'We can wait no longer. It's time to go.'

She studied Caxna, willing him to open his eyes. There was nothing. She must make the decision for him. 'We'll go with you then.'

'You want to take him, knowing it might mean his death?'

'You won't allow me to stay behind, and he'll die on his own, so his best chance is to come with me.' She tried to put all her strength of will and determination in her expression while he scrutinized her.

'As you wish,' he said finally.

IN THE END she lost count of the times she questioned the wisdom of her decision as they made their way downriver. She nearly called a halt to the process when they carried Caxna's litter down the hill and rock face, each jolt causing her to wince. By the time he reached the riverbank, his color had become so grey she would have thought him dead if not for the small pulse at his throat.

They placed him carefully into one of the curraghs, strapping him across two of the seats. Aisling stepped inside and took a seat beside the litter, at his head. The fever thankfully had lessened in the hours before they departed, but she intended to ply him with sips of willow bark tea from the leather flask she had at her side.

The men plied the oars day and night, everyone determined to cover as much distance as possible, taking shifts. Aisling watched Caxna closely, noting every detail of his face and manner for any change. When the boat dipped and bumped along the rapidly flowing water she held her breath, hoping each jolt would be the last. At times she could rouse him enough for sips of tea and a little cold broth she'd brought with her, and he managed them well enough, but he still hadn't regained consciousness. She hadn't dared touch the wound since they'd left the keep and only checked to ensure the bandages hadn't become wet under the protective covering she wrapped around his neck.

It was the eighth day, when the rain had come and soaked them all thoroughly, that she noted with relief that Madog was signalling them to pull over and make camp. It was a nice wide expanse on the riverbank, large enough to hold the three curraghs. She continued to try and shield Caxna from the worst of the rain as Cormac and Owain took him from the curragh and deposited him on the bank, but it was an impossible task. The wool blanket that covered him was completely wet and the fabric covering underneath, she knew, was not much better.

'Is it possible to get a quick shelter built and a fire going?' she asked Cormac.

He looked across at her from the side of the curragh where he was helping to unload some of the packs and then glanced at Madog.

'I'm sure something can be arranged,' he said.

She removed the blanket and covering and was relieved to find that the hide leggings and tunic he wore were only slightly damp. Quickly she chafed Caxna's hands and limbs, trying to stir some warmth within him, eyeing the wan color of his skin with dismay.

Over towards the trees she saw Cormac instructing the men to cut some branches and fashion a crude shelter. He'd been increasingly kind to her and Caxna in the days since she'd arrived, as if somehow her presence had softened his attitude to the world. The poet dreamer seemed to have vanished permanently, to be replaced by someone with a hardened exterior, but there was also a compassion that she appreciated. Madog, on the other hand, seemed increasingly remote, leaving many of the decisions to Cormac. For that she was grateful.

When the shelter was finished, Cormac and Owain moved Caxna to its protection and Owain began the business of starting a fire. It was a slow process, but eventually a feeble flame erupted and with Aisling's encouragement a convincing fire took hold. She busied herself setting water to boil so that she might make a broth out of the dried pemmican she had with her. Beside her Caxna stirred.

'Do not worry, my love,' she said, breaking up the strips of pemmican into the small clay pot. 'I will soon have some hot broth for you.'

'I hope none of those herbs from Xicallanca find their way into it.'

Aisling nearly knocked over the bowl, so startled was she to hear the familiar voice. 'Caxna! You are awake.'

The joy nearly overwhelmed her. She took his hand and squeezed it. She scanned his eyes, looking for traces of fever, and saw none. 'You gave me such a scare. I thought you were gone from me forever. If only I had understood my vision in time.'

'You had a vision?' His voice was thready, but gained a little strength.

'I did. Back in Etowah, of blood-soaked grass. But I had no idea what it meant until I saw you lying severely wounded.' Her eyes clouded with tears at the memory.

'If you had understood, would you have been able to change the outcome?'

'There must have been something I could have done to prevent it.'

'How could you have foreseen Midiwegi's treachery?'

She thought over his words. 'Midiwegi's whole nature was prone to treachery. The canoe—we both know that was no accident.'

'And those things you know through observation.' He closed his eyes for a moment. 'Vision seeking is never a simple clear path where messages are given to be immediately acted upon without any doubt. It is for us to take them in, try and understand what they might mean, if it is possible. It is not always possible. And it is not always possible to change an outcome that you do understand. And when you cannot understand it immediately, or see that you cannot change things, you must not judge yourself harshly.'

She stared at him. 'Such wise words. And yet you cannot see that for yourself.'

He smiled sadly. 'I could not. Perhaps I still cannot, but you have helped me towards that direction.' He closed his eyes again and drifted off until she had the broth ready for him. He took it gratefully, this time swallowing with ease and no assistance until he finished it all. The broth seemed to restore him a little and he made an effort to raise his head, but she stilled it.

'You must remain as you are. I would not wish you to break your wound open.'

'How is my wound?' His voice was stronger this time, a fact that gave her no small pleasure.

'It is bad enough.'

'I recall Midiwegi, wielding the knife at my throat.' He paused a moment. 'He is dead?'

'Yes. And Rhodri, Hirrihigua and Itaba.'

'I see. And we are heading downriver?'

'We are going to the ship.'

'Good. There is a village at the river's mouth. Pakahle's relatives live there. You may leave me with them.'

'I will not leave you. You are coming with us. I am ordering you.'

He gave her a feeble smile. 'You are ordering me?'

'Say no more about it. You must rest now.'

He shut his eyes, too weak to make any further attempts to argue. When she was certain he was in a restful sleep, she went over to Cormac, who was sheltering with Madog and some of the others under a large tree. She saw that they had changed out their wet clothes, something she had yet to do.

'Caxna has improved. He regained consciousness a while ago and took some broth.'

Cormac smiled. 'That's very good news. He certainly is a strong man.'

'He is that,' said Madog. He was hunched down, staring at the ground.

'Caxna spent years paddling to various places to trade, which would strengthen any man,' she said. 'But he is also a man of great courage as well as strength.'

'Yes,' said Madog. 'I can see that.'

'You would do well to have such a man with you,' said Cormac.

Hearing her brother's words, Aisling felt a small leap of joy inside her. 'Caxna has been many places in this land. His knowledge would serve you well.'

'He has knowledge of the journey across the ocean?' asked Madog.

'My lord, you know that we can't immediately return to Wales. The ship needs repairs. There are also stores to gather, animals, cloth for the spare sails.' Cormac glanced at Aisling. 'We must find a place to acquire these things. Somewhere easily reached, but far enough away from the people of Etowah.'

'I'm sure Caxna could show us the way to such a place,' said Aisling. She allowed a flame of hope to gather inside her and watched Madog consider these words.

After a few moments gazing out to the water, he gave a small nod. 'Very well. Your words are full of sense. When he is well enough ask Caxna if he will remain with us for now and assist us.'

She stood on the deck of the ship watching the shoreline recede, the sloping banks, the swaying trees with buds just forming on their branches, a small flock of birds swooping and dipping in graceful unison. The colors too were noted, the deep golds and verdant greens, the clear turquoise of the water. All these details she committed to her memory, so important, critical that each one not be forgotten. There was nothing she would not remember of the place where she had first met Caxna.

'Can you see the beach?'

She knelt down beside the pallet and took Caxna's hand and kissed it. 'I can see the beach.'

He nodded and smiled. She hadn't allowed him to even sit up, too afraid that any kind of exertion might break the careful stitching at his throat or that he might faint. He was still weak. Since their brief stay on the shore, he'd had a relapse and she'd been afraid that all her determined effort had been in vain. But eventually the broth and herbal brews she'd made him sip over the many days of their river journey won out just as it came to a conclusion.

They had arrived at the bay where the ship lay anchored. She'd made no mention to anyone of the village that Caxna had told her about and watched the thatched houses pass as the rowers worked their oars for the few remaining miles. Caxna had dozed, oblivious to the houses in view, but she'd sat at his side, blocking them with her body as much possible. It was only after they'd carried Caxna on board the ship that he looked around him and realized what had happened.

But Aisling was determined that things between them would be different now they were safely on the ship. Now that there was no hope of a marriage with The Great Sun's daughter, he would surely agree to stay with them. He would see that.

'The wind is good,' Cormac said. He came up looked down at the two of them. 'We will make good headway along the coast.'

'That is happy news,' said Caxna. He glanced over at Aisling and made an effort at a smile.

'Aisling says there is another large river further along that can take us to another city?'

Caxna nodded. 'It is a very large river. A good many sleeps.'

'Far enough away that we have no fear that the people of Etowah might find us?'

'I think so.' He frowned. 'I cannot say for certain. But you are not returning home to your own land?'

'No, at least not now. We need to have more time to prepare for such a voyage. There are stores to gather—food, animals, spare cloth to mend the sails, wood to repair the ship and such like. There is much work that needs to be done on the ship as well. Perhaps we might trade with the people of the city for these stores.'

'Ship?'

'This canoe,' said Aisling. 'It is called a "ship."'

He nodded. 'I have much to learn.'

Aisling felt her hopes rise. 'And they have much to learn from you, if you are willing.'

'What do you mean?'

'They would like you to come with us. To help with the trading in this city you speak of.' She glanced at Cormac. 'Please say you will.'

He considered her. 'You would want me to do this.'

She gave him an intent look. 'You know I would. I love you.' She'd said it deliberately so that Cormac would hear it, if he didn't already guess. In the past days she'd spoken her love clearly in all her actions; the meticulous attention she'd given to his care, the fact that she'd never left his side. And now she would state it plainly, for him, for everyone. She didn't care who knew, in fact she wanted everyone to know.

'I am not worthy of such a love. I have nothing to give you.'

'You have the most precious thing in the world to give me and that is your love.'

'Such love would make your life difficult.'

She looked up at Cormac. The past days had taken their toll on him. His eyes were strained and his face drawn, but he attempted a smile. 'You don't need to look to me for a blessing,' he said in Irish. 'I can see you've chosen a worthy man.' He spoke the words again in trader language for Caxna's benefit.

'You see, my brother has no objection and calls you worthy, so you cannot deny me now.'

'I cannot deny you anything. You have my heart, I have told you that.' He kissed her hand.

'And you will see that I will keep it safe, for I will not let you leave now.'

'But your home? Your people?'

'My home is with you. You are my people.'

'You are welcome to remain with us,' said Cormac.

Aisling looked at Cormac and then to Caxna. 'Wherever you

want to journey, I will go.' She leaned across and kissed him. 'Even to the stars.'

Caxna smiled. 'Even to the stars.'

If you have enjoyed this book please post a review. It helps so much towards getting the book noticed.

LOOK OUT FOR OTHER NOVELS IN THE CELTIC KNOT SERIES. There is no particular order and they can be read as standalone. They can be read in any order, though some prefer to read *Selkie Dreams* next and *Raven Brought the Light* last/first.

FOR OTHER WORKS BY THIS AUTHOR JOIN THE MAILING LIST FOR NEWS OF OFFERS, UPDATES AND NEW RELEASES.

www.KristinGleeson.com

HISTORICAL NOTE

Through the centuries since 1169 many accounts of Welsh descendants in America came to light. In Washington, D.C. in 1801, for example, a Lt Joseph Roberts, a Welshman, was seated in a hotel restaurant and spoke in Welsh to the waiter he knew to be from Wales. To his astonishment a Native American chief of some minor tribe in Washington to sign a treaty, approached him and asked Roberts in Welsh, "Is that thy language?"

Roberts told him it was and the Native American said that it was his language too. Roberts questioned him and discovered that the whole tribe, located about 800 miles southwest of Philadelphia, spoke the language and it had been their language stretching back generations.

According to the legend, Prince Madog's father, Owain ap Gruffydd ap Cynan, King of Gwynedd, died leaving ten sons from several different marriages. In Welsh tradition the eldest wasn't automatically the heir, so the throne was up for grabs. The oldest son, Iorewerth, couldn't claim the throne in any case, because he had a deep scar across his face. In Welsh tradition anyone one with such a physical blemish wasn't allowed to be king. Another son, Howel/Hwyel, who was something of a poet and had an Irish mother, Pyvog, seized the throne and held it precariously for two years. He went to Ireland to claim his mother's property and found on his return his brother Davydd had claimed the throne.

Against this backdrop, Prince Madog, a much younger son, decided to take to the seas. Little is known of his early years. Legend would have it that he was born at Dolwyddelan Castle, rather than at the king's seat of Aberffraw and that his mother's name was Brenda. He was raised in secret, because he had a club foot, by a man named Pendaran and it wasn't until he was sixteen, on his mother's deathbed that she told him the truth of his parentage.

He then spent years sailing around France, Spain and into the Mediterranean, trading in various ports. When the king, his father died and the factions formed Owain decided to leave and resume his sea travels. Navigation was still primitive in the 12th century making such a voyage extremely risky, but as a few brave re-enactors of the 20th century have demonstrated, not impossible.

Judging from where he was supposed to have landed in America it is most probable that boarding his ship, the Gwennan Gorn, and with a crew of about 20, he began his voyage in Wales, possibly at Abergwili, sailed around Cornwall to France, then down along the French coast. It was common knowledge at this this time that there were two mighty ocean currents, one that flowed westward from Europe and the other one back again so that it's entirely plausible that the strong ocean currents caught him up and took him into the Canaries and then eventually to what is now the Alabama and Florida coast. There he sailed up along the coast and ended up in what is now Mobile Bay, Alabama. He landed, left a few there, and returned to Wales to bring more colonists. Those left behind travelled upriver encountering friendly and unfriendly natives and built stone structures along the way, until they eventually settled in the Great Plains of the Midwest.

There is no mention of Owain's son in the oldest Welsh chronicles, the Chronicle of Princes or the Annals of Wales, though there were many called Madog whose deeds were recorded. But many of the old records were destroyed by Edward I.There does exist an ancient Welsh manuscript in the Cottonian Collection in the British museum containing a long account of the lineage of Gruffydd ap Cynan, citing him as the father of Owain and the grandfather of "Madawc." In the same collection there's a Latin manuscript that identifies Gruffydd as the son of Cynan and the father of Owain.

The legend attained its greatest prominence during the Elizabethan era, when English and Welsh writers wrote of the claim that Madog had gone to the Americas as an assertion of prior discovery, and hence legal possession, of North America by the Kingdom of England.

ABOUT THE AUTHOR

Originally from Philadelphia, Kristin Gleeson lives in Ireland, in the West Cork Gaeltacht, where she works as a librarian. She holds a Masters in Library Science and a Ph.D. in history and for a time was an administrator of a large archives, library and museum in America. She also served as a public librarian in America and was a professional harper and storyteller for a time.

Kristin Gleeson has also published *The Celtic Knot Series* and *The Renaissance Sojourner Series*, as well as *In Praise of the Bees*, a novel of 6th century Ireland. A free novelette prequel, *A Trick of Fate* is available free on e retailers. In addition to her novels, a biography on a First Nations Canadian woman, *Anahareo, A Wilderness Spirit*, is also available.

If you have enjoyed this book please post a review. It helps so much towards getting the book noticed.

If you go to the author website and join the mailing list to receive news of forthcoming releases, special offers and events you'll receive *A Treasure Beyond Worth* a **FREE prequel e-novelette.**

www.kristingleeson.com

Music is a big part of Kristin's life and many of the books have music connected to them. Listen to the music while you read- go to www.kristingleeson/music and download the files. Keep checking back as more pieces will be added to the library in the course of time.